DISTURBING THE DEAD

Also by Kelley Armstrong

Rip Through Time
The Poisoner's Ring
A Rip Through Time

Haven's Rock
The Boy Who Cried Bear
Murder at Haven's Rock

Rockton
The Deepest of Secrets *Watcher in the Woods*
A Stranger in Town *This Fallen Prey*
Alone in the Wild *A Darkness Absolute*
City of the Lost

Cainsville
Rituals *Deceptions*
Betrayals *Visions*
Omens

Age of Legends
Forest of Ruin
Empire of Night
Sea of Shadows

The Blackwell Pages (co-written with Melissa Marr)
Thor's Serpents
Odin's Ravens
Loki's Wolves

Otherworld
Thirteen *Living with the Dead* *Industrial Magic*
Spell Bound *Personal Demon* *Dime Store Magic*
Waking the Witch *No Humans Involved* *Stolen*
Frostbitten *Broken* *Bitten*
Haunted

Darkest Powers & Darkness Rising
The Rising *The Reckoning*
The Calling *The Awakening*
The Gathering *The Summoning*

Nadia Stafford
Wild Justice
Made to be Broken
Exit Strategy

Standalone novels
Wherever She Goes *The Masked Truth*
Aftermath *Missing*
The Life She Had *Every Step She Takes*
Hemlock Island

DISTURBING THE DEAD

A Rip Through Time Novel

KELLEY ARMSTRONG

MINOTAUR BOOKS
NEW YORK

First published in the United States by Minotaur Books, an imprint of St. Martin's Publishing Group

DISTURBING THE DEAD. Copyright © 2024 by KLA Fricke Inc. All rights reserved. Printed in the United States of America. For information, address St. Martin's Publishing Group, 120 Broadway, New York, NY 10271.

www.minotaurbooks.com

Library of Congress Cataloging-in-Publication Data

Names: Armstrong, Kelley, author.
Title: Disturbing the dead: a rip through time novel / Kelley Armstrong.
Description: First edition. | New York: Minotaur Books, 2024. |
    Series: Rip Through Time novels; 3
Identifiers: LCCN 2023058454 | ISBN 9781250321282 (hardcover) |
    ISBN 9781250360472 (Canadian edition) | ISBN 9781250321299 (ebook)
Subjects: LCGFT: Detective and mystery fiction. | Time-travel fiction. | Novels.
Classification: LCC PR9199.4.A8777 D57 2024 | DDC 813/.6—dc23/eng/
    20240102
LC record available at https://lccn.loc.gov/2023058454

Our books may be purchased in bulk for promotional, educational, or business use. Please contact your local bookseller or the Macmillan Corporate and Premium Sales Department at 1-800-221-7945, extension 5442, or by email at MacmillanSpecialMarkets@macmillan.com.

First Edition: 2024
First International Edition: 2024

10 9 8 7 6 5 4 3 2 1

For those of you who are in a wilderness

DISTURBING
THE DEAD

ONE

"What are your feelings on mummies?"

I look across the drawing-room table at Annis. We're in the middle of a brutal game of cards. Sure, I suspect "cards" and "brutal" should never be used in the same sentence, but this is Annis, who could turn Go Fish into a blood sport.

This particular game is écarté, which is similar to whist, except it's for two people. While playing a card game with my boss's sister might seem like a reprieve from my housemaid chores, it's actually the opposite, because those chores aren't going anywhere. This just means I'll be stuck folding the damn laundry after I should be done with work and chilling.

But what Annis wants, Annis gets, and if she demands I play cards with her, I don't have much choice. Okay, yes, I could refuse. After all, I'm not really a housemaid in 1869 Edinburgh. I'm a twenty-first-century police detective who is—for reasons the universe refuses to divulge—trapped in the body of Dr. Duncan Gray's twenty-year-old housemaid.

Gray knows my story. His other sister, Isla, knows it. But they're not here, having abandoned me for some secret mission that I'm not pissy about *at all*. I'm stuck with Annis, who doesn't know my secret, and if I tell her that entertaining unannounced guests isn't my job? Well, that isn't something a Victorian housemaid tells a dowager countess.

So I'm playing écarté, and she's slaughtering me, despite the fact that

I've actually been getting good at this game. No one plays like Annis. At least the bloodshed is only figurative. This time.

"Mummies?" She waves a hand in front of my face. "Are you listening to me, Mallory?"

"What are my . . . feelings? On . . . mummies?"

"Have you been nipping whisky while my sister is out? That might explain this." She waves at the cards. "The only other explanation is that you feel obligated to let me win. I expected better of you."

I ignore the jabs. With Annis, you choose your battles, or you won't stop fighting until you drop of exhaustion and she declares herself victor.

"I fear, Lady Annis, that I am a poor substitute for Dr. Gray and Mrs. Ballantyne. I do not travel in the proper social circles, and while I am certain there is some custom where one stops in the midst of a card game to ask one's partner's feelings on mummies, I do not know the appropriate response. Please forgive me. I am such a dunce."

Her eyes narrow. "No, you are rude, disrespectful, and sarcastic. Fortunately for you, I find those all admirable qualities in a young woman, so long as she is not *my* maid. Now, mummies. Your feelings on mummies."

"You are talking about Egyptian mummies, yes? This isn't some secret code among the nobility, where 'mummies' really means 'morphine'? I have strong feelings on morphine. It is bad. Don't take it. There, now, I want to discard these." I slap down two cards.

"There is nothing wrong with a little morphine under the right circumstances. The problem is laudanum, which dulls the wits. That I cannot abide. But yes, I mean Egyptian mummies. Have you ever wanted to unwrap one?"

I blink. Did I hear that right? I peer at Annis, focused on her eyes, which seem as cobra-bright as ever. No signs of whisky *or* morphine.

"Have I ever wanted to . . . unwrap a mummy?" I say.

"And see what's underneath all those bandages."

I relax. Right. I remember where I am. Victorian Scotland during the rise of the British Empire, when Egyptian mummies were all the rage. What seems like a non sequitur to me is just Annis making actual conversation. She must have read an article on an excavation and thought it might interest me.

I'm actually flattered that she'd make the effort. That's not usually Annis's style. We do get on, though, despite my grumbling about her roping me into the role of companion. Lady Annis Leslie is not a nice woman. But she is interesting, and as long as she continues to repair her relationship with Gray and Isla, I can admit that I don't mind her company.

"A withered corpse," I say, as I examine my cards. "That's what lies beneath the wrappings. A desiccated human corpse without a stomach, liver, lungs, or intestines. Oh, and the brains. They take out the brains through the nose."

Silence. With most people, I'd presume I'd offended their sensibilities. But the woman across from me is a Gray, born to a father who made his fortune as an undertaker and a mother who shared her love of science with all her children. In this house, no one is going to faint at the mention of pulling brains out nostrils. Instead, it'd be an invitation to a heated discussion of the procedure.

So when Annis goes quiet, I look up, confused.

"Where did you read that?" she asks.

From the way she's staring at me, I want to tartly remind her that I can read, very well thank you. But then she might insist on knowing exactly where I read it, and I wouldn't know what to say, so I tell her the truth. "I'm sure I've read it somewhere, but I've seen mummies, too. In museums."

"Which one?"

I go still as I realize my mistake. This is the source of her confusion—we aren't in a world where kids go to museums on school trips, especially not girls like Catriona Mitchell, whose body I inhabit.

I flutter my hand. "I do not recall. Somewhere on my travels."

"What travels?" She peers at me. "You are a nearly illiterate housemaid who has likely never left Edinburgh."

"I am not nearly illiterate. I realize that I had presented myself as such, before the injury to my head, but I now suspect that I always knew how to read. I chose not to for some unknown reason. My reading skills are, in fact, excellent."

"Head injury" is the excuse given for those who don't know my secret. I crossed over when Catriona and I were both strangled, and she *did* receive a head injury, one that left her unconscious for days. Gray explains my personality changes—and peccadilloes—as brain trauma. It also lets me use my own name—I feel like a different person, and so I have asked to be called Mallory instead of Catriona.

I sip my tea. "Now, let us return to this rousing game of—"

"You have never left Edinburgh, Mallory."

"Of course I have. I was in Leith just last week."

Her eyes narrow. "You did not see a mummy in Leith."

"Are you certain? One sees all sorts of oddities in Leith. Why, on this last trip—"

"There are no museums in Leith."

"Perhaps it is a secret museum. I am sorry, Lady Annis, if you have never been invited to tour it, but they have a strict policy against admitting those accused of poisoning their husbands, even if they were found innocent." At this point, I'm willing to do anything to distract her, including bringing up her recent past.

"I am certain you think that is very amusing."

"As do you, who finds a way to bring it into most conversations. I do not know where I saw a mummy, Lady Annis. That is part of the damage to my brain. I only recall seeing one. Perhaps I heard someone speaking of it, and I misremember the story as having experienced it myself. The mind is a mysterious thing."

"As you keep reminding me, whenever I point out that you do not, in any way, behave like a twenty-year-old housemaid."

"Housemaids behave in all sorts of ways. As Catriona, I was a thief with a clear tendency toward sociopathy. As Mallory, I am, as you put it, rude, disrespectful, and sarcastic. If you prefer sociopathy . . ."

"I do not know, having never heard the word."

"My apologies. Again"—I tap my head—"this causes all sorts of problems, including my propensity for inventing new language. I am only lucky to have found such a tolerant family, willing to overlook my foibles."

"No housemaid should know the word 'foible.'"

"Have I used it incorrectly?"

She shakes her head. "You have far too much fun teasing me with whatever secrets you hold."

"I hold none. Not even in this hand of cards, which is wretched. Now, if I may be so bold, Lady Annis, may I ask why you mentioned mummies?"

"Perhaps because I was about to offer an opportunity a girl like you is unlikely to encounter in her lifetime. However, as you insist on needling me most disrespectfully, I am inclined to rescind the offer."

"You cannot rescind what you did not offer." I peer at her. "It's something about mummies?"

"An unwrapping party."

"A . . . mummy-unwrapping party?"

She flaps a hand. "They call it a scientific demonstration, but it is a party. An evening get-together at the home of Sir Alastair Christie, newly returned from Egypt with two mummies, one of which he intends to unwrap, in what may well be the event of the season—or the week, at least. The unwrapping will be done by Sir Alastair, who is also a surgeon with the Royal Infirmary. Sir Alastair is quite the bore and will insist on lecturing, too, but it is a small price to pay to see a mummy unwrapped."

I school my expression. I've learned to do that a lot here, just as I've learned not to actually speak to outsiders the way I've been talking to Annis.

I'm sure at some point, if Annis remains in our lives, she'll need to know the truth. But no one—particularly me—is rushing to tell her just yet. It does, however, give me the excuse to rumple the composure of Gray and Isla's unflappable elder sister.

As for a mummy unwrapping, yes, I will fully admit that ten-year-old Mallory would have salivated at the thought. Thirty-year-old Mallory is horrified. It's like hosting a party to dig up a grave and ogle the corpse within. Except even Victorian Scots would know *that* was wrong. *This* is acceptable because the person inside those wrappings is Egyptian. I don't expect Annis to understand that, even if Gray—her half brother—is a man of color himself.

Does the idea of unwrapping a mummy offend me? Yep. Would it offend everyone in my own time? Nope. Would everyone in *this* time be okay with it? Nope. I suspect that's one reason this unwrapping is being swathed in the respectable cloak of science.

"You're inviting me to this . . . party?" I say carefully.

"I am inviting Duncan and Isla, who may bring you and that detective friend."

"Hugh, Lady Annis," I say. "His name is Hugh McCreadie, and you have known him more than half your life, as he is your brother's best friend."

"Yes, yes. Hugh. He may come."

"I thought this was an exclusive party. You can just add a plus-four to your invitation?"

"I do as I wish," she says. "I am Lady Annis Leslie." She sips her tea and sets the cup down with a decisive click. "The only reason I have been invited is to add an air of delicious scandal to the proceedings. The notorious widowed countess."

"Ah."

"So I decided that if they want scandal . . ." She trails off with an elegant shrug.

"You'll give them scandal," I say. "By extending the invitation to your chemist sister, illegitimate brother, and their detective friend . . . along with the housemaid your brother insists on calling his assistant."

Her lips curve in a smile. "Precisely."

I sigh. "This sounds like a very bad idea."

"All the best ideas are."

I'm opening my mouth when the back door clicks open. I won't say I've been listening for it. I won't say I have to restrain myself from leaping up like an abandoned puppy hearing her family return. If any of that is true, I blame Annis and this endless game of écarté.

"Go to him," Annis says with a sigh. Then her brows rise. "Oh, do not give me that look, child. The only person you fool is my brother, who is too endlessly distracted to notice."

I don't bother arguing. Let Annis have her fun. I perked up because both Isla and Gray are home, and I might discover what they were up to, which could be something exciting, like the start of a new case.

I walk with all due dignity from the drawing room and down the stairs to the ground level, where I can hear Isla's voice. When my footsteps click closer, she calls, "Mallory?"

"Coming."

I see Isla first. She's a handsome thirty-four-year-old woman, about a half foot taller than me, with pale skin, freckles, and copper curls. Gray is behind her. Three years younger than his sister, roughly six feet, broad-shouldered, with a square jaw, brown skin and eyes, and wavy dark hair already breaking free of its pomade.

They are in the rear foyer, removing winter outerwear.

Isla smiles. "Mallory. We have brought you a present."

She gestures, and only then do I notice the young woman nearly shrunk into the shadows. She is about eighteen, tiny and fine-boned, wearing a brown dress that makes her resemble a wren. A wren ready to take flight at the first opportunity.

"Lorna?" Isla says. "This is Mallory. It is her job you will be taking over as our housemaid."

"Another one?" says a voice. I glance up to see Annis descending the stairs.

"I thought I was choosing a maid for you," Annis says.

"No, dear Annis." Isla folds her gloves with care. "You offered to do so, and we told you no. Absolutely, unreservedly no. We have very specific requirements—"

"Which I understand perfectly, having grown up in this house. What is this? The fourth girl you've hired to take Mallory's place?"

"Third."

"Was there not another one, in September, who lasted barely a half day before—"

"Fine. Fourth."

"In as many months." Annis peers at the girl and says, "No, she will not do."

"Annis . . ." Gray says.

"You wish to consider her? I strongly advise against it, but if you insist, I will conduct the interview."

"Annis," Isla says with exasperation. "We have already hired—"

"Then you can unhire her, with appropriate compensation." She turns to poor Lorna. "First question. You are gathering my brother's shirts, and you realize the red stains are blood. What do you do?"

"Annis . . ." Isla says, but Gray's look says to let her go.

"I soak it in cold water, ma'am," Lorna says in a barely audible voice. "Then I take it to the laundress. I understand Dr. Gray is a surgeon, and even if he does not practice as one, he does assist the police with examining the dead."

"As we have explained," Gray says.

Annis ignores him. "Next question. You are cleaning the funerary parlor downstairs, and you find that my brother has left a jar with a preserved human head on the desk."

"I do not have jars with heads, Annis," Gray says. "That would be the height of disrespect. I have body parts, yes, but only if they are valuable specimens in the study of forensic science."

She turns to Lorna. "There is a floating human head with the eyes open and staring at you. What do you do?"

"I . . ." Lorna shivers before straightening. "I would like to say that I continue to clean the room, but I must admit that I would not. I would close the door and respectfully request that the groom remove it so that I might continue."

"You do not need to involve Simon," Isla says. "Anyone in the household would remove it for you, although personally, I would rather not."

"On the subject of the groom," Annis says. "What are your thoughts on them?"

"On . . . grooms?"

"One of your predecessors was let go for setting her cap on Simon and refusing to take no for an answer. See that you do not do the same. It is pointless. You are a girl. He is not interested."

"Annis!" Isla says, but Lorna seems not to take her meaning and only nods.

"I would never do such a thing," Lorna says, her voice coming a little stronger now, as if she is gaining confidence in this world's-strangest-maid-interview. "It is not wrong to express a romantic interest, but it is wrong to pursue it once it is declined."

"Good answer," I say.

Annis snorts and continues, "Question four. You are walking through the courtyard and see that someone has left open the door to the poison garden. What do you do?"

"P-poison . . . ?"

"A garden filled with deadly plants."

"They aren't *all* deadly," I say, only to realize that might not help.

When poor Lorna falters, Annis goes for the kill. "It used to be my garden. Did you know my husband died this past spring of poison? Unconnected, of course. I have not used the garden in decades. Now it belongs to Isla. I would not overly concern yourself about the poison there, though. It is my sister's laboratory you need to worry about. She—"

"Annis," Isla snaps. She turns to the girl. "Yes, there is a garden of poisonous plants, for study only, and it is never unlocked. Nor will you ever be required to clean my laboratory. In fact, it is also kept locked, and the staff are not permitted entry."

Judging by Lorna's face, this is not as reassuring as Isla intends.

"I . . ." Lorna squares her thin shoulders. "I know you are a chemist, ma'am, and I understand there may be poisonous substances in the house."

Annis eyes her. Then she says, "Last question. What are you?"

"What . . . am I?"

"Thief, pickpocket, con artist, prostit—"

"Annis!" Isla says. "That is enough. She is a maid, nothing more."

Annis looks at Lorna. "I know my sister's hiring practices. There is no shame in saying you have picked pockets or lifted your skirts, so long as you do not intend to continue while you are here. Well, no, if you lift your skirts without charging for it, that is no one's business but your own. Unless you intend to lift them for my brother. He will not properly appreciate it. Nor would I. You are far too young for either of us."

"All right, Annis," Gray says as Isla sputters, unable to form words. "You have had your fun terrorizing the poor child, and the fact she is still standing here is proof enough that she has the constitution we require." He turns to Lorna. "My sister is correct that we typically hire staff who have fallen afoul of the law, sometimes with cause and sometimes without. Their stories are their own business, and I trust you will respect that, Lorna."

"Yes, sir."

He turns to Annis. "Lorna has no such story. In light of our recent troubles with hiring a maid, we decided to make a more traditional choice."

"You hired an ordinary girl?"

"Yes."

"Then no. She will not do." Annis looks at Lorna. "I shall find you employment in my own house and compensate you for the inconvenience. There. The matter is settled."

"You are not stealing our maid, Annis," Isla says.

"I am not stealing her. I am replacing her with someone suitable to your needs, whom I shall choose. This one will not do. She does not suit." Annis waves at Lorna. "Do not bother to unpack your bag, child. You are not staying."

"I will show you to your room, Lorna," Isla says. "Because you are staying, and the first lesson you shall need to learn is this: my sister does not live here, and therefore you need do nothing"—she glares at Annis—"*nothing* she asks of you."

"Oh, I do not ask, dear Isla. I tell."

"Not in this house you don't. I have no idea why you have graced us with your presence, Annis—"

"To invite you to a mummy unwrapping."

Isla stops. She stares. I wait for her to ask what the devil her sister is talking about. Instead, she says, "Sir Alastair's party?"

A look of satisfaction settles over Annis's face. "If there is another, I have not heard of it. That is the only one that matters. The scientific event of the season. I came to invite you, Duncan, your policeman friend, and Mallory. I presume you will wish to go?"

"I—Yes," Isla says. "I very much wish—I mean, I will consider it, of course, if it fits into my calendar."

"I am quite certain you can make room in your calendar. As for this girl—"

"The girl stays," Isla says. "Lorna, come and I will show you to your quarters. Then I will give you a tour of the house."

"I can do that," I say.

"Duncan has need of you," Isla says.

"I am certain he does," Annis murmurs, too low for anyone else to hear. I refrain from attempting to murder her with a glare.

"Quite so," Gray says. "I have brought you something, Mallory." His lips twitch in a faint smile. "A gift that is not fit for present company. Come down to the funerary parlor, and I shall show it to you in private."

Annis starts to say something, but at a look from me, she settles for a very unladylike snicker. I politely take my leave of Isla and Lorna and follow Gray down the hall to the funerary parlor.

TWO

A funeral parlor in the nineteenth century bears little resemblance to what we'd find in the modern era. While Gray is called an undertaker, his job better fits the modern title of funeral director.

This isn't a place to hold a funeral or a visitation. The only bodies that ever find their way to the Gray funerary parlor are those undergoing autopsy in Gray's laboratory. He has degrees in both surgery and medicine but has never practiced. Part of that is because his father died, and despite being the youngest child—and, technically, illegitimate—he inherited the business. Also, he's not allowed to practice due to a small matter of grave robbing. In his defense, he was only trying to prove that a man died of murder when no one would listen to him. But still, the offense was enough to mean he can't practice either medicine or surgery.

So he's an undertaker, and in *that* capacity, he doesn't interact with actual corpses. His job is directing the funeral arrangements. The "funerary parlor"—situated on the ground floor of his family's town house—is for making those arrangements. There's a very comfortable reception room for meeting the grieving families and discussing details. Then there's Gray's office and then, finally, the room no mourner will ever enter: the laboratory.

Gray is not a coroner. He can't be, because, again, he's not allowed to practice medicine. In Victorian Edinburgh, one elected official plays the role of coroner for all suspicious deaths and homicide. That's the police surgeon, a role currently held by an incompetent ass named Dr. Addington.

Being a privileged brat who got the job through family connections, Addington does not actually *want* to deal with the dead. Ew, gross. Also, he doesn't want to conduct autopsies in the police dead rooms. Again, gross. Gray magnanimously allows Addington to work in his own laboratory, and Addington magnanimously allows Gray to examine the bodies once he's done.

Gray's true passion is forensics. He's a pioneer in the field. This arrangement with Addington works out well for everyone, particularly the people of Edinburgh, who get a qualified medical professional following up on—and correcting—their police surgeon's work.

"Did you say you got me a present?" I say as we step into the funerary parlor.

He closes the hall door behind us. "I did."

"Hiring a new maid is a present."

"Only if she works out," he murmurs.

"You don't think she will."

"I remain optimistic. But I have brought a proper present."

"A pony? Tell me it's a pony." I head into his office and lower myself onto the chair. "As a kid, I asked for a pony every year, and every year, I suffered vast disappointment."

He frowns. "Your parents did not buy you a pony? They were quite well off, were they not?"

"We lived in the city. With a yard smaller than yours. And no stable."

"That is no excuse. If a girl wishes for a pony, and her parents can afford one, she should have one. It is only right."

I shake my head. I can't tell whether he's joking.

When I first arrived here, waking up in Catriona's body, I'd found Duncan Gray dour, stiff, and forbidding. It was a long time before I suspected he might be capable of smiling, and even then, I wasn't sure. Now I've seen him smile and heard him laugh, but I've also learned to interpret the barest of lip twitches and glints in his dark eyes. Right now, though, he was already relaxed and in a fine mood, which means it's impossible to tell whether he's kidding.

He might not be. Gray grew up in a world where girls—and boys—of the upper middle class do indeed get ponies. I can tell him stories of the twenty-first century, including the lack of horses, but he can't quite picture it. It's like me, having come here after seeing the Victorian era portrayed many times and still feeling as if I'd walked into an alternate version, where little was as I expected.

Gray lifts a wrapped package and places it on his office desk. "Not a pony, I fear."

"Part of a pony?"

His lips twitch. "That would be wrong. One should not give parts of anything as gifts. Or so I am told." A definite glint in his eyes now.

I look down at the package. It's wrapped in brown paper, as so many things are in a world without plastic or other wrappings. I envy Gray's ability to wrap packages. I know how odd that sounds, but when we've been on crime scenes, I'm at a loss, looking about for some way to transport evidence, and I'll still be looking after he's wrapped it in a waterproof parcel so pretty it makes bloodstained-knife evidence look like a Christmas present.

Of course, if the knife *doesn't* have blood on it, he and McCreadie are just as likely to stuff it in their pocket. Chain of custody for evidence isn't really a thing when courts don't yet admit fingerprint evidence.

"It's too pretty to open," I say as he watches with obvious impatience. "I think I'll just put it beside my bed." I pick up the parcel. "Yes, that seems like a fine idea. I will display this beautifully wrapped package by my bed, never to unwrap it."

"I realize you are teasing me, but I would die of shock if you managed to leave it there, without peeking, for more than a day. Also, I would not suggest storing it by your bed, given the . . . nature of the contents."

I look at him and arch a brow. "Interesting. So it is perishable? Can I eat it?"

That lip twitch, stronger now. "I believe there are laws against such a thing."

I eye the package. "Curiouser and curiouser."

He reaches to take it away. "If you do not want it—"

I snatch it from his hands. Then I take a knife from his desk and cut the twine. It's not *just* brown paper. It's waxed brown paper, suggesting the contents are indeed perishable.

I keep unwrapping it and—

I clap my hands to my mouth with a squeak of girlish delight. "Oh, Dr. Gray! You have brought me a body part!" I wag my finger at him. "Such a tease. You said parts aren't proper gifts, and so I barely dared hope. But no, you have brought me . . ."

I reach and pick up the pickled appendage. "A third hand. This will make cleaning the chamber pots so much easier. I no longer have to use my own hands. I can use this one." I let out a deep sigh of happiness.

"You no longer need to clean chamber pots at all," he says. "We have a maid. Not that I expected you to clean them before that, as you well know."

I don't rise to the bait. That has been an ongoing issue since Isla and Gray realized my real identity. I'm an educated professional woman from the future. I should not be cleaning their chamber pots. That's their opinion. Mine is that chamber pots needed cleaning, and it was hardly their fault the universe threw me into the body of their housemaid.

"I know you are making light," he says, "but I realize it is hardly a normal gift. I only thought . . ." He clears his throat. "I thought it was an intriguing specimen, one we might examine together to determine why it is in such condition."

I smile up at him. "I might have wanted a pony when I was five, but at my age, nothing is better than a puzzle." I set the hand down. "It *is* interesting."

"It is, isn't it?"

He leans over the hand, close enough that I can smell the beeswax and almond oil of his hair pomade. Annis might tease me about her brother but if my heart gives a little patter when he's that close, it's mostly because I'm seeing a secret side of Duncan Gray, one I've earned, damn it. Not just the relaxed version, but the enthusiastic one, so eager to dive into this mystery that he forgets to keep a proper degree of physical space between us.

"I found it in a shop," he says. "They were selling it, which is quite illegal, obviously, but they were claiming it was not an actual hand. With it being so shriveled, I understand why it would seem fake, so I will not accuse them of knowingly trafficking in human parts. On closer inspection, I do not think it is as old as it appears. It seems to have been . . ."

"Pickled?"

"Precisely. Pickled and then dried, so that it might be handled. Then there is something dripped on it, which appears to be—"

"Wax!" I say. "I know what it is. A Hand of Glory."

"A hand of . . . ?"

"Glory. Don't ask me why it's called that." I lift the hand. "If this is a proper one, it was harvested from a hanged man, preferably a murderer who committed the crime with this particular hand. It's chopped off, pickled and dried and then used to hold a candle between the fingers."

Gray's expression says he's insulted that I can't even attempt to devise a more credible story.

I continue, "The hand—with the candle—is then used by thieves."

"Thieves . . ."

"Now, if I'm remembering correctly, there are various explanations for what it's supposed to do. Some say the candle will flicker out if anyone in the house wakes, warning the thief. Others say it will keep everyone asleep. For a thief, though, either way it's . . ." I wave the appendage. "Handy."

His eyes narrow.

"I'm serious," I say. "Look it up. It's folk magic."

"Which you know because, in the twenty-first century, thieves run around using pickled hands to rob houses."

"Sarcasm does not become you, Dr. Gray. I know what this is because, when not dreaming of ponies, I was a ghoulish little brat who thrived on the macabre. In this case, I read about it in a novel, and I was annoyed with the author for making up something ridiculous. So I did my research, and found it's a real thing. And, being so bizarre, naturally I remembered it. You found yourself a Hand of Glory, which you have now given to a thief. Well done, sir."

He shakes his head. "I suppose with that mystery solved, I ought to dispose of it." He sounds so disappointed that I feel a pang of guilt for having accidentally robbed him of his puzzle.

"I think we should still dissect it," I say. "We don't know how it was prepared, which could prove interesting. Also, I think we should discover where it came from, in case someone is . . ." I waggle my brows. "Grave robbing."

He sighs with the slightest roll of his eyes. "You are far too interested in grave robbing, Mallory."

"Oh, I'm not the only one."

"It was a misunderstanding," he says with a mock glare. "But yes, we will put this aside for further examination. However, on the topic of human remains . . ."

"My favorite topic."

"Even if they are wrapped in bandages to be unrolled at a party?"

I make a face. I don't mean to—seeing Isla's excitement, I'd decided to keep my thoughts on mummy unwrapping to myself. I quickly hide the reaction, but Gray catches it and exhales.

"So I am not the only one who finds such a thing in poor taste?" he says.

"You are not." I wave at the hand. "This is different. You rescued it from a shop, and it's only a hand. You'll treat it as a scientific specimen and dispose of it appropriately when you're done. I know they're having a surgeon unwrap the mummified remains and calling it science . . ."

"It would be science if it were the first mummy unwrapped, or if we had reason to believe it was unusual in a way that would prove useful. Experts have already dissected mummies. We understand how the process was accomplished. Now the dead should be left in peace, as that was the intended purpose of mummifying them in the first place. A person who lived thousands of years ago died, expecting to rest for eternity as their religion dictated."

He pauses, looking abashed. "That was a lecture, wasn't it?"

"If so, it was to an appreciative audience. I understand that graves were robbed to advance medicine, and thankfully that's no longer necessary. I agree with exhuming a body if it means catching a killer. But people have the right to have their beliefs respected. So there's *my* lecture."

"Then we are agreed that an unwrapping party is not an event we wish to attend."

I shrug. "I'd be lying if I said I wouldn't be fascinated. Same as I'm fascinated by this." I wave at the hand. "Even as an adult, I still have a macabre turn of mind, as you well know."

A faint smile. "A turn of mind that we share, and I agree. Having never seen an unwrapping, I am curious. If a colleague had invited me to this, I would politely demur. But Isla . . ."

"Isla wants to go, and I don't want to shame her for that."

He meets my gaze. "Precisely. Hugh will also want to go. If you would rather not, I will understand."

"The unwrapping is happening whether I attend or not. I don't see the point in standing on principle, not when Isla might question why I'd refuse something that should interest me."

"So we are going to a mummy unwrapping?"

"It seems so."

THREE

Three days later, we are on our way to the mummy-unwrapping party, with me wearing a gorgeous gown that makes me happier than I ever thought a dress could make me. Chamber-pot scrubbing isn't the only bone of contention between myself and my employers. Wages are another issue. A housemaid makes relatively little on top of room and board. Gray and Isla pay more, of course, but that doesn't mean I can buy dresses for which I have no practical use, especially when they'd cost the equivalent of a designer gown in my own time.

I can't just pop into a discount shop and buy something off the rack either. Even if I chose to splurge, I then need to match it with proper footwear and gloves and jewelry and winter cape and a crinoline cage. I have a decent secondhand brushed-wool "going out" dress that takes me almost everywhere. It will not take me to an exclusive party at the home of Sir Alastair Christie.

Here, Annis plays fairy godmother. Or she does when Isla insists on it. Isla may not have her sister's gift for manipulation, but she did grow up bearing witness to it.

"Annis wants you at that party," Isla said the day we were first invited.

"She wants the shock value of bringing a housemaid to that party," I said.

"Perhaps, but she likes you. You are interesting, and she loves interesting people."

"I'm a puzzle to be solved."

"Also fine company. The point is that she wants you at the party, and so she must ensure you have everything you need. I will insist she play your fairy godmother for this particular ball." Isla's lips twitched. "Please be sure you take full advantage of it. Remember that if Duncan seems well-off, he is a pauper compared to Annis."

I did take advantage. That's not my usual style, but there's a vast difference between accepting the ridiculous wage Gray tried to offer me as his assistant and letting his wealthy sister outfit me in a dress suitable for a party she wants me to attend as scandal-bait.

What I get isn't new. It's too late for that and too extravagant. Instead, Annis had one of her dresses quickly tailored to fit with fresh trimmings. The gown is silk, which I could never afford in this era—and probably not in my own. It's turquoise with rust-brown embroidery and beadwork, trimmed in brown lace. The neckline is high, and the bodice is tight enough that I need help with the strings on my new corset. The crinoline cage is also a hand-me-down from Annis, as is the crinoline petticoat that goes over it. The petticoats underneath are my own. My gloves are white silk, and my slippers are also silk, with thin leather soles.

The accessory I'm most pleased with, though, is my poison ring. It's the first chance I've had to wear it since Gray gave it to me for Catriona's twentieth birthday last month. It's a gorgeous black enamel and gold piece, antique even in this time. The best part, though, is the tiny compartment for, yes, poison. Okay, they're not actually used for poison. Women store pills in there, maybe a bit of scent. But anyone seeing it knows it *could* contain poison.

The ring is in honor of our last case, which had involved a poisoning ring. I'd been terribly disappointed to realize that only meant a suspected ring of poisoners. Gray gave me this to make up for it.

Annis fetches us in her coach. Can I say that's a bit inconvenient? It means McCreadie needs to come to the town house, rather than have us pick him up on the way. Then we have to wait for Annis, and she's late—as usual. Also, coaches really aren't made to fit five people, especially when three of them are women in Victorian evening gowns.

Gray helps me in, and then slides in beside me, which has Annis waggling her brows. I swear the woman is as bad as that annoying friend in fifth grade, always whisper-singing "Jason and Maria, sitting in a tree . . ."

Okay, in fifth grade that annoying friend had been me, but at least *I've* outgrown it.

Gray takes the spot next to me to allow Isla to sit beside McCreadie, because they are the ones who deserve the juvenile singing, and while Gray and I won't subject them to that, we are not above doing everything we can to nudge them together.

After we're all seated, though, Isla sighs and says, "This will not do." She looks at Annis. "Were you not going to mention it?"

Annis only smiles her cat smile.

Isla shakes her head. "We cannot arrive at the party in this configuration. Duncan? Hugh?"

They switch spots without comment, as if they knew better but just weren't going to bring it up. McCreadie sits beside me and Gray between his sisters, for propriety's sake, I presume.

Isla is a widow almost out of her mourning period, and her dress now is a gorgeous rich lilac. Following the death of Prince Albert, there are very strict social rules for a widow of Isla's class, with a two-year public show of mourning for the loss of an asshole that Gray had paid to stay away from Isla. There are, of course, no such expectations placed on widowers. How could one expect them to find a new bride if their dress publicly reminds everyone they lost their last one?

Isla and McCreadie have known each other since childhood. In a proper romantic tale, they'd have grown up together, realized they loved each other, and married. It didn't work like that. Maybe they didn't realize how they felt until it was too late, with Isla married and McCreadie engaged. I don't pry. Oh, I totally would, if that were an option, but when two people refuse to admit they're crazy about each other, you can't exactly ask how long they've been that way and why they've never acted on it. You have to wait for them to figure it out, which is extremely frustrating.

McCreadie is a police detective. A "criminal officer," as it were, a relatively recent position in a relatively recent institution, formal policing only dating to the early part of this century. It isn't a case of Gray befriending a poor boy from the lower classes. McCreadie's family comes from the Grays' social stratum, and the boys met at private school.

McCreadie is now estranged from his family, and again, it's not the sort of thing I can ask about. I only know what I see, which is a very good-looking guy—despite luxurious period-appropriate whiskers—who is clever and good-natured and decent in every possible way, making him the perfect match for brilliant, strong-willed, and kindhearted Isla. But enough about that. For now.

As always, McCreadie is dressed like he stepped out of a Victorian advertisement. Gray might be nattily attired—in a single-breasted mid-thigh silk jacket with a high starched collar and cravat—but next to Mc-Creadie, he looks like he rolled out of bed and pulled on whatever was at hand. It's not that McCreadie is dressed any differently. Men's black-tie wear here is as limited as it is in my time. McCreadie's attire just somehow always manages to be a little better, in the cut and fit and the fabric.

The least fashionably dressed person in our entourage is the one who can best afford it. Annis is in deep mourning, and even coming to such an event could be scandalous. She must wear head-to-toe black, and it can't even be a fashionable black gown. It must be as shapeless as possible, and so on her buxom figure, it looks like she's wearing sackcloth, as if she's being punished for having outlived her husband.

The coach stays in the New Town, naturally. There is a definite "right side of the tracks" in Edinburgh, and it's the New Town. The coach takes us from Robert Street toward grander homes, and it stops at one that I'd mistake for two town houses if it weren't for its single entrance.

Or I think it's only a single entrance. It's hard to tell from our vantage point, at the end of a queue of coaches.

I try not to plaster myself against the window. I haven't been on this street. Gray's town house is stately and beautifully appointed inside, but the exterior could best be described as austere, rather like its current owner. These town houses are fancier Georgian architecture, complete with decorated embedded columns and wide, central front steps.

"Is there some problem ahead?" Annis grumbles. "At this rate, we shall miss the unwrapping altogether."

"We could get out and walk," Gray says. "It is but a few hundred feet."

"It is November, Duncan. *November.* There is . . ." She nods her chin at the sidewalk and says "snow" with the same expression one might give a pile of horse dung.

"It's only a sprinkle," I say. "It looks lovely."

I gaze out the window. With the darkness and the party, the house is so well lit that it twinkles. The coach is cold enough for me to see my breath, and with the fur muff warming my hands, I feel as if I'm heading off to a Yuletide party instead.

Gray leans toward me and whispers, "Would you like to walk?"

I glance toward Annis, expecting some comment, but she is too busy rapping on the roof for the driver to move.

The line inches forward, and I look through the window again. I *would* like to get out. It's both too cold and too warm in here. Too cold on my face and too warm where I'm bundled in layers. We usually do walk wherever we can, but winter fancy-dress parties here are like ones in my time, where you expect to be dropped at the door to avoid needing to bundle up over your party best.

When the coach stops again, I lean to whisper, "Would it be unseemly to walk?"

"Does it matter?" Gray says, his eyes dancing.

I'm supposed to say it doesn't. That's what he expects and what he wants—the Mallory who flouts convention and lets him do the same. I know how much both Gray and Isla enjoy pushing against the constraints they've battled all their lives, and when it comes to that, I'm a terrible enabler.

Gray and Isla exist in a bubble where no one expects them to conform to all social conventions. Coming from a notably eccentric family gives them latitude, as does the fact that they are merely middle class. But bubbles are fragile things, and they must still live and work within this world.

It may seem as if I'm overthinking this. It's just walking a couple of hundred feet to a party. But if walking calls attention to us, and if it invites whispers and sneers and mockery, then that could damage an evening Isla is very much looking forward to.

The coach thankfully rolls forward again. When it stops, McCreadie is the one pushing open the door to look out. He's frowning, as if he heard something, and when I catch it, I kick myself.

I might not be a cop in this world, but for me, a career in law enforcement was more than something that paid the bills. I chose policing because underneath my sarcasm, I'm an idealist and a humanist. McCreadie is the same—a public servant who understands the meaning of the word, committed to being a torchbearer through the shadows. He's heard something concerning outside, and I was too engrossed in my own minor drama to notice.

Now I pick up the sound of angry voices, and when McCreadie steps out of the coach, I start to rise. Naturally, Gray is already moving past me. In his case, it's not so much bearing a torch through the shadows as wondering whether those shadows hide anything interesting.

Annis huffs when I go to follow, but she doesn't stop me, only saying, "Leave your muff in the coach, Mallory. One cannot trust servants, as I am certain you know from experience."

I'm ready to hop out of the coach when I see McCreadie there, hand raised to help me down. Right. Formal event.

"Here, let me help you, Miss Mallory," McCreadie says, loud enough that I know the words are a reproach to his friend, already making his way along the sidewalk, oblivious to everything but the siren's call of adventure.

This particular siren's call seems to be the rather shrill voice of a young woman. She's following two guests up the steps into the town house, haranguing them about something I can't quite catch.

Two footmen slide behind the guests like closing doors. The young woman glares at them and strides back to await new victims. The next coach pulls up, and she is right there, waiting for the guests to descend. When they do not—likely trying to figure out how to avoid her—she spots our party walking along the sidewalk.

Once I'm out of the coach, I realize why Annis and Isla stay behind, other than propriety. I'm wearing thin soled slippers, walking on an ice-cold, snow-dusted sidewalk. Luckily, we don't have far to go.

Gray has slowed enough to notice me and offer his arm, though the gesture seems more reflexive than genuine. I still take it. It's awkward enough walking into a party where I know I don't belong, and I will fully admit that I would rather do it on the arm of a dashing gentleman.

Speaking of gentlemen and dashing, McCreadie dashes in front of us, cutting Gray off from reaching the young woman first. The young woman turns, and I get a glimpse of her. She's maybe in her midtwenties, with dark hair swept back in what looks like an intentionally severe style and spectacles poised on her nose. Her outfit is drab and her boots are scuffed and . . .

Will I sound terrible if I say she looks like a stereotypical bluestocking? There is a type. There has always been a type, and it originated before this time period, and continues to be used in memes right up to the modern day.

See this feminist? See how pinched and unattractive she is? Of course she's a champion of women's rights—she can't win a man to take care of her.

Except this young woman is neither pinched nor unattractive. She seems to be intentionally dressing this way, and I'm not sure whether it's a uniform of sorts, or it's just a way to deflect attention from her looks.

Sometimes, it's easier to be taken seriously if you pull on a cloak of sexual unattractiveness. Unfortunately for me, that's a whole lot harder to do these days, cast into the body of a shapely blond twenty-year-old with the face of an angelic milkmaid.

The young woman disappears from view once McCreadie cuts in front of us, but not before she sees our group heading her way, and her eyes flash like a hawk spotting mice.

"You there," she says, the clacking of boots telling me she's bearing down on us.

"Yes, hello," McCreadie calls back. "I heard a commotion and came to see if you were in need of aid." He takes off his hat, bowing his head. "Detective Hugh McCreadie of the—"

"You're going to this party, Detective?" she cuts in.

"That is my intention, along with—"

"Then I want Sir Alastair arrested. There are laws against disturbing the dead."

"Ah, I presume you refer to the—"

"You do not think it counts? Because the deceased is not a Scot?"

"Perhaps," Gray says, his voice low with warning, "you might let Detective McCreadie finish a sentence before deciding what he does and does not mean?"

"Oh, you wish me to be polite, is that it? Being polite gets us nowhere. The only language your sort understand—"

As she catches sight of Gray, she stops. Her mouth works. Then she finds her voice.

"*You* are here, Dr. Gray? I would have hoped for better, though I suppose that is foolish of me. You are not known for speaking out against injustice. Better to hide behind your family name and pretend you have nothing in common with the poor man whose corpse they are about to defile."

"Defiling requires cutting into it," Gray says, his voice mild now that the rudeness is directed at him. "I do so all the time with men—and women—of every sort. I am an equal-opportunity ghoul."

His smile is all teeth and no humor, and the young woman pauses again. She finds her mental footing quickly, though, and says, "This is not the same, and you know it. This is an outrage perpetrated against a man ripped from foreign soil and brought here for the amusement of bored toffs."

"I would agree," Gray says.

Pause. Pause. Her eyes flash as she tries to regroup. Then she thrusts her chin up. "You agree, and yet you do nothing."

"I *do* something. I attend to ensure the proceedings are as respectful as possible."

"Look," I say. "I understand this upsets you, but I'm not sure who you think you're going to convince."

I wave at a well-dressed couple sneaking into the party behind her, taking advantage of her distraction.

"Them?" I say. "Those other ones back there?" I motion to the queue of coaches as Annis and Isla exit theirs. "They don't care. If you want to have an impact when you do this sort of thing, you need a public record of it. Alert the press. Raise a fuss where it can be heard."

"Yes," Isla murmurs as she reaches us. "I know you are upset, Miss King, but this display will not achieve what you intend."

The young woman looks sharply at Isla. "Do we know each other?"

"I follow news of the Edinburgh Seven most keenly," Isla says. "I supported your fight to be admitted to medical school, and I am delighted that you won it. I have heard Miss Jex-Blake speak, and I am thrilled at what she—what you all—have accomplished."

"You supported our victory? Odd that I have not seen you before. Ah, you *quietly* supported us, yes? From the safety of your drawing room?"

Isla flinches. I know why she doesn't more actively support the Seven. Poking her head over that parapet puts a target on it. She's a woman in a male occupation, doing backflips to avoid being noticed.

"You are one of the Seven?" Annis says, moving forward. "Then convey my words of appreciation to the illustrious Miss Jex-Blake. I do not understand why anyone would wish to practice medicine, but I support her right to do so. I would advise, however, that she keep you"—a feral smile—"on a shorter leash. Now, come, children, we have a corpse-defiling to attend."

FOUR

I'd heard of the Edinburgh Seven before I crossed to this time. To discover I'd arrived in the very year they were making history? Kind of awesome, even if I'd only had the vaguest understanding of exactly what they did.

I know the full story now.

In March of 1869, two months before I arrived, Sophia Jex-Blake applied to study medicine. The academic board admitted her, only for the university court to reject her with the excuse that they couldn't make accommodations for just one female student. So she found six more. They became the Edinburgh Seven. They requested and received permission to write the admission exams. Over a hundred and fifty people wrote that exam, including five of the Seven. Four of the women scored in the top seven overall.

A few weeks ago, they signed the matriculation roll, and the University of Edinburgh became the first British university to admit women.

One part of the story I do remember involves a point still in their future, when during their final exams, male students will do everything in their power to help and support them. No, that's the story my happily-ever-after-loving soul wants, where the young men rise up against their narrow-minded elders to help their fellow students. That is not what happens.

Those male classmates will try to keep the women from finishing their exams by making as much of a ruckus as possible outside, including throwing a sheep—yes, a live sheep—into the room. It won't stop the

Edinburgh Seven, so it's still a happy ending, but I'd prefer one where the male students don't go down in history as frat-boy assholes.

Isla is upset and unsettled by Miss King's accusation, and the best person to handle that isn't the brother who will commiserate or the female friend who will rage alongside her. It's McCreadie, the guy who might not fully understand *why* she is upset but will *want* to understand because she *is* upset, and sometimes, that is the best friend of all.

Once we are inside, McCreadie murmurs something about needing a drink and steers Isla off. Then Annis sees someone she needs to speak to. That leaves me at my first Victorian soiree with Gray to myself, and that is not the worst place to be, not the worst place at all.

We wander through the main rooms. The house is lovely—with decor that is downright tasteful for Victorian Britain. Yet the main scenery tonight is the guests in their party clothes. I am at a Victorian soiree, and it is . . . crowded? I guess I picture massive ballrooms, and this is a very different thing. I catch glimpses of bright fabrics and gorgeous jewels and luxurious whiskers, but mostly we are navigating through very tightly packed rooms.

"Would you like to see the artifacts?" he asks, leaning in to whisper as we head down the hall.

"The . . . ?"

"Sir Alastair's artifacts from Egypt. I have heard he has organized a private display of them here, before they go to a museum."

Am I aware that museums in this time are filled with plunder from other nations? Yes, I am, and that does not stop me from going to them any more than the same problem does in my own day. I fully support all efforts to return them, and if asked to boycott an exhibit, I would, but I also know how much museums have contributed to my understanding of the world beyond my narrow borders.

Mark this particular relationship complicated, but I'm still in it, and I won't deny the spark of excitement that comes at Gray's words.

"Yes, please," I say with a smile.

He gives an exaggerated exhale. "Excellent. I feared you might wish to mingle instead."

I take hold of his arm as he navigates through the crowd. "Then you know me not at all, Dr. Gray."

"Oh, I suspect that if I offered you someone interesting to meet, it would be quite a different story, but the only interesting person I know here is Sir Alastair. And I fear that introduction will not be coming from me. In fact, I rather hope we do not encounter the man, as the last time I saw him, he said he had best never lay eyes on me again."

"Uh . . ."

"Yes, perhaps it seems I should have told Annis that, but if I did, it would only make her determined to perform the introduction herself. My sister does adore fireworks."

We're rounding another corner, and I realize Gray is moving swiftly through the house, as if he knows the layout.

"Dare I ask what you did?" I say.

"Me? Why must you presume it was me, dear Mallory?"

"Was it?"

"Not entirely. Sir Alastair led the charge taking umbrage at my unearthing of the body."

"Ah, the grave-digging incident. Sir Alastair was responsible for making sure you couldn't be licensed because of it? Then perhaps we had best not meet him, or I might be compelled to challenge him to a duel."

Gray looks over with a faint smile. "If I thought you actually would, I might be tempted, just to see him sputter indignantly. Yes, he led the charge, but he had plenty of support. The last time I saw him, he said he had best never see my face in the university again."

"But you go there all the time."

He shrugs. "Sir Alastair travels often. He said he had best not *see* me, not that I had best not *go* there."

"The devil is in the details."

"Indeed. I fully admit that Sir Alastair is a fascinating individual, but you will have to content yourself with his Egyptian treasures."

"Probably for the best."

We turn another corner and someone says, "Mr. Awad?"

A man steps in front of us, looking at Gray. "Mr. Awad. I had not heard you'd arrived." When Gray looks confused, the man says, "Oh! My apologies," and switches to address him in a language I don't recognize.

"I fear you have mistaken me for someone else," Gray says.

The man's eyes widen. "Oh! Yes. Given your accent, I most certainly have. My sincerest apologies."

The man retreats quickly, still apologizing, and is gone before we can say anything.

"Awad?" I say. "That sounds Egyptian. Do you think Sir Alastair brought someone from the excavation to speak? I would like to hear that."

"Let us hope so. If he has brought a local archaeologist or historian, that would cast this affair in a slightly less discomfiting light."

Gray waves toward a doorway. It leads into one of the rooms at the back, with what looks like gardens beyond, closed for the winter. Whatever the purpose of this room, everything has been cleared, right down to paintings on the walls being removed, leaving ghostly outlines on the wallpaper, as if that art might detract from the antiquities on display.

I turn to the first table . . . and gasp. Less than five feet away a set of canopic jars is just sitting there, with no glass box, no barrier, nothing between me and the jars.

"You know what those are, I presume," Gray asks as we step into the room.

"Canopic jars," I say. "Before mummification, the embalmer removed the organs through a slit in the corpse's side. And removed the brain through the nose." I look at him. "Can you do that?"

"The question, I believe, is 'Would I want to do that?' And also 'Why.'" He walks up beside me. "It is an intriguing concept, though. To be quite honest, I am not quite certain how they managed it."

"And you ask whether you want to do it and why?" I grin at him. "Because it's a puzzle. The problem would be finding a volunteer. Preferably dead."

"Preferably, yes."

"You'd need to have a reason to do it, I suppose. Beyond satisfying scientific curiosity. Or would you? It would make a valid paper. You should do it. You just need a body."

When I glance over, I can see that brain of his whirring. Then he shakes it off. "You are a bad influence, Mallory."

"I am the *best* influence, and you know it."

There are four jars, all blue-glazed pottery. Each jar lid is shaped like the head of a god. Fortunately, there are labels, or I'd never know which was which, much less be able to name the gods. On the one with the intestines is the falcon-headed Qebehsenuef; baboon-headed Hapi protects the lungs, jackal-headed Duamutef is in charge of the stomach, and human-headed Imsety takes the liver.

"See these?" I point to the line of hieroglyphics on each jar. "It's a spell naming the deceased and invoking the appropriate god."

I spend a few minutes with the jars. Then I realize I've been so wrapped up in the jars that I haven't looked up to see what else is in the room. Now I do, and I gasp again and take a running step forward, before I remember I'm not wearing jeans and sneakers . . . and not eight years old, setting foot in the British Museum for the first time.

Gray gives a soft chuckle behind me, and when he catches up, his smile is pure indulgence that somehow manages to avoid condescension.

"I've been trying to play this cool," I say. "Recognize the cultural concerns and all that, but when my parents went to London, they'd drop me off at the museum, I'd spend hours in the Egyptian exhibit. History in general isn't my thing, but I loved this stuff."

"Because it is suitably macabre."

"I'm so predictable." I look around. "Are we really the only ones here? This is . . ." I struggle for words as scan the room. "This is literal treasure, right here, to see and smell and touch—yes, I know better than to touch it and I won't, but I *could*. Where is everyone?"

He gives a vague wave. "Talking to people they have not spoken to since the last event a few weeks ago."

"Ugh. Do I dare hope they'll at least pay attention during the unwrapping?"

"Silly lass, of course not. They only want to say they were here. We will need to stand near the front of the exhibition if we hope to hear anything other than speculation on what Lady McDonald might serve at her winter ball."

"Well, I can't complain about having this whole room to ourselves. Wait, is that a funerary mask?"

I practically run over to gaze down on the golden mask that would have lain over a mummy's face.

"Really hope they didn't find this on an actual mummy and remove it," I say. "That's cause for cursing."

"For what?"

"A mummy's curse."

At his blank look, I'm about to tease that he needs to lift his head from his medical journals. Then I remember why he looks so confused.

"That's right," I say. "The curses weren't much of a thing before King Tut."

"King who?"

I glance around quickly, ensuring we are alone. "King Tutankhamun. He went on the throne as a boy and died before he turned twenty. After the turn of the century, an archaeologist will find his tomb. Then people will start dying, cursed for disturbing the sleep of the boy king."

"Is that a real story?" says a voice, making me jump. "Or a made-up one?"

Two small figures emerge from the shadows. Children, maybe ten or eleven. One is a girl wearing a child-sized replica of a ladies' gown, though shorter, with petticoats instead of a crinoline cage. She's tall, with light brown curls and skin that looks as if it has spent more time in the sun than one expects of an upper-class Victorian. Behind her stands a boy with dark hair and eyes, his skin the same shade as Gray's.

"I made it up," I say quickly. "Sorry."

"It is still a very good story," the girl says. "Continue."

The boy rolls his eyes. "You cannot command a guest to continue her story, Phoebe."

Her brows rise. "Then what good is being the host's daughter? If I must endure smiling and curtsying to guests, then I ought to be able to command them to finish the stories they began." She lifts her gaze to mine. "You were talking about a curse on a pharaoh's tomb. Does someone die? I do hope so."

"*Phoebe,*" the boy says with exasperation.

"What? It would be a very poor curse if no one died, and I think some of them should." The girl turns as footsteps hurry down the hall. "Would you not agree, Mimi?"

"Agree with what, Phoebe?" A woman appears and smooths the girl's hair. "Dare I ask what you two are pestering our poor guests with now?"

"'You two'?" the boy squawks. "It was not me, Mama."

The woman who has entered is maybe our age. She resembles the boy, with slightly darker skin. She wears a gown even finer than mine, including what has to be an actual Egyptian artifact around her throat—a broad collar of multiple strands, each strung with dozens of tiny amulets.

Before the children can answer, the woman catches sight of us. Her gaze goes to Gray, and she blinks. Then she gives a light laugh and touches her lips, the gesture self-conscious, as if to hide the laugh.

"I am sorry, sir. For a moment, I almost mistook you for . . . someone else."

"I have already been mistaken for a Mr. Awad," he says.

"Uncle Selim?" Phoebe says.

"He is my uncle, not yours," the boy says.

"As our parents are now married, Michael, that makes him *our* uncle. If you do not wish to share him, I will take him, and you may have my uncle Thomas, who is a right old bore."

The woman sighs deeply. "I must apologize for the children. They have spent too long in Cairo and have quite forgotten how to be proper Scottish lads and lasses."

"Because we're not Scottish," Phoebe says. "I was born in Cairo, like Michael. We are Egyptian." She turns to us. "It is nicer in Egypt, where it is much too warm to wear all this." She pulls at her dress. "And that makes a fine excuse for not wearing it."

I turn to Gray. "Might we go to Egypt, Dr. Gray? Please."

The girl laughs, but the woman gives a sharp intake of breath.

"Gray?" she says. "Dr. Duncan Gray?"

Gray stiffens, almost imperceptibly, and I do, too, fearing what she has heard.

"Oh! Where are my manners?" she says. "I am supposed to be the evening's hostess, however little I might feel it. I am Miriam Christie. My husband is Sir Alastair. These are our children—my son, Michael, by my first husband, and my husband's daughter, Phoebe, by his first wife."

Anyone else looking at Gray in that moment would see only a very polite nod preceding his gracious greeting. But I know him well enough to see that flicker of confusion, and I suspect he did not know the first Lady Christie was dead . . . or that Sir Alastair had remarried.

"You are Dr. Duncan Gray?" Phoebe says.

"Er, yes." His tone says he's dreading what stories she might associate with that name. "And this is my assistant, Miss Mallory Mit—"

"Mitchell?" Phoebe says, her eyes rounding. She elbows her stepbrother and whispers, "It is Miss Mitchell."

"Yes," Michael says dryly. "That is what Dr. Gray was saying. You have excellent hearing when you choose to listen, Phoebe."

I'm opening my mouth to say they have clearly mistaken me for another

Miss Mitchell, when Lady Christie beams and says, "We have been following your cases most ardently, Dr. Gray and Miss Mitchell."

"There is too much about Dr. Gray in them," Phoebe interjects. "And not enough about Miss Mitchell. You must speak to the writer."

"Writer?" That's the only word I can manage.

"I fear I do not know his name," Lady Christie says. "He publishes anonymously, and he has only just begun chronicling your adventures, working through your past cases."

"This is . . . news," Gray says when I cannot find words. "How . . . flattering."

"To you," Phoebe says tartly. "Not to Miss Mallory, who is described only as your flaxen-haired assistant. I presume she is there to do more than look pretty, which does not seem a very useful skill in a detective."

"Oh, you would be surprised," I say.

"Miss Mallory does far more than look pretty," Gray says. "I must take a look at these stories and correct any misunderstanding."

"Miss Mallory was telling *us* a story," Phoebe says. "About a curse on a pharaoh's tomb."

"A made-up story," Michael corrects. "And she was telling Dr. Gray. You interrupted and demanded she continue."

"Because it was a good story. It was about men who are cursed for breaking into the tomb and stealing the artifacts under the pretense of doing it for science. I think people *should* be cursed for such things." She looks at Lady Christie. "Would you not agree, Mimi?"

"Oh dear," Lady Christie says, her cheeks darkening in a flush. "I am so sorry, Dr. Gray and Miss Mitchell. My daughter has . . . very strong opinions. Ones that are . . ." She glances at Phoebe sternly. "Not appropriate at such a gathering."

"Why? Because I am saying that my father should be cursed for unwrapping a mummy as entertainment? He should. Nothing fatal, of course. Boils would do."

"Oh dear," Lady Christie repeats.

I smile at Phoebe. "I think a nonfatal case of boils would not be an inappropriate punishment in some cases." I lower my voice. "But please don't tell your father I said that."

"*Please* don't," Gray murmurs. "Sir Alastair already has a poor opinion of me."

Lady Christie frowns. "Why ever would he—? Oh!" Her eyes round. "You are *that* Duncan Gray. The one his sister—" Her hand flies to her mouth.

"Oh dear," I murmur, and I think it's too low for anyone to hear but Phoebe snickers.

"I am sorry," Lady Christie says. "I failed to make the connection. Not that it is anything of consequence. You were young, and his sister was a widow and . . ." Her gaze shoots to me and she clears her throat. "Nothing wrong with it at all."

Huh. Seems Gray left out part of the story.

"You are most welcome here, Dr. Gray," Lady Christie says firmly. "If my husband says otherwise, I will correct him. I am certain he is over it. Not that he had any right to be offended, as it did not concern him and . . ." She clears her throat again. "Enough of that. Did someone mention a story about a cursed pharaoh?"

Yep, nothing like a curse story to break an awkward moment.

"Shall I continue?" I say. "Or start from the beginning?"

Before they can answer, a man carrying a tray of glasses hurries in, those empty glasses clinking. "Lady Christie? We have been looking everywhere for you. There is a situation." He leans down to whisper something, and Lady Christie's eyes half close, telling me the "situation" is less cause for alarm than annoyance.

"Thank you," she says. "I will find him."

She turns to us. "Children, we must take our leave of Dr. Gray and Miss Mitchell. The demonstration is to begin soon, and there is no sign of your father."

"He will be trapped speaking to some bore who will not release him," Phoebe says.

"Likely yes, and so we must intervene."

"*You* must. I'm staying with them." Phoebe gestures at us.

"Phoebe, you cannot—"

"Miss Mitchell hasn't finished her story."

"But the demonstration will soon begin—"

"I'll watch it with them. Or, if you would prefer, I could wander about on my own, telling other guests what I think of unwrapping mummies . . ."

"She is fine with us," I say quickly. "That will free you to look for Sir Alastair."

Lady Christie hesitates. We both assure her it's fine, and she finally departs. Phoebe waits for her to be gone and then whispers, "You can tell me the curse story later. First, let us show you the ushabtis."

"Ushabtis?" I say.

Phoebe grins and points at a display of figurines. "Servants. For the afterlife."

"Well, that's better than taking the actual servants like the Vikings did," I say.

"We did that, too," Michael says. "The Egyptians, that is. During the First Dynasty."

"Tell them the story about these ushabtis," she says to Michael. Then she looks at us. "It has the most gruesome story attached."

"Now you are commanding *me* to tell stories?" Michael says.

"What else are little brothers for?"

"I am two weeks younger. Two *weeks*."

"And, having been tardy as always, you now find yourself forever cursed . . . with being my *younger* brother. Come now. Tell them the story."

FIVE

We're still in the treasure room, having moved on to discuss the death mask, when Annis's voice erupts behind us.

"Dear Lord," she says. "Leave them alone for an hour and look what happens. They have children already."

"Even Duncan cannot work that bit of scientific magic," McCreadie says. "They merely borrowed these two, testing the idea on for size."

"May I introduce our guests," I say. "Or our hosts, as the case may be. This is Phoebe, and this is Michael. They are Sir Alastair's children." I turn to the children. "These are Dr. Gray's sisters, Mrs. Ballantyne and Lady Leslie, and our dear friend, Detective McCreadie."

"Detective McCreadie?" This time it's Michael piping up, voice tinged with admiration. "The police detective? From the stories?"

"Stories?" McCreadie says, but before anyone can answer, Phoebe walks up to Annis and says, "Lady Annis Leslie? The one accused of murdering her husband with poison?"

"Yes, though that is not usually how I introduce myself."

Isla shoots her a look. "It is *exactly* how you introduce yourself."

"Not to children. That would be wrong."

"You should never have been arrested," Phoebe says. "It was obvious you did not do it. You had no motive. You had your own money, and no need to kill your husband. The police were fools."

"I like this child," Annis says.

"Also," Michael says, "when Phoebe says the police were fools, she does not mean you, Detective McCreadie."

"Good to know," McCreadie murmurs.

"What's this about stories?" Isla asks, turning to me.

I say, "It seems someone has been chronicling and publishing our adventures."

"What? How did I not know this?"

"It appears to be a recent development, and we have been busy."

"Do you think it is . . ." Isla lowers her voice. "Jack?"

"If it is, I'm having a word with her."

McCreadie clears his throat. "I hate to interrupt, but we were seeking you for a purpose. The demonstration is about to begin. Perhaps the children should . . . retire?"

Phoebe huffs at him, and Michael looks disappointed, as if the fine detective just dropped in his estimation.

"Or not?" McCreadie says. "I do not know what your parents wish."

"Does it matter?" Phoebe says.

"As we are your parents' guests," Isla says gently, "it does matter. Disobeying their wishes would be rude."

"So? I would rather be honestly rude than falsely polite."

"I do like this child," Annis says. "If I could have been guaranteed of having one like this, I would have done so."

"All things considered," I say, "you were pretty much guaranteed to have a child like this."

"Nonsense," Annis says. "I had a fifty percent chance of that, and a fifty percent chance of having a mealymouthed brat, who fashions herself as such to spite me. Children do love to rebel against their parents, flouting all their influences."

"Ah," I say. "That is your excuse then. Rebellion."

Her eyes narrow, but she only shakes her head.

"We can take the children with us," I say. "We will be standing near the front, to properly hear the demonstration, and so if their parents do not wish them there, they will say so."

"We are expected to attend," Michael says. "Mother believes we ought to learn as much as we can, and Sir Alastair . . . ?" He shrugs.

"My father does not care what we do," Phoebe says. "As long as we do not do it near enough to disturb him."

"Then you shall need to be quiet, Phoebe," Michael says. "Can you manage it?"

She makes what I presume is a rude gesture, and Michael smiles at her before they lead us to the demonstration room.

I am going to die of heatstroke. That will be my epitaph. Traveled back in time to Victorian Scotland. Survived all the unsanitary horrors of the time, only to die at a fancy party because she was wearing too many layers of dress, stuffed into a room with others wearing too many layers of dress, and no one would open a damn window.

It would help if there *were* windows. We're in an interior room that would comfortably host a dozen people and holds three times that, and as Gray warned, no one is paying the least bit of attention to the fact that there is an actual mummy on the table.

Okay, that's not true. Two boys tried to make a game out of daring one another to touch it, until the stone-faced butler shooed them off. And by "boys" I mean they were in their early twenties. The actual children have been chatting with us, far more politely than the grown-ups in the room, who keep raising their voices to be heard over the din, which of course only adds to the din. We've settled for taking a corner and trying to converse, while sweat drips down our faces.

"This is ridiculous," Phoebe says finally. "Where *is* Father?"

"I wonder if Mama is still trying to locate him," Michael says.

Phoebe harrumphs. "Then why are we all packed into this room like a jar of kippers?"

When a man with a cane moves up beside the mummy, I notice him, mostly due to the sheer number of shiny medals on his suit coat.

"Former military?" I whisper to Gray.

He shakes his head. "Those would be medals earned by his grandfather, who was quite a hero in the French revolutionary wars. That is Lord Muir. He sponsors Sir Alastair's expeditions."

Lord Muir is perhaps in his late sixties. Stout and bearded, with white whiskers and hair and bright blue eyes. He's obviously trying to get everyone's attention, and growing red-faced when he cannot. Finally someone whistles, and that vulgarity has the room dropping to silence.

"Thank you," Muir says. "I hate to be the bearer of bad news, but I am afraid the demonstration cannot proceed. As many of you have noticed, our esteemed host has been unable to join us."

Guests look at each other, clearly conveying that they had *not* noticed. That's why Lady Christie had been able to take time from her hostess duties to talk to us. Not because people were ignoring the second wife, but because they wouldn't have noticed whether the host and hostess were present. They'd been too busy enjoying their hospitality.

"We had hoped Sir Alastair would join us soon," the man continues. "But I fear he continues to be indisposed. I understand this will be a terrible disappointment. Perhaps we can schedule the unwrapping for another day."

"But we're here now," a young man says, chest puffing in a way that suggests a few too many glasses of booze-soaked punch. "We were promised an unwrapping, and I am staying until I get an unwrapping."

A few murmured voices join in with their support.

"You do the honors then," an elderly woman says, waving at Lord Muir.

"The honors?" Muir says.

"Unwrap the thing."

Muir blinks. "I am neither a surgeon nor an Egyptologist."

"What does that matter?"

Gray seems ready to rock forward in protest, but McCreadie catches his jacket.

"I do not like the looks of this," McCreadie murmurs. "I have seen too many dangerous mobs."

I want to laugh. Dangerous mob? This is a party of Edinburgh's wealthiest and most influential. Yet when I think that, the crowd surges toward the central table.

"We should remove the children," Isla says.

"Agreed," McCreadie says.

I expect Phoebe to protest, but she's looking toward the mummy, her eyes clouded with obvious concern.

"Take the children please," McCreadie murmurs to Isla and me. "We will do what we can here."

"You cannot let them unwrap the mummy," Michael says. "They will rip it apart."

Someone reaches out and grabs a loose wrapping, and Michael lunges, caught by Gray, who steps forward, saying, "Come now, enough of this."

"Dr. Gray!" a voice says, rising over the crowd. We turn to see Lady Christie fighting her way through. "Dr. Gray! Yes!" Her voice goes louder. "We do not need to postpone the demonstration. We have a very capable surgeon in our midst."

Gray stops fast.

"Dr. Gray," she says, hurrying over to him. Her smile is gentle but her eyes glow with panic. She turns to the mob. "I am sure many of you know Dr. Duncan Gray. He is perfectly suited for this task. Not only does he possess a surgeon's training, but he is a local undertaker with experience in science of a forensic nature."

"Cutting up dead bodies, you mean," says someone I can't see.

"For science," Lady Christie says firmly. "It is a noble endeavor, and combined with his surgical background, I cannot imagine anyone more suited to this task if my husband is indisposed."

"I-I do not think—" Gray says, too low for others to hear.

"Please," she says, meeting his gaze. "I hate to impose but . . ."

"Either you do it," Annis says, "or they rip that mummy open like a wrapped present."

"Please," Phoebe says.

Gray's gaze shoots to mine. I won't add to the chorus of voices begging him to do this. If he's uncomfortable, he needs to be allowed to make his own choice.

"Would you assist?" he whispers to me.

"Of course," I say.

"I cannot provide the proper historical dialogue," he says to Lady Christie. "I can only report on what I see and the medical implications."

"Michael and I can give the lecture," Phoebe pipes up. "You only need to do the unwrapping."

Gray takes a deep breath and glances toward the table, where the jackals circle.

"All right," he says, raising his voice to be heard. "I will not be able to fully take Sir Alastair's place, but let us see if we can attempt a proper unwrapping."

SIX

"It will be fine," Gray whispers to me as Lady Christie slips away to retrieve her husband's medical tools. "We will be respectful." He passes me a small smile. "For science."

I try and fail to return that smile.

"If you would rather not participate . . ." he says.

"We have an excuse to unwrap a mummy," I say. "I'm not going anywhere. I just know that this is also a bigger share of the limelight than you like."

Gray has always worked off-stage. He presents his findings quietly to McCreadie and doesn't speak at trials or give lectures. That's how he's happiest. Left to work without having strangers accuse him of being a ghoul with an unnatural interest in the dead. He gets enough of that from asshole cops who don't know that the work he and others are doing will revolutionize criminal investigations.

That has started to change, though. His name slipped into the discourse during our first case together, and it was firmly planted there during our second case, thanks to both Jack and Gray's own sister—Annis, of course.

At the time, Gray had said he wasn't concerned because no one would care. He was just a scientist. But now apparently someone is chronicling his adventures, and I can damn well bet the focus isn't on the science. We're in a world just discovering a fascination with detectives, and I'm worried that Gray is going to get caught in it.

"I suspect the curtain over my activities has already been drawn back too far to be closed again," he says. "Which seems to oddly coincide with me taking on a certain assistant. I never had this before, you know, despite my years of working with Hugh."

"Your vast decades of working together? Exactly how many years, Gray?"

His lips twitch, as they often do when I call him that. "Almost three."

"Yeah, that wasn't going to last, with or without me. You're too damn interesting."

"That oddly sounds like a compliment."

"It is one. I toss them out every now and then to keep my boss happy. His ego is so fragile."

Another lip twitch. Gray might be a very private person, but it is not for lack of self-confidence.

"As for these new stories," I say. "If it's Jack, I'll tell her to stop. If she refuses, I'll threaten to kick her ass. She's already said she wouldn't want to face me in the ring."

"Are you saying you would challenge her to a duel to defend my honor?"

"Happily."

That smile grows, his eyes dancing as he leans closer, lips parting to whisper—

"Here is everything you should need, Dr. Gray," Lady Christie says as she appears with a tray of medical implements.

Around us, everyone had gone back to chattering. Now silence falls as Gray takes the tray, and Phoebe and Michael run over to join. It is time to begin.

To the obvious displeasure of the crowd, the children and I insist on beginning with a short lecture, grounding the night's events in their historical context. I leave most of this to the kids and play the role of mediator only when they start arguing over a point of contention in the history.

The kids really *are* amazing. If they don't grow up to play notable roles in Egyptology, I'll be both shocked and disappointed. It seems that Phoebe has spent much of her young life living on excavation sites and, with a father who let her run wild, she indulged her natural curiosity. I suspect she already knows more than most archaeologists of this day. Michael's expertise is the history of his country and his people, and he puts the mummification into its historical, cultural, and religious context.

The children explain the full process of mummification, starting with removing the organs and stuffing incense-perfumed cloth in their place. Then the body is covered in a salty powder called natron and left to dry for about six weeks. After that, the stuffing is removed and replaced, the incisions are sewn up, and the body is covered in resin.

Next come the shroud and the wrappings. The bandages—up to four thousand square feet's worth—are supplied by the deceased's family, which among the poor could include rags and household linens. As the body is wrapped, hot resin is brushed on as a glue. The embalmers will recite protective spells as they work and may place amulets among the layers.

Once the mummy is done, it's put in a cartonnage case, which sounds like papier-mâché made with papyrus and other fibers. Then comes the funerary mask, like the one we saw on display. It will be decorated with a likeness of either the deceased or a god. The cartonnage case is placed into a suhet—a coffin painted to look like a person—and the suhet is ceremoniously taken to the tomb, where it's propped against the wall.

The children impart their knowledge with a liveliness and brevity that even my English prof father could learn from. Sorry, Dad, but you do go on sometimes.

Despite the fact that the children talk for barely ten minutes, the guests' attention doesn't just waver. It never exists in the first place. While a few listen, either out of interest or courtesy, most are too rude to even humor the children, and they resume conversations, as if the kids are on a television playing in the background.

My glares only bounce off the offenders. Well, they bounce off most, though a couple of the men seem to mistake them for flirting. My only consolation is that McCreadie and Isla move to the front and prove as rapt an audience as Lady Christie. Even Annis comes forward to listen, and several others do as well, enough that—I hope—all the children see is an appreciative audience.

As they end, Michael's high, clear voice rings out over the group. "Sir Alastair has brought two mummies to Edinburgh to further advance the study of Egyptian burial practices. As you can see, this one is not well wrapped, and so it is the one we will be examining today, while the other has been delivered to the university for further study."

Phoebe takes over. "This mummy was not found in a proper suhet or even a cartonnage case, which accounts for the condition of its wrappings.

It was located in a corridor, and we could not determine where it belonged. The tomb had previously been robbed, and most of the mummies had been removed from their suhets and taken from the tomb altogether. This one seems to have been partially unwrapped, as you can see, as if the thieves had been looking for amulets or jewels under the layers. We do not know who lies within these wrappings, and that is why my father felt it was acceptable to open the mummy here, so that we might be able to determine who lies within and properly repatriate the remains."

Guests look at one another, brows furrowing, either at the unfamiliar word or the unfamiliar concept.

Michael says, "Dr. Gray? If you would begin, please."

Gray inclines his head in a nod. Then he looks at the crowd. "I will be unwrapping with care, out of respect for the dead. Aiding me is my assistant, Miss Mallory Mitchell."

I don't miss the snicker that goes up at that. Assistant indeed. They all know the truth—Gray has found himself a pretty girl to fetch and carry his implements . . . and possibly more.

If Gray notices the snicker, he ignores it and leans over to whisper a plan to me. This is not a Christmas gift to be easily or quickly unwrapped. It's going to take time, and no one here wants that. So both of us will move as fast as we dare in removing the outer wrappings.

Fortunately, as Phoebe said, the wrappings are in poor condition. The resin that would have glued them together seems to have dissolved, suggesting a cut-rate mummification.

The outer layer shows the classic mummy shape, with the legs together and arms crossed over the chest. It's lumpier than I would have expected. The children had said padding was often used to fill out the form, and I suppose the lumps are another sign of poor—or hastily done—mummification.

I start at the legs with scissors. Yes, scissors, because otherwise, this would take hours. I don't have the luxury of latex gloves, but at least I have silk ones, though I suspect this will be the end of them. The smell of the grave doesn't come off with a simple soak. As we begin, a maid lights pots of incense, and it's not just for atmosphere.

We get the outer layers off more easily than I expected. Then we're down to a recognizable body, with the legs wrapped individually.

"You will note that the legs are bound at the knees," I say. "And that the feet are held apart by packing material. Also, if we examine the wrappings, we can see that some of it is made from old clothing. There's an armhole here." I lift a piece and demonstrate. "I believe that would suggest a relatively poor person inside the wrappings."

"It would," Michael says. "As Phoebe said, Egyptians used whatever cloth was available, including old clothing."

Someone in the crowd audibly sighs with impatience. When someone else makes a hurry-up gesture, McCreadie steps in front of them and smiles.

"We are almost through," I say. "I don't know how many of you will have seen a mummified body, but I should prepare you for what will likely be a disturbing sight."

And with that, the room falls to a hush. A few women raise a gloved hand to their faces, as if preparing to cover their eyes, but those eyes stay trained on my fingers, as I slowly unwrap the mummy's leg.

"I really cannot stress this enough," I say. "If you are faint of heart—or stomach—you may wish to avert your gaze."

No one averts their gaze. Phoebe smirks at me, knowing I'm playing it up for the audience.

"Only a few moments left," I say. "I can see the skin, darkened from the mummification process. If you wish to look away, now is the—"

"Miss Mitchell," Gray says.

I glance over, ready to apologize for the theatrics. If we need to unwrap this poor soul, then I want to make it count and hold their attention. But if Gray has a problem with how I'm treating the procedure, I'll defer to him.

Yet the look he's giving isn't one of warning. In fact, he's not looking at me at all. He's staring down at the corpse.

Gray hasn't been unwrapping as quickly as I have, so his section—the head—is still covered. But he's standing there, gazing down with a deep crease between his brows.

"Hmm?" I say as I move to him.

He looks at me and then down again. I don't see what he's . . .

Oh, that's odd. At my end of the body, the skin appeared dark under the last layers. That's expected, whatever the skin color of the mummified person. But while Gray still has a few layers to go, a poorly wrapped section exposes part of the cheek through the gap. And that skin isn't much darker than mine.

"Something on the face?" I whisper as I move closer. "Some sort of under-the-wrap death mask?"

He motions for me to touch the still-wrapped portion of the cheek. I frown, but I do as he asks.

"Press down," he whispers.

"What the devil is going on?" someone says. "You're almost there. Get on with it."

I ignore the murmur of assent that follows. I press my fingers on the wrapped cheek, and there's give where there should not be give.

"Something went wrong with the desiccation process?" I whisper.

Gray hesitates. Then he says, "Yes, that must be it."

He clears his throat and turns to the audience. "There appears to be an issue with the upper part of the body. It may not have been properly desiccated. We are going to leave that for now and turn our attention to the legs."

A grumble ripples through the crowd.

"We will return to the head," I say. "Once we have ascertained the damage."

The children look at each other. Michael steps up to us and lowers his voice.

"What sort of damage?" he whispers.

"The face is not as we expect it," I say. "It could indicate a failed mummification."

His frown grows. "That does happen but . . ."

"The skin seems very pale. I expected darker, from the process."

He shakes his head. "No, natron dries without the significant darkening you'd see in a natural mummification. There were also paler-skinned people in ancient Egypt, with those who traveled from Rome and Greece."

"That might be it. But the skin also seems softer than I'd expect."

"Oh?" He hesitates. "Oh, that is . . ." He shakes his head. "Perhaps it is a poor mummification, as you said. Forgive the interruption. Continue."

I want to ask what he's thinking, but he's moved away, and now he's in a whispered conference with Phoebe. Lady Christie moves closer to join in the discussion.

Gray is already at the mummified corpse's leg, where I had almost finished the unwrapping.

"We are nearly done here," Gray says, "and seeing what we ought to."

"Yes," I join in as I raise my voice for the audience. "The flesh is hard beneath the bandages, and the desiccation has darkened the skin."

Except, as Michael said, the skin *shouldn't* be darkened. It must really be a poor mummification.

"We are at the end." Gray raises his voice. "We are about to uncover the leg of the mummy. Miss Mitchell will do the honors."

He offers me the end of the bandage with a little bow, as if handing me a rose. Despite the solemnity of the moment, I have to smile. Apparently, theatrics are indeed allowed.

I take the end between my gloved thumb and forefinger. Then I very gently ease it under the mummy's leg and out the other side, pulling it up and over the shin to reveal—

I stop.

I'm not seeing dark and wizened flesh. It looks like cloth, as if the mummy was wrapped while still wearing something over its legs.

"What's that?" someone says. "A trouser leg?"

I let out a light laugh. "It looks like that, doesn't it? It seems we are not at the mummy yet. Something has been wrapped around its leg. Perhaps the deceased was injured in life, and an assistive device was left on to help in the afterlife."

Michael turns to frown at me. Right. "Assistive device" isn't the period-appropriate term.

"A leg binding," I say. "To aid in mobil—with walking."

Gray is already beside me, having taken the bandage from my hand and unwrapping the leg as I speak. He has revealed an entire swath of dark fabric.

Dark and whole fabric. Showing no ravages of time. Because of the wrappings? Would cotton hold up that long? I know Egypt had cotton. Only it isn't cotton. It's wool. Dark wool—

"Take the children out," Gray says to the room, as the reality of what I'm seeing hits me.

Dark wool trousers.

Victorian trousers.

"Children out," he snaps. "Clear the room! Hugh! I need your assistance." He turns to me and lowers his voice. "Someone—"

"—is inside these wrappings," I say. "This isn't a mummy."

Gray is at the corpse's head, unwrapping as fast as he can, and I wonder why until I realize what he clearly has figured out already: we might not be dealing with a corpse.

I hurry to the mummy's head, but McCreadie is already there, helping without needing an explanation. I wildly look around to see a room full of people watching with the same intent interest they'd shown during the final unwrapping.

I bite back the urge to snarl at them to get out. And say what? That someone has been wrapped in mummy bindings? A possibly live person? That this is a crime scene? None of them would leave after that.

I wheel toward where the children were, but Isla is escorting them out, flanked by two members of the staff. Good.

Gray and McCreadie are almost through. I can see the clear outline of a face now. A masculine face with a light tan and a light brown beard. McCreadie is unwrapping a piece around the neck, and when he pulls back the bandages, they're spotted with blood. Clear ligature lines cut around the base of the neck, below the beard. A ligature pulled so deep it drew blood.

A gasp from the crowd.

"Is he dead?" someone says.

They keep unwrapping. A mouth next, and Gray moves down to check for breath as McCreadie takes over unwrapping the upper part of the face. A nose. Then eyes. Brown eyes that stare lifeless at the ceiling.

"Sir Alastair!" someone shouts.

And Lady Christie begins to scream.

SEVEN

I spend the next ten minutes helping McCreadie clear the room. I don't care if I'm not a cop here. I don't care if I get huffs of indignation. Detective Mallory comes out and orders everyone away from her damn crime scene and pushes them there if they don't move fast enough. Several of the men help, as does Annis. Isla has returned and pulled Lady Christie away.

The clock is striking eleven as McCreadie thanks those who lingered to help and then politely but firmly shoos them out. He calls in one of the male staff and sends him to alert both the police and Dr. Addington.

Then the doors are closed, and it's just Gray, McCreadie, Annis, me, and the dead Sir Alastair.

"Lady Leslie," I say. "I am not going to order you out, but I would appreciate it if you would go and speak to Isla. She's going to need help. Maybe take the children for Lady Christie?"

I expect Annis to argue, especially about being put in charge of children, but she only nods and says she'll see what she can do.

I move up to where Gray is unwrapping the body of a sandy-bearded, average-looking man in his late thirties, with the build and callused hands of someone accustomed to manual labor.

"This is definitely Sir Alastair?" I say.

"It is."

"Then . . . I don't understand. You substituted for him because he was indisposed. No one could have murdered him and wrapped him that fast." I stop. "Wait. The mummy was already on the table when we got in here. Before we were told Sir Alastair couldn't make it."

"Yes," Gray says, which is not helpful at all, but it's also a fair answer. He's the doctor and the temporary coroner and crime-scene tech. He's not the detective. That would be me . . . and the guy standing behind us.

I turn to McCreadie.

"We need to discover who said Sir Alastair was indisposed," McCreadie says. "And quickly, before they leave the building."

"I'll help." I turn to Gray. "Is that okay?"

"What I am doing is hardly urgent. *That* is."

I find Isla in a sitting room with Lady Christie. They're together on a settee, and when I walk in, Lady Christie is saying, "I must go to the children. I know I must, but I need to compose myself first."

"Take a few minutes more," Isla says. "They will not need you until then, but yes, they will need you, and you should not concern yourself with seeming distraught. They will expect that."

Lady Christie nods. Her eyes are red rimmed, her face streaked with tears.

I rap on the wall as I enter. Then I half curtsy, because it feels like the right thing to do.

"My sincerest condolences," I say as I come into the room. "I am so sorry for your loss and also sorry that I need to bother you at such a time. I promise I will be as quick as I can, but Detective McCreadie needs me to ask you something before the guests disperse."

Silent apologies to McCreadie for the blame, but he'd understand that I need his authority here.

"Yes," Isla says quickly. "The police must move swiftly in such situations, as I know from Detective McCreadie, and they must ask uncomfortable questions at the worst possible times. If they could wait, they would."

I send Isla a look of thanks as Lady Christie wipes her eyes and says, "I understand."

Here's my opening, and I must proceed with care, because the person most likely to have started the lie that Sir Alastair was indisposed . . . is his wife.

"Do you know who last spoke to Sir Alastair?" I ask. "I understand he was feeling poorly."

Her cheeks darken in a flush and her gaze drops. "No, that was a lie."

"A lie that he was indisposed?"

She nods. "I do not wish to lay blame elsewhere, but saying he was indisposed was not my idea. It was an excuse given when we could not find my husband."

"I recall you were looking for him earlier."

"We were, and we could not find him so Lord—someone else— suggested we say he was indisposed."

"Lord Muir?" Isla says. "I understand you do not wish to lay blame, but the police will require a clear order of events and the people involved."

Lady Christie swallows. "Yes, it was Lord Muir. We had been looking for my husband all evening, and it became clear he was not about, and so Lord Muir said we should say he was indisposed, as saying we could not find him would seem odd."

"It would . . . yet you and Lord Muir did not find it odd that you couldn't find Sir Alastair?"

She flushes again. "This event was Lord Muir's idea, and as he funded the expedition, my husband did not feel he could refuse, but Alastair was not above . . . That is to say . . . He could be . . ." She takes a deep breath. "My husband is—was—a brilliant man, and he did not like intrusions on his studies, and this event was an intrusion."

I recall Phoebe saying something to the same effect—that she could do as she liked as long as she didn't get in her father's way. In the way of his studies and occupations and interests, I presume.

"I realize it paints my husband in a poor light, to say that we were not surprised he had made himself scarce this evening, but Alastair was, as I say, brilliant, and with brilliance comes eccentricity."

Yeah, that's not eccentricity. I live with two brilliant people, and neither Gray nor Isla would leave their friends and loved ones scrambling to cover for them because they were pissy that an obligation interfered with their work. But sometimes brilliance and selfishness go hand in hand. Sir Alastair didn't want to do the demonstration, and because he's a singular sort of fellow—baronet, surgeon, and Egyptologist—he shouldn't have to, even if he would humiliate his wife and sponsor by not showing up.

Except he *hadn't* skipped out, had he? His personality was simply such that no one questioned it when he seemed to be doing exactly that.

"When did you last see him?" I ask.

She fidgets, her gaze dropping. "I . . . That is to say . . . My husband and I lead very separate lives, Miss Mitchell. When he and his first wife lived in Cairo, I was the . . ." She clears her throat. "I was the governess. Penelope—the first Lady Christie—and I went to school together in London. We were friends. That was how she met Sir Alastair—she came to visit me in Cairo." A soft smile lightens her grief. "Penelope was a wonderful woman, so very much like Phoebe. She was my dearest friend and . . ." She blinks up in mild horror. "And that has nothing to do with this. I am rambling, and I apologize."

"Not at all. It helps me understand."

It helps me understand a great deal. The first Lady Christie dies, and who does Sir Alastair choose for his second wife? His wife's best friend and his daughter's governess. Saved him the bother of trying to figure out who would care for Phoebe. Just give the governess a promotion.

Oh, I know that's not necessarily the case, but it's a possibility that gives me some insight into this marriage.

Lady Christie continues, "When my husband was wrapped up in his work, it was not uncommon for me to go all day without seeing him. He took his meals at the excavation or in his offices, and would often return after the children and I had gone to bed. Now that we are back in Edinburgh, he has been busy cataloguing his finds and meeting with museum officials. All of which is an explanation—an excuse even—for what I am about to admit: that I have not seen him since early this morning. We ate breakfast together, and then I took the children for a walk while he worked. When I returned, Alastair was gone. After that, I was busy making ready for the party. I did not think it odd that Alastair did not come home for lunch or tea—that was the usual way of things, much to our cook's frustration. As for dinner, it was a haphazard affair, as we all had to get ready for the party."

"You did not see *him* get ready?"

A long pause. Then, her voice gentle, "We do not share bedchambers or dressing rooms, Miss Mallory."

Right. This is an era where the wealthy have their own rooms. The middle class often try to emulate that, separating themselves from the poor, who must—shudder—share a bed with their spouse.

"Of course," I say, with a small smile. "In a house like this, you could easily go the day and not see each other."

"You truly can. My husband had his own chambers, and when he left, he preferred to walk to his destination—he often complained at how sedentary life is here, compared with the excavation site. The staff were endlessly despairing that they never knew whether he was in or out. I tried to explain that it would help if he told them when he was leaving, but that can be difficult for people to understand if they have not been in service themselves. I believe you were a housemaid, yes?"

"Yes, and you are correct. It helps the staff to know whether their employers are at home. So you didn't see Sir Alastair all day, and then when you realized he wasn't simply late to the party, you went looking."

"Lord Muir and I did. We asked the staff, and no one had seen Alastair since morning. Still, we presumed he'd come in and slipped past unnoticed. It was not until after I saw you and Dr. Gray that I realized there was an easy way to determine whether he was at the party—had he dressed yet? He insists on wearing even party attire that does not require assistance, as he does not like his valet to dress him, so I checked whether the clothing his valet laid out was still there. It was. Which meant he was not at home. That was when Lord Muir suggested we say Alastair was indisposed."

She twists her handkerchief. "I hated the deception, but Lord Muir pointed out—rightly—that the alternative would be humiliating to my husband. We could not admit that Alastair was behaving . . ."

She doesn't fill in the rest. I can. Behaving like a petulant child.

She continues quickly, as if reading my mind, "I thought it could easily have been a mistake. We did not even discuss the party at breakfast. I knew it made him ill-tempered. He could have left and forgotten all about it." She stops, her face twisting with grief. "Or that was what I had hoped, and now it seems . . ." She looks at me. "Is it possible he never left? That we have spent the day presuming he is at work, and he was right here, being . . . being . . ."

She breaks off in a sob, and maybe I should feel terrible for coldly analyzing that sob, but that's my job. I look for signs of actual tears. I look for signs of actual grief. I look for any hint that she's putting on a show. I liked what I've seen of Miriam Christie—and I certainly like her children. But I've met too many killers who—on first and even second and third meeting—I liked very well.

Her grief seems genuine, but even that isn't proof she couldn't have killed her husband. Not everyone who commits murder is a cold-blooded sociopath. An argument. A shove and an accidental death, and then the ligature marks and the mummy trappings to disguise it as murder by persons unknown.

If I must remain impartial, though, that helps me wait out the sob and then push on with my questions.

"Do you know when the mummy was placed on the table?" I ask.

"When the . . . ? Oh!" Her hand flies to her mouth. "Oh!"

I give her a moment to work through the horror of that, while Isla pats her arm in the sympathy I can't show. Yes, Lady Christie has just realized that her husband's dead body had been on display for God knows how long, but knowing exactly how long that was will be vital for the investigation.

"Is there someone else I can get that information from?" I say finally. "Whoever was in charge of the mummy?"

"That was supposed to be Selim," she says. "My younger brother, who has not yet arrived. The plan was for the mummy to be in place this afternoon. Selim was going to arrange it and ensure it was guarded until the demonstration. During the party, he intended to be there, along with Michael and Phoebe, to answer questions but . . ."

She throws up her hands. "He telegraphed yesterday that his ship was delayed, but he was still supposed to be here by noon, and we spent the afternoon expecting him. When the party started and there was still no sign of him, I had two of the men carry the mummy into the demonstration room. We then kept the door closed, so that no one . . ."

Her gaze shoots to mine. "Selim." She inhales sharply. "Alastair was missing, and now he is dead, and Selim has not arrived and . . . Oh!"

Lady Christie turns to Isla. "I must speak to the children immediately, but I also need someone to look for my brother. I know which ship he came in on, and we were going to all meet him at the harbor, but with the delay, we did not know when he would arrive."

"Is your brother familiar with Edinburgh?" I ask. "We bumped into someone who mistook Dr. Gray for him, and he seemed to expect Selim would only know Arabic."

Her hands flutter in annoyance. "That is the way of things. Everyone presumes we are exotic and foreign creatures. My brother went to school in London, just as I did. Our father is a government official who recognized the importance of learning the English language and customs, for children who may one day find themselves subjects of the British Empire." She pauses and winces. "I did not mean to sound quite so tart."

"No need to apologize. I've seen how often people don't expect Dr. Gray to know English. It is frustrating."

Isla makes a tiny noise of agreement. "As someone who has seen him endure that all of his life, I must wholeheartedly agree. It is *exceptionally* frustrating."

Lady Christie relaxes a little. "Thank you for understanding. As for Selim, he is my younger brother, and younger brothers can be somewhat . . . unmanageable in their way."

Isla murmurs, "Once younger brothers decide they are men, they mistakenly believe they no longer need the guidance of an older sister."

"Yes. Selim is reckless and most unmanageable, and while I could rely on him to supervise the mummy, I could not rely on him to come straight here instead of stopping at a public house first. That is why I did not worry when he was late."

"But you didn't need to worry that he might be lost in a foreign city?" I say.

Lady Christie smiles. "Selim knows Edinburgh well enough, and he is at home wherever he goes, which is why . . ." The smile evaporates as she pushes to her feet. "Someone must discover what has happened to him. I said that I was not surprised my husband seemed to be avoiding his own party, but I *was* surprised that Selim was not yet here. That isn't like him. I would have been more concerned about Selim if my attention hadn't been on Alastair."

"If someone can give us his ship information," I say, "we will have it investigated while you speak to the children."

"Yes, thank you. I must . . ." She sways a little, hand going to her mouth. "The children. Phoebe. Oh, my poor Phoebe. First her mother and now . . ."

"She has you," Isla says, rising and taking Lady Christie's arm.

"Yes, of course." Lady Christie straightens. "Whatever has happened, Phoebe will always have me. Let me go and speak to them."

"Would you like me to accompany you?" Isla asks.

A wan smile. "Please. I could use an arm to hold, so that I do not break down in front of them."

Isla holds out her arm, and I open the door for them.

EIGHT

The guests have left. There really wasn't any way for McCreadie to detain them. More officers have only just now shown up, and we don't yet live in a world where a detective can say "There's been a murder. No one leaves until I say they leave" and expect any member of the upper crust to listen.

Instead, McCreadie has focused on the staff. The butler and the house-keeper have gathered everyone into a room for questioning. It's easy to tell *them* to stay. And if the guests are outraged that no one is around to find their coat or hold the door or call their coach? Well, they're welcome to talk to the police while they wait. No one takes McCreadie up on that offer.

I've conveyed Lady Christie's statements to McCreadie, and he's sent a groom to check whether the ship arrived. That's fifty percent courtesy to Lady Christie and fifty percent acknowledgment that if Sir Alastair is dead and his brother-in-law is missing, the answer for that might not be "coincidence."

I itch to help Gray with Sir Alastair's body. I did pop in to see whether he needs me. He didn't say no, but he does say that McCreadie needs me more, and he's right there. Again, my former career supersedes my new one.

McCreadie needs to question the staff quickly, and Gray is in no hurry, with Addington having already told him to convey the body to the funerary parlor, where he'll conduct the autopsy in the morning. The first time

Addington did this, I was appalled. The second time, I was only annoyed on behalf of the deceased, whose death didn't even warrant a sleepless night for the police surgeon. Now, I must admit it works in Gray's favor, allowing him to do all but the internal examination before Addington gets his paws on the victim. In fact, if every murder victim died at night, I'd see it as a blessing for Edinburgh law enforcement.

I leave Gray to his work and help McCreadie with putting together a timeline.

We know the body wasn't moved until after the party began. The footmen who carried it in confirmed that it was eight thirty before they did so. The mummy had been stored in the "artifact room"—a windowless chamber that acts as storage for anything Sir Alastair brings home from his excavations.

Are the artifacts on display tonight usually stored in there?

Yes, but the staff says they were moved out this morning, which was the last time anyone saw Sir Alastair, as he supervised the removal. Afterward the room was closed until the footmen entered to remove the mummy.

Closed? Or locked?

It'd been locked that morning. Sir Alastair needed to unlock it for the footmen, as he had the only key. Once they were done removing the artifacts, he relocked it, and one of them witnessed this. Yet when they went to retrieve the mummy, the artifact room was unlocked, which led them to believe Sir Alastair *was* at home. They presumed he'd opened it for them, knowing they would need access to the mummy.

So the artifacts on display had been removed while Sir Alastair was still at home. Then the door was locked and the only key returned to his pocket.

That happened shortly after nine in the morning. The door was not touched again until eight thirty at night, no one on the staff having any reason to check it in the interim.

It would take a long time to unwrap a mummy and rewrap a body with the bandages. How long? That might require some scientific experimentation. It would likely be hours, though, meaning the nearly twelve hours between that door being locked and reopened should be more than sufficient if you knew you'd be undisturbed. All you had to do was lock the door while you were in there and leave it unlocked when you left.

And who could rewrap the mummy? Did that require special skills? Or could anyone manage it well enough? We'd noted the mummy had seemed in rough shape, which might be a result of amateur rewrapping. We'll need to speak more to someone who'd seen it while it still contained the mummified remains.

Sir Alastair was with the footmen after his wife and the children left for their walk. Then he locked the artifact room. So who saw him last? No one's sure, and I'm not surprised by that. The staff would be intent on their work. They aren't exactly checking their nonexistent wristwatches for the time.

They know Sir Alastair was here when his wife left. They know she was still gone when he was last seen. Breakfast was served at seven. Lady Christie and the children left at about eight thirty and returned "late morning." I need to ask her when they returned from their walk, though she might not know the exact time either.

None of the staff report anything unusual in Sir Alastair's behavior.

"He actually seemed in good spirits, miss," one of the maids says. "Which surprised us because we all knew he did not care to host the party."

"Were there arguments over it?"

"Arguments?" Her eyes round as if I'd said something vulgar. "Lady Christie does not argue. She is far too sweet-tempered. Now the first Lady Christie—"

When she stops herself, I say, "Anything you can tell me is helpful information for catching His Lordship's killer. It is not rumor or tittle-tattle."

"I mean no offense to the first Lady Christie. I liked her a great deal. I have been blessed to have two fine mistresses. But the first Lady Christie was like her daughter." The maid's eyes sparkle. "She's a right firecracker, that one. Ran Sir Alastair to distraction, but Lady Christie knows how to handle Miss Phoebe, just as her mother did. I have heard Lady Christie tell Sir Alastair that spirited fillies should be cherished, not broken, and I thought how proud the first Lady Christie would be to hear that. But what I was saying was that the first Lady Christie had a temper, but she was not ill-tempered, if you take my meaning."

"A spirited mare who had not been broken."

The maid smiles. "Yes, that is it. Sir Alastair did not always seem to know what to do with her, much like their daughter."

"He didn't argue back?"

"He is not that sort of man. When she became angry, he would leave."

"Leave or flee?"

"He made it seem like leaving, but he was fleeing, miss. Not that he feared her tongue, but he liked a quiet household. I always thought that with the second Lady Christie, he would stay at home more, as she kept things quiet for him. But he did not."

Because what he wanted wasn't a quiet household. It was a solitary life where he could focus all his attention on his passions. People were an interruption, even if they were family.

"So when you say you knew he didn't want tonight's demonstration . . ."

"Just because Sir Alastair did not like to argue does not mean he held his tongue, miss. Not when he was feeling peevish. He did not wish to host tonight's party, but Lord Muir insisted, and Lady Christie was left to smooth the waters, lest it cost him his patron. Sir Alastair could never seem to understand that he needed Lord Muir if he wished to continue his work. The master was a brilliant man, miss, but in some things, people like him . . ." She shrugs. "Well, they are not terribly sensible."

Because it is frustrating—and insulting—for a scientist to be expected to entertain like a circus dog. In this, I have sympathy for Sir Alastair. But I have more sympathy for Lady Christie, who *was* "sensible" and understood that just because her husband *shouldn't* need to pander to his sponsor didn't mean he *didn't* need to do it.

"I think he may have also been seeking a new patron because of it," the maid says. "I heard him mutter to Lady Christie that he might not need to put up with Lord Muir's obligations for much longer. She asked why, and he would only say that he'd had enough of this nonsense."

I ask the maid more questions, mostly because she's answering them. If you find a chatty witness, you get everything you can out of them, because others won't be so talkative.

It helps that there don't seem to be any household problems the maid might be reluctant to discuss. Sir Alastair was too caught up in his work to be much bother to the staff. Lady Christie was exacting but also considerate and kind enough to compensate for it. The children were children. Phoebe was a handful, but a good-hearted girl who did as she was told . . .

eventually. Michael got up to just as much mischief, but he also kept Phoebe in check.

Sir Alastair treated his wife and children well. Lady Christie was devoted to the children, and they to her. For a recently blended family, there was surprisingly little friction, probably because they had all known one another for years.

I talk to a few other members of the staff after that, but the only piece of tittle-tattle I get is that two of the staff were released when the Christies returned from Egypt last year, with the former governess and her son elevated to family. One maid and the underbutler did not treat the new arrivals with the proper respect, and they were let go, as much for their behavior, I suspect, as a warning to the others.

Sir Alastair expected his new wife and son to be treated as well as his first wife and daughter, and anyone who had a problem with that would be let go with a month's wages. It was handled firmly but fairly, and while I do take the names of the two staff members, I'm assured that they already had new positions and left without a fuss.

McCreadie and I are in the small sitting room where Isla had sat with Lady Christie, it being the only room where we can speak in private. We compare information. Nothing from his interviews contradicts mine. No one saw Sir Alastair since before Lady Christie and the children returned, and no one went into the artifact room again until after the party was underway.

"So the killer had time to make a mummy," I say. "Strangle Sir Alastair. Get his body into the artifact room."

"If he wasn't already there."

"Good point. That'd make it easier. Get him in there or come in while he's there."

"Which would not be difficult." McCreadie pauses as footsteps pass the closed door. Then he continues, "Sir Alastair could have gone in to check something for tonight's event or he could have been taken in to check something. And if the murder was not premeditated, then the killer decided to use what was at hand to hide the body."

"The staff said Sir Alastair locked the door after they removed the artifacts, but that it was unlocked when the footmen went to get the mummy.

So Sir Alastair locks it, and either is surprised in there by his killer or taken there by his killer. You haven't seen the artifact room yet, have you?"

"I was waiting for you before we searched the house. We should start there, though."

We rise from our chairs and head into the hall.

"We will need a guide for the house," McCreadie says as we walk. "Did any of the staff strike you as particularly suitable for such a task? Excellent knowledge of the house and unlikely to break down emotionally?"

"I can help you," a voice says before I can answer. It's a small voice, hesitant, and we turn to see Michael hovering in a doorway.

"I know the house better than most of the servants," Michael says. "And I . . . I have not broken down yet. Phoebe is very upset, understandably, and I thought it best if I leave her with my mother. I liked Sir Alastair a great deal, but he is not my father." He meets our eyes, one after the other, with a look that is almost challenging, as if expecting to see something there.

"All right," I say carefully.

"He is not," he says as he moves closer. "You may hear that he is, and that is a lie. People think that because my mother and Lady Christie were schoolmates, and I look as if I have English blood, and we all lived together . . . They draw conclusions."

His jaw sets, and I realize he isn't disavowing Sir Alastair as his dad, but as his biological father.

"My father was in the British diplomatic service," Michael says. "He *was* English. He died when I was three, and then my mother went to work for Lady Christie."

"Understood," I say. "If we hear anything to the contrary, we will ignore it as rumor."

That's not entirely true. If it's mentioned in any credible way that affects the investigation, we'd need to confirm it, but I also understand how lurid minds would concoct such a story. Two female friends have children around the same age? One is a brown-skinned governess with a son who seems half white? Clearly the children share a father, and then they're all living together, and what a deliciously naughty bit of specu-lation is that?

"I can show you about the house, if you would like," Michael says. "Or

I can tell you which of the servants would know it best, though even they do not know all the hidey-holes."

I smile. "Grown-ups never know all the hidey-holes. If you feel quite up to it, we would appreciate your services. Could we begin in the artifact room?"

NINE

The first thing I do is confirm that the door on the artifact room will lock from the inside. The lock would hearken back to a time when it'd likely been a guest bedroom, a very dreary and windowless chamber in the back hall, the sort you give to someone you don't want to stay very long. The fact that it can also be locked from the outside might seem a little concerning, but many such rooms can, this being an era where guests often stay for weeks, and they might wish to lock their room when they are out.

The interior lock is important because it gave the killer time to mummify their victim. Sir Alastair had the only key, and so if he was within, being mummified, no one could wander in and disturb his killer. Then the killer had to leave the door unlocked, so the staff could remove the mummy, and we'd all have the horrific moment of watching Sir Alastair unwrapped.

We speculated earlier that the killer might not have known about the party and wrapped Sir Alastair to hide him. I no longer believe that. In retrospect, the wrapping job was too poorly done to disguise the body for long. That's why we'd had no trouble unwrapping him. The chance that his killer just happened to hide him in the mummy wrapping while the staff was bustling about preparing for a mummy-unwrapping party? Slim to none.

The killer didn't want to hide the body. They wanted drama. Sir Alastair's dead body found in the bandages of the mummy he'd taken from Egypt. He'd been planning to unwrap some poor stranger, and instead, the corpse was his.

We're going to need to return to the artifact room for a more thorough search. For now, McCreadie has an officer stand guard with orders that no one—even family—is to be admitted. It's a crime scene, and even if police don't fully recognize the implications of that yet, they understand that McCreadie works differently, and they like him enough to allow it.

Michael takes us on a quick tour of the house. This is mostly for us to understand the layout. We don't know whether our killer is part of the household, but if not, then we need to see all the possible exits.

We are also looking for something. A very important literal missing piece.

The remains that had originally been in those wrappings.

We conducted a quick search in the artifact room, which was the most likely place to stash it. But with all the artifacts on display for the party, there hadn't been many places to hide a desiccated corpse.

That leads to a problem. A rather large one. Killing and then mummifying Sir Alastair in a locked room would have been easily done. Getting the mummified remains out? With a house full of staff bustling about for a party?

"I don't know how it would be accomplished," McCreadie says as we walk while we talk. "But certainly not out the front door."

"Then why not find a way to hide it in the artifact room? Taking it is a huge risk. So why? Is there a black market for mummified corpses?"

"A black . . . ?"

"An illegal network you could sell it to, with buyers on the other end."

"I am certain there is a market for mummies among the wealthy. But this would be the body within, and it is the bandages that make it a mummy."

Michael clears his throat. "If I may?"

"Of course," I say, trying not to smile at how polite he is. That's a mark of a Victorian upbringing, but I suspect it's also his nature.

"The corpse could be sold for medical uses." He makes a face and hurries on. "Fakery, I mean. There is no actual medical use for dried bodies. There was a craze for such medicines in the earlier part of the century, and while it has passed its peak, we must still be cautious. A corpse like that could bring in hundreds of pounds."

"Right. I had heard of that. People would—" Which isn't important right now. "We can discuss it later, and we may need to ask for your expertise, Michael."

He eyes me, as if suspecting I'm humoring him. When he sees that I'm serious, he says gravely, "Certainly."

"For now, we presume someone took the mummified corpse, and they likely weren't just getting rid of it. Would they dare remove it from the house during the party preparations? Or stash it and come back later?"

"We will need to see all your hiding spots, Michael," McCreadie says.

"Yes, but there is something you need to see first."

We are in the subbasement. For most town houses like this, the basement is extended living quarters rather than storage. In Gray's town house, the lower level is the kitchen, the staff dining area, and the housekeeper's quarters. It's a similar setup here, with the first basement being the kitchen and food storage areas plus staff quarters. Some town houses in the New Town have another level—a subbasement. In this one, it's being used for storage. And in the far corner of that subbasement?

"A tunnel?" I say.

Michael gives me a smile that, I suspect, under any other circumstance would light up his face. Under the current one, it's a feeble thing, but he makes the effort.

"Yes, it is a tunnel," he says. "Phoebe and I do not know what it is for. Few know about it, and that does not include Mama or . . ." He glances away. "Sir Alastair. We could not ask about the history without telling them we'd found it, and if we said we'd found it, they'd shut it up."

I can see why the tunnel has gone undetected by all but curious children. To get to it requires taking rickety stairs down and then traversing the whole of the subbasement. At the back is a room filled with moldering crates, as if the staff decided at some point that anything back here wasn't worth getting out again. The entrance to the tunnel is a thick door behind those crates.

Michael opens the door. "The entrance is small, but the tunnel is bigger."

I look down at my dress. There's no way I'm getting in there with a crinoline cage. I'll need to remove it. I should also wear a wrapper to protect my dress, but I can't exactly ask the grieving widow if I can borrow one. I'll just be careful.

I slip into the next room and carefully remove my crinoline cage. The next issue is my slippers. That's when I remember seeing boots on the next level up. I find several pairs, probably belonging to the maids, and I send up a silent apology as I borrow a pair that fits. I also swipe an apron to go over my dress.

Then it's back down to join McCreadie and Michael.

McCreadie has brought a lantern, and he goes in first. While I need to squeeze through the small door, the tunnel within soon slants until we can walk upright.

"Where does it lead?" I ask.

"To a garden at the end of the street," Michael says. "There are side passages, but they are sealed or caved in. Only this main tunnel goes anywhere." He glances back, the lantern casting his face in shadow. "It ends at a hatch that leads into a shed in a private park, and the shed is in ruins, unused."

"A secret exit?" I say. "Is the hatch kept locked?"

Michael shakes his head as he walks. "No, and I told Phoebe that is why we ought to mention it, but she argued that the subbasement door is always kept locked, so no one can sneak into the house that way."

"I noticed it was unlocked when we came in."

"That is because of the party. The servants would have been going in and out of the storage rooms all day."

We continue on. I'm behind McCreadie, who has the lantern, meaning I can't see much more than his back. The floor is earth and silt-covered rock, so it's no surprise when one of my boots slips. My gloved hand smacks into the wall and McCreadie spins, but I lift my other hand to say I'm all right.

I motion for him to go on but, gentleman that he is, he waits for me to recover. He holds the lantern out for me to watch where I put my feet. After a few steps, he starts to turn around, confident that I have my footing. As the light turns, it catches on something by my foot. Something that looks like a charred piece of wood with a pale stick poking from it.

"Hold up," I say. "Can I get that light?"

McCreadie turns as I go to bend over, forgetting that's impossible in an evening-gown laced corset. I inhale sharply, mutter under my breath, and sweep my gown up so I can bend at my knees. As I gather the silk, I'm reminded I'm tramping through a filthy tunnel in a dress worth more than a year's wages. Damn it.

With all my fussing, though, I lose the chance to retrieve what's on the ground. McCreadie has spotted it and—not being in a corset—easily bends to pick it up.

"What the devil?" he murmurs.

He moves the object in front of the lantern. It's maybe an inch long, blackened and dried, with bone protruding from the end.

"A finger," I say. "From the mummy."

Michael has ducked under McCreadie's arm, and he peers at it. "Yes, that's what it is. A finger broke off. The tip, at least."

"So we are on the right track," I say.

"I am going to put this into my pocket," McCreadie says. "I know how much you hate it when we treat evidence so cavalierly but—not expecting a murder tonight—I didn't come prepared."

"Yes, yes," I say. "Just be careful with it."

As we've walked, we've passed a couple of those side passages Michael mentioned—the ones that no longer lead anywhere. Once we continue, we almost immediately reach another one and—

Michael lets out a yelp and dives into the side passage. I resist the urge to shove past McCreadie, though I may give him a less-than-gentle nudge.

Michael is in that side passage, bent beside the fallen figure of a man, and on seeing that figure, my heart does a little jump. In the shadows, all I can make out is brown skin on a smooth-shaven cheek and dark wavy hair falling over a strong nose. It only takes a moment to realize it is not Gray, and in the next moment, Michael is saying, "Uncle Selim!" and shaking the man's shoulder.

I hurry past McCreadie. The man—Lady Christie's brother, Selim—lies on his side, his eyes closed. Blood trickles down the side of his neck. I touch my fingers to his throat and feel a pulse.

"Duncan," I say to McCreadie. "Get Duncan."

We have Selim upstairs in the kitchen. That was as far as Gray wanted the young man's unconscious body carried before a proper examination. During that examination, Selim wakes, and Gray declares he's fit to be taken to his guest bedroom. We're in there now, with Selim slowly rousing as Gray tends to a gash on the back of his head. That gash is presumably what knocked him unconscious.

While Gray tends to Selim, I switch back to my slippers and remove the apron I borrowed. I don't bother with the crinoline cage and extra skirts. I'm sure I'm a mess, but under the circumstances, no one cares.

Michael has been playing messenger, telling his mother that Selim is here and was hurt but is fine. Naturally, she wants to see her brother, but we need to speak to him first. McCreadie handles that by saying Selim is groggy and needs rest, and that is the best thing for him, along with broth and perhaps a bit of brandy. Getting that keeps Lady Christie occupied while we question her brother.

Once Selim is alert and sitting in a well-lit bedroom, there's no chance I could mistake him for Gray. It's only the clean-shaven brown skin and the wavy dark hair and a bit of his profile that resembles Gray. The young man is leaner and a few inches shorter, with lighter eyes and a face that seems more given to laughter than somber contemplation . . . or it would be when he isn't recovering from a blow to the head. Even then, his mouth curves in a wry twist when he explains.

"I wanted to surprise the children," he says, in an accent that matches his sister's: upper-crust English with a melodic undercurrent of what I presume is an Egyptian accent in this period. "I know of their secret tunnel, and so I came in that way. As I was walking, I heard someone. I presumed it was the children. With the party preparations, I knew Phoebe would try to slip away for a bit of fun. I tucked myself into a side passage to surprise them. Yet the figure that passed was neither Michael nor Phoebe. It was someone carrying a bundle of what looked like firewood. I shrank back, intending to slip out after them and see what they were up to. Only it seems the person heard me. I was creeping down the tunnel, thinking they were up ahead, when they leapt out of a side passage and clubbed me on the back of the head. Then I woke here."

"This fellow," McCreadie says. "What did he look like?"

That smile twists more. "I cannot even say it was a fellow. I saw only a cloak and that bundle. The bundle is what caught my attention, as the stick I saw poking out looked already burned, which struck me as odd. I could describe the stick better than the person. I know they were smaller than me. Shorter and slighter of build. Definitely larger than the children, though. And the cloak—or coat—was dark. I fear that is all I can say."

"The sticks you saw," I say. "Could they have been parts of a mummy? The corpse within, that is."

Selim glances my way, as if seeing me for the first time. His brows furrow, as if I do not look like the person who would ask such a question.

"Miss Mitchell is my confederate's assistant," McCreadie says gently. "Please answer her questions as if they were my own."

"Yes, of course." Selim dips his chin. "I did not mean any offense, miss. You asked whether the sticks could have been—" He stops, eyes widening. "Part of a mummified corpse. Yes. That would make sense. I was not aware that Sir Alastair brought back parts, in addition to the mummies. That is . . ." He clears his throat. "I hope he did not. Perhaps they were from a mummified cat or dog?"

I glance at McCreadie and pull back to let him take this next part. He tells Selim that his brother-in-law is dead, his body having been wrapped in the mummy cloths.

"Miriam," Selim says, rising swiftly. "I must see Miriam. And the children. They will be—"

McCreadie stops the younger man from getting up. "As Sir Alastair was murdered and you were discovered in a secret tunnel, I'm afraid I need to speak to you first. Your sister and the children are well, and you will get to them soon."

Selim's mouth sets before he rubs it away. When he says, "Yes, of course," the words are curt. He doesn't like being kept from his grieving sister, but he won't fight us on it.

I say, "Whoever killed Sir Alastair also took the mummified remains. We suspected they went down that tunnel, and that's how we found you. Could what you saw have been a bundled corpse?"

"A whole corpse? No," Selim says sharply. "It would have been pieces. They . . . they broke it up like kindling." Anger sizzles through his voice. "They took a human body and snapped it into pieces for easier transport."

"They just cared about getting it out of there easily," I say.

"Not only that," Selim says. "The only reason to steal mummified remains is to sell it for medicines. You do not need it whole for that."

"Michael did mention something about that," I murmur. "Any information you could provide will help Detective McCreadie, but we can get that later."

"For now," McCreadie says, "we will need as much detail as you can give us on that tunnel encounter. What time you arrived. How you entered.

What you heard. We will also need to know your movements between leaving the ship and arriving here."

"The ship arrived at two yesterday afternoon. I caught a hansom cab directly here. I can give you details on where I was picked up and what my driver looked like. I had him drop me at the corner. I'm not sure which—I can never remember the street names here—but I can point it out on a map. Then I walked directly to the tunnel entrance."

"Do you know what time you arrived?"

"I know I was in the cab at four. I was hungry and knew dinner would be early because of the party. I checked my watch hoping I had not missed it."

"And your bags? I presume you brought some."

"I left them in the little shed, where the tunnel starts. Hopefully, they are still there."

McCreadie asks a few more questions. Then he looks at me.

"In light of what happened to Sir Alastair," I say, "we're going to need to speak to someone who might know how long it would take to unwrap the mummified remains and . . . rewrap a body."

I avoid saying *who* was rewrapped, but the flash of grief on his face says my workaround didn't help.

I continue, "I don't know who we'd speak to about that."

"Me," he says. "I have worked at my brother-in-law's excavations since before he was my brother-in-law. Archaeology is my area of study. I found that particular mummy, and I know it was in poor condition, with little resin holding the cloths in place. One could unwrap it rather than cut it open."

Selim considers for a moment, lips moving as if calculating. "As a rough estimate, I would venture it would take a few hours to unwrap and rewrap. Two to three hours, depending on the expertise of the person doing the work."

"And that was my next question. How much expertise would be required?"

"For remains in such poor wrappings? The unraveling would be simple enough, the speed only checked by a need to note how the wrapping was done. If one took care and did not simply yank off the cloths but paid attention, the rewrapping could be done by anyone."

"Thank you." I look at Gray. "Anything to add, sir?"

"Only instructions for care of that head injury," Gray says.

TEN

McCreadie is busy verifying Selim's alibi. That leaves Gray and me on crime-scene investigation, and we now have two crime scenes to investigate. We start with the one in the tunnel.

"This is most unusual," Gray says as I lead him in after returning to my earlier tunnel-traversing wardrobe tweaks.

"The kids don't know the original purpose," I say. "How old would the houses here be?"

"Not old enough to have a network of secret tunnels beneath them. Those are generally for escape in a time of war or persecution. That would not apply to wealthy New Town families."

"The rich are only persecuted in their own minds."

I get a soft laugh from him for that.

"True," he says. "Every time there is talk of reform, the wealthy do indeed rise up, decrying their persecuted state. Somehow, though, I don't think they were constructing tunnels to escape mobs of the poor."

"Nah, they already did that by building the New Town. Keep the rabble safely across the Mound. What about other reasons for escape tunnels? When would the last battle have been on Scottish soil? Culloden?"

His expression turns somber as he nods. "Yes, and while the Jacobites certainly had tunnels and such, Culloden predated the New Town by twenty years."

"Are subbasements normal around here?"

"In some homes, yes. That is a question to add to the list. Do the other houses in this row have them? And if not, why does Sir Alastair's?"

"They needed a subbasement to get deep enough to build a tunnel. How long has Sir Alastair lived here?"

"It was his childhood home. I am not certain how long it was in the family before that."

"The tunnels have been here long enough for some to cave in," I say.

"Did they cave in? Or were they false starts? Attempts that went through unstable ground?"

"Good point," I say. "And good questions, which may or may not have anything to do with our case. Though it does seem young Mr. Awad encountered our killer."

"If he is not the killer himself."

"I am considering that," I say as I pause to peer into a shallow side-corridor. "We'll need to verify his timeline. Just because he was knocked out doesn't mean he wasn't the killer. Or aiding and abetting the killer. At this point, the suspect list covers just about everyone."

"Even me?"

"You already admitted to having a grudge against the deceased."

"It was not a grudge," Gray says. "He was simply one of several who refused to admit me after I dug up a body without permission."

"Because you dug up a body? Or because you were bonking his sister?"

Behind me, Gray makes a strangled noise.

I glance back. "You weren't bonking her?"

"I . . . I am not familiar with the word."

"Oh, I'm sure you can figure it out."

I resume walking as Gray clears his throat.

"Yes, I had a relationship with his sister," he says. "I was young, and she was recently widowed, and it was . . ."

"Consensual and mutually beneficial. No judgment here. The point is that Sir Alastair seems to have judged plenty. What his widowed sister did with her days—and nights—was none of his business, but he made it his business and unfairly blamed you. While it's probably not a motive for murder, I'll still need to be sure you didn't sneak off on Isla this afternoon and murder him."

"I know you are joking, but I suddenly find myself frantically trying to recall whether Isla can confirm my whereabouts the entire time we were gone."

I glance back again. "I *am* joking. As for Sir Alastair's widowed sister, I'm very sorry if that was part of the reason you were refused your license."

"It played a role, I suspect. I was young and less discreet than I should have been."

"On that note, I should take advantage of this conversation to mention something even more awkward that I've been keeping from you."

"Please tell me it is something that casts you in an equally embarrassing light."

"An affair between consenting adults isn't cause for embarrassment, Gray. And my confession is actually about that."

"You've . . . had an affair? While here?"

"Seriously? When would I have the time? Like I've said before, that is not on my list of coveted Victorian experiences. The affair is yours. *Was* yours, I mean. Catriona had a letter in her room that she'd intercepted. It was for you."

"A letter . . . for me?"

"From a Lady Inglis. I think Catriona stole it from the incoming mail, opened it, and thought it might come in handy, if she ever needed to hold something over your head. I'm sorry."

"She found proof of an affair between a bachelor and a widow? I expected Catriona would have higher standards for extortion material."

"It was . . . Er, so, I apologize in advance. I only read enough to figure out what it was. It seems Lady Inglis wanted to woo you back with, er, detailed descriptions of what you were, umm, missing. After your breakup."

Another of those strangled noises.

"I really didn't read more than a line or two," I say quickly, without looking back at him. "And I'm sorry I saw that much. I hated reading your mail, however inadvertently, and I hated holding on to it, but I couldn't figure out how to return it without you realizing Catriona had it. Super awkward. So I'm leaping on a vaguely adjacent conversation to confess and promise it back."

I turn back to the tunnel, and we walk in silence until Gray says, "Yes, this is exceptionally embarrassing. For both of us. I am sorry you had to find that. But you may dispose of it."

"I really should give it back—"

"I would rather you didn't. I will be happier not knowing what was in it . . . and what parts you might have read."

"Nothing scandalous. I could just tell more was coming and closed it fast."

"Hmm. Well, still, if you *would* burn it, I would appreciate that. It would only be the reminder of a mistake . . ." He inhales. "Let us leave it at that, as I am certain you are as eager to drop this conversation as I am."

"Yep."

"Burn it. Please."

"Done. And, would you look at that. We've reached the spot where we found Mr. Awad. Never thought we'd get here, did you?"

He lets out a soft chuckle. "It was a very long walk."

"Shit!" I turn toward him. "Mr. Awad said he ducked into another passageway and then presumably the killer hid in this one to ambush him. That means the one where Mr. Awad hid would be the way we just came."

"We passed one a few feet back."

We retreat to it, and I bend with the lantern, remembering at the last second that this flips up my skirts at the back, and I need to adjust. There are clear footprints in the silt and soil. The central part of the tunnel is too rocky to show prints, but the dirt is softer here because no one comes into this short passage, which is collapsed after about two meters.

Gray sketches the footprint while I do some makeshift measurements using tape I commandeered from a sewing kit. That's all we find in here. A few footprints, some clear and some scuffed, matching Selim's story that he ducked in here to spook the children.

"The presumed killer was loaded down with a bundle of bones," I say. "Did he have a light?"

Gray takes the lantern and extinguishes it, plunging us into blackness. "I would say yes."

"He had a light, and Mr. Awad must have had at least a match. We'll need to ask. Mr. Awad would have put his light out. Can you ignite that again please and walk down the tunnel? I want to test what I'd see."

"Pass me matches, and I will light it again."

When I don't answer, Gray says, "I am teasing, Mallory." He lights the lantern. "I saw you put down the matches after you lit it. You need to take them with you, in case it goes out."

He backs down the hall. I stand where it seems Selim did, according to the footprints. The problem with our test, of course, is that we don't know what kind of light the intruder had or how they were carrying it, but it wouldn't have been anything larger than a lantern, and Gray gamely emulates how he might hold that with an armful of bundled body parts.

He carries the lantern in the hand closest to me. That would be the left hand, and odds are the person was right-handed, but it provides maximum illumination from my angle.

At maximum illumination, with the lantern in his left hand, angled to shine brightest, all I can see is Gray's sleeve, left shoulder and left hip. Even when I try to look up toward his face, the shadows hide it. I have an impression of a dark-clothed figure carrying an armload of something. As Selim said, I could better describe that armload than the figure itself. I couldn't guess at gender, skin color, hair color, or anything else.

We try the experiment with the lantern in his other hand, in case the reduced illumination actually makes it easier to see more of Gray. It doesn't. I take the lantern and test it with Gray watching.

"I can tell you are in a dress," he says, "and that it is greenish blue. If you had your crinolines on, I would be able to tell you were a woman by the shape."

"But not a maid wearing lesser skirts. Or a lady who'd removed them."

"Yes. And if you were wearing a cloak, the only part of you I might see is your hand. We will have to ask Mr. Awad about that."

"Right. Seeing the hand would suggest skin tone and possibly sex. Unless it's gloved."

"Which could still suggest sex, depending on the glove. Otherwise, his claim that he saw mostly the bundle of supposed sticks is supported by the evidence."

I take one last look around, but there's nothing else to see here. It was mostly about confirming that Selim's story was, at least, plausible. Now it's back to the other caved-in partial tunnel, where he'd been left.

The marks in the dirt here also support his story. Again, the middle is too trodden to pick out footsteps, but at the entrance to the side tunnel, drag marks show where his unconscious body had been moved from where he fell in the main tunnel.

"The question then," I say, "is how strong does one need to be to drag a person Mr. Awad's size." I eye Gray. "You're slightly bigger than he is, so back at the house, I need to see whether I can drag you the right distance."

"The conditions will be different." Gray lowered himself to one knee.

"To replicate them as closely as possible, you must drag me here. In the other direction, of course, to avoid disturbing the initial marks."

"I am not dragging you along the floor in your party best, Gray. Mrs. Wallace would kill you."

"Not if I blame you."

I sputter. "Blame me? What did I do, knock you down and drag you?"

"Exactly so. As she has long feared, you intended to do something nefarious with me, knocked me down and dragged me through the muck. I escaped, luckily."

"You joke, but she might actually believe that."

Gray is already lying on his back.

"For science," he says, and lifts his hand for me to grab.

I could argue that Selim's attacker probably dragged him by his jacket, but if it was a woman, she'd have struggled to bend that far in a corset. She really would need to drag him by the arms. I grab and heave. It's not easy, but the dirt seems to help, and I can indeed drag him the correct distance.

"Someone my strength could do it," I say. "With rest breaks, someone slightly smaller could also do it. It would also be easier if I were wearing my maid corset, being less restrictive. Again, then, if the culprit is a woman, it's unlikely to be someone like Lady Christie . . . unless she switched out her usual corset."

Gray gets up and dusts himself off as I begin taking a closer look for footprints. He joins me, but soon says, "There are far too many."

"Yep," I say. "From Michael running in there, and then me, and then Hugh, and then you . . ."

I don't grumble about that. We'd found someone in distress—no one was thinking about preserving the scene, and even if I had thought of it, I'd have put Selim first. Otherwise I might have been investigating another murder instead of an assault.

"I'll sketch the imprints I can make out," I say.

He plucks the paper from my hand.

"Hey, my sketches are fine," I say. "It's my handwriting that's the problem."

"It is your handwriting that is the *greater* problem."

"Are you insulting my manual dexterity? I'll have you know that I have a seventy-words-a-minute typing speed, even on a cell phone."

"I am sure that is impressive," he says. "However, having nothing that requires those skills in this world, I would suggest you practice more with a pen and pencil. I will sketch the prints. You will measure them."

"Yes, sir."

As we do that, we look for other signs of trace evidence in the tunnel. I find a few hairs, and I do take them, but I suspect they belong to Selim, having come from approximately where his head was lying.

Once that's done, we continue on down the tunnel. There isn't much farther to go before we reach a rusted ladder. Gray examines it.

"Old," he says. "We shall need someone to take a better look, but I would say this ladder predates the current residents."

I'd agree. Even in these damp conditions, it wouldn't rust so badly in a decade or two.

"I will ascend first," Gray says. "As you will have difficulty in those—"

I grab the ladder. He sighs behind me.

"I was merely being chivalrous," he says.

"By leaving me below, in a dark tunnel frequented by killers? You just wanted to be first up the ladder."

Once I start climbing, I realize he actually had a point. Even without the cage, my dress is not meant for climbing. Also, I'm wearing crotchless underwear. All bloomers in this time are crotchless, and when I feel that tickle of air, I'm reminded of it . . . and the fact Gray is below me. Luckily, he's too much of a gentleman to look up my skirts.

With far too much effort, I reach the top. It's a hatch with no sign of a handle, so I give it a shove and it pops open. An oath erupts from above as the hatch clatters open. I look up to see two men in constable uniforms. One I recognize as Iain, a young Highlander who has helped us before. As I climb from the hatch, the other officer gapes at me, and I realize I might not be exactly what he expects to see emerging from a subterranean lair.

Iain grins as he leaps forward to help me out. "Greetings, Miss Mallory."

"Greetings to you as well," I say. "Lovely evening for a tunnel crawl, is it not?"

His grin grows, and he lifts the lantern to survey me. "That's a fine dress you're wearing this evening, Miss Mallory."

I twirl my skirts. "Isn't it just? I had it specially made for fleeing through filthy tunnels. The color goes so well with dirt."

His companion's gaze glides over me, and I realize my joke could be taken for flirting. Damn it. Back in my time, colleagues would know I was goofing around. Here, in Catriona's body, with guys who are not actually my colleagues, it's a very different thing. Hell, as Catriona, I only need to breathe deeply, and my heaving bosom can be interpreted as flirtation.

I glance back at the hatch. "Dr. Gray. There you are. Took you a while, sir."

"I have no idea why," he grumbles. "It is not as if there was someone above me, with dirty boots, clods falling on my head." He gives himself a shake and looks around. "I presume Hugh sent you, Iain?"

"He did." Iain lifts a satchel and a suitcase. "Came to fetch Mr. Awad's bags."

"They were right here then? Where he said he left them?"

"They were."

"All right. If you can return those, Miss Mallory and I will take a look around. We will close the hatch when we are done and come around the street way."

"You . . . may want to shake some of the dirt from your clothing before you do."

Gray sighs. "Of course. Thank you, gentlemen."

ELEVEN

We find nothing in the shed. As Michael said, it's a small and ruined building in a private garden. I remember coming to Edinburgh's New Town in my time, seeing gardens on the map and going to one for a pleasant walk, only to find gates barring my way. Locked gates. The gardens are owned by a private collective, and you can apply for membership and get a key. I'd been baffled by the idea that huge gardens in a downtown core were not open to the public.

This is a small version of that. The shed would have been for the gardener retained by the collective. But there's another shed in a more convenient location near the entrance, and this one has been left as an ivy-covered ruin.

The old shed is kept locked, but Michael—and Selim—have keys, the children having located two in a drawer of old keys after they first found the tunnel.

After a look around, we leave and make it back to the house without neighbors shrieking about the two vagrants wearing fancy clothing they clearly stole from corpses. I could say the lack of attention proves I don't look as bad as I think I do, but I suspect it has something to do with it being three in the morning. Also, might I point out that it's very cold at three A.M. in late November when you're dressed only in party attire.

We ask Selim about his attacker's hands. He hadn't thought of that, but looking back, he remembers what was either dark skin or dark gloves. He didn't see well enough to be sure.

Next we examine the exhibit room. McCreadie joins us, but really, both the detective and I would admit that the person best suited to this task is Gray.

Gray says that I'm better at figuring out people—seeing clues and connections in their speech and mannerisms and expressions. Maybe that's true, but it feels like he's tossing me a bone to make up for the fact that the actual detective is worse than him at, well, detecting. Gray has an eye for detail that I can't match. It's not quite on Sherlock Holmes's level, but sometimes it feels that way.

I find Gray crouched over a clod of dirt, examining it with the end of a pencil.

"Let me guess," I say. "That comes from the tiny village of Cearc, where they only have that specific composition of soil."

"Hardly. Everyone knows the soil in Cearc is largely composed of nitrogen and potassium, given that the land is apparently inhabited by chickens." He glances at me. "I applaud your commitment to studying Gaelic, Mallory, but you might not want to use it just yet."

"Hey, Chicken is a perfectly valid town name. There's one in Alaska. It was supposed to be called Ptarmigan, but the founders couldn't spell that."

He looks up to see if I'm joking. Then he shakes his head and turns back to the soil. "This might not be from the fine village of Cearc, but I do believe we will be able to confirm or reject it as coming from the tunnel. The soil there was somewhat different from what we see outside, possibly owing to the age or depth. We will take this and compare it."

McCreadie walks over. "Because if it does come from the tunnel, that suggests our killer not only fled that way but entered that way." He glances at me. "Do I even want to know what that discussion of chickens was about?"

"Just Dr. Gray questioning my knowledge of geographic etymologies."

"He is terrible for that, isn't he? And while I do hate to interrupt such an important discussion, I believe I have located the murder weapon."

We move so fast we bash into each other. Gray waves for me to go first, which is the proper gentlemanly behavior, though as always, he hesitates before gesturing, as if it takes effort to relinquish the lead.

McCreadie steers us to a rear corner. "I have left it in situ."

A length of rope lies in the gap between a desk and the wall. It hasn't been hidden as much as discarded. Oh, I'm sure the killer wouldn't have left it lying in the middle of the room. That would raise suspicions that might have ruined the fun of having us open a mummy to reveal their victim. Still, there's no need to truly hide the murder weapon, in a world that isn't examining fibers or blood yet. Taking the weapon increases the chances of being caught with it.

"May I borrow your pencil?" I ask Gray.

"If you intend to use it for fishing that rope from in there, I believe we have already established your poor manual dexterity." He moves in front of me and bends. "May I get a light?"

McCreadie fetches a lantern, and Gray shines it into the narrow space.

"Is there anything other than hair that I could be in danger of dislodging?" he asks me.

I shake my head. "I doubt we could even get fingerprints off it. Mostly, we'd be looking for hair, but if it's the murder weapon, any hair would likely belong to Sir Alastair."

He nods and still takes great care extracting the rope before lifting it with the pencil and gingerly putting it onto the desk as if it's a venomous snake.

Using the lantern, Gray examines it. "That looks like blood. There was an abrasion on Sir Alastair's neck where the rope dug in deep. I can check whether the burns seem to match this particular length of rope. I would presume it does."

"Yep, in this time, there'd be no point in planting a fake murder weapon. Well, not really much point in *my* time either, given the science for matching weapons to wounds, but that doesn't keep people from trying it."

"So the police get smarter and the criminals do not?" McCreadie says. When I glance his way, he says, "Humor me, Mallory. Tell me that something gets easier."

"The police absolutely get smarter," I say. "And, if anything, the criminals get dumber. That's why they let women on the force, you know. The job gets so easy, even women can do it."

I get a smile from McCreadie for that one.

"What would you be able to test for on this rope?" McCreadie asks.

"The fabled DNA, yes?" Gray says. "From the blood, and also the skin shed by the victim and possibly even shed by the culprit. Unless they wear gloves."

"Which they will not," McCreadie says. "Because criminals are all much less intelligent in the future. Mallory has promised it, and I believe it."

"Then ask her to tell you about the town called Chicken because no one could spell 'ptarmigan.' At least someone will believe that tall tale."

"Hey, can *you* spell 'ptarmigan'?" I say.

"I do not even know what a ptarmigan is, and I am quite certain you are making up that, too."

"Actually, she's not," McCreadie says. "It's a type of grouse found in very cold regions. Do not ask me to spell it, though I am pleased to know something you do not, Duncan."

"You know much that I do not. Most of it useless trivia, but occasionally your repertoire includes bits of practical information."

McCreadie makes a rude gesture, paired with a smile. They've been friends since they were children, and I envy them that. I have plenty of college friends and colleague friends, but I lost track of ones from my childhood, as we so often do in our world, where being Facebook friends seems enough.

I move to look closer at the rope. Then I start circling the room.

"Uh-oh," McCreadie says. "Mallory is prowling. While we are making light, she is making connections."

"Maybe, maybe not," I say.

I spot a couple of crates under a table. Packing crates. I'd briefly noted them earlier, but I hadn't paid much attention because they weren't big enough to hold the mummy, and that's what I'd been looking for. Now, gloves on, I bend to tug one out . . . and yep, still wearing an evening-gown-laced corset. McCreadie gallantly comes over to pull one out for me.

"Packing materials," I say. "For transporting artifacts. Including . . ." I point at a length of hemp.

"Rope," McCreadie says. "It looks like the same type, though Duncan will need to examine it. If it is, that suggests a crime of opportunity rather than intent. The killer did not bring rope with them. They used what was at hand."

"So they were in here and either found the rope or a length was lying out in plain view," I say. "Have we located the actual crime scene? Any blood on the floor?"

"There was not enough blood lost for that," Gray says. "It really was little more than an abrasion. I do think I see *another* crime scene though, now that we are over here."

He walks a few feet and bends.

"Ah," McCreadie says. "I believe I may know what that is." He takes the mummified finger from his pocket.

"Is that . . . a finger?" Gray says.

"A finger joint."

"And Mallory accuses me of stuffing evidence in my pockets. At least I do not do that with body parts. I am surprised you are not worried about the stink it might leave."

"I wrapped it in my handkerchief," McCreadie says. "I brought it out because I believe it explains what you are looking at."

I look where Gray is bending. There are bits of dark material that seem to be like ash or coal dust from here. Except there isn't a fireplace in this room. I find a bit far enough away, and I try to bend, only to have the usual fashion issue. Gray rises and hands me the lantern.

I angle it as best I can while I squint down at the floor. I could fit several of the tiny bits on my nail, which means they are nearly impossible to see on the carpet.

"Do you have any—?" I begin, only to see Gray holding out a piece of paper.

"Thank you."

He uses the paper to get a speck onto it and brings it up for me. I peer at it under the lantern light. McCreadie has evidently given Gray the finger, literally, and Gray silently holds it out. The skin is the same color. It's leathery, but rough at the edges, where it looks almost exactly like this.

"So this is probably where the killer broke up the mummified body," I say.

"I would say yes," McCreadie calls over. "Considering what I see under this."

I glance to see him bending by a display case. I shine the light under it and see a small brown object.

"Is that . . . ?" I begin.

"Another finger? I believe it is."

With some effort, I rise. "So the killer decides to break the body into smaller pieces. That isn't easy. It's desiccated, not carbonized. A finger flies under there. Another falls off in the tunnel. Helluva way to treat a dead body."

"I have seen worse," Gray says mildly.

"Same," I say. "I'm just more offended because of how old it is. Someone dies over a thousand years ago, and their mortal remains are carted around like a sideshow exhibit and then broken like a stack of kindling. Of course, considering what the killer did to Sir Alastair, I suppose I can't expect them to respect the dead."

A rap at the door. I'm closest and push it open to see Isla, trying for a smile through obvious exhaustion.

"I know you are busy," she says. "Miriam is with her brother now, and the children are with them, so there is little need for Annis or me to stay. She is going to drop me off at the house. Then she will send the coach back after it takes her home. Is there anything I can return with the coach? Tools you might need?"

I look at Gray, who shakes his head.

"Whatever we need to analyze, we can bring home with us," he says. "Tell Annis not to bother with the coach. We will walk."

Isla's gaze slides up and down both of us.

"No, you will not," McCreadie says. "You will accept Annis's offer and hope she does not get a look at you before she leaves, or she might rescind it and *make* you walk."

"Yes, yes. Mallory looks a fright. I was being polite and not mentioning it."

"Me?" I say. "Would you like a mirror, sir?"

Isla waves us off. "Go back to your work. Expect the coach in an hour. I will ask Mrs. Wallace to prepare an early breakfast, which will be ready whenever you return."

"Breakfast?" Gray takes out his pocket watch. "Ah."

"Yes, breakfast," she says. "I will endeavor to get a little sleep myself, but I shall rise by nine so that we might discuss the case."

TWELVE

McCreadie goes to ask the household our list of questions while Gray takes me to see the body. He's waiting until a more reasonable hour to send for Simon and the hearse. In the modern world, that might horrify us—leaving the body in the house so the hearse driver isn't woken early? But there's a reason Victorian undertakers don't actually deal with the corpses. Embalming isn't a thing yet, and so bodies often remain at the family home until they are ready for burial. The women of the household will handle the bathing and the clothing of the dead. So having a body in the house isn't as distressing for Victorians as it would be for us.

It helps that Sir Alastair isn't exactly lying on the kitchen table. The room where we unwrapped him is shut off, with a constable making sure no one enters. We slip inside and close the door behind us.

One reason for that guard is that Gray has left Sir Alastair partially unclothed. It's just an open shirt, but in this world, that would be scandalous and disrespectful for a man of Sir Alastair's position.

"I thought you would like to take a look before I clothe him for transport," Gray says as we cross the room. "As you already saw, the most obvious injury is to his neck."

I peer down at the bruises and abrasions I'd noted before. Then I check under Sir Alastair's eyelids.

"Strangulation seems to be the cause of death," I say.

"Presumably, yes. The classic sign of petechial hemorrhaging is present. If you'll check the hands next . . ."

"Signs of defense?" I lift and notice small cuts on the sides of his fingertips. "No, that's—"

I stop short, an image flashing, the memory of the night I crossed into this time. Grabbed from behind by a rope going around my neck. Struggling to pull it away from my throat.

"Yes, defensive wounds," I say quietly. "But defending himself against the rope instead of the attacker." I shiver convulsively. "I remember that."

Gray inhales sharply. "I blithely showed you something that would trigger a past traumatic event. My sincerest apologies, Mallory. Let us stop this. You do not need—"

"No, I'm fine. It was just a flash. I'm tired, and my mind is wandering." I give a quick shake and check the hands again. "The attacker gets the rope around Sir Alastair's neck. Sir Alastair grabs it and tries to pull it away, but his attacker is stronger. Or . . ." I note the angle of the neck abrasions. "His attacker was above him. Pulling up. Same as . . ." Another deep breath. "My attacker was taller than me, and he got me up onto my tiptoes, which is why I couldn't fight. I was just dangling there, like a rag doll. All my self-defense training, all my fighting skills, and I couldn't even kick properly without strangling myself . . . Damn it!"

I take a deep breath. "I really am tired."

I look up, but Gray isn't in front of me anymore. Fingers rest on my arm, the touch tentative, checking whether I'll pull away. When I don't, he squeezes my arm.

"I would offer a hug," he says. "You did that for Jack, when we rescued her, and she seemed to appreciate it."

I smile a bit at the memory. At first, Jack had been appalled. A hug? Certainly not. She wasn't the type, and this wasn't the era of comforting embraces.

"I am offering," he says, "though I doubt you will take me up on it."

"That depends," I say, through eyes suddenly glassy with tears. "If you're only offering to be nice, then I'm fine."

He puts his arms out. "I am never nice. Ask anyone."

That makes me laugh, and I step into his embrace, careful, knowing how the Victorians feel about touching. But when his arms close around me, I let myself lean a little against his chest, and his arms tighten and I fall onto him. I don't mean to. I just do, and before I can think to be horrified, he's holding me and I'm feeling my eyes fill again, not from the memories of the attack but from the sheer relief of being held.

Is "relief" the wrong word? It feels like relief, as if I can finally let go and relax.

I'm still careful, too aware that this might be awkward for him, and I soon pull away, blinking back the tears and making some half joke about staining his jacket.

"If anything, you cleaned away some of the filth," he says. "I am sorry if I rekindled those memories. I was not thinking."

"If I didn't think of it, no one else should be expected to. And if I *had* thought of it, I would have brushed it off." I dry my eyes. "I've talked to so many victims of violence who blame themselves for not doing anything, and I didn't think I'd feel that way, but I guess, deep down, I do. It happened so fast, and I wasn't prepared."

"Well, I consider myself an excellent pugilist, and yet you have witnessed several occasions where I was caught off guard and soundly trounced. Now, I believe I hear a coach outside, which may be Annis's. We can leave if you would like."

"No, I want to finish the examination." I inhale and look back at Sir Alastair. "What I was saying is that Sir Alastair seems to have been strangled from an upward angle, which would have put him at a disadvantage. But Selim's account suggests we weren't dealing with a particularly tall person. Sir Alastair is above average height himself, and he is in really good shape for a Victorian."

"For a Victorian?"

"You guys aren't exactly going to the gym three times a week."

"Many men do exactly that, Mallory."

"Yeah, for a rousing game of cricket."

"Cricket is not played in the gymnasium."

"You know what I mean. You're swimming and such, not pumping iron."

He frowns at the unfamiliar term.

"Weight lifting," I say.

His brows shoot up. "Why would we do that? We are not sideshow strong men."

"The point is that Sir Alastair is in really good shape, suggesting he didn't just stand around the digs giving orders. He was in there heaving shovelfuls of earth."

"You keep saying 'really good' shape, which suggests that this sort of musculature is a positive and even attractive trait."

"Fine, he's in strong physical condition. Better?"

I bite my lip as I see the wheels turning in Gray's mind. Oh, I know what he's thinking. Like I said, the guy has an ego, and he's weighing his own "physical condition" compared to Sir Alastair's. I could tell him he's fine, being more active than most Victorian men, and he also has the kind of physique that naturally fills out with muscle. But I'm going to amuse myself by letting him stew on that.

"The point," I say, "is that the smallish figure Mr. Awad saw doesn't seem like they'd have been able to strangle a man of Sir Alastair's size."

He snaps out of it. "Yes, of course, and I have already solved the answer to that riddle. It's the reason I left him partially unclothed."

He spreads Sir Alastair's shirt farther apart. I wince when I see the man's stomach. An ugly bruise mars his abdomen.

"Punched in the gut." I get a closer look at the bruising. "Looks like two bruises."

"I am postulating a fist and then a boot."

"The attacker hits him in the stomach. Sir Alastair doubles over. A kick to the same spot takes him down and disables him enough for the killer to get the rope around his neck. Sir Alastair is on his knees, and so the angle helps the killer get a grip and pull upward."

"There is also a bruise on his back, suggesting the killer braced a foot against Sir Alastair's back while tightening the rope. That would explain why the rope dug in so deep. It also means that we cannot presume a strong—or male—attacker."

"A punch to the stomach doesn't need to be hard if it catches someone off guard. Add in the kick and then the bracing, and a woman of average strength could do it."

I walk down the length of the body. "Rigor mortis is still active, which aligns with time of death being sometime between midmorning and early afternoon. Midafternoon would be the latest because the killer needed time to unwrap the mummy and wrap the body, and we believe Selim saw them in the tunnel around four. I would say, though, that we're likely looking at death in the late morning, probably before Lady Christie and the children returned, which would make it easier to pull off."

"The children are out, the staff is busy preparing for the evening, and Sir Alastair goes into his artifact room and never comes out."

I nod. "Which no one notices because he's known for coming and going as he pleases."

The door opens. McCreadie pops his head in. "Annis's coach is here."

"And I believe we are ready for it," Gray says. "Come, Mallory. Our evening is finally at an end."

I'm back at the town house and up in my room, getting ready for breakfast. I couldn't sleep even if I tried, and also, if Gray and McCreadie are having breakfast together, I want to be there. They'll be discussing the case, and my position is still precarious enough that I need to stay front and center in the investigation, lest they forget that I no longer have housemaid duties.

When I look in the mirror, the situation is not as dire as I feared. The dress can be salvaged. There is one bit where the lace caught and ripped, but otherwise, a sponging will do the trick. That's the advantage to dark lace—it looks remarkably good even after being dragged through a tunnel.

The biggest mess is me, with a dirt-smeared face and a hairstyle gone haywire. I can see why no one wanted me walking through the New Town. I'd likely be arrested for solicitation. Well, not that anyone would think I'd actually be soliciting looking like this, but they'd presume I was heading back to the Old Town after a night of hard-core carousing—possibly involving mud wrestling.

I'm unpinning my hair when someone raps at my door.

"It's me," Alice says. "Come to see if you need help with that dress."

I check the pocket watch on my dresser. It's a recent splurge purchase. No one else understands why a housemaid—or even a forensic scientist's assistant—needs one. I can't break my modern-day obsession with time. It doesn't matter that there's a clock downstairs, and I can hear the hourly chimes even up here. I need to know *exactly* what time it is whenever I want.

Right now, it's almost five thirty. Normally Alice would just be starting her shift. Today, though, with the party, Isla and Gray would have been having a late breakfast. Even now that Isla requested it early, Mrs. Wallace would have had Lorna do Alice's duties and allowed her to sleep in. That wouldn't happen in a normal household, but things work differently here, where Alice straddles the line between parlormaid and ward.

I open the door. Alice nearly falls in. At twelve, she's just topped five feet following a growth spurt. No matter how much she eats, she's rail thin, with little sign of puberty. We don't wear uniforms, but her work dress is a simple blue gown, white apron and cap.

She eyes me from top to bottom. "You *are* a mess. I will bring warm water and help you wash up."

"Uh-huh." I lean against the doorpost. "You're up when you could have slept in. You're offering to help me with my dress. Now you're going to haul warm water all the way up here? You want something. Please don't tell me there's a problem with the new maid."

"Her?" Alice sniffs. "She's barely said two words. She seems very dull."

"Dull is exactly what we need in a housemaid. Just like we need parlormaids who are sweet natured and helpful to their sisters in service, and offer to draw them baths for no reason at all. However, we don't always get what we want, do we?"

"If you don't wish my assistance . . ."

"I want to know the conditions that come with it."

"No conditions. I simply hoped for conversation. Unlike the new maid, you are very good at talking. I will help with your gown, and you will tell me all about your evening."

"Ah, the truth comes out. You wish to hear about the lovely party, all the pretty dresses and delicious food and delightful music."

She rolls her brown eyes. "I want to hear about the murder. Obviously."

I'm opening my mouth to answer when Alice stiffens and turns to the hall.

"What do you want?" she snaps.

Lorna's soft voice barely carries to me. "I came to see if Miss Mitchell needed help."

"She does not."

"Might I bring her a cup of tea? I heard she had a terrible night."

"If she needs tea, I shall bring it. You should be tending to Dr. Gray and Detective McCreadie."

Through narrowed eyes, Alice watches Lorna depart. I resist the urge to comment. Catriona had bullied Alice, and it took months—and a shared adventure—to convince her I was no longer *that* Catriona. She finally trusts me, and if she's marking her territory with the new girl, then I won't argue. I don't have time to get to know Lorna right now anyway. That will need to come later.

To Alice, I say, "I would appreciate that bowl of hot water for washing. I need to have breakfast with Dr. Gray and Detective McCreadie."

"Need or want?"

"Sometimes, it is the same thing."

I've taken off the dress, which Alice moved down to the basement for spot cleaning. As I scrubbed up, I told Alice what we'd found. She made me go over the mummy unwrapping twice, grumbling that I was skimming over important parts. By skimming, she seems to mean "not providing sufficiently lurid detail." She also wants to see the finger.

"I've never seen a mummy," she says. "They had one at the museum, but you needed to be a scholar to see it."

"Mrs. Ballantyne or Dr. Gray would have taken you."

She shrugs and doesn't answer. That would be a boundary she isn't ready to cross. They are her employers, and when they are too kind, it makes her nervous. That is not the proper way of things.

"You say the children grew up in Egypt?" she says.

I smile at that. "Children? They are only a year or two younger than you."

"If their father is a baronet, they are *much* younger than me. Like helpless kittens who would starve without someone to bring them their dinner."

Pride sharpens her voice. She has a point. As intelligent and mature as Phoebe and Michael seem, it's hard to believe they could be of an age with Alice, already working for a living.

I take down my usual dress.

"You cannot wear that," she says, taking it from me. "You aren't a maid anymore."

I hesitate. She's right about this, too. While the dress isn't a uniform per se, Isla buys our work clothes so that we don't need to, and they are work appropriate, which means it's meant for scrubbing floors, not interviewing witnesses.

"I'm going to need more appropriate clothes," I say as I take down one of my two nonwork dresses.

"You can buy them with your increased pay," Alice says as she takes the dress and brushes off a bit of lint. "For being Dr. Gray's assistant now."

"Hmm."

She glances over. "He is paying you more, is he not? If he hasn't mentioned it, then you must ask. He may forget that you are entitled to a higher wage now, as his assistant."

Gray has already increased my pay, supposedly to acknowledge the extra work I do as his assistant, but mostly, I think, because the situation is equally awkward for them. I'm not a housemaid or an assistant. I'm a police detective. But it isn't their fault I can't do that job, so I want to be paid for my actual work, not slipped extra money like a relation who's fallen on hard times.

I put on the dress and open my door to see Lorna right outside it, frozen in the horror of being caught.

Finding her there suggests she was coming to speak to me. While that's hardly a crime, I can see why she might be nervous, after Alice snapped at her.

Now Alice snaps again, with, "What are you doing up here?"

"I—I was coming to say that breakfast is ready and the gentlemen . . . They, uh, seem to expect Miss Mitchell to join them."

Her expression says she's baffled by this, maybe thinking she misunderstood. I might be Gray's assistant, but I'm still staff, which means I should not be joining the family for meals. Yep, things are different here, as she'll figure out.

"It's Mallory, not Miss Mitchell," I say gently. "And they will be expecting me to take notes."

She relaxes at that. This is not yet a world with female secretaries, but at least it makes more sense than me joining them as an equal.

"Do you need anything then, miss?" she says. "Paper, pen?"

I smile. "I have both, thank you."

"Do you prefer tea or coffee? I will have it ready for you."

"She's going downstairs right now," Alice says. "And I will be serving the breakfast."

Again, Lorna looks confused. There are very clear rules about which staff members do what. Those overlap more with a relatively small staff, but still, the parlormaid doesn't serve meals unless the housemaid isn't around.

I know why Alice wants to serve. It's not so much about being territorial as about wanting to eavesdrop on chatter about the case.

"Alice will do it this morning," I say. "I fear the case is a disturbing one, and we do not wish to scare you off quite so soon."

"Yes," Alice says quickly, straightening. "I am accustomed to these things. You are not."

With that, Alice sweeps from the room, herding me downstairs to my breakfast.

THIRTEEN

We are taking breakfast in the library, which is not entirely proper. Food is to be consumed in dining rooms. Even if you wished to read while eating, you wouldn't eat in here . . . nor would you take the book to the dining room.

As long as Isla is asleep, the men have the excuse of, well, being men. It's not even so much that they are above the rules as that they can't be expected to know them. That's the job of the "angel of the house."

I once teased Isla with that moniker, and her response was shockingly— and delightfully—profane. The angel of the household is one of those Victorian concepts wrapped in bows and sparkles to hide the rotten core inside. It's supposed to honor women and raise them on a pedestal to be cherished as something good and pure in a filthy world. Instead, it's a gilded cage that traps them both physically and psychologically, forcing them to be those good and pure beacons of light.

The angel of the household is expected to be sweet and mild, her life given over to one purpose: keeping the house pleasant and ordered for her man. Look at the stereotypical fifties housewife and you can see how the concept crept through time. Her man has been hard at work all day, and he deserves to come home to a peaceful and tidy house, and a primped and pretty wife with a tumbler of whisky in her hand.

The problem with peaceful and tidy, sweet and mild, pleasant and or- dered? It's boring as hell. So middle-class Victorian men don't *come* home after work. They go to their pubs and their sports clubs and enjoy them-selves before they must return home, sit on a spindly chair, and read the paper while their wife does needlepoint and the children are kept out of sight and out of mind.

Isla is not the "angel of the household" here. No one wants her to be. But she's still the lady of the house, and things run a little differently in her presence. Without her, we can have breakfast in the library, and Mrs. Wallace will only roll her eyes with affectionate exasperation.

Well, it's affectionate for the guys. I just get exasperation—with a generous dose of suspicion. Winning over Alice was like conquering the bunny hill. Mrs. Wallace is my Everest.

I'm on my second cup of coffee, the best defense against yawning and having Gray suggest I take a nap. Yes, coffee is a thing in Victorian Scot-land, much to my surprise. I won't say it's good coffee, but it exists. I long to experiment with the brewing methods and with foaming milk to make myself something resembling a proper cappuccino. To do that, though, I need access to the kitchen. To get that access, I need to convince Mrs. Wallace that I'm not evil Catriona, who may have spent the last six months ingratiating herself with the bosses only to poison them.

For now, I drink what's available and enjoy the underrated pleasure of fresh warm bread dripping with butter. I'll add jam soon. I'll also avail myself of the ham and eggs. But for now, it's coffee and carbs.

We're deep into conversation on the case when a tap comes at the closed door.

I'm closest, so I open it. Lorna half curtsies in the opening. "I was told not to open closed doors when Doctor Gray is investigating a case."

I nod and smile. "That is correct. Thank you."

"There is a guest for the master. A Lord Muir. Shall I show him into the drawing room?"

"Please. I'll bring the coffee tray."

"Thank you, miss," she says, and scurries off.

We're still walking down the hall, coffee cups in hand, when Lord Muir comes barreling toward us, Lorna at his heels, squeaking, "The drawing room is in there, sir," as she points.

Muir's face is red with exertion as his cane clicks along at top speed.

"You!" he says, homing in on McCreadie. "You are the criminal officer in charge of Alastair's murder, are you not?"

"I am, sir." McCreadie moves his coffee to his left hand and extends his right. "My sincere condolences on the loss—"

The man ignores McCreadie's outstretched hand. "I am so glad to see the murder of a baronet has not put you off your breakfast, Detective. One might think you would be a bit busy—catching a crazed killer—but apparently that is not a priority."

McCreadie's voice is mild. "I have been on the scene all night, Lord Muir. I am here to discuss the case with Dr. Gray and await the police surgeon's report. While I do that, I am eating, so I will be fully prepared to continue the investigation."

"You can eat all you like once you have the killer in custody, and I am astounded that you haven't arrested her already."

"Her?" I say.

"That . . ." He flutters his hand. "Girl."

"You will need to be more specific," McCreadie says. "If you are accusing one of the maids—"

"No, that King girl."

Neither McCreadie nor Gray answers. They are racking their brains. So am I, and it hits me first.

"The young woman protesting outside the party last night?" I say.

"Of course." Muir wheels on McCreadie. "Tell me you have her in custody."

"I know she was upset about the unwrapping demonstration," McCreadie says. "She was stopping people as they came in."

"Upset about the demonstration?" Muir snorts. "She does not give a fig for the demonstration. It was an excuse to embarrass Alastair. Or that is what I thought at first. But now I realize it was a ruse to divert attention in case she was spotted at the scene of the murder. Also, being outside allowed her to hear the commotion caused by her foul deed."

"I believe I am missing something," McCreadie says. "You thought Miss King wanted to embarrass Sir Alastair because . . . ?"

"Because of what he did. To her and the others. And what he was continuing to do."

"What he did . . . ?"

"With those women. He was hell-bent on stopping them."

"Miss King is one of the Seven," I murmur. Then I turn to Muir. "Is that what you mean? The seven women who are studying to become doctors."

"Studying *medicine*. They will not become doctors."

"All right," I say. "The seven women permitted to study medicine. You're saying Sir Alastair tried to stop them?"

"He lobbied for the university court to reject Miss Jex-Blake's application," says a voice behind Lord Muir. Isla appears, wearing a receiving wrapper, having apparently been warned we have a visitor. "Last night, when we met Miss King, I recalled some connection between the Seven and Sir Alastair. It took a while to remember specifics. He was one of those responsible for the university court rejecting Miss Jex-Blake. Now that she has gathered the other six and been admitted, he continues to lobby for them to be removed or be placed under further restrictions."

She meets Lord Muir's gaze. "Because apparently it is not enough to refuse them access to lectures and force Miss Jex-Blake to teach them herself. We cannot have women studying with the men. How will they concentrate with all those . . ." She flaps her hand. "Feminine body parts in the room."

Lord Muir chokes. "It is a distraction."

"That is odd," she continues. "I certainly am not above noticing handsome men, but I have never found myself so distracted by them that I cannot focus on my studies. And if I did, then the problem would be mine to overcome. I would have expected better of young men bright enough to be admitted to medical school."

I expect Muir to bluster, but he backs down with a nod. "You make a fair point, ma'am. Please forgive me. I am upset over my friend's murder."

"Understandable," Isla says. "I presume you are suggesting that Miss King murdered Sir Alastair to remove a vocal opponent to her studies. That seems rather extreme, but as she was on the property and has an issue with the deceased—" She stops short, gaze cutting to McCreadie as if realizing she's treading on his turf.

"Miss King will be investigated," McCreadie says.

"Immediately," Muir says.

I bristle, and I wait for McCreadie to push back. When he doesn't, I see my mistake. I can say that it's the fault of this world and how they treat the nobility, but if I were working a case back home, I'd be expected to give the same deference to any powerful person. They have loud voices and deep pockets, and we might say the law treats everyone the same, but it doesn't.

"I will speak to Miss King myself," McCreadie says. "Dr. Gray will stay to obtain Dr. Addington's report once the autopsy is complete."

"You will speak to her?" Muir says. "Or arrest her?"

"Speak to her and then convey my findings to those who can make any arrest decision." To his superiors and the procurator fiscal. McCreadie doesn't say that. He's not giving Muir a list of targets to harass.

"Acceptable," Muir says. "I will expect a full report this afternoon."

McCreadie's jaw twitches at that, as if chewing over words he'd like to say, but he only murmurs, "I will convey your request to the appropriate parties. Good day, Lord Muir."

Here is where the line between my new life and my old one blurs. Technically, I am Gray's employee, first as his housemaid and now as his assistant. But if McCreadie needs my help with a case, that takes precedence, which I appreciate. Oh, there are times when duty requires me to help McCreadie when something more interesting is happening with Gray, but even if I'm no longer a public servant, I still feel the obligation of that old life.

Today, McCreadie wants me to accompany him to speak to Miss King. There are many situations where being a handsome police officer helps when the interviewee is a woman. But our guts tell us that Miss King will not be susceptible to McCreadie's easy charm.

There are also many situations where being in the body of a young woman helps me with female interview subjects. I put them at ease, looking as little as possible like an officer of the law. Again, I don't think Miss King is going to respond to that.

What she might respond to is an odd and outspoken doctor's female assistant. Isla would be even better equipped to impress Miss King, but I'm the one with the interview experience. So Gray promises he will not examine Sir Alastair post-autopsy until I return, and I'm off with McCreadie.

Isla does help us here, with her more complete knowledge of the Seven. She tells us that they have a home base, so to speak, and where to find it. She's been there herself, offering support and baked goods. Despite what Miss King implied, Isla has been supportive in all the ways she can be, and I know it frustrates her to put her own career concerns above the cause of women's education, but I think she's struck the right balance.

I suggest she join us, but she doesn't think it will help enough. Her time is better spent analyzing the dirt and other samples retrieved from the scene. McCreadie agrees, and we take our leave.

The Seven's base is a unit on Buccleuch Place where their leader—Sophia Jex-Blake—has taken up residence, along with another of their group. According to Isla, the women use it as a study hall of sorts. That's where McCreadie and I head, with a cab dropping us off nearby.

"Nice party until the murder," I say as we walk.

McCreadie laughs. "That does tend to put a damper on the festivities."

"Was Isla enjoying it? I know she was upset after our run-in with Miss King."

"She came out of it soon enough." He smiles fondly. "Isla cannot resist a good party."

I look over at him, surprised. I'm about to say I haven't known her to attend any. Then I realize why that might be.

"Does she not attend because she is still, strictly speaking, in mourning?"

McCreadie takes a few steps as if considering his answer. "Perhaps, in the first year or so. Now I fear she is . . . less comfortable than she was once. Isla used to *adore* parties. We'd go together. Well, with others, of course. Duncan was never one for parties, and so she kindly accompanied me. Then Lawrence came along . . ." He shakes his head sharply. "Much changed after Lawrence came along, including Isla herself."

Another couple of steps before he quickly adds, "I do not mean that as an insult. She is still herself in most ways. Just . . . more cautious. Less open. She is coming around, though. Being more her old self, with her old confidence. You help with that a great deal. She sees your confidence, and it buoys her own."

"Maybe, but sometimes I worry I might set . . . not the best example. Like the friend who has lots of money and spends it freely, and you try to keep up with them only to realize you aren't in the same position. I can afford to be odd. This isn't my world. I don't know how much longer I'll be here. But then, when I worry about that, it feels patronizing."

"You need to let Isla make her own choices," he says softly. "She is not a child."

My cheeks heat. "I know."

"I need to do the same. Do I love the thought of her rushing into danger with you? No. But if I laugh at Duncan for doing it and fret about Isla, that is wrong."

"Yes, you really should worry more about Duncan."

He laughs softly as we cross the road. "True."

"I know what you mean, though," I say. "You do a good job of not hovering over her."

"Then I am an excellent actor, because that is exactly what I wish to do. It is what I have wished to do . . ." He takes a deep breath. "Enough of that. We are here."

I look to see we're across the road from the Buccleuch Place residence, a narrow door between two others.

"Now here is the awkward part," McCreadie says. "The police are never popular with those who espouse strong political beliefs. We are seen as the enemy, sometimes rightly so."

"Yep. I remember what happened the last time." I'd suggested speaking to some young men with very strong anti-immigration views, and things got ugly when they spotted McCreadie's constable outside. "In this case, you aren't able to send me in alone, because it's a proper police investigation and I am not proper police. However, if you're thinking we should play some role to get them to open the front door, it's already too late. They've spotted us."

His gaze lifts to a window, where the curtain has been pulled back, the pale oval of a face pointed in our direction. McCreadie curses under his breath.

"If I thought we should trick them," I say, "I wouldn't be standing here. These are young women accustomed to being treated like children. I'd suggest we don't do that."

He dips his chin. "Of course. I did not think of that."

We cross the road. McCreadie knocks on the door. When no one answers, he calls, "Detective McCreadie of the Edinburgh police. I am sorry to disturb you ladies, but I fear I must ask a few questions of Miss King."

He's raising his hand to knock again when the door jerks open. There stands the one member of the Seven I can both name and recognize. The leader, Sophia Jex-Blake. Her dark hair is pulled back in a severe style and her small mouth seems to be in a permanent moue of distaste, but her eyes are gentle, if wary.

"*Mrs.* King is not here," she says, holding the door, barring entry.

"My apologies, ma'am. Mrs. King then. I need to speak to her most urgently and I was told she might reside here."

"She does not. While she is often here in the evenings, she rarely spends the night. We did not see her last evening, but I presume you know why and that is the reason you are here."

"Er, yes, I fear she was outside a home where—"

"A murder took place. Yes, she has spoken to me about the events of last evening."

"Already?" I say.

Jex-Blake turns a cool look on me. "What she does on her own time ought to be her own business, but she recognizes that it could affect all if it draws attention to one. Murder does tend to draw attention. You are Miss Mitchell, I presume?"

I must look surprised, because she says, "It behooves me to know who I am dealing with. Mrs. King mentioned she had an encounter with a detective—Mr. McCreadie here—and that he was accompanied by Dr. Gray, his two sisters, and his young female assistant. You would be the assistant, as I recognize from the accounts of Dr. Gray's adventures, which wax most poetic on your golden curls and cerulean eyes."

I turn to McCreadie. "Remind me to hunt down that writer as soon as we've solved this case."

Do I imagine a twitch to Jex-Blake's lips?

"Please do," she says. "It paints a most vexing portrait of you, if you are indeed Dr. Gray's assistant, and not a pretty face to light his days."

"One can be both," McCreadie murmurs, and I glare at him.

"As for Mrs. King," Jex-Blake says, "she confessed to protesting against the mummy unwrapping, which occurred before the murder." She pauses. "No, I suppose it occurred before the *discovery* of the murder, but Sir Alastair must have already been dead, if his killer wrapped him as a mummy. That would take some time. Rather fitting, though." Her gaze rises to McCreadie. "Is it against the law to say that about a member of the so-called nobility?"

"Not yet."

"Mrs. King confessed to being at the house and to being recognized by Mrs. Ballantyne, which she realized could cause problems for us. She intended to tell me about that when we next met. Instead, she heard of the murder and came straight to me."

"What time would that have been?" McCreadie asks.

Jex-Blake sighs. "This is going to be a proper interview, isn't it? Then you might as well come in. The longer I have the police at our door, the more people will be certain we are all—finally—about to be arrested."

We enter and find ourselves in a foyer with a wood floor as worn as the faded yellow wallpaper.

"Miss Mitchell?" she says. "As I have decided to cooperate, I will do so fully. You may check for signs that I have lied about Mrs. King being here while I speak to Detective McCreadie. I would prefer *you* did it, as one of our group is currently sleeping in the back and would be quite alarmed to wake to Detective McCreadie in the room." Her lips twitch. "Or perhaps not so much alarmed as disappointed to learn he is only there for Mrs. King. Come, Detective. I just put a kettle on the stove for tea."

FOURTEEN

It's a quick enough search. Oh, if I thought I'd find evidence connected to the crime, I'd have taken full advantage of being left alone. But there's a reason Jex-Blake let me go off unaccompanied. Even if Mrs. King was guilty, there'd be no evidence of that guilt here. I *would* like to poke about, to satisfy personal interest in such a fascinating part of history unfolding before me. But that would be a violation of privacy.

As Miss Jex-Blake said, the only other person in residence is the young woman who'd fallen asleep while studying. I don't ask her name. Again, that'd be prying. I can tell she isn't Mrs. King and so I move on with a quick apology for the disturbance.

When I return to the sitting room, Jex-Blake rises to meet me.

"So," she says, "are we harboring murderers under the floorboards?"

"No, but there's enough food lying around to attract rats from under the floorboards."

"I know," she sighs. "We really do need a maid. I do not suppose you would volunteer your services?"

"Sorry, I've moved from crumbs to corpses."

She tilts her head. "Does this mean you are considering a career in medicine, Miss Mitchell?"

"No. I enjoy the science mostly for solving crimes. I would make a terrible doctor. I have no bedside manner."

"Oddly, I have heard the same said about myself. Well, if you change your mind, we can always use more young women joining our cause."

"I'm happy to join the cause of improving opportunities for women in any way I can . . . as long as it doesn't involve studying medical texts myself."

She gives me a genuine smile then. "I appreciate your candor and your support. Please give my regards to Mrs. Ballantyne. And tell Dr. Gray we would very much appreciate it—presuming he supports his sister's right to a career—if he might lend his support to *our* cause."

"While I hate to speak on Duncan's behalf," McCreadie says softly, "I can say that he does support you, but he fears his open endorsement would do more harm than good. He is a divisive figure within the medical community."

"Have him speak to me. I will convince him otherwise. Until then, good day to you both."

Jex-Blake has given McCreadie an address where Mrs. King lives, apparently with her husband. Yes, the use of "missus" implies she's married, but that's not always the case. While I don't think our housekeeper is a widow, no one would call her "Miss." In this case, there is indeed a Mr. King, a fellow medical student, in fact.

We arrive at the address. It's in the Old Town, but a decent part of it. The apartment, though, is located on the top floor, up five flights of very suspect stairs. In other words, the couple can't really afford this neighborhood, but it's safer than most for a couple of young students.

I rap at the door this time, with McCreadie behind me. We aren't going to pretend to be anything other than police, but seeing a woman's face first might help.

The door opens to a young man, maybe twenty-four, slender and dark-haired. I suspect he'd be quite handsome if he got some sleep. The textbook in his hands and the ink staining his fingers suggests it isn't late nights at the pub keeping him up. Seeing us, he straightens and runs a hand through his hair, smearing ink on his forehead.

"Oh, you must be here for the Ryans," he says. "They are the next door over." He lowers his voice. "They really do appreciate the baskets, even if

Mr. Ryan grumbles. It is a kind thing you do, bringing them food while Mrs. Ryan is ill. We have offered what little help we can—my wife and I are both medical students—but they see even that as charity."

"We are not here for the Ryans, I fear," McCreadie says. He tips his head. "Detective McCreadie of the Edinburgh police. If you are Mr. King, I met your wife last night, outside Sir Alastair's home."

The young man's face spasms. "Detec—My wife? Outside Sir—whose home? I fear you have the wrong person. My wife was here with me all night. Yes, all night. And evening." He lifts the book, his hand trembling slightly. "We were studying together."

"One of our companions identified your wife," McCreadie says, not unkindly. "Mrs. King did not dispute the identification, and she later told Miss Jex-Blake that she met me."

King's mouth works. Then he slumps. "I am sorry, Detective. I asked Florence not to go there last night. I said it could cause trouble, but she was determined. I presume you have come to arrest her for disturbing the party."

"No, I need to question her about something far graver."

King goes still. "Did she break a window or such? If so, it was an accident."

"May we come in and speak to her?"

King hesitates.

McCreadie says, "It will be better for all if we do not have this conversation in the corridor."

The young man motions for us to come in and shuts the door. "She is not here. You may search if you like, but as you can see . . ." He waves at the room with a rueful smile. "There is little to search. We have only been wed two months and are still furnishing."

McCreadie nods to me, and I enter ahead of him.

"Miss Mitchell will look about," McCreadie says. "She works for a consultant with the police."

There really isn't much to search. The single room is a couple of hundred feet square, with two privacy screens. I check behind each as McCreadie questions King.

"When did you last see your wife?" McCreadie asks.

"Perhaps an hour or so ago? She came in briefly to tell me she would be out for the day. I protested—we were supposed to walk in the park—but she promised we could go tomorrow. I had the sense something had come up."

"Did she say what?"

King shakes his head. "I presumed it was to do with Miss Jex-Blake and the others. Sometimes it is best if I do not know what they are up to." He quickly adds, "I believe my wife has as much right to study medicine as I do—and to become a doctor. That is how we met. This past spring Miss Jex-Blake held a talk for the male students who wished to know more about their cause. I was . . ." He makes a face. "I regret to say I was one of the few who attended. If I am not privy to all their plans, that is because my wife thinks it best. She fears it could jeopardize my own career. I say that does not matter, but she insists one of us needs a job." A wry smile. "Florence is a very practical woman, which I appreciate, because I am not a very practical man."

I've checked behind both dividers. Now I glance over at King, but he has his back to me. I slip into the bedroom section of the room.

McCreadie continues, "You mentioned her act of protest at Sir Alastair's party last night. I presume your wife *did* tell you about that?"

I don't catch the answer. I've struggled down to the floor to look under the bed, which smells of slightly moldy straw. It's tidy, though, the sheets pulled up, and there isn't so much as a dust bunny under it.

I glance over my shoulder. The men are still talking. Good.

The only other piece of furniture in the tiny space is a makeshift nightstand stacked high with books. It has a single drawer. I slide it open soundlessly. Inside are what I recognize as the current version of condoms, the cheaper ones made from some kind of animal skin. King wins a point for that one. He might say he supports his wife's studies, but this proves it. A baby would be a convenient excuse to convince Florence King to give up her dreams and be a "proper" wife.

There's nothing else in the drawer. I slide it all the way out and check in behind. Nope, still nothing. I look around and my gaze goes to the bed.

With a sigh of resignation, I lift the mattress. Sure enough, there are two opened envelopes under it. That's the thing about a world that predates crime shows. People pick the most obvious places to hide things. It's almost disappointing.

I make sure the men are still talking. Then I tug out the contents of the envelopes. One holds a key. The other has several sheets of paper with tiny feminine handwriting. No way am I going to be able to read it before King realizes I'm gone. And if his wife knows the police were here, she'll hide anything.

Well, this is one *good* thing about doing detective work before proper crime-scene containment and chain of evidence. With a silent apology to the patron saint of law enforcement, I tuck the envelopes into my pocket.

I slip back out just as King seems to remember I'm there.

"There is no sign of Mrs. King, sir," I say to McCreadie.

"And you have no idea where she might be?" McCreadie says to her husband.

The young man shakes his head. "I would try the rooms Miss Jex-Blake keeps. I can provide you with the address."

"We have it, and your wife is not there."

King wipes his brow. "I am sorry then. I truly do not know." He quickly adds, "But that is not unusual behavior. When she is troubled, she often takes long walks, usually along the Water of Leith or up on Calton Hill. She did say not to expect her for lunch, but that she will return for tea."

"All right. Tell her it was Detective McCreadie again. I need to speak to her urgently, and if she does not present herself at my police office by nightfall, I will be forced to send men here to bring her to the office, which will be most embarrassing."

"Y-yes, sir. At the police office by sundown. Where is that?"

McCreadie gives directions. Then we leave.

We're barely outside when a young constable runs up.

"Sir," he says. "Detective Crichton is looking for you."

In a time before cell phones—or even police radios—the communication system in the police force is rather astounding. It helps that Edinburgh is, in this time, not an overly large city. If someone needs McCreadie, the word will go out, along with what neighborhood he might be in. Officers will keep an eye out while doing their regular duties, and if they spot him, they'll pass on the message.

When the constable leaves, I tell McCreadie about the envelopes and pull them out.

"Now *you're* stuffing evidence in your pockets?" he teases.

"You and Dr. Gray are terrible influences. Should I have left them there?"

"No, you are correct in taking them. If the envelopes are important, the Kings would have moved them in case we returned to make a more thorough search. At worst, we can put them back later."

I try not to cringe at that. Then I ask his thoughts on Florence King as we walk.

"Before Lord Muir insisted, I did not consider her a viable suspect," he says. "I am still not convinced she is. However, I do not like this running-off business. Even if it is her custom, it is suspicious."

"Particularly as she does it when she is troubled."

"Hmm."

"Do you want these?" I ask, holding out the envelopes.

"No, take them to Duncan. Examine them there, and I will come around when I am able."

FIFTEEN

I enter the town house through the back door, and I'm still removing my outdoor boots when feet tap on the stairs. The steps are too light to be Gray's, and even too light for Isla. Too quick for Mrs. Wallace. Too heavy for Alice. Then who . . . ?

Lorna pokes her head around the corner. Ah, right. New maid.

"Miss Mallory," she says, and I don't correct her. If she's not ready to call me by my given name, this is close enough. "Dr. Gray said to send you down to his offices when you return, and Mrs. Ballantyne said you are to have lunch with her and that Dr. Gray may attend if he insists." She lowers her voice. "I think she was teasing about that."

I smile. "She was."

"She said you will discuss the case over luncheon, so you are to bring your notes. But first, you must attend to Dr. Gray." She puts a hand out. "I will brush those for you."

I hesitate until I realize she means my boots. Usually I am the one brushing off everyone's boots, including my own. But that is a housemaid's job, I remind myself, and I am no longer a housemaid. Still, even when we had other temporary maids, none of them had offered to clean my boots.

"I will brush them later," I say, "but I do appreciate the offer."

"May I bring you tea?" she asks.

Huh. None of the other maids offered that either. I could get used to this.

I check my pocket watch. "It is almost time for Dr. Gray's morning tea and biscuits. I will have some with him. Thank you."

She half curtsies. "I will bring them down."

I put on my indoor boots and head downstairs. Gray is in his laboratory, looking down at the body of Sir Alastair.

"Is he saying anything interesting?" I ask.

"Sadly, no. Even his corpse is a rather dull conversationalist." He makes a face. "And that was petty and rude. Sir Alastair could be very engaging. I admired his passion for his work, and I always had the feeling we would have gotten on well, if he could have gotten past . . ."

"The color of your skin?"

"To be honest, that was never an issue. In medical school, I developed a rather finely honed sense for determining who claimed to have no concern with a brown-skinned doctor but obviously did. But that was not a problem with Sir Alastair. At that point, he had already worked for years with Egyptians, experts and professionals as well as laborers. The problem was, well . . ." A quick glance my way. "The affair with his sister. Although, again, I do not believe his reaction had anything to do with my skin color. He would have been as outraged if Hugh were the man involved."

"As a widow, his sister was his responsibility. So was her virtue."

"I am not certain it was that so much as a fear that she would be hurt. She was the one who, well . . ." He clears his throat. "She initiated the relationship. I think he presumed I had taken advantage of her. A misunderstanding, but not one that would reflect as poorly on him as considering his sister to be his property. His wife—his first wife at least—was very forward thinking, as is his sister, and he did not ever seem to mind that."

"Yet he did have a problem with women joining the medical school?"

His lips purse. "I thought that was odd. Perhaps his respect for women's intelligence had limits? I can only imagine that if his first wife had been alive, she would have roundly thumped him for speaking out against female students."

"His current wife doesn't seem like a shrinking violet either. Just maybe not as confident in her voice yet."

"Yes, perhaps they had not been married long enough for her to feel comfortable objecting. Also, I believe Lady Christie was in Cairo when Sir Alastair argued against the young women's admission. She stayed with the children and helped her brother supervise the dig." He shakes his head. "But enough of that. You are here to discuss the autopsy."

"Dare I hope it went well?"

"That depends on whether you—"

A tap at the door, almost inaudible.

I call a hello, and Lorna enters with the tea tray.

"Where would you like this, sir?" she asks.

Gray waves distractedly at a table right beside the dissection table. To her credit, Lorna doesn't hesitate. She sets the tray down two feet from a naked corpse with a bit of cloth over his groin for privacy. Then she begins pouring the tea.

"You need not do that," Gray says.

She smiles. "I am fine, sir. It is not often I get to serve tea beside a dead body."

"You're doing very well," I say.

"Thank you, miss."

We wait until she's done pouring tea and leaves.

When the door closes behind Lorna, I say, "About the autopsy? You said whether it went well depends on . . . ?"

"On whether you are in the mood to be amused by Addington, rather than wanting to smack your head against the nearest wall."

"That good, huh?"

"He allowed me to attend the autopsy, mostly because he wanted to be done before Lord Muir returned. He asked what I thought, and I made the mistake of saying it seemed to be strangulation. He then declared, without even looking at the body, that Sir Alastair died because he had been wrapped in the mummy's bandages and could not breathe."

"Did you explain the difference between strangulation and suffocation?"

"Oh, that is only the first of many issues with that scenario. He then proceeded to wax poetic on what a gruesome and terrifying death that would be, waking to discover one is entombed in a mummy's wrappings. He seemed very taken with the image. I will admit to being somewhat concerned."

"'Somewhat'? I'm the macabre one here, and I don't even want to think what it would be like to die that way. However, I know I sure as hell wouldn't just lie there and let myself suffocate . . . when I could struggle a bit and get out of the damn wrappings."

"Tosh, Mallory. What a ridiculous thought. Fight your way out? Why not simply lie there and revel in the horror of your inevitable demise?"

I shake my head. "Please tell me he changed his cause of death after seeing the very obvious ligature marks around Sir Alastair's neck."

"He did, thankfully. And while he failed to note the bruising on the back or the angle of the ligatures, he did notice the abdominal bruises. He also performed the autopsy correctly and concluded that it was indeed suffocation brought on by strangulation. I would concur."

"So Sir Alastair died the way we thought he died."

"Yes. Otherwise, as I said, Sir Alastair has very little to tell us."

"And the rope?" I say.

"Ah, yes. I actually had time to check that before Addington arrived." He points to the rope. "Would you like to give it a try?"

I smile. "I would, thank you."

Matching weapon marks is one thing they *can* do in this time. Or Gray can do it, though the validity for court is still in question. There are three basic steps here. The first is comparing the size and pattern of the rope sample to the marks. I do that and agree that it appears to match, which is as conclusive as that can be. The next step is examining a fiber from the wound and comparing it to one from the rope. Under the magnifying glass, they do indeed match. The third step is the most conclusive, but that involved Isla. She took these two fibers for comparative testing and found a match. Apparently, I missed that demonstration, too.

"I have also confirmed that it is the same type of rope we found in the packing crates," Gray says.

"Which suggests it wasn't premeditated murder," I say. "Yes, I know, that doesn't matter here—it's still murder, and the killer will still go to the gallows. But it does affect the investigation."

"Because grabbing a murder weapon from the supplies at hand suggests that the killer didn't plan to murder Sir Alastair."

"Right," I say. "Either Sir Alastair caught them doing something, possibly in the artifact room, or they argued and the killer lashed out."

"It must have been a quiet argument if no one overheard."

"Fair point. Considering—" I stop. "Isla wanted to discuss this over lunch. Should we wait?"

He checks his pocket watch. "I would rather not wait to decide our next move. However, I agree Isla should be part of the conversation. Shall we see whether she is free to join us for this tea that we've let go cold?"

"Good idea."

We're in the dining room with fresh tea and biscuits and Isla, who was indeed ready to join us. We bring her up to speed quickly. She confirms that her analysis on the rope matched fibers found in Sir Alastair's neck and that the length of rope used is from the same skein as the rope found for packing, meaning the murder weapon was already at the scene.

As for the dirt, the traces found in the exhibit room are not a conclusive match for the dirt in the tunnel. They could still be from the tunnel, but we can't say with certainty that the killer came in that way.

Then I say, "So we seem to have an unplanned attack. Something happened in that room, and Sir Alastair was murdered without raising enough fuss to be heard through the closed door. Did he walk in on the killer?"

"Stealing an artifact," Isla says.

"That's the most obvious answer. The door was unlocked while they were being removed. Let's say the killer sneaks in before it's locked again. Then Sir Alastair enters."

"Could the killer have had a key?" Isla asks.

"No, only Sir Alastair . . ." I stop. "But we haven't recovered the key, meaning it's still out there."

I remember the hidden key in the Kings' apartment. I take the envelope from my pocket and explain where it came from.

"That is not the key to the artifact room," Gray says. "While we were at the house, I examined the lock to see whether it could be opened the way you do it."

"With my handy hairpins?"

"Yes, and it is a more complex mechanism. That key"—he points to the one on the table—"is for the simpler sort."

He's correct, of course. This is a classic Victorian key, the sort we in the modern world consider an old-fashioned key. My grandmother had locks like that in her home, and I'd delighted in opening them with my junior-detective-kit picks.

"So three options," I say. "One, the killer snuck in while the artifacts were being carried out. Two, they came in while Sir Alastair was in there with the door unlocked. Three, Sir Alastair took the person inside himself. Except the house had no visitors that morning. Which suggests the killer was part of the staff."

Isla shakes her head. "They were preparing for a party. People would have been coming and going, and the staff wouldn't consider them 'visitors.' Someone could have easily entered through the back door if they were dressed in any sort of service or trade clothing."

"Also," Gray says, "while the staff may have not admitted any visitors, Sir Alastair was not the sort to stand on ceremony. If he were expecting a guest and the staff were busy, he'd have let them in himself."

"With that sort of chaos—planning for a fancy party—getting into the house would have been easy," Isla says.

"We will need to have Hugh's policemen continue questioning the staff," Gray says. "Now, about that key . . ." He pulls it over and frowns. "It is very old."

Old . . .

"The tunnel?" I say. "The shed at the top is locked. Selim had a key, and Michael. How many keys would there be?"

"I will ask for Mr. Awad's and see whether it is a match."

"Good idea. Now, this letter . . ." I spread it out on the table with my gloved hands and squint. "The writing is so cramped, I can barely read it."

Isla reaches out, and I hand it to her. Then she shakes her head and passes it to Gray.

"The problem is not the small writing," she says. "It does not appear to be in English."

"No," Gray says. "I think it *is* English. But a cipher."

"Oooh, a code?" I say. "You're good at those, right?"

"I know a few," he says. "This is not any of those."

"So we copy it out, give the original to the police, and then try to solve it."

"Yes . . ." Gray says, with obvious hesitancy.

"Is that a problem?"

"If it's too complex for me to easily solve, then it will take time, and unless we consider Mrs. King a strong suspect, we'd spend hours deciphering what would likely turn out to be a love letter. They *are* newlyweds."

"Ah. Fair point. Then we set this aside for now. The primary lead, of course, is the mummy itself."

Gray frowns. Then he says, "Of course. Yes. Whoever killed Sir Alastair undoubtedly also took the mummified remains. There was little point in concealing them—and great danger in being caught with them. Meaning they had a purpose for them."

"Both Michael and his uncle mentioned the resale value for medicinal purposes. What do you two know about that?"

"I do not deal in quack medicines," Gray says loftily.

"Well, then, you're no help at all."

"Fine," he says. "I am aware that mummia—"

"What?"

"Mummia," he says with some impatience. "The powdered remains of mummies."

"There's a name for that? Wow."

"As I was saying, I am aware that mummia has been used in medicines. Human remains have been thought to have medical uses throughout history. In the second century, Galen thought burnt human bones could be used in the treatment of epilepsy. In the sixteenth century, Paracelsus believed in using human fat, marrow, and, yes, mummia, to treat various conditions."

"Also excrement," Isla says.

"I was not mentioning that," Gray says.

I shake my head. "If we're talking about eating dried bits of people, I'm not sure eating feces is a whole lot worse."

Gray continues, "When the remains of mummies began to be used in Europe, it included both the powder and a liquor form made from the liquid leaked during the mummification process."

"Tell me you are joking."

"I never joke about medical history. It is believed that the original mummia was the material used in mummification—a bitumen. A Western translation error led to that being interpreted as first the leaked residue and later the remains themselves. Mummy remains were most popular as medicines between the fifteenth and eighteenth century, when they were used primarily for treating cuts, bruises, and fractures. At the height of its popularity, however, people naturally began to falsify the ingredients, and what was most commonly available was not powdered Egyptians but powdered corpses of Europeans. That led to the decline in popularity."

"What is the world coming to when you can't even trust your mummy powder to be actual mummy."

"The same as when you cannot trust your sugar to be actual sugar or your coffee to be actual coffee," he says dryly. "If it can be adulterated, it will be."

I'd never given much thought to food regulations until I came to this world where, as Gray says, adulteration is rampant, whether it's medicine or food.

"So there's no market for mummia now?"

He gives me a hard look. Isla only shakes her head.

"Right," I say. "Dumb question. If it was a recognized medicine in the past, there will still be a market for it. You just won't be able to find it in a chemist's shop."

Isla nods. "Whenever a medical ingredient goes out of fashion, there are still those who will cling to it and clamor for it, that knowledge having been passed down through generations."

"Like people in my world who still think you can catch the common cold—or catarrh—by going out in cold weather, despite the fact we've known for generations that it's caused by a virus."

"Catarrh is caused by . . . what?" Gray says.

"Whoops. Sorry. Spoilers. Moving right along. I get your point. Just because mummia is no longer a common medicine doesn't mean there won't be a market for it. The next step, then, is to investigate that. Do we talk to Selim Awad first?"

"I agree we should speak to him at some point," Isla says. "But for now, it might be better to exhaust our own resources first. Give the police time to retreat from the Christies' house and allow the family a brief respite."

That's not how we'd do things in the modern day, but I understand her thinking. Here, if someone of Sir Alastair's caliber told McCreadie to come back and question his family tomorrow, he'd have to do it unless he had enough evidence to push the point.

"Our own resources first then," I say. "Do you know someone?"

"No, but you do, and I've been rather eager for the excuse to meet her." I frown.

"Queen Mab, of course," Isla says. "While her expertise is in preventing—and ending—pregnancies, she is known to deal in rare and illicit ingredients that I cannot obtain myself. I do not expect her to sell powdered mummy . . ."

"But she might know someone who does. The problem will be contacting her. We know where she lives but showing up there would be rude, even threatening."

"Then you approach her the same way you did the last time."

"The last time, we sent a message . . ." I look over at her. "Through Jack."

Isla smiles and takes a bite of her biscuit.

"Jack," I say, "whom we already want to talk to—about these detective stories—but we can't afford the time to do that while we're on the case."

"And now the two purposes have cleverly intersected." She smiles again. "How convenient. I will allow you and Duncan to tackle Jack—literally, if necessary—as it is your story she seems to be writing. Then Mallory and I will pay a visit to Queen Mab."

SIXTEEN

To find Jack, we need to go to Halton House. That sounds very proper, as if we're visiting a lovely manor for tea. Halton House is a fight club. Oh, it's supposed to be a rooming house, but management doesn't make more than a token effort to pretend. Just enough, really, that the police can claim they had no idea what's going on there, and they certainly aren't being paid to look the other way.

Isla and I discovered the truth of Halton House on our own, in search of a mysterious young woman with connections to a broadsheet writer known only as "Edinburgh's Foremost Reporter of Criminal Activities." The young woman is Jack. I also suspect she's the person writing those broadsheets and these accounts of our adventures.

As for Halton House, McCreadie already knew about it because, yes, it's one of law enforcement's worst-kept secrets, secrets that are kept through payoffs. I don't begrudge the police that money. They're poorly paid, and they'd already be expected to turn a blind eye to fight clubs for the upper classes. It's a time-honored system for dealing with so-called victimless crimes.

Gray and I set off on foot. While I doubt we'll find anyone at Halton House so early, it'll be an excuse to convince Gray that we really should pay Selim Awad a visit, propriety be damned.

We reach Princes Street. As in my time, it's a major thoroughfare, and probably just as wide, which makes it practically a superhighway for coaches. On this side, it's mostly shops, with colorful awnings to attract customers and tourists. There's a streetlight-lined sidewalk wide enough to walk four abreast, and it's actually—by Victorian standards—clean . . . because it's a major shopping avenue for the wealthy New Town and those aforementioned tourists.

We continue across the street and down to where a boy sells newspapers.

"Good morning, Tommy," I say as we walk up.

He dips his chin. "Good morning, Miss Mallory." His gaze cuts to Gray. "Good morning, sir. Come to fetch news of the mummy's curse yourself?"

So much for thinking mummy curses weren't a thing yet.

"If you are referring to Sir Alastair's demise," I say, "we will take the papers on that, if you please."

While it's barely noon, there *will* already be stories on that. News distribution here is remarkably efficient. Broadsheets will have been hastily written and hastily printed—and newspapers that missed the print deadline will have included an oversheet with as many details as they could get.

I skim the first broadsheet and sigh as I murmur to Gray, "Well, we know where Dr. Addington got his story."

Apparently, Addington has a habit of checking the news sources before conducting an autopsy. I say "apparently" only because I'm still hoping it's a joke, even though he claimed to do so right in front of me.

How else would I know what killed the chap?

The fact that I only sigh over it now suggests I might never be able to go back to being a modern-day detective. Stuffing evidence in pockets? Letting people pay to access crime scenes? Checking the papers for cause of death before conducting the autopsy? Shrug. These things happen.

To keep from completely abandoning all faith in the system, I will acknowledge that Addington is a decent surgeon who can usually tell dead people from the living. It's the cause of that death that eludes him, that's all. He just needs a little help. From the press.

Okay, fine, I'm going to tell myself that he checks that early news to help him understand the situation, and that even if he does occasionally— *often*—mess up the cause of death, the legal system has a fail-safe in Dr. Duncan Gray. They really should *pay* him for it, but Gray has enough money and he considers this a public service, and I can't fault him for that.

From this broadsheet, with its lurid sketch of a mummy in the throes of—well, I'm going to guess it's death and not passion, though the sketch really *is* sketchy—Addington must have gotten the idea that Sir Alastair suffocated in the bandages. That's exactly what it says here, complete with lovingly rendered detail of the baronet's corpse when it was opened, a nondescript male face with grotesquely contorted features and bulging eyes.

Really, I do hand it to Victorian writers. When your readers don't have TV and movies, you get a lot of creative license, and writers use it to full potential, creating the most vivid images in pictures and words. Victorians might grumble at the sight of bare ankles, but give them splattered innards, and they're a happy bunch.

Gray takes the rest of the papers and broadsheets as he tells Tommy to add them to his account.

"Do you have any tips for me?" Tommy says. "I know your friend is with the police."

"He is and . . ." I lean down to whisper, ". . . we were the ones who unwrapped poor Sir Alastair's corpse."

Tommy stares at me. Then his eyes narrow, sensing a joke at his expense.

"Miss Mitchell is correct," Gray says.

"As for a tip," I say, "you may tell people that I thought we saw the body move."

"Did you?" Tommy asks, his eyes round.

"No, but it's a good story," I say with a wink. "I did think, for a second, that I saw a tremor, as if Sir Alastair was struggling to sit up . . . but it must have been a trick of the light."

Gray sighs. Deeply. Yes, this is unprofessional of me, but compared with Sir Alastair being mummified alive, it's a safe enough tidbit for Tommy to pass on, one that will help his sales. As for admitting we were the ones who unwrapped the mummy, if that's not already public knowledge, it will be soon. Especially since Gray seems to be garnering a bit of ink himself. Which reminds me why we really stopped here.

"Tommy," I say. "I have it on good authority that someone is writing accounts of Dr. Gray's exploits with the police."

Tommy's face screws up. "They are?"

"That is what I heard. From two reliable sources. It seems quite a recent development. Someone is penning broadsheets or pamphlets detailing his past cases."

"Then I will need to find them, miss. I've not seen anything like that, but I only sell the news. If they're telling stories of what he's done in the past, that would be a very different thing."

"Do you know where I'd find those?"

"I'll find them for you, miss, and have them sent to the house."

While that's very kind, he's also protecting his position as our primary news vendor. I don't argue. We thank him and then move on toward the Old Town and Halton House.

We have arrived at Halton House, and to my surprise, Elspeth is already at her place behind the desk. She seems to be busy with paperwork. I suppose that makes sense. They don't open until late evening, but if she's the manager—or even the owner—she'll have work to do during the day and being at the desk helps maintain the fiction that it's a boardinghouse.

The front desk does look like it belongs in an inn. A decent inn, too, for this neighborhood. Yes, the NO VACANCY sign is dusty and pages in the sign-in book are yellowed, but it certainly doesn't look like a fight club. You'd never know it was one at this hour, not unless you're Gray, who—on his first visit—picked up the faint smell of blood and sawdust from the basement.

The woman behind the desk is maybe forty, with gray streaks in her dark hair. She's stout and bespectacled and dressed in a simple brown plaid dress and bonnet.

"Come to take me up on that offer, lass?" Elspeth says without glancing up from her account book. "Ready to go a few rounds in the ring?"

"Five months after you asked?"

"Took you some time to make the right decision." Her gaze lifts then as she sets the pen down. "Good morning, Dr. Gray. You look well."

I cross my arms. "Better than he looked the last time you saw him, after your goons tried to kill him?"

She sighs. "They did no such thing, lass."

"They knocked him out and then threw him down the stairs."

"I have had a talk with them. They should have *either* knocked him unconscious *or* thrown him down the stairs. It's the combination that's a danger. The problem with fighting men is that they aren't terribly good at foreseeing consequences. I would say they're dumb brutes, but I would hate to insult the present company." She looks at Gray. "I have heard you know how to throw a punch or two, Doctor."

"He can," I say. "When he's not caught unawares by brutes you set on him."

Gray lifts a hand. His look says he appreciates my defense, but I can take it down a notch. After all, we're here for Elspeth's help. I know that. I just can't help still being furious about what happened. He really could have been killed.

"I don't suppose you came here to try the ring yourself, Dr. Gray," she says.

"Hardly. I do not resort to pugilism unless absolutely necessary. I find it distasteful."

Wow. He can even say that with a straight face. It's the accent that sells it, that snooty upper-crust one, combined with a lofty look down his nose.

"We're looking for Jack," I say. "I haven't seen her in a while, presumably because we didn't have any interesting cases for her. Now that's changed, so I'm sure she'll be happy to speak to us. On her writerly friend's behalf, of course."

"You mean that baronet's murder? The one who was wrapped in mummy bandages? What will people think of next." While her expression mimes shock, her tone is pure wonder, tinged with admiration.

"We need to speak to Jack," I repeat.

"I can pass along the message. It isn't free, though." She smiles. "Nothing is free."

Gray turns on his heel and heads for the door. Oh, he isn't averse to offering bribes. He's actually very quick with them. But there's a difference between a freely offered bribe—*a little something for your time*—and extortion.

"Tell Jack we tried to speak to her," I say to Elspeth as I follow Gray. "And if that costs money, too, then don't bother. We can get what we need without her, and it saves us offering information for her broadsheets."

"For her broadsheets?"

I turn and give Elspeth a look. She's an old friend of Jack's, and if Jack is "Edinburgh's Foremost Reporter of Criminal Activities," Elspeth knows it.

We leave Halton House. I don't expect Elspeth to chase us into the streets. That would be undignified. But I did think she'd call a resigned "Wait" before we got out the door.

"Did we overplay our hand?" Gray asks as we head down the busy street.

I shake my head. "Elspeth nearly had you killed because she thought we'd kidnapped Jack. She's as protective as a mother hen. A really vicious mother hen. She'll also be protective of Jack's business interests, since that's what puts food on Jack's table. She was just testing our boundaries."

"Seeing whether I will pay a bribe?"

"Elspeth is the sort who takes her pounds and her pence wherever she can get them, because even if she doesn't need them now, she did need them once, and after you've needed them once, you're never certain you won't need them again."

"The calluses on her fingers. They suggest years working in a mill. That is not an easy occupation." He glances over. "Excellent deductive work."

"I never saw the calluses. My deduction comes from the way her eyes light up at the thought of adding a few extra coins to her penny jar. Also, the fact that she let us walk out—hoping to call our bluff—means she's not giving up a payday so easily, even though her clothing suggests she's not in dire need of the half crown you might offer."

"Then our combined observations suggest we did not overplay our hand. She is simply more than averagely hopeful of a bribe. You expect she will make contact with Jack—once she is certain no bribe is forthcoming. I agree. I could have hurried the process with that bribe, but my sense is that it would set a dangerous precedent."

"Yep. If she can get a half crown out of you so easily, there's no point giving you anything for free." I glance over. "I'd like to speak to Selim Awad. I understand that Isla wants us to wait, and that's probably the proper thing to do, but in my world, we don't stall on a lead out of respect for the grieving, whatever their status. We understand it's an imposition, but we have a murder to solve and the longer we wait, the colder the trail becomes."

"I would agree, particularly as it is the victim's brother-in-law we need to speak to, and not his wife or children. We will do so while intruding as little as possible on the family's grief. I would suggest we catch a hansom to the Christie house, as it will look more proper than walking up in dusty boots."

"Catch a hansom to Sir Alastair's house?" a voice says behind us. "Mind if I tag along? I would love to see the inside of that place."

We turn to see what appears to be a young man, average height and very slender, dressed in the typical garb of a working-class youth—second-hand trousers, an ill-fitting jacket, and a shirt with sweat stains.

It's Jack. From what I can gather, she doesn't present as male because she identifies as male. It's just a useful disguise. She still goes by "she" . . . at least to those who know she isn't actually a teenage boy.

I turn to her. "Since you're here, we aren't going to Sir Alastair's. Do you want to talk at a public house? Or in your quarters at Halton House?"

Her brows lift. "What makes you think I live there?"

"Uh, the fact that it took you . . ." I consult my pocket watch. "Six and a half minutes to catch up to us. That's just enough time for Elspeth to decide she's not getting a bribe and walk upstairs to fetch you. Also, your red cheeks suggest you ran, as much as you're trying to modulate your breathing." I glance at Gray. "How'd I do?"

"Excellent. Also, her cap is askew. You might want to adjust that, Jack, before your hair falls and gives you away."

She makes a face but still tucks her curls up under the newsboy cap. "Just because I came from Halton House does not mean I live there."

"You have obviously pulled on your trousers over several layers of under-garments," Gray says. "Also, you are wearing women's boots."

Jack looks down and lets out a curse.

I laugh. "Nice. I missed that. You were in a hurry and grabbed whatever was at hand. The fact you grabbed the wrong boots means you were in the place where you keep all your clothing. In other words, it's where you live."

She adjusts her trouser cuffs to hide more of the women's boots, which no one would notice without a close look.

"World's End," she says. "Meet me there in ten minutes."

SEVENTEEN

We head to the pub, which is up on the High Street, along the Royal Mile. The pub's name—World's End—comes from the fact that the pub's walls were once part of the Flodden Wall, meaning the pub marked the edge of Edinburgh. The end of the world, at least for those living within it in centuries past.

As Gray and I make our way through the narrow pub, I look around. We settle at the farthest table, and I say, "Wow. This place hasn't changed much."

His brows arch. "I do not believe it ever changes. When were you last here?"

"Mmm. Two years ago, I think. I came to Edinburgh to visit my nan, and one of her friends insisted I meet her grandson in this pub. I thought it was just a meet-up. Turns out to have been a blind date. Guy spent the entire time snarking about how touristy this place is . . . and he's the one who picked it. The bar was the only interesting part of that evening."

Gray's brows go higher. "You meant that the public house hasn't changed much between now and *your* time. Where it still exists."

"Most of the buildings here exist, but this one is a pub with the same name, though I seem to recall it's been a few other things along the way."

I twist around. "In my time, that's the kitchen behind us. Also . . ." I nod to the next table, where two working-class men drink pints. "The glasses are much cleaner."

Gray sighs. The state of drinkware in this world is an ongoing issue with me, at least in these Old Town pubs, where I suspect it's been weeks since the glasses met soap.

Jack arrives, tipping her hat to the bartender as she slips past to our table.

"It's been a while," she says as she slides in. "I will not mention that you ignored my request for an interview after the incident at the Leith docks."

"There was nothing to be interviewed about," I say. "It was a minor adventure."

"You set a boat on fire. With some sort of incendiary device."

"It was an old boat, infested with human traffickers. Once they get in, you need to burn the whole thing down or you never get rid of them."

"Human traf . . . ?" She trails off and then shakes her head, as if she figured out the term in context. "You ignored my request because you were still angry with me for running out on you at a bad time. But now I suppose I have been forgiven, because you need something."

"We don't *need* anything. We would *like* an audience with Queen Mab. We know where to find her, but showing up doesn't seem the polite way to handle this, so we're asking you to act as intermediary again."

"And in return my friend gets exclusive information on the Christie case?"

"That depends. Are we going to keep pretending you're not 'Edinburgh's Foremost Reporter of Criminal Activities'?"

Her brows shot up. "You think *I* write those? I can barely scratch out my own name."

"Whatever. I don't actually care. I just don't want you negotiating to pass messages between us when I'm pretty damn sure you're the one getting those messages. Sweet setup, though, making people pay you a fee for access to yourself."

"I have no idea what you mean."

"Again, whatever. I don't care. But speaking of your writerly friend, let's discuss those accounts of Dr. Gray's adventures."

Her gaze shoots to Gray, who has been quietly sipping his pint. "Accounts?"

"It has come to our attention that someone has been writing about Dr. Gray's adventures. Not as news articles, but as stories. Recounting his past cases and selling them."

"What?"

"If it's you—or your writerly friend—tell me now, because if you deny it, and I later find out that it's you . . ."

"I honestly have no idea what you're talking about, Mallory. I cover—" She coughs. "I help my writerly friend cover the crimes you have been involved in, but we do not center the stories on Dr. Gray. If someone is doing that, then I . . . Well, had I heard of it, I would have presumed you had entered into an agreement with the scribbler who pens them, and I would have been put out that you did not ask my writerly friend to do it."

"So you really haven't even heard of these fictionalized versions?"

"No."

"Isla loves true-crime broadsheets. Yet she had no idea these existed. Neither did our local newsboy. Neither did you. How is that even possible? Who's writing them, and who are they being marketed to?"

"They are being sold at the market?"

I wave a hand. "The 'market' meaning the people who will buy them. The consumers."

"You have such an odd way with words."

Gray sets down his glass. "Yes, she does, but her meaning is clear. My sister is a prime consumer of such stories, yet she has never heard of them. Even if they are apparently new, I would presume someone would have mentioned it to me." He pauses. "Which is what occurred, I suppose, but I am surprised it did not happen sooner. So who are these stories being sold to? Through what venues?"

"Who told you about them?"

Gray and I glance at each other. Then I say, with care, "So, you might have heard we were at the Christie party last night."

"Why do you think I ran to catch up with you? I heard Dr. Gray here unwrapped the mummy, and you assisted."

"Someone there had read the stories. A woman whom I would not consider the primary market for such things, although I do not know her well. She had read them with her children."

"There!" Jack smacks the table. "Now that makes sense."

"It does?"

"You said they are being written as stories, and that this wellborn lady reads them with her children. That is the market, then, as you call it."

"Children? For stories of murder?"

"No, for stories of *detection*." Jack's lips curve in a smile. "It's like the Bloody Register."

"The Bloody Register?"

She sips her beer. "You're too young to remember those."

"How old are *you*?" I say.

"About your age, which means I was also too young for them, but my ma had them from when she was young, and I read her copies."

I glance at Gray, who only shrugs.

"The Bloody Register?" Jack says. "*The Newgate Calendar*?"

"Oh," I say. "I know what that is. I've never heard it called the Bloody Register, though."

"That was the subtitle. *The Malefactors' Bloody Register.*"

"But you said they're old, and the calendar is still being published."

"That version doesn't count."

From Isla, I know that *The Newgate Calendar* started out as a simple bulletin, published by the Newgate Prison, listing executions. The title was co-opted by others who churned out chapbooks on the lives of famous criminals, and those are what Jack's mother would have been reading.

The "Newgate Calendar" went through several iterations, finally becoming a penny dreadful that ended a few years ago, according to Isla. The Calendars, though, also sparked a literary movement of "Newgate novels." This part I know from my English prof dad.

Dickens's *Oliver Twist* was considered a Newgate novel in its time, meant as a compliment by crime readers and an insult by authors like Thackeray. On that note, let me just say that I devoured the work of Dickens and have never been able to finish a Thackeray, and if that makes my tastes decidedly lowbrow, so be it. My father didn't raise a literary snob.

"So how does this relate to these stories about Dr. Gray?" I ask.

"Because *The Newgate Calendar* was a way for people to read about horrible crimes and tell themselves it was their duty, as good Christian folk."

I remember that part. *The Newgate Calendar* was considered acceptable for children because the stories were framed as cautionary tales. Of course, that's not why anyone was reading stories about things like child killers—both those who murdered children, and murderers who were children themselves.

"Okay," I say. "I get it now. If the stories about Dr. Gray are marketed as detective fiction, suitable for women and children, then they provide a way to read about murder while pretending it is not a prurient and unsuitable interest in violence."

"Yes."

"I don't think an interest in violence is particularly unsuitable unless one is looking for a how-to guide on committing it. Even then, since detective fiction ends with the killer always being caught, if that's one's interest, it's more of a cautionary tale."

Jack stretches her leg under the table, her boot knocking mine as she does. "Like the Newgate Calendars."

"So would the main market for this be women? Possibly under the guise of reading adventurous tales to their children?"

"From what I hear, yes."

That isn't surprising. Women are the primary consumer of true crime in the modern day. It's not prurient interest as much as self-preservation. They aren't looking for ways to commit murder. They're looking for ways to avoid becoming a victim of it.

"Most of it is fiction, though," Jack says. "The accounts of real detectives are quite a rare thing, although there were the McLevy books, a few years ago."

When I raise a brow, Gray is the one who answers. "James McLevy was the first Edinburgh criminal officer. He published a couple of popular books on his past cases."

Jack nods. "Which is why my writerly friend would be put out by the thought of someone else writing up your cases. They may have a small audience now, but in the right hands, they could be just as popular as McLevy's adventures. And even more lucrative. Which is why you should let my friend write the authorized accounts. They'd give you . . . Oh, ten percent of the earnings."

"I would like to hire you to find the writer of these tales," Gray says. "I will pay you a stipend for the investigation, with a reward if you find them."

"Uh . . ." I look at Gray. "She's already charging people—including us—for introducing them to herself."

Jack sighs. "You are convinced I am a writer. It is most flattering. I wish I were."

I note that she doesn't say she isn't. I'm not pursuing this. There's little point in it . . . yet.

I look at Gray. "What's to stop her from taking your stipend to *not* find herself?"

"I am not the writer of these new accounts," she says, and I note she doesn't say her *friend* isn't that writer.

"That is why it is a stipend," he says. "With the proper payment coming when Jack finds the culprit. That payment being that I will grant her friend exclusive information on my future cases—for their crime broadsheets. The stipend is that she will have exclusive information on *this* case. For her writerly friend."

"You *do* know how to deal, Dr. Gray," Jack says. "If I find this writer, my friend gets to take over? Authorized purveyor of your fine tales of derring-do?"

Gray gives a slight eye roll. "There is less derring-do than one might hope. But no, I am only granting exclusive information for current news articles. The rest can be discussed at a later time, with the understanding that I much prefer to stay in the background of stories that properly highlight the work of the Edinburgh police."

"I understand. You'd rather read tales of the great Dr. Addington."

Gray can't suppress a flinch, making Jack grin.

"Oh, everyone in the business knows about Dr. Addington, sir. I am needling you. Fine then. I find this fellow in return for access to this case and others, with the rest to be discussed later."

"And one more thing," I say. "*We* need access to Queen Mab."

"Right. You did say that." Jack glances between us and lowers her voice. "Is there a problem?"

"Problem?" Gray looks perplexed.

"She thinks I'm pregnant," I say. "And that you have something to do with that."

Gray's eyes go so wide I have to stifle a laugh.

"Absolutely not. That would be . . ." He struggles for words and settles on. "Improper." He hurries on. "For me, of course, to take advantage in that way. Not improper for Miss Mitchell to engage in . . ." He struggles again. "In whatever she might wish to engage in. Improper for me. As her employer. That is what I meant."

Now Jack looks as if she's the one stifling a laugh.

"We need to speak to Queen Mab about the case," I say.

Jack sobers, her brows knitting. "Was someone involved pregnant? Or trying not to become pregnant?"

"Is that all Queen Mab does?"

"Well, no. It is only what she is most known for."

"We have need of her expertise in a matter unrelated to being or becoming pregnant. And if you wish a hint about what that could be . . . ? We'll need that introduction first."

EIGHTEEN

Like I said, we know where to find Queen Mab. She lives in the New Town, with quarters in a house that seems to be occupied by an elderly couple, who act as a front for her business.

The problem right now is that it's still daylight, which means a visit to Queen Mab's place of business is risky. Or so I think, until I realize that having a steady stream of nighttime visitors would be even more suspicious. Queen Mab has figured out a solution to this problem, and it involves that elderly couple.

Jack tells me to bring Isla to the house in an hour, and to arrive at the front door with a bag, preferably containing clothing. If anyone asks—which she assures me they will not—we are visiting Mrs. Morgan, having heard that the expert seamstress is a miracle worker at fixing damaged gowns. It is particularly convenient then that I *have* a damaged gown.

Simon drives us by coach, in proper New Town fashion. Nothing to hide here.

As Isla and I climb the steps to the town house, two ladies are passing on the sidewalk, and I pull out the hem of my dress, saying, "I am not certain anyone can fix this."

"We will give Mrs. Morgan a try," Isla says, patting my hand. "She comes most highly recommended."

We are greeted at the door by a Black man with a spine as starched as his collar. A butler then.

I hate to admit that I've been surprised by the number of nonwhite faces in the city. I shouldn't be. We are in the time of the British Empire, with people moving about as they've never done before. But it's most common to see people of color either in trade or in service, like this man.

"Mrs. Ballantyne for Mrs. Morgan," Isla says. "I believe she is expecting me. I am hoping she might repair my young companion's dress."

The man bows and, without a word, steps back to let us in. He escorts us to a parlor and then half bows and leaves. Inside, an elderly white woman sits under a bright light, and she is indeed sewing. She would have been as tall as Isla in her youth, though her back has hunched. A cane lies beside her, and she wears spectacles.

Seeing us, she smiles and nods. "Please excuse me if I do not rise."

Isla moves quickly to assure her it is fine as she greets the woman and introduces us. Mrs. Morgan eyes the piece of my dress still hanging out of the bag.

Mrs. Morgan smiles broadly. "You really did bring me something to fix."

"If you could, that would be lovely," Isla says. "But it is hardly necessary."

"Oh, I'm quite happy to try. I *am* a seamstress." She winks. "It is easier to maintain the facade when people can honestly attest to my expertise."

Mrs. Morgan pulls the dress out. "My word, what did you do with this fine gown? Roll in the mud?"

"An unexpected trip through an underground tunnel after a party."

I'm making light, but her lips twitch. "Ah, yes, I remember being young. An unexpected trip to an underground tunnel for a lovely roll in mud. Hay is softer, though. You need to find a handy stable."

My cheeks heat, and Isla's hand flies to her mouth as she laughs.

"It wasn't that," I say.

The old woman sighs. "Youth is indeed wasted on the young. Perhaps next time. And forget tunnels and stables. At a party, there is always an unused guest room or two. Simply remember to lock the door. Oh, and also remember to visit Her Highness *before*hand, rather than after. That is much more convenient. As for the dress, it will require lacework repair, which is fiddly."

She quotes a price, and before I can comment, Isla says, "Yes, please. Thank you."

Mrs. Morgan rings a bell, and a maid appears. She's also Black, and no more than sixteen.

"Please escort these ladies to the queen," she says. "And when they are done, take Her Highness a plate of lunch and make sure she eats it. She gets too wrapped up in her work."

"Yes, ma'am."

The maid leads us down the stairs. I catch sight of another member of the staff, an older Black woman. This is no coincidence, I suspect.

Queen Mab herself is Black. Part of her staff choices may be about offering good employment to domestic servants of color, but they would also provide camouflage for Queen Mab herself. The neighbors will have noticed that the Morgans employ Black staff, and so they will think nothing of it when they see Queen Mab coming and going.

The maid takes us downstairs to a tiny library.

"Miss?" I say. "I know the trick. May I show my friend?"

The maid smiles shyly, nods and leaves without a word.

"The trick?" Isla says.

"Oh, I'm going to let you figure it out. There's a secret door behind the bookcase. You need to remove the right book."

Isla's face lights up, and she fairly pounces on the bookshelf. She scans the books and then laughs.

"Queen Mab," she says, and tugs on the copy of *A Midsummer Night's Dream.*

The bookcase opens, and I can't help grinning along with Isla at that. We slip inside and pass through to where Queen Mab is working in her lab.

Queen Mab has a physique that befits someone who names herself after a fairy and a dress that befits someone who names herself after a queen. She's less than five feet tall and slender, with dark skin and hazel eyes. Gold combs hold back her dark curls. Her gown would have turned heads at the mummy party, and yet apparently, that's just how she dresses, even when working in a laboratory. Today's gown is silk, golden brown and olive, with black lace trim at the collar and three-quarter sleeves, and black buttons that I'm sure are semiprecious stones.

I'd say this gown represents the advantage to having a first-class seamstress as a tenant, but I suspect the tenant is a first-class seamstress *because* it's to Queen Mab's advantage. Her only concession to work is an apron, which is better quality than any of my dresses. Oh, and goggles. Like Isla, she wears goggles in her laboratory.

Queen Mab lifts the goggles. "Mrs. Ballantyne," she says, her accent a mix of London and Paris with an undercurrent of the West Indies. "You will excuse me not sitting down with you for tea. I am in the midst of a delicate procedure that I cannot leave, but I am free to talk."

As Queen Mab lowers her goggles, Isla takes a moment to openly survey the laboratory. Her gaze pauses on a dried pink flower.

"Is that balmony?" Isla asks.

Queen Mab smiles as she measures something into a flask. "It is."

Isla sighs with envy. "My source for North American herbs is ridiculously expensive, and their products are in dreadful condition when they arrive. I can barely tell one from the other."

"Then you must allow me to help you find a new supplier."

I leave them to their shoptalk while I resist the urge to poke about the room.

"And Miss Mallory is being exceedingly patient with us," Queen Mab says finally, "but I have heard she is here on official business, that being the investigation of Sir Alastair's murder last night."

"It is," I say. "Thank you for seeing us."

Queen Mab lifts the flask to goggle level and peers into it. "Thank you for going through Jack. I appreciate the consideration. In future, if you wish to speak to me, simply have one of your staff ask Mrs. Morgan for an appointment time." She lowers the flask and looks at Isla. "And I would like to have tea with you someday, my dear, if you can spare the time."

Isla beams. "I would be delighted."

"I know we approach the science from different aspects—yours being chemical and mine primarily herbal—but I would love to chat about medicine."

"As would I."

"Now, Miss Mallory . . . I am most curious to know how you think I can help with a man who, by all accounts, died of either strangulation or suffocation." She takes a jar from the shelf. "Or, if it was suffocation, being bound in a mummy's wrappings, then he would have needed to be sedated. That, however, would be more Mrs. Ballantyne's area than mine."

"Actually, it's not about his murder, per se. Before I ask, I'm not saying you're involved in the sort of thing that I'm asking about, only that you might be able to set us on the trail. We're looking for those who trade in illegal medicines."

"Oh, now that *is* interesting. While I appreciate you clarifying that you do not think I would trade in such things, it is unnecessary." Her lips twitch. "I have traded in many substances that are considered less than legal if they seem the best way to treat an ailment."

"Well, this isn't a way to treat anything. It's quack medicine." I pause, uncertain that's a word used in this time and place. "I mean it's fake."

"Yes," Queen Mab says. "I know what 'quack medicine' means. I am nothing if not well traveled. There is a great deal of that out there, and I am familiar with most of it, particularly substances derived from the horns of large beasts."

"Elephant and rhino tusks," I say.

"And unicorns. Nothing is as valuable as the horn of a unicorn. Did you know any poisoned food placed into it will immediately become safe?"

I look from Isla to Queen Mab.

"She is having fun with you," Isla says. "You must forgive Mallory. Being new to the world of medicine, she is never quite certain which old beliefs we still cling to."

"It is true that people did believe in the purifying quality of unicorn horn," Queen Mab says. "After all, the beasts are associated with virgins. Pure as the driven snow. They sold for astronomical fees, mostly to royalty. The unicorn horns, that is, although I'm sure the virgins did, too. Then explorers traveling north discovered a true dragon's hoard of treasure. Unicorn horns, right there on the beach."

Both their gazes rest on me, and if I feel like a child being given a riddle, I don't begrudge them their fun. At least not when I have the answer.

"Narwhal tusks," I say.

"Clever girl," Queen Mab says.

"But aren't narwhal tusks as long as a person? How big were these unicorns?"

Queen Mab sighs. "You are bringing logic into the realm of fantasy. Also, have you not seen medieval tapestries of unicorns? The horns are very long and thin."

"Because they were based on narwhals. The horn part, at least. Got it."

"As for elephants and rhinos, yes, their horns are used, along with parts of other wild beasts. Some of it is traditional medicine from those areas, but when it is used here, the appeal is the exotic qualities of the beasts. Everything from a foreign land can be magical, including the people. A woman like Mrs. Ballantyne can be accepted as a chemist, even if some might be suspicious of her motivations. They will still suspect her of brewing poison because that is what women do, like the witches of old tales. As for me, I must be brewing potions from deepest Africa, even if that is not where I was born or raised. My herbalism must derive not from a knowledge of plants, but from a knowledge of magic."

"Ugh."

She shrugs. "Sometimes, it is to my advantage. I have given up being taken seriously, so I surrender myself to being Mab, queen of the fairies. If you have questions about so-called quack medicine, though, I suspect I *can* be of help. I do not dispense such cures, but I am asked about them often enough that I know where to send people. One of these days, a man is going to find his way to my doorstep looking for my excellent male shields. Until then, I need to know where they can buy what they really came for."

"Aphrodisiacs?" I say.

Her eyes glitter. "If they ask me for that, I can help. I give them something harmless. Aphrodisiacs exist in the mind. They only need to think they have been given one." She sobers as she checks her flask. "And more often than not, I suspect they want the aphrodisiac to slip into some woman's lemonade. In such a case, at least if I sell it, I can be certain it is harmless. No, most men who come to me are looking for extra help. Their sword metal has softened over the years. Or they wish for a longsword when they possess a dagger. Or a broadsword when they have a rapier. Or their sword has the bend of a scimitar, and they wish to straighten it. If men spent as much time worrying about their swordplay technique as their equipment, women would be much happier for it."

Isla's face flames. That's the thing about having red hair and pale skin. She can't hide a blush, and if she blushed any harder she'd incinerate. But she's also smiling and nodding in agreement.

Victorian women aren't the prudes we might imagine. They simply don't have experience discussing sex, even with friends—at least not if they're in Isla's social class. Here, the old saw "good girls don't" would be "rich girls don't."

"This isn't an aphrodisiac," I say. "Or any other male aid." I pause. "Or I hope not. I *really* hope not. It's about mummies."

Her brows shoot up. "Mummies? As in the Egyptian dead?"

I nod. "You know Sir Alastair was wrapped as a mummy. Well, the original mummified remains are gone. Someone broke them into pieces and secreted them out."

Queen Mab stares at me, slow horror replacing her usual amused glint.

"Sorry," I say. "I could have phrased that better."

"You do not need to cushion the truth for my sake, child. I am appalled by the thought, but I am not surprised. You think they took the body for medicine? Could they not have merely removed it for disposal?"

"There were places in the room to hide the remains, and taking them out was a much greater risk than leaving them. Someone wanted the body, but not enough to keep it whole, which means it isn't for a collector. It could be for science, but Dr. Gray doesn't know of any significant demand for mummy parts. According to Lady Christie's brother, though, there is a medical market for powdered mummy, which Dr. Gray and Mrs. Ballantyne have both heard of."

"Unfortunately," Isla murmurs.

"As have I," Queen Mab says. "Also unfortunately. So you are not here to confirm that, but rather to understand where one might sell such remains."

"Yes."

"The underground market."

I nod. "That's what I figured. Some sort of secret network of tradespeople."

Queen Mab laughs softly. "Oh, I did not mean that figuratively, Miss Mallory. I meant the actual underground market. A market that is, well, perhaps not 'underground' in a literal sense, but held in what we call the underground here. The vaults."

I know about Edinburgh's vaults. They're under the South Bridge. When the bridge was built, the areas under it were divided into a warren of rooms, some as small as a few meters long. Larger ones were sold or rented for storage, while smaller ones became shops. That was at the end of the last century. In this century, they became slums, with brothels and pubs and all manner of criminal activity. I thought that was largely gone, but apparently not.

"So down in the vaults, there's an actual marketplace that sells stuff like this?" I say.

"'Stuff like this,' and so much more." Her eyes twinkle. "But you would have no interest in visiting such a thing, would you? Such a sweet and pretty child, who would not care to dirty her white gloves and muss those golden tresses—"

"Where can I find it?"

That makes Queen Mab and Isla both laugh.

"I fear the market only opens every fortnight," Queen Mab says. "But you are in luck. It will be open tomorrow. That does not resolve all our problems, though. First, I must take you, as both an escort and a sponsor. However, vouching for you is not enough. You would need something to offer."

I frown. "But I'm looking to buy. That would be my cover story. I want to buy mummy powder."

She shakes her head. "The market does not operate like that. Do you know what a goblin market is?"

When I hesitate, Isla says, "Ms. Rossetti's poem. 'Goblin Market.'"

"Oh!" I say. "I know that one. My—"

I'm about to say my dad teaches it, but I stop myself. I wasn't even sure the poem had been published by now.

"When did that . . . ?" I begin carefully.

"It came out a few years ago," Isla says.

Queen Mab continues, "In the poem, the girl has no money so she trades a lock of her hair. The goblin market of folklore uses a barter system. So it is here. Of course, transactions for money are not unknown, but you must have something to offer in order to enter."

"I have lots of hair," I say.

"Will you let them shave it off for a wig?"

"Er . . ."

Isla smiles. "Our Mallory is not vain, but nor does she wish to try conducting her secret investigations as a bald woman. Could I help? Something I can concoct?"

"Can you make anything magical?"

Isla and I exchange a look.

"The market is a place of magic," Queen Mab says. "Not true magic. I don't believe in such things. But it is a place of superstition and lore, particularly regarding the fairy folk. I think that is why they allow me in. They cannot believe that the queen of the fairies does not traffic in magic.

Surely I must, for those I trust. Which means they all want to earn my trust." She smiles. "It is very beneficial."

"Fairy . . . folklore . . . superstition . . . Wait! I have a Hand of Glory." Queen Mab's brows shoot up.

"It's from folklore," I say. "I don't know whether it's fairy lore or not. It's a hand that's used—"

"For thieving," Queen Mab says. "The hand of a hanged man, coated in wax and used as a candle."

Isla slowly turns to stare at me. "Where on earth did you come by that?"

"Your brother gave it to me last week. As a gift."

Isla stares harder, and Queen Mab bursts into musical laughter, which Isla joins with a sputter.

"Such a lovely present for a young lady," Queen Mab says. "So much better than a bouquet of flowers. Far more useful, at least. Your brother is terribly romantic, Mrs. Ballantyne."

"He does know the way to a woman's heart." Isla sneaks me a sly look. "Or to the heart of one woman, at least."

I roll my eyes. "It's not that kind of gift. He found it in a shop and brought it home for us to dissect together."

"To dissect together," Queen Mab says with a swooning sigh. "And to think I only meet men who want to take me on promenades and picnics."

Isla snickers.

I lean against the lab table. "While I do hate to interfere with your fun, you do realize the stereotype you are perpetrating, right? That no man is going to offer a woman a job unless he wishes to get under her skirts. Really, I expected better."

Queen Mab gives me a stern look. "You aim low, Miss Mallory."

"She always does," Isla says with a sigh. "Fine. We will stop teasing you, now that you have called us out on it, but be aware that you *have* spoiled our fun, and we shall certainly hold it against you. Also . . ." She leans toward me. "We are well aware you only said that to make us stop."

"Like the queen said, I'm not above low blows. So I have a Hand of Glory. The problem is that Dr. Gray does expect us to dissect it, and I'm not sure it was meant as a gift in the sense that it belongs to me. He found it, thought it was interesting, and gave it to me as a joke. More of a shared project than an actual gift that I'm free to dispose of as I like."

"Duncan is always willing to lend a helping hand," Isla says. "Even if it is not his own."

I snort at that and shake my head. "Fine. If the hand would work, I can talk to him. Will it work? And would I need to give it away?"

"It will most certainly work," Queen Mab says. "For giving it away, that will depend, but you had best be prepared to do so, though I would expect something in trade for it. Perhaps a severed leg?"

"He already has one of those. Keeps it in a jar. Okay, so the hand gets me in. Who else can come? Mrs. Ballantyne? Dr. Gray?"

Queen Mab shakes her head. "Neither could affect a proper disguise, and the fewer people I bring, the better."

"So I need a disguise?"

"Oh, no. You are a pretty housemaid who works for a notorious mad scientist. That is all the disguise you will need."

NINETEEN

You wish to abscond with my Hand of Glory, use it to gain entrance to
a secret goblin market . . . and leave me behind?" Gray stands behind
his desk, arms crossing. "What, pray tell, have I done to deserve such ill
treatment?"

"I—"

"Have I not taken you in? Endured your twenty-first-century peculiar-
ities and your inability to start a proper hearth fire?"

"Hey, I learned—"

"I have raised you to the position of my assistant, and allowed you to
accompany me on my investigations, even when your recklessness almost
gets me killed."

"*My* recklessness? How often are you the one leading the charge into
danger?"

"Only half the time. You are a bad influence, Mallory, but I allow it."

I make a rude noise.

His brows rise. "What was that?"

I curtsy. "Please, sir. I do apologize. You are correct. I am the worst influence, encouraging you to embrace your most unsuitable inclinations. I will
do better, starting with not giving you this box"—I raise a cardboard box—
"of cream pastries that I picked up. Eating sweets is terribly bad for your
health, as sure to get you killed as leading you into dangerous situations."

"You thought to buy me off with pastries?"

"*Cream* pastries." I wave the box. "From your favorite shop."

"I should be offended that you thought me so easily mollified."

"Delicious cream pastries. Best enjoyed with a coffee and a generous splash of whisky."

"Which you will enjoy with me, I suppose."

"Only to keep you company. As your faithful assistant, who really does hate to steal your severed hand and take it to a goblin market."

He sighs and comes out from behind the desk. "I know. And I hope you know that I was teasing you. Mostly. I am, of course, a little put out, and I may sulk for a while."

"Understandable."

"You also did not need to bring me the pastries, though I do appreciate them. Come. Let us enjoy them while we talk, and then perhaps we can examine that hand before you take off with it."

We end up taking the Hand of Glory to tea. Actually "to coffee," though that doesn't sound the same. We retreat to the laboratory and set out the cream pastries on one lovely linen napkin and the severed hand on another . . . and then lock the door so Mrs. Wallace doesn't happen by and see what we're doing with her linens.

I have brought coffee, and Gray has added whisky that is far too expensive to ever be used as a mixer, but what's the point of having money if you can't occasionally do gauche things like add single malt to coffee?

We sit on the floor and examine the Hand of Glory while having our little laboratory picnic. We don't actually touch the hand, of course. Oh, Gray would have, but he knows I frown on handling dead things while eating finger food.

Instead, we visually examine it and use probes. When actual touching is required, we don gloves. Mostly, it's just an external examination with discussion and note-taking. And cream pastries. Lots of cream pastries. Lots for Gray, at least. I do feel bad about cutting him from the underground-market trip tomorrow, and I make up for it by letting him have four of the half-dozen small treats.

"I would like to cut into the hand," he says.

"I know."

"Perhaps take a small piece for testing."

"I figured you would."

"Removing a section from the stump would work. As long as it is not readily apparent that we have sliced into it."

"If someone at this market wants the hand, they won't care if it's missing a chunk or two. We can rough it up to look like prior damage." I eye the blackened and twisted hand. "It's pretty rough already."

"Which is to our advantage. I will remove a piece for examination and analysis and then—"

A sound outside the door. We both go still.

"Hello?" I say.

"Miss Mallory?" Lorna calls through the door. "I am sorry to disturb you. I was waiting for you and Dr. Gray to finish speaking."

The knob turns, and I leap to my feet. I *try* leaping, anyway. Even after six months here, I forget that I can't just scramble up from the floor, especially when holding a cup of coffee. A Victorian corset and skirts presumes that a lady is never going to be sitting on the floor and therefore does not need to vault to her feet.

I nearly spill my coffee, and I'm still setting it down when Gray reaches the door. I rise as quickly as I can and straighten my skirts.

"I am so sorry, sir," Lorna says as he opens the door. "I did not realize it might be locked."

"We were examining a potentially disturbing object and did not wish to startle anyone," Gray says.

Her gaze drops to our little picnic setup, with the patisserie box and napkins and bottle of scotch.

"The remains of our tea," I say with a smile. "We should have cleared that before we returned to work on this."

Gray scoops up the Hand of Glory, hopefully moving too fast for her to see what it is . . . or that it's wrapped in a linen napkin.

"What is that?" she asks.

"Nothing for you to worry about," Gray says.

"It looks like a hand."

Gray hesitates and then says, "Yes. Which is why we closed the door. It is a severed hand that I have been examining."

She nods, seeming not at all perturbed by this. "You need not fear I shall balk at such things. I grew up on a farm and—Oh!" Her cheeks flush. "I forgot why I came down here. I am so sorry, Dr. Gray. There is a young woman at the door for you. A Mrs. King? She seems . . ." Lorna bites her lip. "Out of sorts? She would not tell me what it was about."

"That is all fine, Lorna. Please show her . . ." He glances up, toward the living areas of the town house, and then says, decisively, "Show her in to the front waiting room of the funerary parlor and bring tea."

"Yes, sir."

TWENTY

We put aside the Hand of Glory, and I use a dampened cloth to wipe my face and dress and insist Gray do the same, which irks him. In this world there are far fewer opportunities to see oneself. Water closets don't necessarily contain mirrors. Nor do bedrooms, other than a small one for shaving.

Mirrors are used in decoration, but Gray isn't the sort of man to pause at one before he leaves the house. That could be a refreshing lack of vanity, but it's more that he's focused on a goal and pausing would be an interruption, and if it means he goes out with ink—or blood—on his face, well, no one else cares so why do I make such a fuss over it? Probably because he fails to notice people crossing the road to clear his path when he has blood spattered on his collar. Or maybe that's the point—getting people out of his way—and I'm ruining everything.

I leave him with the cloth, and I head toward the front parlor, murmuring for him to give me a moment alone with Mrs. King. She's standing at the window, looking out at the street, and on hearing footsteps, she turns, seeming annoyed, as if she's been waiting for hours.

"I am here to speak to Dr. Gray," she says coolly.

"Mrs. King," I say. "I must apologize for last night, when we referred to you as Miss. That was a dreadful presumption. Please, sit. The maid is bringing tea. And you must excuse her as well. She is very new. Less than a week at a job I used to do myself." I sweep my skirts elegantly behind me as I sit.

"You were a maid?" she says as she sits.

"Yes. Dr. Gray recognized my interest in his work and was in need of an assistant, so he allowed me to take on the position." I smile. "It is so much more enlightening than scrubbing floors. We were just working on something when you rang. A human hand preserved for supposed magical purposes. The process of how it came to be that way—the desiccation and treatment—is fascinating, as is the folklore behind it. I believe it dates all the way back to medieval times." I laugh softly. "The lore, that is. Not the hand."

Gray opens the door and enters, and Mrs. King blinks up at him, thrown off-kilter by me, which is the point, of course. Don't be what she expects. Don't act like she expects. Don't make the small talk she expects. After our encounter last night, she came here with a chip on her shoulder. I need that knocked off before we start.

"Thank you so much for coming, Mrs. King," Gray says. "We can only imagine this has been very unsettling. Might I presume you have already spoken to Detective McCreadie?"

She seems to try to find some of her anger, only to realize it will indeed sound peevish, when we are both being so genteel and considerate.

"I do not trust the police," she says finally, keeping a touch of sharpness. "There have been incidents, and the police have treated us like hysterical women."

"Incidents with the male students?" I ask, remembering the stories I'd read of the Seven.

Her gaze pierces mine, half surprised and half searching. "Actually, that has been a growing concern of ours. The male students do not seem as if they will be inclined to treat us fairly, but they do not know us." She relaxes a little. "I cannot help but believe that is true for most who oppose us. If they got to know us, they would see we are earnest and serious in our pursuits, and no threat to them. As for the male students, it is early days yet, and we have hope."

"Hope is good," I murmur. "But so is caution. I heard many of you outscored them on the entrance exams. They will not take kindly to that. Just . . . be wary and be prepared. They will see you as competition and use your sex to say you are unsuitable for the occupation or that you are receiving preferential treatment."

That gaze continues to search before she gives a quick nod. "You are correct, Miss . . ."

"Mitchell. Mallory Mitchell." I settle into my seat. "But you will have allies among the male students. Your husband certainly seems to be one."

Her expression softens and she even smiles. "Yes, Emmett is truly an ally. He understands we are not competition, that there should *be* no competition in such a profession. We are all striving for the same purpose—to help others."

"A noble goal," I say. "And I am glad you have your husband's support. That will make things infinitely easier. As for what you have experienced requiring police assistance, I presume it is harassment of some sort? From a specific quarter?"

"No, not a specific quarter. I would almost prefer that. An organized opposition gives us something to fight. This is so general that it is . . . well, discouraging."

"It would be. Please understand that you will have allies in the police force as well. Detective McCreadie for one, and he can recommend others you should speak to. In the event of trouble, you need resources within the department. Going straight to the nearest policeman—or nearest police office—might not be useful in your situation."

She stares at me long enough that I worry I've misspoken. That is how one reports crimes in this pre-911 time, isn't it?

"Miss Mitchell is correct," Gray says, a little tersely, as if annoyed she seems to be questioning me.

"Y-yes, of course," Mrs. King says. "I only . . . I appreciate the suggestion. It is very wise and very insightful, in regards to, as you say, our situation."

Ah, that's the problem. I was talking like a cop experienced at handling such situations. I wish I could say that everyone in "such situations"—be it abuse or assault or harassment—could just expect their local police department to handle it properly, but no one pretends that this is the case in my day, and it certainly isn't in this time.

"I will ask Detective McCreadie to provide you with contacts," I say. "And, who knows, maybe someday there will be women among the police as well."

She gives me a smile for that. "Perhaps there will be. Thank you, Miss Mitchell. I will admit that I am feeling rather defensive about being summoned to speak to the police regarding Sir Alastair's murder. I understand that murder is far more important than harassment, but I cannot help but wish we received a wee bit of that time and attention."

"It must rankle to have the police immediately on your doorstep for this when they ignored your own concerns. As for being on your doorstep, we had a murder last night at a home where you were situated outside."

She tenses. "Yes."

"We must ask whether you saw anything."

She exhales a little, though she tries to cover it. "Oh. Yes. Of course. You wish to know what I saw."

"We do."

"Very little, I'm afraid. I went directly from the apartment I share with my husband. I walked to the Christie house and took my place outside and did not leave it until your Detective McCreadie made me realize perhaps I should."

"But you did not go home, as you apparently heard of the murder and went to speak to Miss Jex-Blake."

Mrs. King swallows. "Yes, I retreated, but I did not leave. I was angry. I paced. I walked away and came back. Paced some more, and then walked away and came back again. When the body was discovered, I was close enough to hear the screams."

"And then?" I say.

"I . . . went to where the servants had left open a door."

"Which door was that?"

She relaxes a little, apparently relieved that I don't gasp in outrage at her getting closer after hearing screams. As far as I'm concerned, the only people who *wouldn't* get closer are those who are afraid they might be called on to help.

"Down the steps on the left. There are two doors down. I took the one on the left, leading into the servant quarters."

"You went inside."

A pause as she realizes what she said. Then she lifts her chin. "Yes. They may say I can never practice medicine, but I have been training as a doctor all my life. My father is one."

"So you went inside to determine whether help was needed, and what did you see?"

Again, she relaxes at my tone. "Not much," she admits. "Servants came running down the stairs, alerting the others that the master was dead. I hurried out before I was discovered."

The door opens, and I remember we'd asked Lorna to bring tea. She starts to pour, but I get to my feet.

"I still remember how to do this," I say. "Thank you for bringing it."

She hesitates and glances at Gray.

"Mallory will serve the tea," he says.

Lorna nods. Then she says, "Mrs. Wallace wishes to know whether you will still be dining at seven."

Gray checks his pocket watch. From here, I can see it's already six thirty. We were up all night and on the go all day, and I've lost track of time and meals.

"Shortly after seven," he says to Lorna. "Tell her I expect Hugh to join us. Thank you."

Once she leaves, I serve the tea as I resume the interview. "You hurried out before you were discovered. And then what?"

"I was not certain what to do then. Clearly, I could not help. In Dr. Gray, they had both a doctor and an undertaker at the party. I was leaving when I heard one of the maids inside say it was murder. That is when I left the area altogether. I knew I could not be found there, and because I had been recognized earlier—by a policeman no less—I had to warn Sophia. Miss Jex-Blake, I mean."

"Which you did after three o'clock this morning. The murder was discovered before eleven. There are four hours remaining."

A wan smile. "You miss nothing, do you, Miss Mitchell? I am beginning to wish I had gone to the police for this interview instead."

"That wouldn't have made it any easier. Detective McCreadie and I discussed what to ask you before we arrived at your home. My questions would have been his. Also, your husband says you returned home this morning and then left again. I am going to need a full accounting of your time."

She sighs. "Of course you are. All right then. I say I realized I had to speak to Sophia, as if I knew that immediately upon leaving. I only wish I were as clearheaded as she is." A faint smile. "Sophia knows what she wants and how to get it, and woe betide anyone who stands in her way. I am not nearly so decisive. I left the house and went down by the Water of Leith to walk and think, and I fear it took a good few hours before I realized I had to warn Sophia. Even when I left the Christie house, I had not realized the full import of what happened, only that I dared not be found there."

I finish the tea service and sit down with my own cup and biscuits.

Mrs. King continues, "I was with Sophia for a couple of hours. She needed to calm me, and that involved both whisky and distraction. We ended up talking about murders—a man in my village who died and a case she had followed for the medical implications. When I left there, it was past dawn. I knew Emmett would be worried sick, and so I bought fresh bread and some butter for his breakfast. I took that home and found him deep in his studies, having not even realized the hour."

She smiles again, that affectionate smile. "My husband lacks the advantage of a physician father and a good education. He must work harder than I do, and seeing him like that, I knew it was not the time to burden him with my mood. I explained what happened and said I needed to walk. He offered to accompany me, but I persuaded him not to. I walked, and I walked. When I got home before noon, Emmett had left for a lecture. He returned late this afternoon and told me the police wanted to speak to me. I decided to come here instead, after learning where to find Dr. Gray."

I sip my tea. Then I say, "Backing up a little. You said Miss Jex-Blake knows what she wants, and woe betide anyone who stands in her way. I understand Sir Alastair stood quite firmly in all your paths."

"And so we murdered him to clear the way for our progress?" A bitter smile. "If we began that, we would never stop. Those who oppose us are like ants at a picnic. There are too many to kill, and even if you managed it, more would march in to take their place."

"Had you ever met Sir Alastair before?"

She sets her teacup down. "That would depend on how you define 'met,' Miss Mitchell. If you are asking whether we were formally introduced, no. If you are asking whether I have exchanged a word with the gentleman, no. I have, however, 'met' him in the sense that I was in the room when Sophia spoke to him. Or, I should say, when she tried to speak to him. Sadly, he was busy. Terribly busy. This came after she had tried, repeatedly, to set up an appointment to do so. We waylaid the man, and he fled."

She pauses, fingering the saucer of her teacup. "I admit it was very disappointing to all of us. Of all those affiliated with the university who oppose us, Sir Alastair had seemed the most reasonable. The most likely to listen and perhaps even be swayed. Our hopes were dashed after that."

"You say he fled. Your choice of words seems significant."

She glances over.

I say, "He did not walk away or refuse to see you or shut the door in your faces. He fled."

"Perhaps that is the wrong word, implying he took flight and ran off down the hall." Her lips quirk. "That is not anything I could imagine him doing. He was a very dignified man. When I say he fled, I mean he made haste to leave."

"And your group had tried multiple times to arrange a meeting with him, while he was in Edinburgh, but he refused."

"'Rebuffed' is a better word, if we are choosing them with care. Perhaps even 'dodged.' He did not refuse to see us. He was simply busy. So very busy."

"And when you waylaid him, as you called it? Did he say anything?"

"He was in his office at the university. Sophia got in while the secretary was away from his desk, and we marched into Sir Alastair's office. Took him quite by surprise. He said he was terribly sorry but had someplace to be, grabbed his jacket, and rushed off. We tried to follow, but by then, the secretary had returned and stopped us."

"So Sir Alastair wasn't refusing to speak to you as much as avoiding doing so. Dodging, as you said."

"Precisely."

His maid suggested Sir Alastair avoided confrontation. Is that the behavior I'm seeing here? It would seem, though, that a man of Sir Alastair's position would not flee before a group of women. He would simply tell them no, he would not speak to them, and please stop bothering him.

This behavior speaks of discomfort. Like a politician ducking a question on a policy he doesn't really believe in, but he has to toe the party line.

Both Isla and Gray have noted that Sir Alastair seemed an odd choice to join the opposition against the Edinburgh Seven, much less take a leadership role.

Did he really believe these women posed a serious threat to the future of medicine?

Or was he toeing the party line?

Not just toeing it, but being pushed into the forefront of the charge.

And who would be the "party"? Who would be doing the pushing?

I make notes of all this. Then I say, "For your whereabouts when you were walking, do you have anyone who could provide an alibi?"

"Alibi?"

"Someone who might have seen you—perhaps you stopped to purchase something?"

"Ah." She thinks. "Not between the time I left the house and went to speak to Sophia. At that time of night, I avoid being seen. Between Sophia and Emmett, I bought the bread and butter. After I left Emmett . . ." Her eyes roll upward. "I bought a newspaper with an article on the murder and later I stopped for a cup of tea in the New Town. I can provide addresses for all of those stops."

"Thank you. I would also like to know where you went walking both times."

"Certainly."

"And then I will need your itinerary for the day before, between nine A.M. and four in the afternoon."

She goes still. Then her gaze rises to mine. "I presume that is when Sir Alastair died?"

"Roughly, yes."

"I was with the other ladies until noon. We met for a late breakfast and studied together. After that, I was studying at home."

"Which your husband can verify?"

"Yes—No, actually, he cannot. He was in class. But I *was* at home. I returned around twelve thirty, after spending the morning at Buccleuch Place with the other ladies."

Meaning her afternoon lacks a witnessed alibi. Would that give her time to kill Sir Alastair and wrap his body and encounter Selim in the tunnel after four? I'm not sure. Of course, I'm also not sure I consider her a viable suspect anyway.

Stopping Sir Alastair's opposition would be, as she said, pointless. But the murder doesn't seem to have been premeditated. Could Mrs. King have gone to speak to Sir Alastair at home, after he evaded Miss Jex-Blake? Killed him in the heat of the moment?

She showed a temper last night, and she is not a tiny woman. She could have done it after delivering those punches to knock him down and then leveraging the rope with that foot on his back. If I could drag Selim, she could as well.

"Thank you," I say. Then I turn to Gray. "Do you have any questions to add, sir?"

"I do not. If you would like to take the rest of Mrs. King's statement, I will leave you to that."

TWENTY-ONE

McCreadie shows up in time for dinner, and he understandably grumbles over Mrs. King coming here instead of the police office. It's a soft grumble, though, one laced with understanding for her distrust of the police. He will need to speak to her officially, but he'll wait until he has any new questions. I've covered everything he'll need for now, leaving him to pursue more viable leads.

McCreadie is investigating Sir Alastair's business dealings, which are mostly related to his excavations. Sir Alastair does lecture at the university enough to earn him an office, but that's mostly to honor his reputation rather than the amount of work he does there. It's also about the university maintaining a link to someone who brings in important artifacts.

McCreadie gets the sense Sir Alastair treated the lectures the way some researchers do, where teaching students is a necessary evil rather than a calling. My dad genuinely loves what he does, but he became an English professor because he wants to share his passion, not because he needs the affiliation to support his research and provide a laboratory.

Sir Alastair strikes me as a scientist more akin to Gray than to my father. His Egyptology might have leaned into the arts—history more than medical science—but his passion was getting out into the field and making discoveries.

It wasn't just lectures that got in the way of that. It was that damned filthy lucre. Gray is lucky there. His family's wealth means he only needs to work a few days a week, maintaining his father's undertaking business with no interest in growing it. Also, his own brand of research requires very little in the way of supplies. Cadavers aren't what I'd call cheap, but I haven't seen him purchase one since I got here. They're brought by the police looking for answers. As long as Gray has time and equipment, he's set.

Sir Alastair was different. He needed money—a lot of it—to fund his expeditions. That's where Lord Muir came in, but having a sponsor also meant Sir Alastair had to do things like put on that humiliating mummy-unwrapping demonstration.

Had there been more tension between the men?

That's all on McCreadie's investigative plate. Tomorrow, he will keep digging through the business side while we wait to follow up on Queen Mab and her goblin market.

We have a quiet evening in. Once we finish dinner, the exhaustion of yesterday's sleepless night hits. Isla and I retreat to the library to read, and after McCreadie leaves, Gray joins us.

There are many things about this new life that frustrate me, and at least as many that I love. One of the parts I love is the quietness that can settle over an evening like this.

We might be in the middle of an investigation, but no one has anything urgent to do for it, and so we just let ourselves rest. In my world, even on a quiet evening, my brain would whisper that I couldn't get too wrapped up in a book or a TV show or a video game. A brief rest was all I could afford before I needed to be productive again. Answer email. Reply to a text. What am I missing? What else should I be doing? Am I forgetting some obligation? I must be, if I think I have an entire evening free.

Here, we put the investigation aside and give our brains and bodies a much-deserved rest. I'm reading a first edition of *The Moonstone*, published last year. Isla has the equally recent *Little Women*, which I finished last week. Gray—well, Gray has the latest edition of *The Lancet*, so he's kind of working, but this is his idea of leisure activity, so I'll let him have it.

We sit in silence, with only the ticking of the clock to mark the passing of time, and I read until I can't keep my eyes open. When I make to leave, the other two agree we should all turn in, and we say our good-nights and head off to bed.

Gray, Isla, and I are taking breakfast together. I could get used to this. Oh, they've always invited me to join them, but taking meals with our bosses while Alice served would have been awkward. I would dine with them when I could put on my assistant hat, but even then, I'd insist on serving. Now I can rise at a normal hour without Mrs. Wallace giving me shit for showing up five minutes late and serving Gray his morning coffee less than piping hot. I can dress properly and at my leisure, and then I can read a newspaper or check in on Gray or Isla before breakfast.

This morning, we eat upon waking. We all slept until eight, and we need to be ready for our day.

"I have sent Simon to fetch the newspapers," Gray says. "If young Tommy has not uncovered any of those stories about us, I would propose that we seek them out."

"I agree," Isla says, "though you will need to take Mallory for that. I have a lunch engagement that I should not break without just cause."

"Mallory?" Gray says.

"Sounds like a plan. I'd also like to—"

A tentative knock at the door.

"Yes, Lorna?" Isla calls.

Lorna pokes her head through. "Sorry to interrupt, but this came for you, Dr. Gray." She holds an envelope out, quivering slightly, as if suspecting this should have waited until after breakfast. "It's from Lord Muir, and the boy said it was very urgent. Lord Muir will be waiting for you at the Christie house."

Gray bites off a sigh and finds a suitably neutral expression. "Thank you, Lorna."

She hesitates and then ducks her head, as if embarrassed at the two-second pause before realizing that was a dismissal. Gray waits until she is gone and then releases the sigh in a long exhalation.

"I understand that working with men such as Lord Muir is part of Hugh's job," Gray says. "But it is yet another reason why I prefer to avoid calling too much attention to myself."

"Because if men like Muir don't know you're involved in the investigation, they can't send messages demanding you wait on them like a common footman?"

He wrinkles his nose. "That makes me sound rather superior myself, doesn't it."

"Nah. I'd get that when I was a cop, and it rankled. Technically, I was a civil servant, but that didn't give anyone the right to order me around. What does Muir want? Besides us dropping everything and rushing to the Christie house at his convenience."

"Which I shall not do," Gray mutters. "Perhaps I do have too high an opinion of myself, but I will not set such precedents."

He slaps the envelope onto the table and picks up his coffee. Isla and I share a knowing look. Gray manages to get one sip of coffee before reaching for the envelope again.

"I shall read this and return a message," he says.

"Mmm," I say, "if it really is a summons to the Christie house, we might actually want to use the excuse to pop by and talk to Selim Awad about mummia. We just shouldn't drop everything, as you say."

When Gray keeps reading, my own curiosity spurs me to say, "Did anything actually happen? Or is Muir ordering us to deliver a status update in person?"

Gray's frown grows as he reads. "They have discovered several artifacts missing from the collection."

Isla puts down her cup with a clink. "Truly?"

"That was checked right away," I say. "It's the obvious motive for murder—Sir Alastair caught a thief in the act. But the staff said everything was there."

"They did. And now they say it is not, and Lord Muir believes he knows who took them. He's waiting for us at the house now."

"Then I guess we really are dropping everything and leaving."

Before we walk to the Christie house, Gray dispatches Simon with the coach to track down McCreadie and bring him, if he's not already on his way. While the note was addressed to Gray, that might only mean Muir doubled his chances of a response by messaging both men.

We arrive to a very quiet house. Black crepe wraps the outside pillars, and a black ribbon wreath at the door warns visitors that this is a house in mourning.

Inside, more crepe is hung over the doorways. Clocks have been stopped at the rough hour of Sir Alastair's death and the mirrors have been covered.

I remember Nan saying that the mirror-covering is from an old superstition that sees mirrors as portals to the next world. If they're left uncovered, the soul of the dead could be trapped in there. Is Lady Christie really worried about that? No, I suspect the staff did it, and even then, it was just a custom, the meaning probably long lost.

The thought, though, reminds me of my grandmother. I'd come to Edinburgh to sit at her deathbed, and I'd been flung here before she passed. Did she die thinking I'd vanished? That I'd died? And what about my parents? What do they think happened to their only—

I cut off the thought. I've gotten better about compartmentalizing my grief and worry. Someday I'll get home and explain everything. That has been my mantra since I left, and if it has faded, that's only because I know my goal and don't need to keep repeating it and reminding myself that I have no damn way of achieving it. It's not that I've become comfortable here. It's not that I'm no longer sure I want to go home. I've just set the whole thing aside. That's all.

The butler leads us wordlessly through a house that seems empty, but I've been in service long enough now to hear the swish of skirts and tap of soft indoor boots as the maids retreat. The butler opens the door to the artifact room and inclines his head and—again without a word—seems about to withdraw when I clear my throat.

Gray takes the hint. "I am sorry," he murmurs, "but I must ask, for the investigation, if we might speak to Mr. Awad afterwards. I promise we will keep the conversation brief."

"Mr. Awad is not here, sir."

"When do you expect him back?"

The butler's gaze cuts farther inside the room, and I realize Lord Muir is there, within earshot.

"I do not know, sir, but on his return, I will tell him you need to speak to him."

"Thank you," Gray says.

The butler closes the door behind us as Muir walks over.

"You came," he says.

"We did, Lord Muir," Gray says. "I have also taken the liberty of notifying Detective McCreadie. I am certain you had done the same, but he will be out of the police office today and my man might stand a better chance of finding him."

"I do not much care whether he comes or not. You are the one I messaged. He is merely a criminal officer. Lady Christie needs a detective."

"Hugh McCreadie *is* a detective," Gray says. "That is his rank. He investigates crimes, such as murder."

"Yes, yes, but he is a mere *police* detective."

"Who has brought several murderers to justice."

"With your help. My daughter reads all about your adventures, Dr. Gray, and it is very clear who is the brains behind this operation."

"Not at all. Hugh McCreadie is—"

"A fine policeman, which is an admirable achievement for someone from the lower classes."

Gray opens his mouth, and then stops, and I can read his thought process there. He'd been about to protest that McCreadie didn't come from the lower classes . . . and then realized that would sound as if that meant McCreadie shouldn't be lumped in with "common" police officers.

Muir continues, "My daughter loves detective fiction, and she says that the police detective is never the one who solves the mystery. He is the one bumbling about until someone such as you steps in to guide him in the right direction."

I wince. Apparently, this was a problem even before Doyle penned his famous amateur sleuth. I do love Sherlock Holmes stories, but I'll admit I didn't much appreciate the portrayal of the police, one that continues to prevail in detective fiction. The cops are buffoons who need the clever private detective to guide them from the fog of their own ineptitude. While I can grumble, I know that, for fiction, it makes sense to downplay the police if your protagonist is an amateur sleuth. It just has the unfortunate effect of making real-life police detectives seem like the amateurs.

"That is not true in this case," Gray says firmly. "While I have not read these stories, from what I have heard, they give me far too much credit. They have been fictionalized to conform to public tastes for a single central figure rather than a collaborative group."

"Yes, yes, dear boy," he says, slapping Gray on the shoulder. "It is admirable that you wish to deflect credit to your associates, but see that you do not become too adamant about doing so." He meets Gray's eyes. "The world will be quick enough to take credit from you, on account of your background. Do not allow that. You deserve better."

Huh. Well, that wasn't what I expected. Muir had made his stance on higher education for women clear, and so I presumed his bigotry would spread further. That's not always the case, though. Someone can support equal rights for one group while denying it for others.

For Gray's sake, I'm just glad Muir isn't as quick to dismiss him as he'd been to dismiss the Edinburgh Seven. If only that opinion hadn't come at the expense of denigrating McCreadie and the working class.

"I appreciate that you have faith in my competence," Gray says carefully. "I have still summoned Detective McCreadie to join us. In the meantime, though, I will respect your time by beginning the investigation along with my assistant here."

Muir smiles. "The lovely Miss Mitchell. I apologize for not having understood who you were before now. My daughter has schooled me most soundly. She is exceedingly fond of your character in the stories and says you are very charming."

Yeah, we definitely need to see those stories. Many words have been used to describe me. "Charming" is never one of them.

I return the smile with a half curtsy as I murmur, "I do my best, sir."

"You said artifacts are missing," Gray says, looking about. "I fear that is rather unwelcome news. It does put another spin on the case entirely. The staff seemed confident they were all accounted for."

"They were. That is the problem."

I take out my notepad and pencil.

"The artifacts were all here after the murder?" Gray says.

"Yes. I have done a little sleuthing of my own." Muir's blue eyes sparkle. "I knew you would need to question the servants again about the missing pieces, presuming they had somehow been overlooked in the inventory. They were not. The two footmen who checked were using a list. Alastair was very particular about that. He had a list of all artifacts in this room, and he made a note of which ones were to be placed on display last night. The footmen had to mark those removed and returned. Alastair was most particular."

Muir crosses the room and brings us a sheet of paper. All the artifacts are catalogued, and there are notes beside each showing when they have been removed and returned, like proper museum exhibits. Whoever moves them must sign them in or out. Even Sir Alastair's own signature is there when he was the one doing the moving.

"The final column was added last night," Muir says. "The footmen documented each artifact as it was returned, as well as checking the others. They are all clearly accounted for. I took the list to the footmen, who insist the missing artifacts were here when they shut the door last night."

"Shut it but did not lock it?" Gray says. "As the key is still missing."

"Correct. I believe, with the door being opened and closed so often, the thief took advantage of the household's grief and distraction to steal the artifacts, presuming the crime would be blamed on the murderer."

Muir looks almost shyly pleased with himself, as if envisioning his own portrayal in the next installment of Gray's adventures. The venerable Lord Muir, secret sleuth. I'm not inclined to like this guy, but I have to wonder how much of my dislike is based on his title and entitlement, rather than the man himself. Yes, one could argue that the sense of entitlement is part of his personality, but it's also the times and its classism.

"That seems a very solid conclusion," Gray says.

Muir beams.

"What can you tell me about the missing artifacts?" Gray asks, and here, Muir falters, looking like a boy who proudly stood up in class with the answer, only to realize he's missing half of it.

"No matter," Gray says without waiting for an answer. "I was unsure how well versed you are in Egyptian antiquities yourself."

"Not at all, to be truthful." Muir relaxes, seeming more human with each passing moment, first in his enthusiasm and now in his honesty. "For me, sponsoring Alastair's work was a philanthropic investment in the pursuit of knowledge. I find all this"—he waves at the room—"beautiful and fascinating, but the importance of it is an abstract concept to me, as with most art." An almost self-deprecating smile. "My wife and I buy art that we like and must rely on others to tell us the meaning of it."

"My view of art would be the same," Gray says. "I only know what I like."

"Precisely." Muir looks about the room. "That is why I sponsored Alastair. He was doing worthwhile things. First a surgeon and then an

Egyptologist? He makes the rest of us look quite indolent, sitting in our country homes, having our little parties."

Muir says this with a smile, his tone light and jovial, but there's a wistfulness in his eyes, and I'm reminded that in this time, having a title often meant you *couldn't* do much else. The title and its responsibilities were your job.

Muir clears his throat. "I can tell you that the thief did not make off with what I would consider the most beautiful of the artifacts—the jewelry and masks are still here. I believe those to be the most valuable, but the sale value and the historical value could be very different."

"They could be," Gray says.

Muir perks up. "And knowing which ones the thief took might tell you why he could have taken them. To sell to a private collector or to sell to a museum. All that would help you find the thief." He hesitates, his enthusiasm faltering. "Except you do not need to do so, as I know very well who stole the artifacts."

Right. He'd mentioned that in his note.

"It is young Mr. Awad," he says. "Lady Christie's brother."

TWENTY-TWO

We have moved farther into the artifact room to lessen the chance of being heard by Lady Christie. As we relocate, Gray lets Muir move ahead and murmurs to me, "Take over this interview, please."

I know what he means. I'd just started to see another side of Muir, and now those hopes for his character have plummeted. Accusing Selim Awad is like accusing the housemaid when the silver goes missing. That's not to say housemaids would never steal silver—I'm in the body of one who did—but it seems like a knee-jerk accusation. Of course the thief would be the shifty, working-class maid granted access to valuables by a trusting employer. Of course the thief would be the young foreigner granted access to valuables by a trusting brother-in-law.

Whatever we might think, though, we need to treat the accusation as respectfully as we did Muir's one against Florence King. I'm better equipped to do that, having spent my working career interviewing hundreds of people who insisted that the homeless guy in the alley must have picked their pocket or the kids hanging out on the corner must have vandalized their home. Most times they were wrong, but I needed to listen without judgment.

"Lord Muir," I say with a curtsy. "Please forgive my impudence, but Dr. Gray has asked me to take over the questions here, as I am learning his detective trade so that I might be a better assistant to him."

Muir's smile is pure indulgence. "Of course, child. What would you like to know?"

"First, and I do hate to ask this"—hoping that sounds sincere—"where were you yesterday, between the hours of nine and two?"

He blinks at me, and I'm pretty sure I hear Gray choke, but he also doesn't stop me.

"We must ask everyone," I say. "Again, forgive my impudence."

I give the slightest curtsy, and his indulgent smile returns.

"You are truly a detective, aren't you, child? Of course you must question everyone who did business with Alastair. I spent yesterday morning at my solicitor, on a matter unrelated to my Egyptian dealings. Then we went to lunch with two other fellows. That lasted until nearly three, at which time I returned home to prepare for the party. I will provide you with the names of those who can vouch for me."

"Thank you, sir. Now, I suppose the obvious next question is what leads you to believe Mr. Awad is responsible for the thefts."

Muir rubs his beard. "That is . . ." He exhales. "I have your discretion in this, I hope? I am very fond of dear Miriam, and I would hate to see her upset at any time, but least of all under these circumstances, which is why I hope to resolve this as quietly as we can."

I hesitate. To me, resolving it quietly would be speaking to Selim himself rather than summoning the police with an urgent message. But maybe that's *why* he summoned us instead. Or maybe by "resolving it quietly" he means whisking Selim off to jail with the minimum amount of fuss.

Arresting a new widow's brother for stealing her dead husband's artifacts, it's all just so unseemly. Can we just . . . get it over with? Quickly?

"Alastair suspected Selim has been taking artifacts for a while now," Muir says, lowering his voice until I have to strain to hear him.

"He consulted you about it?"

"Not . . . precisely. I was in his office at the university, and I found a letter he'd been writing to Selim, saying he needed to speak to him most urgently about the missing artifacts. Alastair was very understanding. Selim is young and, you may not realize this, but he spent a number of years in London."

"Going to school, yes."

Muir nods. "I remember that time of life myself, when I may have amassed some . . . embarrassing debts." His gaze cuts to Gray. "You will know what I mean, being closer to that age yourself."

Somehow I can't imagine Gray ever running up debts anywhere but a patisserie. Oh, he's been to fight clubs and he frequents public houses, but I suspect that even when he was young, he'd paid his tab at the end of the night. Yet to imply he didn't incur those debts as a young man would sever a connection here. Muir obviously likes Gray, and that helps him open up.

Finally, Gray says, "Yes, of course. There are many ways for a young man to find himself indebted to others when he only sought a little youthful extravagance."

"Exactly." Muir beams at him. "Nothing wrong with enjoying one's youth. Yet there are always people willing to prey on a young man's inexperience. That is what I presumed happened with Selim."

"And the letter said that he needed to speak to him about the missing artifacts."

"Urgently."

"Did it mention theft?"

Muir's brows shot up. "Alastair would hardly put that in a letter. But the meaning was clear."

"Do you have any more information about what had gone missing in the past?"

Muir shakes his head. "I wanted to discuss it with Alastair, but he was annoyed with my plans for the mummy party, and it seemed best not to bring it up. The artifacts belong to both of us, you see. I take a share in consideration of my sponsorship. I am certain what was taken would have come from Alastair's share—he was very careful and open in his accounting. Yet if I mentioned the theft while he was annoyed with me, he might think I was accusing him of cheating me out of my full share."

"By not including stolen artifacts in the tally."

"Yes. I decided I would wait until after the party, when he would doubtless be in a better mood. With his death, I forgot all about it until I was informed that more artifacts were missing."

"Who informed you?"

"I received a note from Miriam last night. It seems the children went to look at something and it was not there, and that began the chain of events leading to Miriam deciding I ought to be informed."

"Lady Christie's note said *more* artifacts were missing? She presumed you knew about the others?"

He shakes his head. "I misspoke. She said several artifacts were missing. That is all. I can show you the note. I have not mentioned the past thefts to her, so I do not know whether she is aware of them. I suspect not, if Alastair thought her brother responsible. Selim has . . . been in trouble before, and she has needed to get him out of it."

"Trouble with the law?"

"Oh no. Certainly not. Youthful trouble. That is all I know. I did not think Selim responsible for this theft myself, and perhaps not even the others. With these current ones, I thought the artifacts had been misplaced. Or Alastair's killer took them. Then I arrived to find that Selim has been gone since last night."

"Ah."

He glances toward the door, voice lowering again. "Alastair would not wish the police involved in this. I only want the artifacts returned and Selim spoken to, most sternly."

We have taken our leave of Muir and had a maid show us to a room where we might talk—a small music room.

"Well, this is a problem easily fixed," Gray says. "Find Selim Awad. Insist on the return of the artifacts. Then speak to him. Sternly."

"*Most* sternly." I take a chair by a pianoforte. "At least Muir didn't demand we deport him to Egypt."

"Hmm. There is that." Gray stands by a window overlooking the back garden. "What do you think of all this?"

I sigh and sink into my chair. "I don't know. It's easy to paint Muir as a bigot who automatically points fingers at a foreign relation, but that doesn't seem to be the case. He didn't even seem to think Selim responsible until he went missing."

"And the letter?"

I throw up my hands. "Not sure how to interpret that. We can ask Selim about it, but if Sir Alastair was accusing him, he could just lie."

"And the fact Mr. Awad is now missing?"

"It looks suspicious, but it isn't proof of anything. If Sir Alastair suspected Selim, that would be a solid lead . . . *if* we were investigating missing artifacts."

"Because the missing artifacts do not seem to be connected to the murder. The thief only took advantage of the household's mourning to steal them. I would say we have no place in this artifact investigation at all except . . ." Gray glances toward the door.

"Except that if we refuse, Lady Christie may call in the police, not realizing the prime suspect is her own brother?"

"Hmm."

"If we must look at Selim, is it only for artifacts? He couldn't have committed the murder, right? His ship arrived too late."

"Unfortunately, that did not clear him. It arrived closer to one than two, and Hugh cannot find the driver who allegedly dropped him off here past four. While arriving at the house around two would give him a compressed timeline, he would know how to unwrap and rewrap a mummy, making him quicker than the average person. Also, it would mean we could not say the killer left after four, as the tunnel encounter would be a lie."

"Damn."

I rise and walk around the room, thinking. "The theft of the artifacts might not be directly connected, but talking to Lord Muir did provide a potential connection of another sort. We already knew Sir Alastair chafed at being indebted to Muir."

"Yes."

"Yet he had to stay indebted if he needed to continue his work. In return, he owed Muir a share of the artifacts, and he had to agree to things like that mummy party. He was under Muir's thumb. Is that an accurate understanding of such a relationship?"

"It is. Many men in Sir Alastair's position would have made the best of it. Curried favor with their sponsor. The Sir Alastair I knew would have, as you said, chafed."

I pause by a harpsichord and run my fingers over the keys. "Last night, I was thinking about Sir Alastair avoiding Miss Jex-Blake. As both you and Isla said, he didn't seem the type to oppose women in medical school. He married a strong-willed woman and had one for a sister. The issue didn't affect him personally, and he seemed much too wrapped up in his work to fuss with academic politics. My sense, after what Mrs. King said, was that someone was putting him up to it. He had a position on the medical faculty and some person or group demanded he use it to oppose the female students."

"Lord Muir."

I glance over. "Does that make sense?"

"Unfortunately, yes. We have already heard Lord Muir's opinions on Mrs. King and her studies. He does not believe in higher education for women. Yet he has no standing in the medical or university communities."

"Sir Alastair does."

"He does indeed. I think, then, that as much as we would like to leave Lady Christie to her grief, we need to better understand the full state of the relationship between Lord Muir and Sir Alastair."

When we ask to speak to Lady Christie, it's clear the maid disapproves. Then fate intervenes, in the form of a handsome and charming police detective, who is terribly sorry that we need to intrude on Lady Christie's time of grief, but it really is important, and she may take all the time she needs to prepare. We will wait quietly in the music room.

"You're a lifesaver," I say to McCreadie. "I think she was going to refuse to even check with Lady Christie."

"At least I am good for something," McCreadie says as he falls into a chair with a deep sigh. "I am contemplating retirement, as it seems my services are no longer required. First Mrs. King and now Lord Muir, everyone calling upon my consulting detective instead of the actual detective. Why, even in those tales of your heroic adventures, I barely warrant a line or two."

"Who told you that?" I say.

"One of my men found copies, and I read them over breakfast. I think I receive four mentions in nearly fifty pages."

"You—you have them?" I say. "And you haven't shared them with us?"

"I know you are not interested, and so I burned them after reading." He catches my glare. "They are with Simon, awaiting your return. Now you, Miss Mallory, receive ten times the ink I do. The golden-haired maiden with womanly curves and eyes like sapphires, lips like a rosebud, voice like a songbird."

I snort. "Now I know you're joking. Catriona might have the hair, eyes, and curves, but this is not the voice of a songbird."

"Oh, but that is what it says in the stories. Over and over. I believe the writer is quite smitten with you. Or simply trying to enlarge his male readership. At least you get flattery. Do you know what he calls me? One adjective, mentioned every bloody time he pens my name. 'Vigorous.'"

"'Vigorous'?"

"Yes, 'vigorous.' What does that even mean?"

"Full of energy."

"Yes, yes, I know that. But how does it apply to a *person*?"

"It applies to a man, and it means he is . . ." I waggle my brows. "Vigorous."

McCreadie sputters.

I smile. "Do not be too quick to presume the writer is male. Whoever it is, they find you very . . ." Another brow waggle. "Vigorous."

Gray clears his throat. "Before Lady Christie arrives, perhaps we should tell Hugh what we have discovered and why we are speaking to the widow."

"Don't you hate it when he's reasonable?" I say to McCreadie.

"You think it is bad now?" McCreadie says. "Try having a friend who is that reasonable when he is still a child. There was no mischief to be had. Not at all."

"Not even digging up dead bodies?" I ask.

"That was his idea, which made it acceptable." He turns to Gray. "All right. We are done now. Tell me what has happened."

TWENTY-THREE

While we're talking, the maid pops her head in to say it will be at least twenty minutes, as the mistress was asleep. She obviously hopes we'll return later, but we promise to wait. That gives us more time to confer.

McCreadie agrees about the letter Muir saw. It isn't proof that Selim took these artifacts or the ones that went missing before. It does, however, mean we need to investigate him. As for Muir pressuring Sir Alastair to oppose the Edinburgh Seven . . .

"That makes sense of some correspondence I found," McCreadie says. "Before I received your message, I was reading through business correspondence from Sir Alastair's office. There was some rather heated back-and-forth between him and Lord Muir that I put aside to follow up on. It mentioned 'the young women' and Sir Alastair fretting that Lady Christie and Phoebe might find out. Out of context, I thought it might suggest affairs, though it would seem odd to worry about his young daughter discovering that. This makes far more sense. His wife and daughter were in Egypt while he was speaking against the medical students, but the more he spoke up, the greater the chance they'd hear about it on their return."

"Yeah, they wouldn't have been happy," I say. "My sense is that Lady Christie would be disappointed, and Phoebe would be *furious*."

"Lord Muir's reply chastised him for such worries. Women under his roof should accept that he knows best."

I snort.

McCreadie smiles. "I agree. We can examine their correspondence later, in this fresh light. For now, I am troubled about Mr. Awad. Are we certain he left of his own accord?"

"We need more information," I say, just as the maid raps on the door and tells us Lady Christie will see us now.

We are led to the garden, where Lady Christie sits by a small pond with the children. Phoebe is leaning against her, and Lady Christie strokes the girl's hair while Michael pokes a stick into the water, his distant expression saying he's barely aware of what he's doing.

The gardens have been cleared and covered for winter, but it's still a pleasant spot, the stone walls blocking the wind. One red ribbon on the ground tells me the bushes had been decorated before someone hastily removed the decor after Sir Alastair's death.

When we appear, Phoebe jumps to her feet and wipes tears from her eyes. Lady Christie lightly touches her back.

"Lady Christie," McCreadie says, removing his hat and dipping his chin. "Again, my sincerest apologies for this intrusion."

"You are conducting an investigation. I understand it is necessary. Please, ask your questions."

I glance at the children. When Phoebe only goes to stand near Michael, I look over at McCreadie and Lady Christie, expecting one of them to tell the kids to go inside.

McCreadie clears his throat. "The children might be more comfortable—"

"With me," Lady Christie says, her voice firm. "They will be more comfortable with me, if that is their wish."

"All right then," McCreadie says. "Let us begin with the theft of the artifacts."

So he's really going to interview their mother with the kids right there?

Gray walks over to Michael and murmurs something. Michael nods and follows Gray to another part of the garden. That leaves me with Phoebe, and I'm going to guess that was also my cue to distract her.

"Shall we walk?" I say.

She nods and joins me as we head in the other direction.

Phoebe doesn't say a word, and I'm shuffling through my options. Leave her to her silence? Ask something distracting? Ask something pertinent to the case despite her being a ten-year-old witness without a parent present?

"Lord Muir thinks one of the medical students killed my father," Phoebe says, when we reach the far corner. "One of the women."

I turn, my shock genuine.

Her gaze is down, and she has Michael's stick in her hand and is dragging it through the dirt as she walks.

She continues, "He says one of them was at the house that night, and she murdered Papa because he opposed their entry into the university."

I open my mouth, but before I can say anything, she continues, "Mimi thinks that is silly, and I said we should speak to you and Dr. Gray, but she says we cannot interfere. We must trust everyone to do their jobs properly. I still think you should know."

"We are aware of Lord Muir's suspicions, and they are being accorded all proper consideration."

She glances over. "I hope that is a fancy way of saying you are ignoring them."

"Ignoring them wouldn't help. If someone is a suspect, they need to be cleared. Otherwise, in a trial, the barristers can say the police overlooked a suspect."

"That makes sense." She walks a few more steps, stick still dragging a line beside her. "It is true, then. That Papa spoke out against the women students, as Lord Muir says."

Shit.

"I'm sorry."

She keeps walking, and then says, "Papa always said he believed girls were just as smart as boys, that Michael and I could both become Egyptologists, if we liked. Or I could be like Mama and help with my husband's work. Or I could be like Mimi and teach children."

Her eyes glisten. "But he only said what we wanted to hear, didn't he? Because Mama and Mimi would not have married him if he believed otherwise. He pretended because it made them happy."

"I think," I say slowly, "that such a thing would require too much pretending. At home, we wish to relax and be ourselves."

"So you think he lied to others. That he pretended to think women shouldn't study medicine when he didn't believe that."

"I don't know what your father did or what he thought, Phoebe. I only believe that he was not lying when he told you that you could be whatever you like, that you are as capable as any boy."

"But Papa must have opposed the women students for a reason." She fingers the needles on an evergreen and then says, "Perhaps he did it because of someone else. Like in a book I read, where a boy at school said mean things because he wanted other boys to like him."

"I cannot speculate on that, Phoebe, and I am not sure it helps you to do so."

"But would that not be *worse*?" she says. "It is bad enough to think women should not study at university. Is it not worse to think they should . . . and yet try to stop them? At least if you believe in an idea, you think you are doing the right thing. Like Lord Muir. He believes women should not be in university. That is terrible, but it is also sad, because he believes something that is wrong."

She stops short, stick swinging up. "Was Lord Muir the one pushing Papa to say those things?"

"The police are investigating every angle."

"I do not trust the police," she says tartly, sounding more herself at last. "There are no women among them, and so they cannot be trusted to truly understand cases that involve women. That is what Mama always said. You must have women in a group if the group is supposed to be for everyone. Just like you need Egyptians on a job that is in Egypt. You must have them in positions of influence, Mama said, and Papa agreed." Her voice cracks a little. "Or he said he did. Did he hire Egyptians just to make Mama happy?"

"I cannot see a man molding his hiring practices to appease his wife."

She worries her bottom lip with her teeth and then blurts, "I did not want Papa harmed."

I frown at her. "All right . . ."

"I know I said he should be cursed for unwrapping a mummy for entertainment, but I did not mean it."

I lay a careful hand on her arm. "You were clearly teasing, and even then, you said you would only hex him with boils. What happened has nothing to do with you. Curses aren't real."

"I know," she says, her voice dropping. "He was a good papa. He would complain if we were underfoot or making too much noise, but he took us to the excavations and he talked to us and listened to us as if we were grown-ups. Michael liked that. I did, too."

"Then that is the part you remember," I say. "That is the part that counts."

She resumes walking. Now she's tapping the stick ahead of her, the movement almost agitated. When she stops, it's so abrupt that I nearly crash into her.

She turns sharply and looks up at me. "If Uncle Selim took the artifacts, he had a good reason."

I go still.

Her chin lifts. "He did, no matter what Lord Muir might say."

Damn it. In the modern world, I'd be obligated to let this drop—or at least take her to Lady Christie before she went further. But whatever she's saying, she's not going to say it in front of Selim's sister.

"All right," I say carefully.

"He is not a thief."

"All right."

"If he took them, he has a reason and it is a good one."

I speak with as much care as I can. "Do you have cause to suspect he might have . . . removed artifacts from the house?"

Silence. Shit. If she was merely defending him, she'd have been startled by the question, rushed to say no, of course not.

Her chin lifts again. "Uncle Selim is not a thief. You cannot steal what is, rightfully, already yours. The history of Egypt belongs to the Egyptians."

I exhale. Okay, then. Well, that puts a very different spin on this.

Egypt is not yet part of the British Empire, although I think it will be in a decade or so. Right now, it's under the Ottomans, in a relationship known as a suzerainty, similar to Puerto Rico's relationship with the United States. The British are moving in, though, and they're taking whatever artifacts they can.

I want to press more, to ask whether Selim has ever protested the removal of the artifacts from Egypt. I can't ask, of course, because she's a ten-year-old girl who would be offering evidence against an uncle she obviously adores, and she would be telling me in hopes of helping him, not condemning him.

Phoebe is too young to realize what she's doing, so I need to back off and only note that we cannot, unfortunately, dismiss Selim as quickly as we hoped.

We're walking in a garden. Not the one at the Christie house, but one of the not-public gardens near Gray's town house. These gardens have been private since they were created about fifty years ago for the exclusive use of neighboring homeowners. Gray has a key, and he lets us in and then shuts the gate behind him.

There's no one else in the garden, with the flowers put to bed and no winter decorations to entice anyone. Without snow, it's closed flower beds and bare trees and bushes of dead leaves, nothing like the Christie yard, where even in November, the gardens felt like a pleasant place to spend some quiet time. At least we get the quiet part.

"I believe I may know who took the artifacts."

I'm not the one saying that sentence. McCreadie is. I tense, ready for him to say Lady Christie fears her brother is involved. Instead, he says, "It seems there was a dispute regarding the artifacts between Sir Alastair and Lord Muir."

"Dispute?" I say.

"As Lord Muir told you, he is entitled to a portion of the findings. But that is done under very strict restrictions imposed by Sir Alastair, to protect the historical and scientific value of his finds. While Lord Muir takes half the finds, Sir Alastair is allowed to remove up to twenty percent before Lord Muir makes his choices."

"Twenty percent that Sir Alastair deemed notable."

"Yes."

I move aside an untrimmed branch. "Twenty percent that Sir Alastair promises he will donate."

"He *does* donate them. Lady Christie was clear on that and says Lord Muir will not attempt to claim otherwise. Sir Alastair donated the artifacts he said were of significant historical value."

"But I'm presuming that's still where the dispute arose. Sir Alastair was removing artifacts Lord Muir wanted."

"Yes. They had come to this agreement at the start of their working relationship, and Sir Alastair was choosing twenty percent to donate, as they agreed. But Lord Muir had come to realize that 'valuable' in a historical context could also mean 'valuable' in a monetary one."

I remember Muir's words, breezily acknowledging that the most valuable of artifacts might not be the most *historically* valuable. Except they can be, to a discerning buyer.

I'm turning a corner when my heel catches on a loose cobblestone. Gray's hand shoots out to steady me before I can do more than wobble. I glance over with a grateful smile. He's been silent so far, listening and assimilating.

I say, "Is Muir keeping his share of the artifacts or selling them?"

"An earl does not dirty his hands by selling anything, my dear Mallory. He has people for that. But, yes, while Lord Muir chooses a few for his own collection, most are sold."

"And he's come to realize that savvy collectors don't just want a pretty jeweled scarab. They also want artifacts they can brag about, like saying they have a rare scroll taken from the tomb of a pharaoh."

"Precisely. Lord Muir wanted to renegotiate their arrangement so that he could take half of his allotment off the top. Lady Christie believes her husband was conducting a negotiation of his own. Mollifying Muir in other ways."

"Like speaking out against the female medical students. Throwing them under the bus to preserve his artifacts."

McCreadie nods. "Likely so. Lord Muir apparently accepted such conciliatory efforts as his due and the matter seemed closed."

"Hmm." I realize we're heading for the exit and take the next turn to loop us through the garden again. "Were any of the previously missing items among the disputed artifacts?"

McCreadie smiles. "You were a detective for a reason, I see."

"No, I know *you're* a very good detective, which means you wouldn't consider Muir a feasible suspect for the thefts unless you had more evidence, such as the missing artifacts being ones he wanted."

"Of the four items taken the last time, two were ones they had argued over."

"Because only taking the ones he wanted would be too obvious. Now you think Muir hadn't dropped the matter. He used the chaos after Sir Alastair's murder to make off with more artifacts, which is easy because he'd have been in and out of the house. When Lady Christie messages him about the theft, he races over and takes charge, summoning us, pointing the finger at Selim, and even making a point of suggesting the missing artifacts *weren't* the most valuable."

We continue down a row of hedges.

McCreadie looks over. "You lay out a solid argument, but I have the feeling you are merely repeating what you believe my argument to be . . . and that you disagree."

"No, I don't disagree. I'm just struggling with extra information."

I tell him what Phoebe said about her uncle.

"Ah," McCreadie says. "That does add a complication."

"It doesn't mean Selim did anything. Phoebe might only have heard Muir blame him, so she's leaping to his defense. Perhaps she fears he may have done it to reclaim his country's treasures. That he objects to the plunder and therefore, by logical extension, *could* have taken them."

"Yes."

I glance at Gray. He continues walking, but his gaze is sharp enough that I know he's thinking it through.

"That does make sense," Gray says. "Lord Muir makes off with the artifacts and blames Mr. Awad as a convenient suspect, who is also conveniently unavailable. However, that leads to the question of where Mr. Awad is. Michael says they do not know."

McCreadie nods. "That is what Lady Christie said as well. He was not in his rooms this morning, and at first . . . Well, you remember when we would do the same thing as young men. Isla would discover your room empty, and likely heave a great sigh of exasperation before covering for your absence with your parents. Lady Christie found the room empty, rolled her eyes at her brother's youthful ways, shut the door and told the children he was still abed."

"Expecting him to sneak back in after a night of carousing," I say.

"Then Lord Muir arrived and wanted to question Selim, and she had to admit he was not at home."

"But not being at home wasn't initially a cause for surprise. Suggesting it wasn't unexpected behavior."

"Lady Christie was most circumspect." McCreadie nudges a stone from the path with his boot. "But she did suggest he has . . . a friend he meets while in Edinburgh."

"Got it. Any chance we can check in with this nighttime friend?"

McCreadie shakes his head. "Lady Christie, being a proper lady, has no idea who he was seeing. However, she did say that he always returned home before dawn. She presumed, with the tumult over her husband's death, Selim thought he could linger longer."

I check my pocket watch. "Linger past noon?"

"Yes, that is concerning."

"Lord Muir mentioned something about 'youthful troubles' in Selim's past. . . ."

McCreadie waves a hand. "He was exaggerating, it seems. There was trouble with a few boys at his London school, who mocked Selim's accent. He claimed to have put an ancient Egyptian curse on them, which caused some commotion."

I smile. "Good. But yes, that's hardly what I'd consider youthful troubles."

"Agreed. I told Lady Christie I would return to the house. I will need to search Selim's room." He catches my look. "No, I did not warn her that I would be coming back to search, giving her time to remove anything she considers private, which might include information on his 'night friend.' I only said that I need to return to speak to the staff."

I'm about to ask whether he wants our help, but a look from Gray stops me. McCreadie has already had two people contact us instead of him. Better not to say anything that might suggest he needs help. If he wants it, he'll ask.

"Mallory and I shall return home," Gray says.

"Get some rest," McCreadie says, and then adds with a sly smile, "I have left you some reading material."

TWENTY-FOUR

Back at the house, we don't just have the "reading material." We have two copies of it, one from McCreadie and one from Tommy. They're in two formats, though. The ones McCreadie found are bound chapbooks, selling for . . .

"A half crown each?" I sputter. "That's more than a properly published book."

Isla says, "That is intentional. It will keep them out of the hands of common folk and make the well-to-do readers feel they are receiving something special."

"Who would pay that much for a book they've never heard of?"

She picks up what Tommy found, which is serialized pamphlets. "They will have heard of them through these, which are priced at a thruppence each. Triple the price of penny broadsheets, but reasonable enough to find an audience of middle-class thrill seekers, who will carry the word to others, who will then purchase the chapbook, it being the same price as buying all ten pamphlets."

I still shake my head. I know there's an appetite for stories of crime and murder. The interest lingering from *The Newgate Calendar* is now morphing into an interest in detective fiction. But it still astounds me that these stories could have been circulating for weeks now, somehow finding a market that extended all the way to Lady Christie and her children.

"The title is ridiculous," I mutter as I glare at the first volume. "*The*

Mysterious Adventures of the Gray Doctor? *The Mysterious Adventures of Doctor Gray* would flow better *and* make sense."

"I would have used 'undertaker' myself," Isla says. "*The Mysterious Adventures of the Curious Undertaker.*"

She glances at Gray, but he's staying out of the conversation, leafing through the pamphlets with a growing fissure between his brows.

"Mallory?" Isla says softly, pulling my attention back. When I look over, she murmurs, "He is fine."

I want to grumble that he might be fine, but *this* is not fine. It's not fine at all.

Gray has kept out of the limelight because he doesn't want it. He just wants to do his damn work, and I get that. As a cop, I'd cringed anytime I got in the papers, and if I had the chance, I'd direct attention to a more deserving officer.

Part of it was that I felt there *was* always someone more deserving, and if I got my photo in the paper instead, it was because someone making those decisions thought I had a better "look" for the piece. Young, female, and attractive enough. I had a pleasant and open face. Cute, as I'd been told, which was a whole lot more flattering when I was a whole lot younger. In interviews, I was, well, me. Friendly, approachable, a little bit outspoken, a little bit sarcastic. A good choice for a sound bite that was honest but never *too* biting.

So I understood why I got more ink than my colleagues, but I hated it. I'd literally cringe when someone joked that I was in the papers *again*. I just wanted to do my damn job.

This isn't a photo or a mention in the paper. These are entire stories dedicated to Gray, written by a stranger who is profiting from Gray's earnest attempts to quietly help the police and further the state of forensic science.

I might be snarling about the shitty title, but really, I'm snarling about the whole damn thing. And that's before I start reading.

"Oh hell, no," I say after two pages. "If this is Jack, she had damn well better never show her face around here."

"Perhaps," Isla says gently, "but it is no worse than you would read in the papers, Mallory. In your time writers might have better ways to describe people who do not resemble the dominant population, but this is normal."

Maybe, but the fact that she didn't need to ask what I'm snarling about tells me she noticed it, too. McCreadie might have grumbled about the adjective "vigorous" being attached to his every mention, but in two pages, the writer has made three different references to Gray's skin color and two to his "foreign visage."

"Perhaps you would like to read elsewhere?" Gray murmurs.

The words are soft, with no sense of rebuke, but my cheeks still heat.

"Sorry," I say. "It just pisses me off."

"Then we shall reach an agreement. You have registered your disapproval of these descriptions. Now I will say that if this damnable writer mentions your bosom one more time, I shall be forced to challenge them to a duel, even if it does turn out to be Jack."

Isla snorts. "Oh, but her bosom is mentioned so prettily, Duncan, so as not to offend women and children." She lifts the book. "'Miss Mallory leaned over the victim, the firm mounds of her maidenly bosom rising and falling in panicked breaths. "Sir!" she cried. "Do you think he is dead?" She clapped her pretty hands over her pale breast and gazed beseechingly at her employer through her lovely golden lashes.'"

"That is *not* for women and children," I say. "It's soft-core porn disguised as detective fiction. For the record, I don't give a damn how many times Catriona's boobs are mentioned. *I'm* going to be challenging the writer to a duel for portraying me as a simpering fool."

"At least we know the writer has never met you," Isla says. "That would seem to strike Jack from the list of suspects."

"Unless she's doing it to piss me off. Panicked breaths and beseeching looks," I mutter under my breath.

"Now, now," Gray says. "I have seen you look at me most beseechingly from under those golden lashes. You do it every time there is only one cup of coffee left in the pot."

"Like the way you look at me when there's only one pastry left on the plate?"

"While I hate to interrupt your adorable banter," Isla says, "I must assure you both that I have now gone two pages with nary a mention of Mallory's bosom. There is only this rather unremarkable tidbit." She raises the book again. "'Miss Mallory noticed a mark on the floor, and in her haste to examine it, she lifted her skirts—'"

"What?" Gray looks thunderous.

Isla raises a finger. "'She lifted her skirts *most decorously,* revealing no more than a sliver of milky skin above her fine boots, and then she arranged the skirts to allow her to crouch on all fours—'"

Gray starts to make strangled noises, his expression murderous now.

"'To crouch on all fours,'" Isla repeats, clearly enjoying herself, "'with her rounded posterior in the air.'"

"A duel," Gray grinds out. "This requires a duel."

"'She crouched there, on her hands and knees, rounded posterior lifted as she bent to examine the evidence on the floor, which . . .'" Isla chokes on a laugh. "'Which turned out to be nothing but a speck of dirt.'" She claps a hand to her mouth as her shoulders shake with laughter, tears welling. "Oh, my."

"Yep," I say. "Soft-core porn, Victorian style."

Isla's eyes dance. "May I presume the existence of the term 'soft-core' implies there is a hard-core?"

"Definitely."

"What exactly would constitute—?"

Gray clears his throat, loudly.

Isla looks at me. "Men might say they avoid such conversation so as not to scandalize women, but as you can see, that is but an excuse. The ones we must truly fear scandalizing are the men themselves."

"If you are finished," Gray says, "might we return to reading these . . . ?" He struggles for words.

Isla grins. "Mysterious adventures of the very foreign doctor and his lovely assistant's lovely body parts?"

I sputter a laugh. "All right. We've registered our shock and disapproval. Now let's read and see if we can figure out who is writing this trash."

"So I may challenge them to a duel?" Gray says.

"So we may tell them to—in the name of all that is holy—stop writing. Or it may be their murder we're investigating next."

Gray smiles, a little too broadly, and I pick up another pamphlet to read.

"So we agree it's complete and utter trash," I say as I put down the last pamphlet.

"As well as 'soft-core porn,'" Isla says with a smirk my way.

I roll my eyes. I have to admit I'm almost impressed at the way the writer wove those bits in, using every excuse to have my bosom aflutter or my ass in the air, even if that's not physically possible while wearing a corset. In one part, I'd even, for a brief moment, been kneeling in front of Gray. All in the most innocent of contexts, of course.

The stories might allegedly be for children, but someone was making sure they didn't ignore the male market. I can't even grumble, having seen too many detective dramas where the camera lingers a little too lovingly on naked young female corpses. Hey, at least I'm alive in these stories. And fully dressed.

What actually pisses me off about my portrayal is that I seem to be the equivalent of a magician's assistant, there to look pretty and hold things for her genius boss. That role is also a time-honored one in detective fiction—the wide-eyed ingénue who asks endless questions that give the protagonist a chance to pontificate and look like the genius he is. I'm a foil—Gray's Dr. Watson.

So I'm not *truly* pissed off about the portrayal of myself. It just tells me that the writer either doesn't know me or is intentionally tweaking me.

When I say that, Gray makes a noise deep in his throat.

"Yes, I realize that isn't as helpful as we'd like," I say. "It doesn't answer the question of whether it could be Jack or not."

"Given these descriptions of you," Isla says, "I must presume the writer has developed something of an infatuation. I did not get that impression from Jack."

"She finds me interesting, but not that way."

"And her preferences in general . . . ?" Isla says, circumspectly. "Do we have any indication of that?"

"She likes men," I say. "She's made comments to that effect." Admiring McCreadie, though I won't say so in front of Isla. "That doesn't mean she doesn't also like women, but . . ." I leaf through the pages. "Presuming Jack is 'Edinburgh's Foremost Reporter of Criminal Activities' this writing is shit compared with hers. It's possible Jack *isn't* writing those broadsheets but tried her hand at these without any writing experience, which would explain the terrible prose, but that feels like too many ifs for me. Jack slipped up the other day. She started to say *she* covered crimes before switching to saying her writerly friend covers them."

"You caught that, too," Gray murmurs.

"Oh, I caught it. I just wasn't going to call her out on it. My gut says *this* isn't Jack. It's not just the bad writing or the weird obsession with my body parts. It's not even the racism, which doesn't sound like Jack either. This is ninety percent fiction. There are things Jack knows, especially about the poisoning case, that she would have included for a better story. This is written by someone who knows nothing more than they'd glean from the papers."

"And someone who has met you and formed an unhealthy attachment," Gray says.

I wrinkle my nose. "Have they, though? Or is that just marketing?"

"I believe someone disinterested in women could pen this," Gray says. "But my sense is that the writer does find you attractive. I even speculated briefly whether it could be Dr. Addington. He would certainly pen those bits. But the portrayal of him is dismissive, and he could not bring himself to do that, even to hide his identity."

"Let's look at that, then," Isla says. "You are the clear star of these stories, Duncan. The writer exoticizes you in an uncomfortable way, but not an overtly negative one. They have nothing but praise for your abilities. They fail to realize Mallory's contributions, but she plays a significant and equally positive role. As for Hugh, it is clear that the writer considers his detecting skills far inferior to Duncan's. Dr. Addington is written as equally superfluous. They are bit players in your drama, Duncan. I am completely absent from the pages as anything other than 'Dr. Gray's widowed sister.'"

"*Handsome* widowed sister," I say.

She rolls her eyes. "Yes, but there is no mention of my chemistry, even when it played into the last case. My sense is that we are not looking at a writer who is part of our social circle, even our wider circle. This is a stranger who has absorbed Duncan's story through the papers and broadsheets and maybe uncovered a tidbit or two through gossip, but has stitched the rest out of whole cloth."

"I think you're right," I say. "Which is not going to help us get rid of these. Or even just control the narrative."

"That is why you have Jack," she says. "We believe she works in this milieu. Let her investigate. We have a murder to solve, and Mallory has an underground market to infiltrate."

"Not until this evening. It is only . . ." I check my pocket watch and curse.

"Teatime," Isla says. "You both missed lunch, and so I shall insist on tea. Later, we must find you proper attire for your mysterious late-night excursion."

We'd hoped for an update from McCreadie, but he's obviously busy with the case. After tea, Isla slips off, saying we will worry about my outfit later. Gray and I spend some time in the lab with the Hand of Glory, in case I need to give it away tonight.

After dinner, Isla enlists help designing my costume. *Who* she enlists has me doing a double take.

"Mrs. Wallace?" I say, and then look at the housekeeper's hands, expecting to see she's only bringing something into Isla's rooms. They're empty.

"Mrs. Wallace has graciously agreed to help us with your outfit for this evening," Isla says as she closes the door behind the housekeeper.

"Er . . ." I say.

"That was a thank-you," Isla says to Mrs. Wallace. "Mallory is struck dumb with appreciation."

"I do appreciate it," I say. "I just . . ." I glance at Isla. "Have you explained where I'm going?"

"Not yet."

Oh, this should be fun.

"I decided you can do the honors," Isla says to me.

Double fun.

"Er, uh . . ." I glance at Isla. "I'm not sure how much I should say." When she doesn't seem ready to help, I turn to Mrs. Wallace. "We are working on the investigation, obviously. There is reason to believe that the, uh, mummified remains may have been taken for, uh, medical reasons. Medicine, that is."

"Mummia," Mrs. Wallace says. "I have heard of it. Ridiculous notion, but one cannot blame people for being willing to ingest almost anything that might restore their health."

"Right. Yes. So that's what we think, but it's no longer readily available, so if the remains are sold, they'd be sold at a black—at a market for illegal and mystical substances."

Her eyes narrow. "You are planning to go to the underground market?"

"You've heard of it?"

She answers with a snort and then says, "If you are counting on the 'old' Catriona having contacts that will allow her into the market, you will find yourself stopped at the entrance. If you can even *find* the entrance, which I doubt. I myself have never gained admittance, and I was more than a mere thief."

I open my mouth to ask what she was then, but this isn't the time—and I know she won't answer.

"That part is handled," I say. "Someone is taking me there and getting me in."

Her eyes narrow more. "Who would have the influence to not only obtain entry but to be able to take a guest? No one short of—" She rocks back on her heels. "You are working with Queen Mab."

"We are working with someone," I say firmly. "I can divulge no more."

"It must be Queen Mab. I wondered whether you had approached her during the case with Lady Annis. I know it was whispered that she was responsible for selling the poison that killed those men. Now you have made a contact, which you are using." Her eyes are all but slits now. "Does she know who you are?"

"Whoever is helping us knows I am Dr. Gray's assistant. That is enough."

Mrs. Wallace makes a shockingly rude noise. "That is certainly *not* enough. Someone must tell her who you are."

"Who Mallory *was*," Isla says gently. "Before her accident. That is immaterial in the current context."

"It is hardly—" Mrs. Wallace softens her voice. "I am sorry, Mrs. Ballantyne, I did not mean to speak to you that way."

Isla's faint eye roll suggests Mrs. Wallace's show of deference is for my benefit. While I know how much Mrs. Wallace adores Isla and Gray, it's with the adoration—and occasional exasperation—of an aunt who dotes on her younger relatives but sees the need to nudge them now and then, to keep them on the path.

"Yes, yes," Isla says. "You may speak freely here, Mrs. Wallace. Duncan and I have no concerns that Mallory will do anything untoward at the market nor use the visit for anything but the intended purpose, which is to represent herself as a young woman with an item to trade and possibly hoping to pave the way for future enterprise."

"What are you taking to trade? It cannot be some bauble, however valuable."

"A Hand of Glory. That's—"

"If you are hoping to pass off a mere severed limb as a true Hand of Glory, they will see through that ruse in an instant, and you will damage Queen Mab's reputation."

"It's an actual Hand of Glory. I can show it to you, if you like. It's downstairs."

I have, for once, rendered the indomitable Mrs. Wallace speechless.

"Downstairs?" she says.

"Duncan found it," Isla says, "and bought it for Mallory as a gift."

Mrs. Wallace assimilates this. Then her gaze hardens. "If Dr. Gray bought you this item as a gift—and I cannot believe I am saying that—and you are traipsing off to the underground market to give away something he purchased at great expense—"

Isla cuts in. "Duncan is aware of what we are doing, and he agrees with Mallory using the hand to gain entry in hopes of furthering the case." Isla meets the housekeeper's gaze. "If you believe you know who Mallory is meeting, then you know we would not attempt to misuse her in any way. We would not dare."

Mrs. Wallace looks from me to Isla. Then she says, "I will accompany Cat—Mallory."

She's making a concession here, calling me Mallory, but Isla shakes her head.

"If someone else could go, I would," Isla says. "Or Duncan."

"No disrespect, ma'am, but that would be, frankly, ridiculous. Your brother's growing reputation makes it impossible for him to disguise himself in a place that is expecting disguises. And you are a proper lady, unable to act as anything but a proper lady."

Isla's expression makes Mrs. Wallace's grim countenance soften in a near smile. "That is not an insult, Mrs. Ballantyne."

"It most certainly *is*, and one I will rectify at another time, with Mallory's training."

"Aye, something tells me Miss Mallory would be an excellent teacher for such things."

"And that," I say, "*I* will take as a compliment."

"You cannot go, Mrs. Wallace," Isla says. "Our contact was clear on that. Only Mallory may accompany her."

"I know Queen Mab. I have not seen her in several years, but she will take me. I had oft thought of asking her to take me to the market, but by the time I was in a position to do so, I was no longer engaged in work that would benefit from such a visit."

"That work being . . . in the circus?" I prompt.

"I will accompany you to the meeting point," Mrs. Wallace says, ignoring my question, as expected. "If Queen Mab does not wish to take me further, I will not argue the matter. That is settled. On to dressing Miss Mallory appropriately."

"Fairy wings?" I say. "Please tell me I get to wear fairy wings."

Mrs. Wallace looks at me. Then she gives a slow smile. And with that smile, I know I'm in trouble.

TWENTY-FIVE

"I am not wearing this in public," I say as I stand in front of Isla's full-length mirror.

Behind me, Gray's lips twitch. "I think you look ador—"

"If that word is 'adorable,' stop now or suffer the consequences." I glare at my reflection. "Who the hell am I supposed to be? Glinda the Good Witch? I just need my magic wand to sprinkle fairy dust through Munchkinland, and while I'm at it, maybe I'll grant Mrs. Wallace a heart. No, a sense of humor."

"You realize none of that makes any sense to us," Gray says. "However, while I have wondered about Mrs. Wallace's lack of humor, I no longer do. Seeing you in that outfit, I am assured a very keen wit lurks behind that dour facade."

I turn my glare on him. Then I look back at the mirror, where Isla is eyeing me contemplatively.

"I am not certain it is . . . quite right," Isla says.

"You think?" I gather layers of skirts. "I look like I'm ready for a freaking communion."

I'm dressed in white. All white. Except for the very top layer, it's all underthings, and I could argue on that point, but they've been arranged in a way that disguises their true purpose, leaving me in a frothy confection of white linen and silk and lace.

That's not even the worst of it. My hair has been curled and frozen in place with fixative, and I look like a twelve-year-old who got carried away with a curling iron. A light rub of something on my cheeks and lips makes them rosy red, my lips a perfect cupid's bow.

"You guys can see she's mocking me, right?" I say. "How the hell am I supposed to walk down the street like this."

"You have a point," Isla murmurs.

"Thank you."

"You will need to be hidden under a long coat. I have one with a hood. That might—"

"Queen Mab will not take me into the goblin market dressed like a freaking angel."

Gray frowns and tilts his head. "They might find that intriguing, provided of course that you add a few more eyes and animal heads to properly resemble a biblical angel."

"More eyes and animal heads might help," I grumble. "I am not—"

A brief commotion outside the door cuts me off.

"Dr. Gray's room does not need cleaning," Mrs. Wallace snaps. "Go."

A moment later, the door opens and Mrs. Wallace walks in, shaking her head. "That girl."

"Lorna?" Isla says.

"She will not last, ma'am. I am sorry to say it, but we have no place for a timid mouse like that."

She cuts off Isla's response by lifting something in her arms. It's an overcoat . . . I think. It looks more like something worn by a medieval minstrel, all strips of varying colors and fabrics. Without a word, she puts it on me. It's too long and nearly brushes the floor, but the added girth lets it button over my breasts. Mrs. Wallace promptly *unbuttons* that part and arranges the jacket bodice so that it is otherwise open, showing my white and frothy garments beneath.

I look in the mirror. The effect is interesting. That showy and dramatic jacket with a glimpse of the angelic costuming.

Mrs. Wallace walks up behind me and plops a hat on my head. It's a low top hat, made of the same multicolored fabric. It seems intentionally small, and she has to fasten it in with pins.

"There," she says when she's done.

I look in the mirror. "Huh."

"Are you done caterwauling now?" she says.

"I am." I swing around, watching the jacket swing with me, the white peeking out through the half-fastened opening. "You know I have to ask where you got this hat and jacket."

"From the circus, of course. Now we are going to need Simon to drive us. You cannot walk about like that. Let me dress, and we shall be off."

Gray joins us in the coach. He isn't happy about the prospect of leaving me with Queen Mab. At first, he'd only been disappointed that he couldn't go along. Now, as night falls, he's concerned about what I'm doing and the fact that I'm not doing it with someone he trusts to have my back. Oh, he trusts Mrs. Wallace. He's even seen her teaching Isla and me how to use a knife, so he knows she's capable of defending herself in a dangerous situation. But *will* she defend me? That is the question, and while I tell him there's nothing to worry about, I'm lying through my teeth.

If we run into trouble, I have absolutely no expectation of Mrs. Wallace's help. The most I can hope for is that she won't use the chaos of a fight to slide a blade between my ribs.

I have Catriona's switchblade. I also don't expect to need it. Queen Mab isn't going to take me any place where I might be shivved and tossed onto a trash heap. That would be bad for business.

I understand Gray's concern, and I do wish he could join us. With that being impossible, I appreciate that he promises he won't try to sneak after us . . . or ask Simon to do it for him. In the past, he has sent Simon to secretly watch Isla's back and mine. It's the "secretly" part that's the problem. We have agreed that he will instead make his concerns known and, if he strongly disagrees with my assessment of danger, he can insist on sending Simon or coming himself. It's a difficult line to tread for a Victorian man, and I appreciate his restraint.

Queen Mab wants to meet near the entrance to the vaults. To understand Edinburgh's "underground," one needs to understand how the city was constructed. For centuries, with the Flodden Wall around it, the only way to build was up. There are areas where new buildings were just constructed over old ones. Literally over them. Edinburgh being a city of hills makes that easier. What is considered underground actually lies above ground level. It's just underneath the city.

The vaults mostly come from another bit of historical reconstruction.

The Old Town is, well, old. And mostly impoverished. If you're traveling from the New Town and you want to get past the Old Town to the wealthier areas on the other side, you don't want to actually have to go into the slums, right? Yuck. All that filth and poverty and reminders that some people are living in homes you wouldn't consider fit for your livestock. No, what you need is a road that goes over those icky parts. Thus the South Bridge was built.

Under that bridge there are vaults. Mazes of rooms and corridors that eventually proved unfit for storing goods, but perfectly fine for storing people, namely those desperate for free shelter. The vaults are also a place for black-market trade, and so it's not surprising that the underground market will be there.

Simon takes the coach over the bridge and then down to where we're to meet Queen Mab. It's a dark street where I wouldn't walk by myself at this time of night. Hell, I might not even walk it with Gray. It's both too empty and not empty enough. Too empty to make a mugger think twice, and yet in every dark shadow, I catch the movement that tells me people are there, people who don't want to be seen.

When Gray raps on the coach roof, Simon only slows Folly, as if he's not sure he really wants to stop. He finally does and calls back, "Are you certain this is the place, sir?"

"It is," says a voice from the shadows.

Through the window, I see Queen Mab step out. She's making no effort to disguise herself in shabby clothing. Quite the opposite. She's wearing a gorgeous scarlet wool cape with black embroidery and silken tassels along the hem. Underneath, I can see a green and gold dress. She has a boy with her, of no more than thirteen. We've seen him before. I don't know his name, though we suspect he is a relative, maybe grandson or great-nephew. I peer into the shadowed alley, but there's no one else with her. Just the boy.

Simon hops down to open the door, but Gray is already swinging it wide.

"I am not staying," Gray says to Queen Mab as he alights first. "Though if you have changed your mind on that, I would happily do so. You do not seem to have a proper guard."

The boy bristles, and Queen Mab's hand lands on his arm.

"I meant no offense," Gray says to the boy. "Only that I expected multiple guards."

"To bring a guard would suggest I need one," Queen Mab says. "As if I cannot trust my reputation to keep me safe. Gustav here is quite capable of fighting, should the need arise, and I have heard Miss Mallory is as well. We—"

She stops as Mrs. Wallace gets out the coach, Gray helping her down.

"Well, hello, Paulina," Queen Mab says. "I did not expect you. You are part of Dr. Gray's household?"

"His housekeeper."

"Really? I have wondered where you ended up. I should not be surprised."

"I will be joining you," Mrs. Wallace says. "I do not trust Mallory in this. Or in anything."

Queen Mab's brows shoot up. Then she laughs softly. "You always did say what you think."

"It's easier."

Gray sighs. "I respect Mrs. Wallace's opinions, but I assure you that I trust Mallory implicitly. I do not know how much you understand of Mallory's past . . ."

"That she used to be a demon with an angel's face?" Queen Mab says. "A ruthless thief who double-crossed everyone she met?"

Simon makes a small noise. He'd been Catriona's friend, and—as far as I can tell—the one person she'd never betrayed.

Queen Mab continues, "Then there was an incident, a near-death experience during which the girl struck her head, and now we have Miss Mallory instead, who is neither angel nor demon, but something far more interesting. An enigma."

"Wrapped in a mystery," I say. "If Mrs. Wallace can join us, I'm fine with it. I understand that she doesn't trust me, and I accept that, as Catriona, I gave her reason for that."

I think I'm being reasonable, but Mrs. Wallace's hard look says she hears only mealymouthed platitudes, and she isn't falling for them.

I let Gray help me out of the coach. Once I'm in Simon's lantern light, Queen Mab says, "Oh, my. Now that is a bit of clever costuming."

"Do I look a delightful confection?" I say with a half twirl of my skirts.

"You look like a fairy changeling, ready to shed her colorful skin and play the role of a sweet human child. Clever indeed. Also appropriate, in light of your transformation. I commend your ingenuity and your sense of humor."

"It was Mrs. Wallace's idea."

"Then I commend hers."

"It's not too showy?" I say.

Queen Mab looks pointedly down at her own outfit and arches a brow.

"All right," I say. "Showy is good, I take it."

"*Interesting* is good, as is that sense that it suggests one is more than one appears. Your costuming is perfect. I presume you brought the hand?"

I lift a carpetbag. She waits until I open it. Then she lifts it out for a closer look.

"It is indeed authentic," she says. "Yes, this will do nicely. Now, Dr. Gray, while I know you long to accompany your fairy changeling, I am going to need to ask you to leave with your coach. It is not safe here. I will see that she is properly returned home in my own conveyance."

Gray nods. He murmurs, "Be careful," to me and then, louder, "If she is not back by two, I will return. That is no threat, ma'am, only a precaution, in case anything befalls you both in there."

"Nothing will befall Miss Mitchell while she is under my protection. Come along then, ladies. We have a goblin market to infiltrate."

TWENTY-SIX

We head up the alley, which is pitch black. Young Gustav lights a match, but that is all the illumination we get. More than once I hear scuttling in the shadows, and I suspect it's something much larger than a rat. Finally, we reach a metal door. Liquid drips down it, forming an ice-crusted puddle that I gingerly avoid.

Queen Mab raps twice. A peephole grinds open, metal on metal. Then the door unlatches.

"Quickly," Queen Mab says to us.

She enters first, lifting her skirts over the stairs. I follow, then Mrs. Wallace. Once Mrs. Wallace is in, the door shuts and I hear Gustav, still outside, checking to be sure it's latched.

Only once that door is closed does a lantern hiss to life.

"Your Majesty." The voice sounds like that metal peephole opening, a deep grinding. I can't see the speaker. He has the lantern positioned so it casts a near-blinding glare on us and obscures himself. "You have brought guests."

"Yes, and you are being most politic, not demanding immediate explanations. That is appreciated."

"I would not demand them of you, my lady. But I must ask, all the same."

"And I will happily answer. The caution you show toward us is the same caution that protects us. I would like to introduce my young friend, Miss Cat. I bring her tonight because she is seeking a special ingredient for a cure, one I do not provide. In return, she has brought something of interest."

Queen Mab motions for me to open the small carpetbag. I take out the Hand of Glory. The guard grunts in appreciation.

"Authentic, as you can see," Queen Mab says. "I hope this item—along with my own seal of approval—will be enough."

"And the other lady?"

"Miss Cat's governess. My friend, as you can see, is quite young, and she requires governing."

I bite my lip to keep from snorting. That's a good way to describe the situation. Mrs. Wallace is indeed here to "govern" me.

"May we proceed?" Queen Mab asks, with all the concern she might display asking whether she may remove her hat, certain her request will be granted.

"Certainly, my lady. Enjoy your evening, and I bid fair welcome to your young friend. She will brighten the gloom nicely."

I swear Mrs. Wallace sniffs. I only give a half smile and incline my head toward the voice in the shadows.

There's another grinding creak, this one an interior door constructed of even heavier metal. It opens into absolute darkness. Queen Mab strides through, and we all carefully follow. The door shuts behind us, and my heart pounds, my fingers going into my pocket for my knife as the darkness envelops us.

Then a match is struck. A hiss and another lantern is lit. This time, I can make out the shape of someone behind it, but nothing more. The figure silently heads down the corridor, and we follow.

"Silence in here," Queen Mab whispers. "Voices carry."

We do as we're told. The escort leads us down one narrow corridor and then another, along stone so cold I feel it through my boots. The ceiling is so low that Gray would need to duck. Water drips down the walls, and I remember this is why the vaults didn't work out as storage units—they weren't waterproof.

Finally, our escort stops and raps on a metal door. The process repeats. We step through into darkness, handed into the custody of another, and only once the door shuts behind us does our new escort light their lantern. This time, though, the light is barely needed. We're in a much larger stone corridor, at least six feet across, with a half-circle ceiling. Closed doors line either side. Voices tumble from the distance, and the dim glow grows brighter until we reach a wooden door with light shining through the slats. Our shadowy escort half bows and opens the door, and we step into the market.

The first thing I see is light. The flickering glow of candles and hearth fires. Then the sounds—fires crackling over a steady chorus of murmured voices. I think we must still need to go through another door, because the voices are muted. Then I see figures. Lots of figures.

The room is cavernous. One of the larger vaults, I presume, with double-height ceilings. There are dozens of people, yet the voices don't rise above a murmur.

I start to step in and stop abruptly. My gaze swings down. There, on the stone floor, is some kind of mystical symbol drawn with soot and chalk. And we're walking over it.

"Is that . . . a problem?" I say, looking down.

Queen Mab chuckles. "Only if you believe in magic. Do you believe, Miss Mallory?"

I hesitate, and she looks over sharply.

"Well, that is interesting," she murmurs. "You strike me as a young lady who would have no patience with such things. I was teasing, and yet you hesitate." Her dark eyes bore into mine. "Had a mystical experience yourself, child?"

I give myself a shake. "It just unsettled me, that's all. My family was superstitious. Can't help picking up a bit of that."

Her piercing gaze calls me a liar, but she decides not to pursue it, only saying, "That symbol is supposed to compel you to be honest in your deal-ings. It is only a problem if you do not intend to be . . . and if you believe in such things." Her voice lowers. "Which I do not."

I nod, still unsettled as I follow her in. Do I believe in magic? I'd say no, and yet I'm walking in a world that existed over a hundred years before I was born. What is that, if not magic?

I shake it off and look around. What strikes me next isn't the sights or sounds. It's the smells. I catch dozens of them, coming from every direc-tion, faint scents that have me sniffing the air like a bloodhound.

Queen Mab gives me a quizzical look.

"I'm trying to place the scents," I say. "Some are familiar, but I can't name any of them."

She inhales. "Myrrh and frankincense oil, always popular at this time of year. Also aniseed and . . ." She lifts her chin, taking a deeper breath, and then makes a face. "Now that smell I would know anywhere. Someone has cheese fruit."

"Cheese fruit?" I say. "I like cheese, and I like fruit."

"You most assuredly would not like this. It is also known as vomit fruit."

"Yum."

"It is a starvation food in the tropics, meaning it is only eaten if one is starving. It is also said to have medicinal properties, which is why it is here, but I have never found it useful myself."

As we walk, people glance over. No one does anything as indiscreet as turn around, much less gawk, but by the way they quickly look away, I get the sense that even those subtle glances are considered rude.

Most gazes go to Queen Mab. They recognize her, and they nod, even bow or curtsy. When they see me, their interest sharpens. Something new. Something interesting, as Queen Mab said. Whispers trail in our wake.

"You are causing a stir, my dear," she murmurs. "Excellent."

"May I look around?" I whisper. "I'm dying of curiosity, but I don't want to stare."

"And you should not. Discretion is key. You may look, though. Keep your chin up, and let your gaze sweep about you, as if you are simply taking it all in."

Mrs. Wallace has been silent behind us, and I look back, but she has her gaze forward and her expression impassive.

I do as Queen Mab suggested. I survey my surroundings like a princess, curious but taking this in as if it is rather commonplace.

It is not commonplace. What I see around me is part smoky dive bar and part mystical fairyland. The fires mean there's plenty of smoke, and only a small hole for it to escape . . . somewhere. That leaves the ceiling a low-hanging cloud of swirling fog that slips down to wreath the tops of rickety wooden market stalls. Candles flicker from scores of candelabras. Some burn red and orange, while others dance with mystical flames of green and blue and white. When a dark shape flies overhead, I nearly drop to the floor. A raven lands on the post of a stall and eyes me with disdain.

There have to be close to a hundred people in here, half behind stalls and half browsing them. At least a quarter of the stalls are unmanned, as if their owner is among the browsers.

Underground-market attire seems to come in two varieties. So dull and dreary that the wearer vanishes into the smoke or so bright that they glitter even when that smoke swirls around them. Those who want to be noticed . . . and those who wish to disappear into the shadows.

When Mrs. Wallace slows at a stall, I fall back a step, eager for any insight into our housekeeper. I have no idea what would catch her eye, and when I find her skimming a table of *shuriken*, I'm not sure whether I'm surprised or completely unsurprised.

"Oooh, throwing stars," I say. "If I bought one, would you teach me how to use it?"

She moves on without comment, and I tell myself that if I catch her looking at anything else, I need to be stealthier.

Queen Mab has also slowed. She's eyeing a cloth covered with what looks like bits of gnarled root. When her fingers reach down to touch a root, the stall keeper tears herself from another customer and races over.

"You have fine taste, my lady," the woman says. "That comes from darkest Arabia, where the unknown plant was found growing from the footprints of a djinn."

Queen Mab looks at the shopkeeper. Says nothing. Just looks until sweat beads on the woman's forehead. Then Queen Mab murmurs, "You have mistaken your audience, ma'am," and moves on, ignoring the woman's entreaties and apologies.

Another stall catches her eye. This one is jewels, mostly raw and unpolished, some little more than cut stones showing the treasures inside.

Queen Mab looks at a few. Then her gaze settles on a stone with a sliver cut away to show brilliant green.

Again, the shopkeeper—this time a middle-aged man—hurries over.

"If you tell me it is a dragon's eye, you lose a potential customer," she says. "I have no time for that nonsense."

"Yes, my lady. I know who you are, and I would not make that mistake."

"Excellent."

She lifts the stone. The man tenses, as if he would stop anyone else. For her, he only stays tense and tries to smile as she tests the weight and lifts it to her eye and then uses a magnifying lens from her pocket.

"I might be interested in this. What sort of trade are you seeking?"

He licks his lips. "The one you have brought would do nicely."

Queen Mab glances my way. My gaze falls to my carpetbag, and my grip tightens on it.

"What I bring?" she says.

"Yes, my lady. It is a rare specimen. Priceless, in fact, and I know you are not offering it for possession, but only for the borrowing. For one evening, I would give you that stone."

"An evening with . . ." My gaze returns to the bag.

"That is not what he means." Queen Mab's voice is ice. "Although he may wish it was."

"Then what does . . ." I look up to see the man's gaze fixed on my half-bared bosom. "Oh."

When Queen Mab speaks again, her voice is cool silk. "You wish to buy my young friend."

"Borrow, for an evening. That is why she is here, is she not? For trade."

"You believe I would trade a human being? Look at me, and tell me whether you honestly think I would trade a person."

Her voice is still low, but all around us, people have gone still to listen.

"Even America no longer trades in human beings," she says. "And yet you think I would?"

"N-not trade. M-merely lend."

"Lend *her* body for *my* gain? How would that make me any different? This young woman is a friend of mine. A *friend*. That is not a polite euphemism." She meets his gaze. "You see a pretty girl and naturally presume she is for sale?"

He stammers wordlessly. Seemingly from nowhere, a woman appears, dressed in gray the color of the swirling smoke. She's on the other side of the stall, and I tense, expecting trouble, but she says to the man, "You are no longer welcome here. Pack your things."

"No," Queen Mab says. "Please do not expel him on my account. He has made a mistake and paid the price of a lost sale. That is enough."

The woman nods and melts back into the darkness as Queen Mab turns and walks away. When she realizes how fast she's moving, she slows to let me catch up.

"I apologize for the insult," Queen Mab says to me.

"You aren't the one who made it."

"Perhaps, but I should have realized that assumption would be made, purely on the grounds that you are young and pretty and female. Clearly you are what I am offering in trade tonight."

"They might have still presumed that even if I weren't female."

"Hmph. That is part of the reason I insist Gustav wait outside. I do business with these people, but it is not only the mystical leanings that keep us from being more than mere associates."

"A market for the mystical can mean a market for everything. Every taste."

"It will not happen again. Everyone who thought I brought you for that now stands corrected. I will pause my own browsing and take you where you want to be."

TWENTY-SEVEN

We keep walking until we have reached the farthest row. It only takes a glance to realize it's Medicine Lane. There's a young Asian man demonstrating acupuncture to a woman with knotted hair and dirt-stained clothing, looking like a medieval herbalist who just wandered in from the woods. At another booth, a Middle Eastern woman rubs something onto the gnarled hands of a tiny elderly man dressed in a bright green suit that screams "leprechaun" and also "arsenic." A third booth has a tent behind it, the flap drawn. I slow, curious, until a muffled gasp from within makes me jump.

"Flagellation," Queen Mab says, still walking.

"Flag . . . ?"

"Whipping."

"Oh, I know what flagellation is, but it seems more appropriate for a brothel than Medicine Lane here."

She glances over with a barely suppressed smirk. "And what would a lovely young woman like you know about such things?"

"I'm not as young as I look."

"Why do I get the feeling that's even more accurate than it might seem?" she murmurs. "In this context, the flagellation is for driving out inner demons, therefore it is medicinal. However, if you look all the way at the end, there's another closed tent specifically for women suffering from nerves and discontent. Do you want me to tell you what they're getting inside?"

"Orgasms?" I say, lowering my voice. When her brows shoot up, I say, "I've heard of that. I'm sure it does make them feel better, though self-medicating is certainly cheaper."

A sputter of laughter that turns into a cough. Only it doesn't come from Queen Mab, who's only smiling. I glance behind me as Mrs. Wallace stops coughing and fixes me with a remarkably blank stare, as if I imagined the laugh.

"You are far too clever for your own good," Queen Mab says. "Admittedly, while I do not begrudge those ladies their treatment, I am saddened to think they need to come here to get it. And saddened to think that it works. Imagine a society that has twisted basic human nature to such a degree that those women do not even recognize their dissatisfaction and longing for what it truly is, and how easily it is remedied. I am glad you do not have that problem. If you do, I would suggest you ask your in-house doctor for the remedy."

I roll my eyes. From behind me comes a sound suspiciously like a growl.

"I know you are teasing," I say to Queen Mab. "But beware Mrs. Wallace. She already believes I have my sights set on the boss's bed."

"Why shouldn't you? If I were ten years younger, I would."

"Only ten?" Mrs. Wallace murmurs.

"Only ten." Queen Mab gives her a look that dares her to challenge that. "Your employer is a handsome and virile man, but more importantly, he is clever and interesting and also considerate, which make him very likely to provide what the ladies entering that tent lack in their own lives."

"Ma'am . . ." Mrs. Wallace says, her voice laced with warning.

"Oh come now. It is not disrespectful to speak of Dr. Gray like that. If you are concerned that I am putting ideas in Mallory's head, then I would point out that you seem to think she already has those ideas. And I would counter that, even if she does, she has no intention of acting on them, sadly. I thought you a better judge of character than that, Paulina."

"I believe that is the stall you were looking for," Mrs. Wallace says, nodding to her left.

"Ah, it is. And do not think I didn't notice that sudden change of subject. Speak to me later, Paulina, and I believe we ought to make a wager on whether Miss Mallory's goal involves bedding her employer or not."

I decide to end this conversation by taking great interest in the stall. It specializes in herbs, but tiny labels in calligraphic script list things I wouldn't expect to find in Isla's laboratory, and maybe not even in Queen Mab's. Some of them I recognize, like red lotus. Others, such as a "dream herb" from Central America—*Calea ternifolia*—I don't.

There isn't anyone manning the booth, but after we stop there, a young woman approaches from her own browsing. She's dressed in an off-white gown suitable for a moderrn bride, complete with headpiece and a veil drawn over her face. Raven-black hair falls over her shoulders.

The stall keeper doesn't rush over, as the others did. As she approaches, she dips her chin and says, "Mab." I haven't heard anyone else call Queen Mab that. Even I don't mentally reduce her name. It seems too disrespect-ful. There's no disrespect in the woman's musically high voice, though, and Queen Mab inclines her own head, murmuring a greeting, as if they are equals.

"I hear you have a shipment of Egyptian blue lotus," Queen Mab says.

Through the veil, I can only make out dark eyes and bright red lips, and those lips curve in a smile.

"I do, and if you did not come this evening, I would have sent my girl around to see whether you wanted any. I admit, half my reason for buying it was in hopes of drawing you out. It has been too long."

"It has indeed. You do not need blue lotus to draw me out. I am always available to you, dear lady, to discuss herbs and medicines. In return for the lotus, I presume you wish the usual?"

"If it is not too much to ask."

"Never. I will take the lotus then, and perhaps a few other things. But I come tonight for a secondary reason. You will have noted my young friend here?"

"I have."

"She is on the trail of an ingredient you no longer carry."

The veil turns my way. "If I no longer carry it, then it is not useful."

"It *is* not useful," Queen Mab says. "She realizes that and has another reason for seeking it out. More specifically, she is interested in knowing where one might sell such an ingredient. To those who still trade in it."

"Ah. That is another thing altogether. Tell me what it is, and I will tell you whether I can help."

"She is looking for those who might purchase the remains of an Egyp-tian mummy."

"Mummia?" The woman hesitates. Then her veiled face rises sharply. "Is this in regards to the murder of that baronet?"

"I would not bring you anyone involved in a murder, dear lady. Or, perhaps more correctly, I would not bring you anyone involved in the committing of it."

Silence. I feel the veiled woman's gaze on mine, and I keep my expression open and still.

"You wish to know where someone might sell a mummy?" she says finally. "The human remains within, rather than the trappings or the mummy itself."

"Yes," I say. "If someone had those remains, would they be easy to sell? Or would finding a buyer require specific knowledge and connections?"

"It is a rare ingredient, little used these days. For it to be at all valuable, one must indeed know where to sell it. I know where you might find information on that."

"Thank you."

"That information does not come free."

"She has something to trade," Queen Mab says. "Show her, please."

I lift the bag onto the booth front and open it. The woman peers inside. She lifts a gloved hand to open the bag further, but then makes a grumbling noise, as if she still cannot quite see. Very carefully, she moves the veil. She doesn't lift it entirely. In fact, I catch only a glimpse of her neck, and I bite back an inhalation of surprise. From the high voice and the jet-black hair and the white dress, I was certain we were speaking to a woman about Catriona's age. What I see, though, is a neck so lined that she must be older than Queen Mab.

It's a disconcerting dichotomy, with that bridal gown, and my first thought is *Miss Havisham, I presume.* I bite my tongue before I say it aloud. That's a literary reference that *would* be understood . . . and not appreciated. The woman's age does explain why she greeted Queen Mab as an equal, though.

The lifted veil only reveals her neck for a moment before it drops again.

"May I remove the hand from the bag?" she asks.

Queen Mab looks about.

"Back here," the woman says, nodding to the counter behind her. "If I may."

At Queen Mab's nod, I move around the stall and set the bag on the back counter. Then I discreetly remove the hand and set it down on the cloth the woman has laid out. She moves in to block the view of anyone passing, and Queen Mab and I do the same on either side, while Mrs. Wallace stays on the other side of the booth.

The woman pokes and prods the hand with a metal probe, not unlike what Gray and Isla might use. She also employs a magnifying glass.

"I will accept this as genuine," she says. "Where did you obtain such a thing?"

Queen Mab answers for me. "It was found quite by accident, by someone who did not recognize it for what it was, but my friend here did. It has been in her possession, and when I mentioned needing something to trade, she remembered this."

The woman keeps examining it, not raising her veiled head as she says, "You should tell your employer to be more careful, child. He already has a reputation as a ghoul. Being seen purchasing such a thing would not help."

I try not to react and keep my gaze on the hand.

"I do not believe we said she was here on behalf of any employer," Queen Mab says smoothly.

The woman turns to Queen Mab. "Please give me some small credit for intelligence, old friend. I might not be a detective myself, but I can put together simple clues, enough to know I am speaking to an actual detective. Or, at least, the assistant to one."

When we don't answer, a sigh ripples her veil. "You said it was purchased by someone who did not know what it was. How many people do you think see a severed hand in a shop and declare they must have it?"

"More than you might imagine," I murmur.

"Perhaps, but I also know your question is connected to the mummy murder. You are seeking information on selling a mummy but not seeking to actually sell one. That told me I was almost certainly speaking to the young lady from *The Mysterious Adventures of the Gray Doctor*."

"The *what*?" Queen Mab says.

"Is everyone reading it?" I mutter.

"I am not," Queen Mab says. "I do not even know what 'it' is."

"Someone is fictionalizing Dr. Gray's investigations," I say. "And doing a very poor job of it, too."

The woman looks my way. "You mean your role is not to examine imaginary bits of evidence on the floor, as an excuse to put your pretty bum in the air?"

Queen Mab snorts. "Now I do need to read them." She addresses the other woman: "Does it matter who my friend is?"

"It might. While this Hand of Glory gets my attention, I could not use it myself. I would need to trade it, which is too much trouble. Also, it is an unfair trade. That hand is more valuable than my information. What I would like in exchange is what I trade with you, Mab. Except from the good doctor's sister."

I frown at Queen Mab.

Queen Mab sighs and says to me, "I offer my services as a herbalist, mixing her ingredients into concoctions that require my skill and equipment. She would be asking the same from Mrs. Ballantyne."

"I can't agree to that on Mrs. Ballantyne's behalf," I say.

"Understood," the woman says. "I will tell you how to contact me with the answer, and when I have it, I will give you what you need."

"Is there anything I can offer instead?"

"I do not think so, child, as your only skill seems to be picking up imaginary evidence off the floor, and I fear I am the wrong audience for such delights."

I can't see her face, but her tone says she's teasing. Still, I say, "I would really rather not pass on the burden for this to another."

"It will not be onerous," Queen Mab says. "She mostly wants to make Mrs. Ballantyne's acquaintance, to add a chemist to her resources."

I'm not happy about it, but it's obvious that I'm not making any other deal here, and Queen Mab seems satisfied with the one being offered. That means it's as good as I'm getting. Like she said, the hand mostly bought me credibility. It's not actually going to buy what I need.

As we're leaving, Queen Mab says, "I know you do not wish to put this responsibility on Mrs. Ballantyne, but it is not *your* responsibility to take either. You are trying to solve a murder, one a case for which Dr. Gray isn't even being paid."

I say nothing.

"You are not getting this information for your own use," she says.

"I would still rather pay for it myself."

"Which is admirable. You were reluctant to give away the hand, because it was a gift. You are reluctant to ask Mrs. Ballantyne for her services, because it is not her job. That reflects well on you. But this case is a matter of public good, and you cannot let your personal ethics interfere."

"I know, but I can still sulk over it."

We've walked a few more steps when something catches my eye. We've left the medical section and we're walking down a row with some seriously interesting stuff—like brass knuckles with tiger claws and a tiny gun worn as a ring—but I don't do more than glance at it all. I'm pissed off for good reason, and I'm not going to let any cool bric-a-brac spoil that. But then I see a table of objects that are obviously Egyptian in origin, and that yanks me out of my sulk.

As I walk over, Queen Mab murmurs, "If you are hoping to find another source for that information, I would not recommend it. The White Lady is far more reliable than this fellow."

"Artifacts have been stolen from Sir Alastair's collection," I whisper. "I would not expect them to be on the market so soon, but apparently, they aren't the first thefts."

"Ah. In that case, let us peruse."

I'd made a mental note of all the artifacts reported missing. There's nothing on the man's table that matches the descriptions. My gaze falls on a necklace that looks like the one Lady Christie wore to the party, but then I pick up subtle differences.

"Do you like that, lass?" the man behind the table says. He's not much older than me, with a greasy look that has nothing to do with the actual grease slicking back his hair. "Now that particular piece was found in the tomb of . . ."

I tune out the rest, recognizing sales-pitch bullshit when I hear it.

"It is very pretty," I say. "But I am more interested in things like paddle dolls."

At his frown, I say, "I do not know what you would call them but they are paddle-shaped pieces of wood, carved to look like stylized women, with beads for hair. They have been found in tombs and are believed to represent dancers of the god Hathor. Have you seen any of those?"

He blinks. His gaze goes from me to Mrs. Wallace, standing dourly a step away, as if guarding me. Then it moves to Queen Mab, and he gives a slight start, as if he'd been so focused on me that he hadn't realized who I was with.

"Your Highness," he says, with a tug on his cap.

Queen Mab regally inclines her chin. "Please answer my friend's questions regarding these objects, and understand that she is here with me, and also that she knows precisely what interests her and has the wherewithal to purchase it."

"Y-yes, ma'am. Of course, ma'am."

The man turns back to me. "I would be most pleased to assist in whatever you might need, lass—my lady. This represents only a small portion of my collections. I have excellent sources. Straight *from* the source, in fact." He glances around and lowers his voice. "An Egyptian chap who works the excavations."

My brows shoot up. "Truly?"

"Truly."

I let my enthusiasm dim. "I suppose that would be an excellent source for some of the simpler items, more easily obtained, but what I need is more . . . singular."

"Oh, my contact is no common workman, my lady. His sister is wed to one of the gents who runs the digs."

My heart thumps. Shit.

The man looks again at Queen Mab and fairly licks his lips. She'd said she didn't trust him, which means she doesn't deal with him. Here, he sees not only a potential sale from me, but a way to prove himself to a very powerful member of this community.

The man lowers his voice again. "In fact, I have had word that a new shipment is arriving shortly."

"How shortly?" I ask.

"I cannot say exactly. The objects were delayed between him and me. A bit of a family tragedy, with the police sniffing around and all that. But they are in a safe place, and will be retrieved soon."

"Do you know what is coming?" I ask.

"There are several objects, and I will likely receive one or two. I cannot say exactly what—I will not know until they arrive—but I can guarantee they will be far rarer than what you see here. Crowning jewels for any collection of Egyptian antiquities. If you tell me how to contact you, I can do that as soon as I have them."

Queen Mab cuts in. "Excellent. Please let us know where we might find you, and we shall reach out in a few days."

I barely notice that we're leaving the market. My brain is spinning. It seems that Selim Awad did take the artifacts, and that we've found one of his buyers. The guy said receipt had been delayed by what I presume is the police investigation. I thought the culprit had used the murder to hide the theft, and he probably did, but clearly all the police searches of the premises caused problems. Selim couldn't get them out. So where would he leave them?

In the tunnels.

That might not be the only answer, but it's the most likely one. We'll need to investigate the tunnels again in hopes of finding those artifacts before Selim can whisk them away. Wherever they are, he's not going to leave them there for long. He might even have removed them by now.

We rejoin Gustav and walk to where Queen Mab's coach is hidden. Her town house is closer than Gray's, and she apparently has another task for her driver after we've been dropped off, so she has him stop at her house first, and she takes her leave of us.

"Let me know Mrs. Ballantyne's answer, and I will act as your intermediary there," she says before she leaves.

"Thank you."

"As for that other fellow, if you need to contact him, I would do so with care, but I suspect you already have what you want."

"I likely have as much as I can get from him. Thank you, again."

We say our goodbyes, and she takes Gustav and leaves. Then the coach rolls forward again, and it's barely pulled from the curb before Mrs. Wallace says, "You think you know where those Egyptian items are hidden, don't you?"

I give a start. "Hmm?"

"The stolen goods from the Christie house. You think those are the items that lad was referring to, and you think you know where they have been stashed."

When I don't answer, she snaps, "Do not ask how I know antiquities were stolen from the Christie house. I have ears, girl, and none of you discuss your investigations in hushed tones. Half the time, I can hear you from the kitchen."

"Yes," I say. "I believe they may be the same goods, and I have an idea where they might be held."

"And now you are going to drag Dr. Gray off on a wild chase in the middle of the night."

"No," I say evenly. "I am going to convey my theory to him, and he will decide what we should do."

She snorts. "You know what he will decide. That he should go haring off with you at this ungodly hour. You think nothing of waking him in the night. You think nothing of dragging him into it."

I struggle to keep my tone calm. "I am not asking him to join me for a drink, Mrs. Wallace. This is an investigation. I have been out investigating, and I very much doubt he will have retired yet, given that he said he'd come after us if we weren't back by two. If these stolen goods are hidden, the thief will seize his first chance to recover them. Which will be tonight, after everyone has gone to bed."

"Then I will go with you."

When I open my mouth to protest, she says, "If this is truly about recovering the goods or catching the thief, you will accept me as your companion. Otherwise, it has little to do with that and everything to do with Dr. Gray."

My fingers white-knuckle the carpetbag. She's goading me. There's a perfectly good reason why I'd speak to Dr. Gray, rather than take her along. He's my damn partner on this investigation. Hell, as far as she knows, he's my boss. The lead detective.

If I say that, she'll only find fresh arguments. The truth is that I *could* take her. She'd be adequate backup, and if we don't stop at the town house, we stand a greater chance of beating the thief to the tunnels.

Do I trust Mrs. Wallace to watch my back? Not really. Do I trust her to watch the back of Gray's assistant? Yes. She'll do this for him.

"Fine," I snap. "Do you have a weapon?"

She produces a knife from her boot. Then she reaches into the pocket of her wool coat and takes out a derringer. I bite back a surge of envy. I want a gun. I've joked about it, but I'm not really joking. I know McCreadie would help me find one, but then I'd also need to learn how to use it, as I'm sure it's nothing like what I'm used to.

"Fine," I say. "I believe the thief is, unfortunately, Lady Christie's brother, who is from Egypt and worked with Sir Alastair on the digs. There are tunnels under the Christie house, and Mr. Awad definitely knows them—that's where he was knocked out the other night. He uses them to sneak in and out of the house. There are places in there where he could hide the artifacts. They were thoroughly searched yesterday, so he wouldn't expect the police to look in there. Does that make sense given what you heard?"

"It does."

"Then I guess we're giving the driver a new destination."

TWENTY-EIGHT

It took me a moment to decide where the driver should drop us off. Too close and it could draw attention to us entering the tunnel. Too far and, well, it's not late enough yet for me to stroll through the streets of the New Town dressed in a multicolored frock coat and top hat.

I settle for having him stop a couple of streets away, and we alight as quickly as we can and then get into the shadows before he pulls away. I draw my coat tight to hide my blindingly white dress and then hurry to the shed that marks the entrance to the tunnels.

I reach for the door, and there's a massive new lock on it.

Without a word to Mrs. Wallace, I take out a hairpin, bend, and . . .

The lock is open. Oh, it *looks* as if it's shut, but the shackle hasn't been pushed down. Someone has left it like this so they can get back in without it appearing open. Someone who had access to a key . . . but didn't count on having it for long.

I find a hiding spot for my carpetbag. Then I pull a box of matches from my pocket. I light one and show Mrs. Wallace the ladder before I position myself and put out the match as I descend. Only once I'm at the bottom, where no one will see the light, do I strike another match.

I move into the tunnel. I don't wait for Mrs. Wallace. If she insists on coming, she can either keep up or bring her own damned matches.

To give her some credit, she doesn't grumble. Or, if she does, it's silent.

She follows right behind me and when I glance back, she has her derringer in hand. Better yet, it's not even pointed at me.

I relax a little and begin my search. I check the partial passage where we found Selim. Nothing there. I check others. None go beyond six or seven feet deep, and when I find one that seems to have been destroyed by a collapse, I wriggle partway into a crack between timbers, only to find a solid wall of dirt behind it.

I check another dead end that seemed to be the victim of structural collapse and find the same thing. As Gray suggested, these were almost certainly test runs, where those building the tunnel headed in one direction or another, only to find that it wasn't a good spot to dig.

Not an old system of tunnels then, but a single one.

We haven't determined the nature of the tunnels. Lady Christie knew of them, and said that, despite what the children thought, Sir Alastair knew of them, too, but hadn't used them since he was a boy.

McCreadie's investigations have revealed that no other houses on this street have subbasements. That suggests the one under Sir Alastair's house was built for this tunnel. An exclusive secret passage just for the occupants.

It must be a smuggling tunnel. For getting illicit lovers and shady business partners in and out of the house? Or for transporting illegal goods? Whatever the original purpose, they've been co-opted by the children and Selim . . . and the killer.

I continue my search. I'm nearly out of side passages when I reach another one that looks collapsed, with a gap big enough to crawl through. I crouch and shine my match inside. Deep in the hole is a burlap bag.

"There's something there," I say as I pass the match to Mrs. Wallace. "I'm going to crawl inside."

I'd love to take the match, but the hole is too small to crawl with it in my hand, and I don't trust this outfit to be fireproof.

I remove the frock coat. Then I hike my skirts and tie them awkwardly, in hopes I won't drag them through the dirt and ruin them.

Mrs. Wallace only watches. When she doesn't complain, I presume she doesn't care what I do to the dress. After all, it's really not a dress at all but undergarments. Still, I don't want to give her any reason to grumble.

I get down onto my hands and knees and crawl past the half-broken barrier between the tunnel and the solid ground beyond. What I discover past it is a hole dug into the earth, just over two feet in diameter.

It's a tight squeeze for me. Was this something the children dug while they were bored? Or a hiding spot for smuggling tools and goods, hidden before that barrier broke?

I'm in past my hips when I can finally touch the burlap sack. I tug, but it sticks. A bigger tug has it coming free and, even in the dark, I can tell it's empty. I push it past me and then reach my hands into the spot where I'd pulled it from. I touch dirt on all sides. It's the end of this little passage, and there's nothing else there.

I squirm backward until my hips are out. "Nothing. Just an empty—"

"Stop."

I go still and whisper. "Did you hear something?" but the dirt swallows my words. I resume wriggling and something presses into the small of my back. Something hard and exactly the size of a derringer barrel.

"Are you holding a gun to my back?" I say, twisting my head so Mrs. Wallace can hear me.

The barrel presses in, answering that question. Anger surges, but I resist the urge to fight. For one thing, there's a gun pressed to my spine. For another, I have a feeling we are about to have a long-overdue conversation, one Mrs. Wallace prefers to hold at gunpoint.

"Who are you?" Mrs. Wallace says.

I sigh and resist the urge to drop my face into the dirt. "You know who I am. If you think I'm conning Dr. Gray—"

"You have them fooled, lass, but that is only because they've never met the likes of you. I have. I used to see her in the mirror."

That gives me pause. I work out what she's saying. "You're a con artist?"

"A what?"

"A grifter. A hustler."

Silence.

"You used to run confidence schemes," I try. "Trick someone into your confidence and defraud them. With the poisoning-ring case, Mrs. Ballantyne said she was going to talk to an expert. The next time I saw her, she was coming up from the basement. I thought she'd returned from her visit and gone down to speak to you about dinner. But it was you she was talking to, wasn't it?"

"I have run more schemes than you could imagine, and the only reason I was caught was because I trusted someone who was not nearly as skilled at them. I know a confidence scheme when I see one. Some are short and quick, but the most profitable ones go on so long that those involved are thoroughly fooled."

"And my intention is to become Dr. Gray's mistress, at which time, he will shower me with gifts. Like severed hands and medical journals."

"You scoff, but that hand is very valuable. It is also such an odd item that no one would ever suspect your motives, the way they might if he gave you fancy rings and jeweled hairpins. And he *did* give you a ring. You are wearing it tonight. Yet, again, because it is a joke between you—a poison ring—there is an excuse for accepting it. You were very pleased with the ring, and now you are pleased with the hand, and so he will continue to find things that please you, because you might say you are not wooing Dr. Gray, but he is wooing you, and that is all that matters."

My snort sends dirt into my nose, and I cough so hard I half expect to jostle the trigger on her gun. "That would be the oddest sort of wooing."

"An odd wooing for an odd girl."

I sigh again. "Yes, I'm odd. Dr. Gray finds that interesting because he's not exactly average himself. When I hit my head—"

"Tell that lie one more time, girl, and I will smash this pistol on your kneecap."

I hesitate. For one thing, my kneecaps are on the ground. For another, a smack might break that pistol. Still, I get her point. She's angry, and she believes the only way to get honest answers is to threaten me.

"So you think I'm still Catriona," I say.

"No, I do not think you are Catriona at all. There is too little of Catriona in you, and too much that does not make any sense. You speak words I do not understand. I have looked in Webster's dictionary, and they are not there."

"It's the blow to my—"

"Stop. You will answer my questions satisfactorily, or I will leave you in this tunnel nursing a bullet wound. I will not kill you. Not unless I decide you are a threat to anyone in our household. But I will shoot you and lock the garden exit, and you will need to go through to the Christie house and explain what you are doing in their tunnel. If you say I shot you, I will lie. I am excellent at it. You, however, are not."

"I—"

"Tonight, you made jokes about that tent for women. Catriona might have been a demon, but she was as prudish as an old maid. Yet you speak like that as if it is the most natural thing."

"Maybe because I realize—in my new mind—that it is."

"Catriona would not even know what an 'orgasm' was, much less be able to speak of it. You know many things she did not. She could not read, and I once heard her tell Simon that words muddled, and so she never learned. Yet you can."

"Because I was taught, and that knowledge—"

"You are *not* Catriona. You do not speak like her, think like her, walk like her, gesture like her. There is nothing of Catriona in you except your face, and therefore the explanation is obvious. You are her twin sister. If not, then you are a very close relation who looked enough like her to pass as her."

"After being found unconscious in an alley? Where is Catriona then?"

"I believe she is the one who attacked you. You met with her. Perhaps she demanded something. She strangled you and thought she had killed you, and that went too far even for her. So she exchanged clothing with you and fled, leaving everyone to think she was dead."

"That is . . . elaborate."

"Are you mocking me?"

I try to wriggle again, but she only digs in the gun barrel.

"I'm not Catriona," I say. "Does it matter who I really am? Whether I'm here with an addled mind? Whether I'm her twin sister taking her place? Whether I'm a fairy changeling? What matters is that I have no ulterior motive, and if you discover otherwise, you're free to take any necessary steps to protect your household. Also, as I've told Alice, if I ever become Catriona again, I want you to warn Mrs. Ballantyne and Dr. Gray immediately, so they get her the hell out of your lives."

"You realize you do not even *sound* like a proper Scottish lass."

"Because I curse."

"No, because of how you talk. The patterns of your speech are wrong. You will usually find correct ones when you address me, but you do not bother when you think you are alone with Dr. Gray or Mrs. Ballantyne. Now that I have you at gunpoint, you have slipped out of them again. Whatever story you have told the mistress and the master, it means they do not question your oddities, whether in your speech or your mannerisms or your ideas. I want the story you gave them."

"I gave them the truth." I pause, and then I go for it. "And that's going to have to be enough for you."

"I beg your pardon?"

"You know they are intelligent people. Yes, they are kindhearted, and someone could use that to take advantage of them. They might also be a little sheltered and naive. Dr. Gray can be easily distracted. But do you honestly believe that if I gave them a preposterous story, they would accept it without investigating? They're scientists. That's what they do. They challenge theories."

"So your story is preposterous?"

"Is that really all you got from that little speech? Of course it's preposterous. Slightly less than your changeling theory, but more than your identical twin or doppelgänger one."

"Doppel . . ."

"Germanic folklore to describe someone who looks exactly like you. In the lore, it's an evil spirit. In common parlance, it means someone who just happens to look like you, which is actually more possible than you might think. There are only so many combinations of the DNA that make up our physical features, and people who aren't related *can* look alike. There's a theory, mostly urban legend, that everyone has a doppelgänger out there. As for how I know about the German lore, it's the same way I recognized the Hand of Glory. Reading. I like the weird stuff. Always have. Helps to have overly indulgent parents with an academic bent, who encouraged their only child to study anything she likes, however strange. Kinda wish I'd studied history more, though. It'd sure be helpful now."

I'd done the same thing with Isla, bombarding her with information that she'd struggled to process, in hopes it would make my story easier to handle.

"You're right, Mrs. Wallace. I'm not Catriona. However, if you know any physical trait that would separate her from a twin—scar or such—tell me where it is and I'll show it to you. This is her body. I'm just not her."

Silence.

I continue, "I'd like you to just trust that Mrs. Ballantyne and Dr. Gray know my story and accept it, however unbelievable it is. So does Detective McCreadie. Three people who aren't going to swallow anything without testing it from every angle. They accept it. Now, can we please finish searching? I'm no threat to your employers. I'm only here to help them, and if I haven't proved that by now, I don't know what else I can do."

"Tell me who you are." The barrel drives into my tailbone. "Now."

"We're really doing this?" I settle back on my haunches. "Fine. My name is Mallory Elizabeth Atkinson. I'm thirty years old. Born March 20, 1989, in Vancouver. My parents are Scottish. Mom came to Canada after she went to university here in Edinburgh. She's a lawyer—a barrister, you'd call it. Dad's family emigrated . . . well, around now, actually. He grew up in Vancouver. He's a university professor. English lit. Especially the Victorian era, which is about all the insight I get into this world."

I try to glance back, but I can't see her. "There. Is that weird enough for you? I'm from the future."

Silence.

I continue, "If you want to test me, can we do that later? I'm not going anywhere. Kinda stuck here, in the body of a Victorian housemaid who was a really nasty piece of work. Seriously, if she ever shows up again, get her out of the house. She's probably a sociopath. I've met a few. In my world, I'm a cop. A detective, like Hugh McCreadie."

"And how did you end up in Catriona's body?"

"You want that part, too? Fine. My world. 2019. My grandmother is dying." My voice hitches there, but I push on. "I was sitting vigil in her final days. After she fell asleep, I slipped out for a jog—running for exercise. I needed to get away. Clear my head. It was late at night, but hey. I'm a cop. I can handle myself, right? I hear a woman in trouble. I run into an alley in the Grassmarket. I see what looks like the image of a young woman in Victorian dress. Catriona, as I realize now. I thought it was some kind of macabre tour video. This young woman was being strangled. At that same moment, I got grabbed by a guy who'd been stalking me. He strangled me as she was being strangled in the same spot a hundred and fifty years earlier. I woke up in her body, and I'm really—really—hoping she didn't wake up in mine, conning my family—"

There's a thud behind me, as if she's rocking back hard. The gun is gone from my lower back.

"Does that mean I can come out?" I say.

No answer.

Someone else might be rendered speechless, not sure how to even answer such a preposterous story. But that's not Mrs. Wallace. She'll have lots to say, and I might find myself locked in this tunnel while she decides what to do with me.

Either way, she's no longer holding a gun to my ass, so I'm taking full advantage. I start reversing out when hands grab the back of my dress and haul me.

"Hey!" I say, twisting.

My hand moves to plunge into the coat pocket for the knife. Except I'm not wearing the multicolored coat. I'm wearing the equivalent of under-things, which have no pockets.

I'm being dragged from this narrow tunnel, fingernails scraping the ground on either side as if I can stop myself. I can't stop myself. I can only prepare to fight like hell once my attacker hauls me out—

Hands grab my hair and rip so hard I scream, my head jerking back. I kick and twist to punch, but my attacker has my hair wrapped around their hand. Something soars over my head in a blur. A cord cuts into my throat, and my brain goes wild, torn between raw animal panic and dis-belief.

You're hallucinating. You're mistaking something brushing against your neck for a rope, and you're panicking when you need to be fighting.

There cannot be a cord around my throat. I just explained to Mrs. Wallace how I got here, saying I'd been strangled by a rope, so this cannot be happening.

Except it is happening. My hands fly to my neck and catch the cord. A smooth silken cord.

Mrs. Wallace is killing me. I told her my story, and she's decided I'm a madwoman, and she needs to protect her family from me. I'd claimed to have been strangled, so that's what she's doing to me. A fitting end.

I wedge my fingers under the cord. A foot slams down on my back, so hard that pain rips through me. I'm on my knees, being lifted aloft by the cord around my throat, the foot on my back now a knee pressing me down, keeping me from fighting.

I *should* be able to fight. I don't know whether I could beat Mrs. Wallace in a brawl, but I'm strong enough to fight back. Yet I can't do more than grip the cord around my throat, that knee plus the cord giving me no leverage however much I struggle.

I manage to twist, trying to see Mrs. Wallace, to let her see my face, to hope she might not be able to murder me if she sees my face.

A makeshift torch that Mrs. Wallace stabbed into the earthen wall illuminates the darkness, but it's a poor light, with a sputtering flame. When the knee slams into my back, my head jerks down and I see Mrs. Wallace . . . lying on the ground behind me.

I also see the legs of the person hauling me out. Two trousered legs set in a wide stance.

The thud I heard was Mrs. Wallace being knocked out.

Knocked out? Or murdered?

I can't worry about that. I just need to fight. Selim must have come to retrieve his artifacts and found us here, and I underestimated the danger.

Hands grab mine and wrench them from between the cord and my throat. I twist again, looking up, and I see a face over my shoulder. A face set in a twisted mask of determination.

It's not Selim's face.

It's Lord Muir's.

I see his face . . . and then I don't see anything at all.

TWENTY-NINE

I wake gasping and grabbing for my throat. When my fingers touch fabric, I panic, thinking it's the cord. Then I realize I'm touching bandages, and I'm not lying on the cold dirt of the tunnel floor. I'm in a bed.

I exhale and relax.

Lord Muir didn't kill me. Someone stopped him. Mrs. Wallace woke up or someone came into the tunnel and Muir fled, and I'm at the town house, recuperating. My eyelids feel leaden, but I crack them open to catch a sliver of dark curling hair and brown skin.

"Duncan," I croak.

My voice is strange. From the strangulation, I guess. I force my eyes open another fraction, looking up at the face . . .

At the face that does not belong to Duncan Gray. It's a man I don't recognize. I struggle up.

"Whoa, whoa!" the man says. "Easy now, Ms. Atkinson." He smiles. "Glad to see you're back in the land of the living, but you need to take it easy."

He has a thick Scottish brogue, but it's wrong. The cadence, the word choices, the phrasing.

Then I realize exactly what the man said. What he called me.

Ms. Atkinson.

I bolt upright and stare at the man in scrubs, a gleaming modern hospital room behind him.

I've returned home.

I'm in my own time.

No, no, no. I have to get back. I have to see whether Mrs. Wallace is all right. I have to tell Gray who attacked me. I need to . . .

I need to . . .

The thought sputters out as something floods through my veins. It should be relief. I am home. I am finally home.

It's not relief.

It's horror.

My shock knocks me back onto the bed, my horror mingling with overwhelming guilt.

All these months of desperately wanting to go home, and now that I am here, all I can think is that I want to go back.

I rub my eyes. It feels strange, as if I'm moving a body that's not mine. Except it is mine. I look down and see my hands, my arms, and they are as foreign to me as Catriona's had been six months ago.

I don't notice the doctor leaving. I'm only dimly aware that the room has gone silent. Then the door bursts open.

"Mallory!"

My mother rushes through, with my dad right behind her. She grabs me in a crushing hug . . . and I fall against her and start to cry.

The next half hour passes in a blur. I'm in shock, not quite able to believe that I've come home. I don't ask any questions. I just hug my parents and cry on their shoulders and hug them some more.

"I don't think I've gotten this many hugs from you since you were a little girl," Dad says as I lean against him, inhaling the familiar smell of his aftershave. "I could get used to this again."

I hug him fiercely, my eyes filling.

"Hey, now." He takes my chin in his hand and wipes away my tears, and I see his own eyes misting behind his glasses. "You're okay, sweetheart. Everything is okay."

I blink past the fog of shock and force my brain to begin working again, processing that I'm in a hospital.

Have I been in a coma for six months?

My fingers reach to touch the bandages at my throat. When I talk, it hurts, meaning I wasn't strangled six months ago.

"How long—?" My voice rasps, and I try again. "How long have I been out?"

"Since the night before last," Mom says.

"The night before . . . ?"

"You'd gone for a jog and someone tried to . . ." Mom's voice catches. "Tried to . . ."

"Strangle me," I whisper. "That was the day before yesterday?"

Mom nods.

It's been less than forty-eight hours since I left.

"And I've been unconscious ever since?" I ask.

Mom and Dad nod in unison.

So Catriona was never in my body. I was attacked and found, and my comatose body was brought to the hospital, and then Mom and Dad arrived—

My head jerks up. "Nan. Is Nan . . . ?" I swallow. "Is she . . . ?" Another harder swallow. "Am I too late?"

Mom's gaze drops, and I wait for the dreaded answer.

"She doesn't have much time left," Dad says gently. "But no, you aren't too late."

"I need to see her. Now."

I'm heading to the hospice. Mom's driving because we're in a hurry and Dad's "left side of the road" driving skills are even worse than my own. Dad had crawled into the backseat of the very tiny rental car, and I was too numb to balk.

My grandmother is alive. I'm not too late to say goodbye, and that is a dream come true except . . .

Except that it means the past six months have been nothing but a coma dream. Isla, McCreadie, Alice, Simon, Mrs. Wallace . . . and Gray. All figments of my sleeping brain.

That's the only explanation. I've been unconscious in a hospital bed while my brain told me this wild and wonderful story.

And none of it is real.

None of *them* are real.

I can't even hold on to a shred of hope that I really traveled through time, because the ending proves it was just a dream. I'd been in a tunnel, held at gunpoint by Mrs. Wallace, and I'd literally just finished telling her how I got there when I was strangled again and ended up back in my own time.

It is as if my brain knew it was about to wake up, and it had to finish the story fast, so it came around full circle to the beginning.

I want to curl up in a ball and sob for something I've lost. Something I never actually had.

My brain only wanted to entertain me while I slept, and instead, it feels like a betrayal. Like those dreams where I finally got on the major-crimes squad or I met an amazing man or discovered the doctors had been wrong about my grandmother's cancer. It's waking up to the disappointment of realizing my dream-come-true was only an actual dream.

I look back and poke at the oddities and tell myself those prove it was fake. I just happened to land in a progressive family? People I would like as friends? A suffragette chemist and her forensic-scientist brother and their police-detective friend? That should be proof enough that I dreamed it. Pass through time for real, and I'd have ended up the wife of a lout who spent every cent on booze while I worked my hands raw and popped out squalling children.

I had fallen into a fantasy Victorian life. But even knowing that, it *still* feels real.

When we reach the hospice, I gather my grief and stuff it away for later. Nan is still alive. I've spent what felt like six months thinking I'd missed her last days, and I hadn't.

How many times did I imagine walking these halls, seeing Nan's door ahead, my step quickening as I realized I wasn't too late after all.

I find my smile then. I head down that hall, walking and then striding and then breaking into a run that has my dad laughing behind me. I wheel into the room, and she is there. A tiny woman on a huge bed, surrounded by flowers and books and half-eaten boxes of chocolates.

I run in, and she's resting with her eyes closed. They open, slowly at first and then popping wide as her face lights in a smile, arms reaching for me.

"Mallory," she says, and I burst into happy tears as I run to embrace her.

It's evening. I'd arrived around lunchtime, and Mom made me go out to dinner with Dad. Now I've come back, and we've made Mom go out for a late dinner with Dad. My father is never one to turn down multiple meals.

Nan has been asleep since I got back, and I'm trying to read one of her books, but I haven't turned a single page. I'm actively avoiding thinking about Gray and Isla, which is taking all my mental energy, like holding back a dam.

"What's wrong?" Nan's voice says softly.

I startle from the fake-reading to see her watching me intently.

"You're doing an excellent job of hiding it, as always," she says. "You and your mother put on a good face until you think no one's watching, and then it falls away."

I stand and roll my shoulders. "Tired, I guess, despite sleeping for two days straight."

"There's something else. Something making you sad."

I tap the tray of pills at her bedside. "Huh. No idea why I'd be sad."

"There's no reason to be sad about that. I had an incredible life, and I'm ready to say goodbye. It's leaving others behind that's the hard part. What else is bothering you?"

"I . . ." I struggle for words, and then I blurt, "I had a dream. While I was in the coma."

She tilts her head, sharp eyes studying me. "One that made you sad."

I roll my shoulders again, as if I can slough off the melancholy. "It was a good dream. Weird and strange, but good, and I thought it was real and . . . and it's not, and I'm having a bit of trouble dealing with that. Which is . . ." I wrinkle my nose. "Also weird and strange."

"What did you dream?"

My lips quirk in a smile. "That I fell through time, into the body of a Victorian housemaid working for a forensic scientist."

Her eyes glitter. "Now that does sound like fun. Tell me more?"

I lift one shoulder in a shrug. "It was just a dream."

"So you'll tell me later?"

"Sure."

"How about next Tuesday? You can sit at my graveside and tell me the whole story."

I glower at her, but she only smiles back. Yep, I really did get my love of the macabre from Nan. Her death isn't something I want to joke about, but this isn't about my comfort, is it? These next few days are all about her.

"Tell me a story, Mallory Elizabeth," she says. "A story about my granddaughter falling through time." She takes a chocolate from an open box and then pops a tiny pain pill with a sip of water. "There. I'm ready. Entertain me."

I get as far as the death of Annis's husband before my parents come back from dinner. I stop there. I'm fine entertaining my grandmother with my weird dream, but I don't want to get into it with my parents. Besides, Nan is almost asleep, and the nurses come to give her a little something extra for the pain. Then Mom stays with her while I return with Dad to our rented flat, and I take the sedative the doctor prescribed because there's no way I'm getting to sleep without it.

I'm back in Nan's room before dawn, sending Mom to breakfast with Dad. Nan had a rough night. The end is coming fast, and she's putting on a good face, but I can only imagine the pain she's in. She half wakes once or twice, seeming confused, only to slip back under. She's still sleeping when Dad takes me for his second breakfast, but when I return, Nan's awake and even alert, tapping away on her iPad while Mom dozes.

"Take your wife to bed, Glen," she says to my father. "I don't want to see her again before two P.M. That's an order."

Dad smiles and gently wakes Mom and gets her out of the room. Then I take her place beside Nan's bed.

When I yawn, she glares over at me. "Do I need to send you to bed, too?"

I heft a giant coffee-chain cup. "Nope, I'm good. I haven't had a cappuccino in . . ." I trail off and struggle for a smile. "Well, three days, apparently. It just feels like months."

"About your story, I want to know more about your friend Duncan Gray."

I groan. "He's an *imaginary* friend, Nan. Like Angus when I was five. Remember Angus?"

"Dr. Duncan Gray," she says, making me groan again. "Born August 12, 1838, in Edinburgh. Son of Irvine Gray and his wife, Frances. Attended the Royal High School and then the University of Edinburgh, where he graduated with degrees in both medicine and surgery, though he was never licensed to practice."

"Because he dug up a body to confirm a theory on cause of death." I sip my cappuccino. "Are you just going to recite my own stories back to me?"

"Did you tell me his birth date, Mallory? Or where he went to school? I don't even think you told me what his degrees were in, besides being medical. As for why he wasn't licensed, you definitely didn't tell me that story, but now I want it very much."

I go still, lifting my head from my coffee cup. I stare at her. My brain is sluggish this morning from last night's sleeping pill.

Nan waves the iPad. "There's not much here, but even a non-detective like me was able to track down that much."

"I . . . I must have read about him somewhere. While studying forensics."

She reads from the iPad. "Sisters Isla Ballantyne, chemist, and Lady Annis Leslie, who took over her husband's business after his death from poisoning at the hands of . . . Well, you know who killed him, I presume, though I'm a bit disappointed to have this spoil *that* story for me."

I can't speak. My mouth is dry, my brain suddenly blank.

"Is anything I just said incorrect?" Nan asks.

I still don't answer.

"I have read you the facts," she continues. "You believe you must have stumbled over some mention of Duncan Gray and then put him into your dream, which means you imagined all the details. Which ones that I recited are wrong?"

I struggle to focus. "Wait. It said his mother was Frances Gray. That was his adopted mother in my dream."

"Yes, in your version, his father brought him home, as his illegitimate child, and his wife raised the boy as her own. Which has me thinking I would like Mrs. Gray very much . . . and would like to curse her husband to the second circle of hell. But I am reading a brief biographical note focused on his place in science, where they would not delve into the exact nature of his parentage."

When I still hesitate, she says, "Describe your Duncan Gray. What does he look like?"

I stumble over the words, spitting out bits and pieces. She turns the iPad around.

"Like this?"

There, on the screen, is Gray. He's older, maybe in his early forties, graying at the temples, but it is definitely him, and seeing that photo . . .

I burst into tears.

Even as I do, my hands fly up, covering my face in horror at the sudden outburst.

"Well," Nan murmurs, "I always did tell your mother that it would take a very special sort of man to capture my Mallory's heart. I just never thought she'd need to travel a hundred and fifty years into the past to find him."

I wipe my eyes. "It's not like—"

"It's not like that, yes, yes. He's a friend, and he's only part of the reason you were happy there. You aren't drowning in despair because the man you love is a figment of your imagination. It's the loss of everything. Which is true. It's Isla Ballantyne and Hugh McCreadie and Alice and Simon and even Mrs. Wallace. It's that world and that life. But it's also, in part, that man."

"I'm not drowning in despair."

Nan rolls her eyes heavenward. "God forbid you admit it. Or admit how you feel about a man." She meets my gaze. "A man who is very real."

"*Was* very real," I say, my voice suddenly a whisper. "A hundred and fifty years ago. What else does it say—"

"Nothing." She flips the iPad over and holds it down. "You will not look up any of that. Promise me."

"I—"

"I'm a dying woman, and I'm entitled to my deathbed promises. This is the first of two. You will look up nothing regarding Duncan Gray or anyone else you knew from that world."

"What's the second?"

"Agree to the first."

"Fine. I'll look up nothing. Now the second promise?"

She meets my gaze and holds it, seconds ticking past before she says, "That you'll go back."

THIRTY

I have spent the last hour arguing with my dying grandmother, who wants me to travel back in time after she's gone. I shouldn't argue. I should just say "Yes, Nan, whatever you want, Nan." But I'd never patronize her by making a deathbed promise I can't keep.

"Fine," she says finally, slumping against the pillow. "Let me amend that. You will *try* to go back. Whether you can or can't may not be up to you. But you will try."

I throw up my hands. "I wouldn't even know where to begin."

"We'll work on that. I had a dream last night . . ." She trails off. "Let me think more on it. For now, you need to promise me that you will try to go back."

"To the nineteenth century? Where they don't even know what botulism is? Or penicillin?"

Her lips twitch. "Is that really your biggest concern?"

"Oh, I have a lot of concerns. It's freaking terrifying, Nan."

"And you loved it." She looks at me. "You found your place there. A place where you were challenged and happy, surrounded by people who made you happy, even when they had to be prodded to scrub their hands after dissecting corpses."

I say nothing, and she lets the silence stretch.

"I'd never leave Mom and Dad," I whisper. "Can you imagine? Mom loses you, and then I'm gone, too? Her only child?"

"They thought they lost you already, Mallory," she says softly. "The doctors believed you'd never wake up."

"So now we'll tell them that I *want* to leave forever?"

"They love you. They love you *so* much. They only want what you want, what makes you happy, whatever the cost to them." She pauses and looks at me. "May I speak to them?"

"No," I say. "I'm back where I should be, where I want to be, and I'm staying."

Nan is fading fast. There are lots of whispered discussions between Mom and the doctors, conversations I am not allowed to be part of. Conversations about hurrying the end along? I know Nan had considered medically assisted death, but when the end came, it came too fast for that.

Is it too late to do anything? Too late legally . . . but too late for mercy? I have no idea what the laws are here. I only know that I don't need to be part of those conversations to understand what they are about. And even as the little girl in me screams that I want every last moment with Nan, the adult agrees that if the end can come faster, while she's lucid and the pain is controlled, then that is the truest definition of mercy.

Nan and I talk when she's awake. She wants to know more about my life in 1869. She doesn't mention me leaving again. She just wants to know more, and if it gives her something to distract her in these final days—and gives us one last secret to share—then that is the greatest blessing I could ask for.

That evening, after Nan falls into a deep sleep, I head to the rental apartment, on Royal Circus. Standing at the window, looking out at the quiet circle, I remember when I'd last seen it, strolling here with Isla. We'd walked along the Water of Leith, the same route Florence King wandered the night Sir Alastair died. We'd bought hot pies, and we were heading home when I recognized the apartment I'd rented and stopped to show it to her.

I'm looking out, smiling as I imagine us standing right under this window. Then I realize I'm not alone and wheel to see Mom there.

"I didn't hear you come in," I say.

Without a word, she walks over and hugs me. Hugs me tight, and I fall into her embrace.

"I love you so much, Mal," she says, stroking my hair. "I want you to be happy. That's all I've ever wanted."

I stiffen. "Did Nan say something?"

She doesn't answer. She just holds me even tighter, and I know my secret isn't a secret anymore. Does Mom believe it? It was one thing for Nan to accept it—the woman who claimed she didn't believe in the fair folk but also avoided stepping in mushroom rings. Convincing my defense-attorney mom? That'd be a whole other level, and I can't imagine how Nan would even try. But for now, Mom doesn't say a word. She just hugs me.

Death comes for Nan the next morning. When Mom and Dad hurry me into the room, I swear I see Death waiting by the curtains dancing in the breeze, and it's not the Grim Reaper with his scythe, but Death from the Sandman comics I devoured as a teen, gentle and kind and waiting patiently to lead my grandmother to the other side.

I expected to howl and rail at these final moments. But Nan is ready to go, and I am ready to let her go. Not ready to release her from my life—I'd never be ready for that—but ready to release her from her own.

I am calm enough to insist Mom be the first at her bedside, in case the end comes too quickly for us all to get a chance. Dad and I stay outside the room while Mom says her goodbyes. Then Dad joins Mom for a few moments.

When it's my turn, I ask my parents to stay, and they agree, just stepping aside to give Nan and me our moment together.

I say everything I've dreamed of saying since I thought I'd lost my chance. I share my most cherished memories of our time together. I tell her how important she was in my life and how much I love her, and how I regret being too busy with work to come over for more than a few days at a time.

"You came," she says. "That was all that mattered. Children grow up, and they start their own lives, as they should. But you called and you wrote and you came, and I never once wished for more."

I hug her. Then she takes my hand and squeezes with more vigor than I expect, startling me.

"I believe everyone has a place they are supposed to be," she says. "For me, it was here. I was born here, grew up here, met your grandfather here, and never left, and I counted myself lucky to have been born in exactly the right spot. Your mother's spot was across the ocean, and that hurt, but I was so happy she found it. Then I only had to wait for you to find yours. You thought you had, but it wasn't quite the right fit. You needed to find the place where you belonged, completely. A place where you could make a difference. You did. It just wasn't where anyone would have looked."

I go to speak, but her hand tightens on mine.

"You could be happy here, Mallory," she says. "And if you must be, then you will be. But your place is back there. You think it was some wild coincidence that landed you in that time, in that place. It wasn't. It was the universe correcting itself. You went to where you were supposed to be."

She reaches up for a hug, and I lean down into it, her frail arms going around me. "You will find your way back, Mallory. I've seen what you will do there, the life you will lead, and I could not be happier for you."

I hug her again and step to one side, nodding for my mom to come closer. We hold Nan's hands, with Dad coming up behind us, his hands on our shoulders. And, with a few final breaths, Nan quietly passes from this life.

The last twenty-four hours have been hell. Mom planned everything in advance, because that's my mother, but it doesn't keep there from being an endless list of things to be done—final arrangements, people to be notified, staff to be thanked—when all I want to do is find a quiet place and grieve. But then there will be a lull in the activity, and the grief is so overwhelming that I long for activity again.

Everything that can be done has been done. Mom being an only child means there isn't a cadre of relatives who need to fly in. Nan's family and friends all live locally, and the funeral will be in two days.

We're driving back to the apartment, heading down Princes Street, when Mom turns in to a parking lot.

"Let's grab something to eat."

I want to protest. It's midafternoon, and I couldn't eat even if it were mealtime. Yet I must always remember that, as much as I loved Nan, my mom has suffered the greatest loss, and if she wants to eat, we will eat.

Dad says nothing. He just gets out of the car—the passenger seat now—and takes her jacket from beside me, shakes it out and helps her into it.

Nan joked earlier about me needing to cross time to find a man worthy of me. The truth behind that joke is that it's not about me finding a "worthy" man, but finding one who might give me the sort of love, respect, and support I expect, based on my parents. They have set the bar so high that anything less is settling, and I've never settled in my life.

I lag behind to watch them, hand in hand, Dad carrying Mom's purse, as if even that would be too much of a burden for her right now.

We're on the south side of Princes Street, and I'm trying so hard not to think of all the times I've walked along here with Gray and Isla, Simon and Alice, even Annis, who dragged me there two weeks ago shopping, because Isla refused to go and I soon discovered why. Shopping with Annis was like going to a restaurant with that one friend who always sends something back. She'd—

I yank from the thought. None of that.

None of what? Memories? I've accepted that I really did pass through time, which means those aren't scenes from a dream. Am I going to box them up permanently? Hide them on a shelf in hopes I'll forget where I left them?

"I'd like to go up," Mom says.

I startle from my thoughts to realize she stopped. I follow her gaze up to see the Gothic splendor of the Scott Monument.

"Come," she says, taking a credit card from her pocket. "I'll buy tickets."

My knees lock. I look up, and I remember this past spring, Gray and me climbing the steps after dark, following our first visit to Queen Mab.

"Mallory?" Mom doesn't even look back, just waves, like I'm twelve again and dawdling. "We're going up."

My feet drag the whole way, first to get the tickets, and then climbing those steps. I hear the clang of them underfoot, and it's 1869, a warm June night—

None of that.

I steel myself and continue up while focusing on everything that screams twenty-first century. The honking cars. The trams rattling down the middle of the road. The tour buses, and the tourists, so many tourists.

Stay in this time. Don't let my mind wander. Don't remember. Don't break down.

When we reach the viewing platform, I stay by the steps, but Mom steers me to the railing. Then, as Dad moves up to my other side, Mom murmurs, "I know where you went."

I glance over sharply.

"Your nan told us everything, and she made us promise not to mention it until . . ." Her voice catches but she clears her throat. "Until she was gone. That was best anyway. I wanted to focus on her, and I also needed time to . . . process. I've been doing that, processing and investigating and trying to wrap my head around it."

"You don't need to," I say, my voice a little brusque. "It's over, and it's nothing we ever need to talk about."

"We never need to talk about something that had a profound effect on my daughter?"

"I'd rather not."

She's quiet. Dad reaches for my hand, squeezes it and holds it. We look out over the city.

After a moment, Mom says, "Every time we drive past this monument, you look up at it, and your face . . . It breaks my heart."

I stiffen. "We *really* don't need to discuss—"

"You came here, back then. Tell me about it."

I say nothing, just set my jaw, ignore the ache in my throat, and stare out.

"Mallory? Just . . . talk to me."

I shake my head. "Can we not do this? Please? You don't believe I actually traveled through time. Don't humor me. Please."

She lays her hand on mine, gripping the railing. "But I do believe. I have to."

Dad murmurs, "'When you have eliminated the impossible, whatever remains, however improbable, must be the truth.'"

My eyes fill at the Sherlock Holmes quote, but I manage to smile at him. "Pretty sure time travel is the very definition of impossible, Dad."

"Mmm, not according to some very intelligent people. People much smarter than me."

I lean against his shoulder, and before I can hold it back, I blurt, "I called Dr. Gray a consulting detective once, and now he's using it, and I feel like I owe Sir Arthur Conan Doyle a huge apology."

Dad's arm goes around me as he chuckles. "Consulting detective, huh?"

I tense as I realize what I said, and I want to pull it back, to pretend I was joking or frame it as a dream. But I let it sit there, and I listen to their breathing and try to analyze it, to tell whether they're holding back the obvious worry that their daughter seems to actually think she traveled through time.

As if reading my thoughts, Dad leans over and whispers, "We believe you, sweetheart," and my eyes fill with tears as I lean against his shoulder.

Mom's hand tightens on mine. "Now, tell me what happened up here?"

When I don't answer, she adds a soft "Please." Then, "We'd really like to know. Something happened up here . . ."

"Nothing bad," I say finally. "Not even anything big. Duncan—Dr. Gray, that's the—"

"The scientist you work for." Mom's lips twitch. "As a housemaid."

"World's worst housemaid. Well, no, I'm actually not too bad, thanks to parents who made me get work experience cleaning homes for seniors."

"Didn't I say you'd thank me someday?"

I roll my eyes.

"So you were out with Dr. Gray . . ." she prompts.

"We were passing here, and I said I've always wanted to come up here at night. So he brought me. It was late and quiet and . . ."

I gaze out and shrug, unable to find words. No, that's a lie. I can find them. Special. Magical. Enchanting. But those aren't the sort of words I ever use.

"It was nice," I say finally. "We talked about what the view was like in my time and then about . . ." My throat catches. "About me wanting to go home. That was tough for him, knowing I'd leave the moment I got the chance. He'd just gotten used to having me as an assistant, and yet he knew if I got the chance to go home, I'd snatch it. I said that didn't mean I wasn't happy there. I just . . . I had a life here, and maybe it would have been easier if . . ."

I take a deep breath. "Easier if I didn't have an amazing family I wanted to get back to."

Dad's arm tightens around my shoulders.

I continue, "Duncan said he'd never wish for me to have had a worse life."

"And then?" Dad prods.

"Well, and then someone yelled 'Murder' below, which totally spoiled the mood."

Dad pulls me over to kiss the top of my head. "I'm sure it did."

We stand there, Mom's hand on mine as I lean against Dad. When I glance at Mom, she's watching me. She says nothing, though, and we just stand there, in peaceful silence, together.

THIRTY-ONE

The funeral is perfect, of course, because Mom's in charge, and part of that means that every detail is covered, but it also means that she asked what Nan wanted and made sure she got it. The result is a Scottish funeral that's really more of an Irish wake, with lots of laughter and lots of whisky, and a parade of people telling me what a wonderful woman my grandmother was.

The next day, I'm in the rented apartment, trying to catch up on work emails, but my brain keeps turning to the mummy case. I remind myself that is not my responsibility. It's long solved, and I promised Nan I wouldn't look up anything from that time.

I'm trying not to worry about that. Did she find something in her research that she didn't want me to see? If she did, then is it something I can change? *Should* I look?

No, my gut tells me that I should not research anything or anyone from that time, if only to avoid knowing something I shouldn't, good or bad. Also, I remember Nan's final words to me.

I've seen what you will do there, the life you will lead, and I could not be happier for you.

That's good, right? Of course, it does make me wonder *what* she saw—

"Mallory?" Mom calls from the living room. "Tea?"

I walk into the room to find a full spread waiting. I take my seat at the tiny dinette with my parents, and we dig into a plate of scones with clotted cream and jam. The quintessential British "afternoon tea," even if it wasn't what Mrs. Wallace served on Robert Street.

I think of saying that, but we haven't discussed my "trip" since that day on the monument, and I've decided that's intentional. My parents let me know they accepted my truth, and we've moved on, and they aren't comfortable discussing it again.

"I've been thinking of your nan," Mom says. "Well, obviously, but about something in particular. When I told her I was staying in Canada. I wrestled with that for so long. I . . ."

She glances at my father, and then back at me. "I almost broke it off with your dad because I couldn't bear to tell my mother that her only child had moved across the ocean forever."

She reaches for my dad's hand. "That would have been the biggest mistake of my life, but it shows how upset I was. Your nan was disappointed, obviously. She'd hoped we'd move to Scotland together. But your dad's roots were in Canada, and my new roots were there, and the opportunities were there, and it was where I wanted to be. That was what mattered to her—that was where I wanted to be. There were phones and there were planes, and we'd be fine."

Mom shifts in her seat. "But that got me thinking about what it was like for families in the past. Like when your dad's great-grandparents emigrated to Canada. It was permanent. There were no phones and no airplanes and no money for monthlong steamship voyages. People went to Canada, and they never saw their families again. All communication was by letters. I couldn't imagine what that would have been like for parents. But now, having a daughter of my own, I think I understand. We want for you what my mother wanted for me—for our child to be happy and free to find her own joy. We don't raise our children to look after us in our old age anymore. We raise them to fly on their own, to soar if they can."

Her eyes meet mine, and they glisten with tears that she quickly blinks back.

"What would be keeping you here, Mallory? What would keep you from going back to 1869?"

"I can't *get* back—"

She lifts a hand. "Pretend you could. Consider this a thought exercise. Would you stay here for your job?"

I shake my head.

"For your friends? I know you have plenty, but I also know you've drifted from the truly close ones you had as a girl. Would you stay for them?"

I shake my head.

"So, imagine you could walk through that door." She points at the front entrance. "And be back in 1869. Would you do it?"

"No."

"Because of us."

I pull away. "No, it's just . . . a lot of things. It isn't my world and—"

"What if you could walk out that door, but every now and then, you could come back, and we'd be here. Would you leave then?" Her gaze cuts into mine. "Give me honesty, Mallory. Would you leave then?"

My throat closes, but I nod.

"So we *are* what would hold you back," she says, with the decisiveness of delivering the final argument in a court case. When I go to protest, she continues, "Your Dr. Gray wouldn't hold you back, would he? If he were sitting here, and that door was the way to the twenty-first century, he'd tell you to go because it's what you wanted."

I don't answer.

"You can say he just didn't want to lose a new assistant, but that's not it. That's not it at all, and yet, if the way opened, he would have told you to go. Knowing he'd never see you again, he would want you to go because he wouldn't hold you back. Your happiness is more important than any happiness you might bring him."

Her gaze locks with mine again. "It's the same for us, Mallory. We raised you to soar, and we want to see you soar . . . even if it means you leave us behind."

I love my parents for saying that. Lots of tears follow. It's a moot point—there is no door for me to walk through—but I love that they would let me go, even knowing I might never come back.

When the tears—and the tea—are done, I say, "I should call my sergeant. I need to discuss my return to work."

"Not yet," Dad says, gathering the teacups. "First, we need to try getting you back to 1869."

I look over, certain he's joking, even if a squeeze in my gut whispers it would be a cruel joke, and my dad is never cruel.

Mom makes a face and then sighs. "Don't get her hopes up, Glen." She looks at me. "Your grandmother had dreams before she died, about you and how you passed back through. She left a video for you to watch."

"With a method for returning that came to her in a *dream*?"

"I know." Mom rolls her eyes. "Mostly, I just want you to know that if it ever happens, for any reason, and you end up in the nineteenth century . . ." She trails off and takes a deep breath. "I want to have had this conversation. If you disappear or fall into a coma again, we understand where you are and you have our blessing to stay there. Also . . ." She stands. "I want to have a way for you to communicate."

"Uh . . ."

"You will take out personal notices in the papers."

Dad says, "Because, as I know from Victorian novels, personal notices were a common way of communicating."

"I will also require your name in that world," Mom says, "and any personal information you can supply."

"Well, someone's been chronicling our cases," I say. "You can just read those . . . if you don't mind seeing your daughter portrayed as a pretty and empty-headed magician's assistant."

Mom's brows shoot up.

I sigh. "We were working on putting an end to them. I'm sure there wouldn't be any trace of them these days. They were just serialized stories. *The Mysterious Adventures of—*"

"*The Gray Doctor*?" Dad says.

Now my brows shoot up.

"Your nan found a reference to it," Dad says, "in relation to Dr. Gray. She wasn't able to find any actual copies online. I can search my sources. There might be something in an academic collection somewhere."

I shudder. "I hope not. All I do is exclaim over how brilliant Duncan is and bend over to check nonexistent evidence, as an excuse for the writer to wax poetic on my ass."

"Your . . . ?" Mom says.

"Catriona is blond, buxom, and very pretty." I sigh again. "It is a trial. Useful, though, in its way." My head jerks up. "I wonder what happened to her. I thought she might have crossed into my body, but it doesn't seem she did."

Mom shrugs. "If she did, then she was not there when you woke."

"There was another coma patient," Dad muses. "It was the oddest thing. She woke up and . . ." He waves a hand. "And that has nothing to do with getting you back to the past." He smiles. "I will need to find those adventure serials, though. If only to get a laugh."

"You will," I say. "You get to see your daughter bumble about while her boss changes history."

"At least in part because he met my daughter."

I frown. "Is that a problem? Is it all a problem? All the changes I might have wrought? That damned butterfly effect?"

"Well, according to the latest quantum physics theories, changing one thing in the past would *not* have endless ramifications in our time. So you're safe there."

"But how *does* it work?" I say. "Six months passed there and two days here, which suggests separate universes. Is it the same timeline? Parallel ones that overlap?" I rub my temples. "It makes my head hurt."

"And, not being a quantum physicist or a philosopher," Dad says, "I'm not even going to try to answer that question."

"Don't look at me," Mom says. "All I can see are enough loopholes and inconsistencies to make my lawyer's brain scream."

"How it works isn't important," Dad says. "It does work. At least for you. Now, you should watch your nan's video."

"Don't get your hopes up," Mom warns. "She was on a *lot* of drugs."

Dad looks at me. "What your mom *isn't* saying is that your nan has had prophetic dreams before."

Mom snorts. "If by 'prophetic' you mean things like dreaming I made a surprise visit and then I actually did . . . a month later."

"Your nan believed she had a touch of something," Dad says, "and she thinks that might explain why you crossed over."

"So many drugs," Mom mutters. "Also, remember she was a young adult in the sixties, which meant more drugs and all that mystical counterculture nonsense—"

Dad cuts in, "Your nan also believed that, being on the cusp of passing into her next life, her dreams—which were particularly vivid—meant something. That she was seeing across the veil."

Mom continues to mutter, only half under her breath. She's never had any patience with Nan's more colorful beliefs, and when I was young she'd have Dad take me aside to explain the role of superstition and folklore in people's lives. This time, though, she only says, "I don't want to get your hopes up."

"If I stay here, I'll be fine, Mom. I expect to stay, and that's okay." I manage to say it like I believe it. "But I agree with figuring out the personal ads, in case it ever does happen."

It takes a while before I can watch the video through. Hell, it takes a while before I can even process what I'm hearing. I see Nan and hear her voice, and the grief washes over me, and not a single word sinks in. But eventually I'm able to watch, and when I can, I focus on her theory for getting me back.

Is it wrong to say I'm disappointed?

I'm struggling with the idea of going back. Struggling with *wanting* to. For six months, I've been saying my life is here.

It's rational to make plans in case I accidentally go back. But to pursue it as a goal?

I think, in some way, I like not having an actual choice, so I don't have to make it. On a deeper level, though? When I think of never going back? Of never seeing that world and those people again? I start to panic.

So when Nan says she thinks she knows a way, part of me spirals in panic . . . and a deeper part leaps in hope. Then I hear her plan.

I want her to give me magic. Do this special thing to go back. I'd even settle for the obvious answer of having someone throttle me until I pass out. Instead, what she says is too close to all the failed things I tried to bring me back to this world.

The entirety of her plan? Go to Gray's town house.

Return to 12 Robert Street, go inside, and the veil, as she calls it, will thin, and I will be able to step through.

I appreciate that she did this final thing for me. I'm also really glad she told Mom not to give me the video until she was gone, so I never had to tell her it didn't work.

When I stop the video, Mom comes in.

"I was kind of hoping for something a little more creative," I say. "Given all the drugs."

Mom chokes on her laugh and hugs me. "I know."

"Even if I did think that would work," I say, "how would I do it? Knock on a stranger's door and ask to come inside?"

Mom's quiet. When I look up, she says, "The town house is a vacation rental. A very posh vacation rental. The family renting it leaves tomorrow morning, and there's an opening."

My heart leaps with that hope before I cast it aside with a hard shake of my head. "It won't work, Mom."

"Probably not, but I've reserved it. At the very least, you can show us where you lived for six months and we'll all have a lovely night in a posh house." She pats my shoulder. "Now, your father has compiled a list of the newspapers and how best to compose Victorian personal ads."

I want to say it won't work. I want to sink into a chair and wallow in my grief over Nan and my disappointment over her "solution" and my guilt over being disappointed.

Instead, I just say, "Thank you," and kiss Mom's cheek. She hugs me again and then says, "After the personal-ad lesson, I want you to tell me about this latest case, with the mummy. See whether we can solve it together."

That night, we do indeed discuss the mummy case. Mom and I hash it out until we see Dad on his cell phone.

"Boring you already?" I say. "I thought you liked detective stories."

"I'm not sure he actually does," Mom says, "since he always skips ahead to the end."

"What?" I squawk. "Seriously, Dad?"

He looks offended. "I go back and finish the book. I only skip forward to check my answer."

"That's still cheating." My gaze goes to the cell phone in his hand. "Wait. Were you trying to skip ahead? See whether the crime was solved?"

"Possibly."

"Did you find it online?"

"It's a unique case. Got a fair bit of press at the time."

"So whodunit?" I say.

"Now who's skipping ahead?" he says, tucking his phone into his pocket. I take out my own phone, but Dad snatches it.

"No spoilers," he says. "Your nan didn't want you looking up anything about your life there. As for who was convicted, it's only a spoiler if this person actually committed the crime."

"So who was it?"

He hesitates, and then says, "Selim Awad was convicted of killing his brother-in-law and Dr. Gray's young assistant, whom he strangled in a tunnel. A week later, she died of her injuries."

The breath goes out of my lungs. "Me. He was convicted of murdering me, which made him seem to be Sir Alastair's killer, too."

Dad nods. "The housekeeper testified that you two went to the tunnel after hearing that Selim had been stealing artifacts from his brother-in-law."

Mrs. Wallace testified. That means she survived.

My father continues, "She was knocked out and you were strangled. While she didn't see your attacker, Lord Muir spotted Mr. Awad fleeing the scene."

"Lord Muir being the actual person who strangled me."

"He framed Selim Awad," Mom murmurs. "Starting with what you overheard at the market."

I glance over and then wince. "Of course. It was strange that the market seller knew so much about who was supplying the artifacts. He'd been fed a story that, if uncovered, would lead back to Selim. So what happened to Selim—?" I stop.

I know what would have awaited Selim Awad. What awaited all convicted killers in that time period.

The hangman's noose.

THIRTY-TWO

We don't solve the mystery of who killed Sir Alastair. Oh, Lord Muir tops the list, but I'd known that when I'd seen who'd been strangling me . . . in the exact same way Sir Alastair had been strangled, right down to the knee in my back.

Except Muir has an ironclad alibi, which McCreadie has verified. I still suspect he's framing Selim, but that will need to be proven. No one else makes an obvious suspect. Mom is delighted by the link to the Edinburgh Seven and fangirls over me meeting Sophia Jex-Blake, but the students' only connection to the murder is that Lord Muir seems to have been using Sir Alastair to speak out against them.

I won't say Selim's fate gives me an excuse to return to the nineteenth century. If there is a choice to be made, then I must make it, and I can't take the cowardly route, casting myself as a martyr who sacrificed her place in the world to save a near stranger. I must go back for *me*, as painful as it is to even think of leaving my parents.

That won't happen by walking into 12 Robert Street. Still, we're going to try, and the next afternoon, we're making our way down the sidewalk, pulling our luggage behind us.

Walking down Robert Street physically hurts. I can't help but think of all the times I walked it with Gray and Isla, or with Simon or Alice, heading out on errands. If I half close my eyes, I can imagine I'm with them . . . until a car rumbles past, shattering the illusion.

No one meets us at the house. It's just us and a lockbox. I push open the familiar door and unfamiliar smells roll out, and I want to back away.

This isn't Gray and Isla's house. It's a sterile rental, stinking of floor polish and disinfectant. It's like a family home after everything has been moved out and cleaned for the next residents, except I'd actually have preferred bare walls and empty rooms. This is fully furnished—in up-scale Scandinavian, like Ikea for the one percent. Normally, minimalist decor suits my minimalist tastes, but here, in this grand old town house, it makes me shudder.

How many times have I grumbled about the eyeball-assault that is Victorian decor? But there was warmth and enthusiasm in the jumble of colors and styles, like when I was five and insisted on a purple bedroom with a princess bed and posters of unicorns and rainbows. I loved that room, and I love my parents for giving it to me without a single "Are you sure?"

As we leave our bags in the front hall, I remind my parents of that old purple bedroom, how much I appreciated it, and how it reminds me of the Gray town house.

"The gas lighting helps," I say. "You can't see as well, so the colors don't completely blind you. I keep imagining the day when the world gets electricity and they realize exactly how garish that gold and scarlet wallpaper is."

"Or they don't care," Mom says. "Remember Aunt Lillian's house?"

"I do," I say with a smile.

We've come in the front door, and the room layouts on this level are also the same. I take my parents into what would have been the "funerary parlor" and I give a mini lecture on undertaking in the nineteenth century, and they are as patient as they'd been when I'd regale them at dinner with whatever weird facts I'd learned at school.

The funerary parlor has been redone as bedrooms, and I smile to think of people settling into the cozy little beds where Addington had performed autopsies and Gray had dissected corpses. Do guests ever wake to the dull splat of an organ being dropped into a bowl? Or hear a distant voice saying, "Hugh? Please hold this severed limb for me"?

Next I go down to the basement. What was Mrs. Wallace's domain— the kitchens and her living quarters—is a children's suite, with two small bedrooms and a den with a TV and game consoles.

Then it's two flights to the second level or, in British parlance, the first floor. This area is the least changed. The rooms remain intact, and even in their original functions, from the dining room to the library. The only difference is that the drawing room has been divided to form a tiny bathroom and a kitchen even smaller than the one in my condo. I guess if you can afford to rent this place, you aren't planning to cook.

We're in the library, where I run my hands over the built-in bookcase. "These shelves are original. Back then, this one here would be for fiction. Over here is medical—"

Footsteps patter up the distant stairs, and I wheel toward them.

"Mallory?" Mom says.

"Someone's here." I follow the patter of those steps overhead. "Maybe the cleaners aren't done?"

"I . . . don't hear anything, Mal," Mom says.

The footfalls have stopped now, and a door creaks.

"There," I say, looking up. "You must have heard that."

They exchange a look.

"No, hon," Dad says. "What do you hear?"

Footsteps on the stairs. Someone running up in . . . In soft-soled boots, light-footed.

Alice running up to the next level and then opening a door.

My mind is playing tricks, replaying a sound I've heard so often I can barely walk through this house without imagining it. Alice scampering about. Mrs. Wallace snapping at me for something. McCreadie's laugh, and Isla's answering quip. And then heavy footsteps, Gray pacing about, deep in thought.

"Let's go up to the top floor," I say, a little too brightly. "I want to show you where my room was."

"I think we should go to the next floor," Dad says. "You heard something up there."

I make a face. "My imagination. It's Alice's fault. She's always scampering about. Isla bought her softer-soled indoor boots, but I swear they still echo like me with my cowboy boots. Remember those?"

"We're going to the next floor," Mom says, and heads that way before I can stop her.

As we climb, I keep up the tour-guide spiel, overeager now. "This is just the bedroom level. Duncan's room first and then Isla's across the hall, and two smaller rooms farther down. I think they use what would have been their parents' rooms, and the others would have been the children's quarters."

I stride into the hall, pointing to my left first. "That's Duncan's and—".

The beige paint seems to shimmer, gold damask wallpaper appearing behind it. I shake my head and the wallpaper vanishes.

"Mallory?" Mom says.

"Is this entire place painted builder-beige?" I say, shaking my head as I pull open Gray's door and—

There's a desk beside the hearth, Gray's papers and books scattered over it, spilling onto the floor.

I slam the door shut, my heart pounding, but the image stays burned on my retinas.

When I look up, light flickers. Gaslight, from a brass fixture down the wall.

"Mal?" It's Dad now, his hand closing on my elbow. "Tell us what you see."

I shake my head.

His voice lowers. "Please, Mallory."

I hesitate. Then I do. I tell them I saw Gray's room and that there's gas lighting in the hall here, and wallpaper shimmers beneath that builder-beige paint.

A noise in a room down the hall has me jumping.

"Mallory?" Mom says.

I don't answer. I just start walking. There's a scrape and a clatter, as if someone is picking up something that fell. Then a voice. The low murmur of a voice that sends prickles through me.

Gray's voice.

I keep walking as if in a trance. My fingers close on the doorknob to one of the guest rooms. The same room I'd woken in six months ago. Under my fingers, the knob feels smooth and modern, but when I look down, it's antique brass, with a key in the hole.

I push open the door. The room inside is dim. No lamps or candles. Just a single window, the light outside fading. White specks hit the glass and slide down.

"Snowing," I whisper. "It's snowing."

I walk in, entranced by that snow. I get three steps, and a deep sigh has me spinning. My hand flies to my mouth, and I stagger back. The bed is there. The bed where I'd woken . . . and I'm in it. *Catriona* is in it, with sheets pulled up to her neck. She's pale and lying flat on her back. Under the sheet, her hands are visibly folded on her stomach, as if she's laid out for a funeral. Only the shallow rise and fall of her chest says she's alive.

Beside her Gray is just sitting there, in the gloom, watching her. Watching me.

I can tell myself I'm seeing a scene from last May. I know I'm not. Gray checked in on Catriona, but he wouldn't have sat with her like this. And there wasn't snow.

Gray shifts, pulling in his long legs and running a hand through his hair.

"Duncan," I say, because I can't help myself.

I say his name again as I step toward him, and his head jerks up. He peers in my direction, as if he heard something, but his gaze doesn't focus on me.

My mom rests her hand on my arm, making me jump. "What do you see?" she whispers.

"Me. Catriona. Well, me. In bed. It's snowing out, and it's getting dark already, and Duncan is sitting beside the bed."

"So Mum was right," she says with a sigh. "As usual."

I glance over.

Dad has moved into the room, too, and he's looking around. When I focus on them, I see what they do—just a regular guest room. As soon as I look away, though, the other room returns.

"You're seeing through the veil," Dad murmurs. "Just like your nan dreamed. That was the key. Get you in the same place you are over there."

I don't know what to say to that. I can't form thoughts. I just stare at Gray. I thought I'd lost him forever, and now he's right there. Except he's not right there. A hundred and fifty years stretch between us, an impassable gulf.

"You said there was a floorboard loose in your room," Mom says.

I startle at the change in subject. "What?"

"You mentioned a loose floorboard. You should put letters in there, and we can rent this place to look for them. But still do the classified ads, of course."

I stare at her. She's calm. Too calm, as if she's sending me off to summer camp and reminding me to email and send postcards.

"I . . . I can't just . . ." I look back at Gray.

"Oh, I think you can, Mallory." She kisses my cheek. "I think you can do anything you put your mind to." She straightens. "Now, where is your room and that floorboard?"

"I'll show—"

Her hand on my arm stops me. "You aren't going anywhere, just to be sure. Tell me where to find the board."

I do, and Dad murmurs he'll be right back. Moments later, he returns with a smile that looks a little forced.

"They haven't done much up there," he says. "It's an overflow bedroom. They've refinished the floors, but that board is still loose. Almost as if it was meant to be loose."

"All right then," Mom says, straightening. "Time to see if this works."

"What?" I say. "I can't just . . . It's not like walking through a door."

"No? Then it won't hurt to try."

When panic washes over me, it's Dad who pulls me into a hug.

"You've got this, sweetheart," he says. "We'll be fine."

I open my mouth to protest. But he's right. They will be fine without me. They raised me and launched me into the world a decade ago. We might live less than an hour's drive apart, but that doesn't mean I see them every day or even every week. As close as we are, most of that closeness these days is in our hearts and thoughts. There are phone calls and texts, but I live my life and they live theirs, and I'm not a vital part of theirs the way I was when we all lived under the same roof.

They have each other, and they will be fine.

Are they right then? That it's time for me to chase my own dreams? I feel as if I've been doing that ever since I left home, but I hadn't been chasing dreams. I'd been pursuing goals.

What do I want?

Everything. I want that damned magical door so I can come and go as I please. To live in 1869 Victorian Scotland and still be able to visit my parents and, if it doesn't work out there, to come home again.

I want the safety net, and that's not an option.

So do I stay where it's safe? Or do I jump anyway, knowing I leave behind part of myself?

"You want this," Mom says, taking my face between her hands and meeting my eyes. "Don't you dare pretend otherwise. You want this, and we want you to have it."

I throw myself into her arms. They both hug me, and we stay there, and it is like being back at Nan's bedside. If I cross over—now or some other time—I might never see them again, and there is so much I want them to know.

I tell them how much I love them and how much this is going to hurt. They tell me how proud they are of me, how glad they are that I found my place in the world, how much they will miss me and look forward to the updates.

Mom also, being my mother, hits the practical notes. They presume I'll lapse into another coma, but they'll be sure I'm cared for, because who knows what would happen if the plug was pulled, though she doesn't say that, of course. They'll look after telling my department and friends what happened—well, that I lapsed back into a coma, not the truth.

Then Mom takes me by the shoulders and says, "Go," and gives me the softest push. I feel her hands on my shoulders and Dad's hand locked in mine and then I let go. I walk toward that bed with my gaze fixed on Catriona.

No, with my gaze fixed on *me*. I am lying in that bed. I don't know where Catriona has gone, but she's not there. That's me. I step up to the bedside, reach forward to touch my cheek, lying in that bed and—

And I gasp, disoriented and flailing, as if I've woken in a strange place. As if I've fallen through time.

THIRTY-THREE

I jerk upright, gaze flying to where my parents had been standing moments ago. There's no one there. Just a dimly lit room . . . and the patter of snow against the window glass.

I follow the sound to see the snow, and to feel the chill of November and the dry heat of coal, the smell of it acrid and familiar.

I lift my hands. They're smoother, younger, and yet as familiar as my own. Because they are my own. My own in this world.

The room is silent, and that stops me dead. I'd seen Gray by my bed. Was I imagining that? I turn slowly and inhale sharply as I see him on his feet and staring at me, his expression so guarded that something in me crumples.

Yes, he'd been by my bedside, but he was just watching over a patient, and if some romantic corner of my soul hoped otherwise, here's the truth of it, in his expression, which is hardly any expression at all.

"Dun—" I swallow. "Dr. Gray."

If there was any light in his eyes, it fades now as his shoulders slump.

"Catriona," he says.

"What?" I stare at him, blinking. Then comprehension hits. "No, it's me. Mallory."

I try for a smile, but it falters as I realize the enormity of what I've done. I once took weeks to decide between two condos, knowing once I made the choice, it would be difficult to reverse. Now I've made a decision that is almost certainly irreversible, one that affects my entire life, and I just . . . did it. Part of me had been so certain it wouldn't work that the choice seemed more symbolic than real.

The voice in my head isn't screaming that I left my real life behind. It's screaming that I took an unbelievable leap of faith in presuming I had a life here. Presuming my home and my job were more than temporary arrangements for a stranded traveler.

I'm about to tell my hosts that I'm here for good, whether they want me or not.

I'm mired in all that fear and indecision, and all Gray says is "Mallory?" and I realize he still isn't sure it's me.

I should start spouting proof. Instead, I hear myself saying, "I came back."

He only looks at me, uncertainty lingering.

How often have I said not to trust whoever comes back? But now I'm here, and proof is easily given—*I last saw you when you left me with Queen Mab, outside the vault market, with me carrying the Hand of Glory in a carpetbag.*

Yet I don't want to *need* to prove it. I want him to look in my eyes and see me, and I know that's childish and illogical. But it's what I feel, and when he keeps looking at me as if he's not sure who has woken in this body, I want to flee.

I swing my legs off the bed, only to realize I'm wearing a nightgown and my legs don't "swing" the way I've grown used to again. I curse under my breath, and Gray goes to catch me, but I brush him off.

"I'm fine," I say. "Is Mrs. Wallace all right?"

He nods, slow, still wary.

"I need to speak to Isla," I say.

He still says nothing. Not one damn word, and that hurts more than I ever imagined silence could hurt.

What did I expect?

More than this cautious, guarded stare. The man was sitting by my damn bedside, waiting for me to wake up, and when I did, I got a single word from him.

Catriona.

With that, I realize he wasn't waiting for me to return. I get a closer look at him in the gloom, and he looks like shit, lank hair and stubbled face and a shirt that isn't even buttoned up correctly. But that's not because I was lying on my deathbed.

He has been sitting vigil against Catriona's return.

I don't think Gray had realized he was harboring a sociopath. Catriona had seemed like just another person with a criminal past that his sister was trying to help, and if she wasn't coming along as well as Alice, well, these things took time. Through me, he fully came to understand that Catriona wasn't someone they could help, that she was someone they needed to get out of their house if she ever returned.

So Gray was waiting, ready to deal with a threat to his family.

"Where's Isla?" I say, and there's more snap to my voice than I like.

"Mallory . . ."

"Yes, it's Mallory. If you want proof—"

"No, I just . . . I didn't think . . ." He exhales. "You are back."

"I am. Now, if you can point me—"

"I'm sorry."

I look over at him, and my heart leaps into my throat, my brain running wild at those words. He's sorry? For what? Has Isla been hurt? Did something happen?

"I know . . ." he begins, and then takes a deep breath. "You said you came back. I presume that means you went . . . home. After you were hurt."

I give a curt nod. "I did."

"Then I am sorry."

"For what?"

"That you could not stay. I know it is what you wanted, and yet somehow you found yourself back here, and I am sorry."

I shake my head. "That's not how it happened. I came back."

"You . . . ?"

"Came back. I . . ."

I want to make an excuse. I came back to solve the case. I came back because, if I didn't, Selim Awad would end up on the gallows.

I want to duck and weave and avoid admitting that I came back because I wanted to. How do I say that?

I came back because I'm happy here.

I came back because I belong here.

I came back for Isla, for the investigations, for the work.

I came back for you.

I remember once when I called him a friend, he said I made such admissions sound easy. They can be, if they are straightforward enough. If they don't risk too much.

"I came back," I say simply. "There was an opportunity, and I didn't think it would work, but I made a choice."

"So you can go back and forth now? Travel from your time to ours?"

Can I? Is it possible? I push past that thought. I must commit wholeheartedly to this. "No. It . . . it was probably a one-way ticket. Can we talk about something else?"

He stares at me. "Something else?"

"Anything else. Please? I just want . . ." I stand and brush down my nightgown. "I'd like to get back to work."

"You've been unconscious for two days. You were nearly killed."

"But I wasn't. Killed, that is. I should get dressed. We have work to do."

"Mallory? You—"

"Has Selim been accused of attacking me?"

"Yes. He was spotted leaving the tunnel after your attack. You need not worry about that. Hugh is hunting for him and—"

"It wasn't Selim. You said someone spotted him leaving the tunnel? Lord Muir, right? That's who attacked me. We need to get word to Hugh—"

"Mallory, please. Sit down. Let me at least examine you. You've been unconscious—"

"For two days. Got it." I meet his gaze. "I'm moving too fast. I know that. I'm pretending everything is fine, when I've just boomeranged between times and chosen to give up everything to come back here, and that's huge. Really huge. But I can't deal with it right now, okay? To you, I've been unconscious for two days. To me, I woke up in my world, where it was only two days since I left, and my nan was still alive. I sat with her while she died. I went to her funeral. And then my parents told me they'd understand if I wanted to come back here, to maybe never see them again, and I . . . I did it and that's . . ."

I inhale sharply. "I can't deal with it, and if you force me to face all that, I'm going to be as useless as I was lying in that bed. I'm back. I'm not going anywhere. Am I fine? Hell, no, I'm absolutely not fine."

I look up at him. "But I need time to work this through, and in the meanwhile, I'd like to solve this case before Selim Awad ends up on the gallows. Okay?"

Silence. The ugly silence that tells me I've overshared. That I've made Gray uncomfortable with my honesty.

"I . . ." He rubs at his throat, and his gaze shifts to the side, and I'm ready to leap in and make a joke or divert however I can when he says, "I thought you were gone. Really and truly gone. I . . . I thought I'd lost you."

"Oh."

Shame washes over me. Yes, I've just spent four days in an emotional whirlwind. And yes, I want to lose myself by diving into work. But it's not as if Gray's been here, carrying on as usual. He's spent two days waiting to see whether I'll wake up . . . and if the person who wakes up is actually me.

I rub my hands over my face. "I'm sorry. Of course, you didn't know who might return, and either way, you've had an unconscious patient for two days. You need rest."

He shakes his head. "I don't. I . . . I know I may have seemed underwhelmed by your return, and I only wanted to be clear that I was in shock. You are back, and if this is what you chose, then while I know that will be painful, I . . . May I say I am happy to see you?"

My smile breaks through at the same time that my eyes fill with tears. "You may. I would give you a hug, but I know that's not done—"

He gathers me up in an embrace before I can finish, lifting me clear off the floor in a fierce hug before setting me down again.

"There," he says. "Now, while Isla and my mother would say I should insist you talk about what you have endured and what you are feeling, I do not see the point in demanding someone unburden themselves for their own good. If you wish to talk . . ."

"I don't. Not now. If I start, I might end up in a puddle of tears, grieving for my grandmother and also for my parents and yet relieved that I actually made it back and—"

Deep breaths as my heart speeds up. "Nope. Pull me back from the abyss, Gray. Preferably with coffee." My stomach growls. "And food. Apparently, I haven't eaten in a while. I should also speak to Isla."

"She is out, but I will get food and let the others know you are awake. Would you like me to keep them at bay?"

"For a while, please."

"Coffee and whisky? Or just coffee?"

I smile up at him. "I won't say no to whisky if the doctor recommends it."

"He does."

I'm back, and it is as if I never left. Or it is once I can fully immerse myself in the case, telling Gray what we'd seen in the papers about Selim and the theory Mom and I came up with, that whoever stole the artifacts—presumably Muir—was framing Selim by spreading word that the seller was the Egyptian brother-in-law of an archaeologist.

Once I'm lost in that, I forget that I left, and even when I remember, I'm reminded that I got to see my grandmother and tell my parents where I am, and that releases a knot I'd been holding inside for six months. I said goodbye to Nan. She doesn't think I abandoned her. Mom and Dad hadn't spent six months dealing with Catriona's treachery. All that is settled. Yet when I feel relief, guilt chases it.

I left my parents behind. Willingly left them. Their only child, gone, right when they also lost Nan. I abandoned my job and my friends and left my parents with the cleanup for a daughter they might never see again.

So, yep, it's really easier to focus on the case. I'll have to deal with the rest, but I will do so the way I dealt with first coming here. Let reality and the emotional turmoil of that reality slowly settle over me, rather than immersing myself in it.

As for someone framing Selim for the antiquity theft, McCreadie has already considered that. When I'd discussed it with Mom, I'd gotten enough distance to realize that, as tips went, the one I got from the underground-market seller was a little on-the-nose. The Selim I met was a well-educated, savvy young man. Would he steal Egyptian artifacts to repatriate? Possibly. Might he even sell the least valuable for a bit of extra cash? Possibly. He's young, and ideals don't buy a round at the pub.

But would he tell his buyers that his brother-in-law was an archaeologist? There are ways to explain where the artifacts came from and prove they're legit without basically handing the buyer a card saying, "Selim Awad, brother-in-law to Sir Alastair Christie."

What kept McCreadie from following up was the fact that, well, Selim really did seem to have stolen the artifacts. Mrs. Wallace and I were in the tunnel looking for them when he attacked us.

He wasn't *just* spotted by Lord Muir—McCreadie would have found that suspicious. He'd also left fresh boot prints that matched the footwear we'd taken after he was found unconscious in the tunnels after Sir Alastair's murder. Moreover, Selim isn't around to provide an alibi or explanation. Except for being spotted allegedly fleeing the tunnel, he hasn't been seen since the night after Sir Alastair's murder, when he disappeared from the house and didn't return.

"At least we know he's alive," I say as we sit in Gray's office, with coffee, whisky, and an assortment of cold meats and cheeses and bread. "The future articles say he went to trial, and they wouldn't have tried and convicted him in absentia."

"Hmm."

I think Gray's going to argue the point. Would it be possible to frame a random young Egyptian man and say it was Selim? Then I realize what he's really thinking.

"Just because Selim *had* survived to be hanged doesn't mean he'll stay alive now that I'm back to send the investigation after Muir," I say. "You said the police are hunting for Selim?"

"Yes, Hugh is with them, in hopes that nothing goes wrong."

By "goes wrong" he means that McCreadie will ensure that Selim is alive and well when he's arrested.

"It would be helpful to know *where* he was found, but all my father could locate was the crime and verdict. Digging deeper would have meant a trip to the archives. Which I suppose I should have done but . . ." I shrug. "My grandmother made me promise not to look up spoilers."

"Spoilers?"

I sip my coffee. "Anything that could predict the future. What eventually happens to you, Isla, Hugh . . . There are things I shouldn't know, and if I came back, things I shouldn't share. She did find you, though. In the history books."

"Along with my date of death, I presume, which is exactly the sort of thing she didn't want you seeing."

"Oh, don't worry. Now that I've returned, you'll die *much* sooner."

His eyes warm at that. "It is good to have you back, Mallory."

"Good to be back, even if it now means I'll almost certainly pay the price by dying of something easily curable in my own time. Also, since I'm apparently staying, I really need to teach Mrs. Wallace how to make a cappuccino." I peer into my cup. "At least a decent café au lait."

"Coffee and milk?"

"Can't be too hard, right? Speaking of Mrs. Wallace . . ." I sober. "Is she okay?"

"She suffered a blow to her head and . . . she has not been herself. For a few moments, I almost wondered if it was like you, that she was literally not herself. She is. She's just . . . distracted. When I told her you were awake, she went very quiet. She only asked if I was certain you were not Catriona. I said yes, beyond any doubt."

"I told her the truth in the tunnels. We had an . . . altercation."

He stiffens. "Did she threaten you?"

"No, no," I lie. "Her concern was for you and Isla and Alice. In the end, I didn't confess to save my life. I just got frustrated and said screw it. I told her the truth."

He blinks.

"Yep," I say. "Pretty sure I'll end up regretting that. I need to be more careful." Especially since I've now told someone with reason to use it against me. "It was a spur-of-the-moment bad decision."

"We will handle it," he says firmly. "I will ensure she knows that if she misuses that information, she is betraying my trust. Mine and Isla's."

"Anyway, that's when Muir knocked her out. She'd trapped me half-way backed out of a hole, so when Muir grabbed me, I figured it was her. Then I saw him. Also, for the record, he did the same thing to me that Sir Alastair's killer did. Put his foot on my back for leverage."

Gray's eyes narrow. "Making him a suspect for Sir Alastair's murder as well."

"Except Muir has confirmed alibis for the entire time the murder could have taken place. Also, framing Selim means he likely copied the murder on purpose. Would he have known how exactly Sir Alastair died?"

"I believe so, as our supposition about the method made its way into the papers."

"Damn. Okay, so he copied it to frame Selim further. Back to my attempted murder then. It seems Muir went down there to retrieve the stowed antiquities, saw Mrs. Wallace facing the other direction, knocked her out, and then . . ."

Gray takes a quick belt from his whisky glass. "Saw an opportunity."

"Me with my butt sticking out of a hole, easy to grab, strangle in the same manner as Sir Alastair, and then blame Selim for both deaths."

"Yes."

"Has anything else been uncovered while I was unconscious?"

"Hugh has been focused on Selim Awad, naturally, both locating him and seeking a motive for him to murder Sir Alastair. The obvious one is the stolen antiquities, yet Hugh would need to prove Selim stole them, which seems increasingly unlikely. While I was tending to you, I turned my attention to the objects found under Florence King's mattress. I do not see how they are connected but . . ." He shrugs as he cuts off a piece of cold ham. "I needed something to occupy my mind."

"Did you solve the cipher?"

"I did. It would, however, be more satisfying if the letter turned out to be anything of importance. It was study notes."

"Study notes? Like for Florence's exams?"

"It seems so. It was nothing more than a list of questions for self-study."

"So why write it out in a cipher?"

"That is the question. I fear, however, that the answer is simple— someone was practicing a cipher and used the study notes. As for the key, Lady Christie was kind enough to allow me to send Simon to the house, where he tested it in every lock. I fear we have stolen a key that has no use to anyone except Florence King."

"And if it turns out to be her only key to something, we're going to feel really shitty. We'll need to get it back to her once this is over. So the key and the cipher—along with Mrs. King herself—are red herrings."

His brows rise.

I take a bite of cheese before explaining, "Clues that aren't related to the case and distract us from it. If I recall correctly, the phrase comes from the strong smell of herring, which could be used to hide another scent. In this case, on the positive side, they weren't completely useless clues. Lord Muir probably intended to send us on a wild-goose chase when he accused Florence King of the murder, but without following up there, we might never have known that Lord Muir was using his leverage with Sir Alastair against the young women."

"Thus giving Sir Alastair another reason to want to sever the patronage arrangement. We—"

The front door opens. Boots click in.

"That will be Isla," Gray says. "Would you like me to speak to her?"

I hesitate. I should do it myself, but even at the thought, I want to crumple in exhaustion.

I was able to blurt everything to Gray and then ask to set it aside. Isla won't allow that. She'll want the full story, and she'll have questions. Like Gray implied earlier, to some people, if you say you don't want to talk about a difficult thing, they think you're "just saying that." You really do want to talk but need to be pushed. Or you don't want to, but you should, for your own good.

"I will speak to her," he murmurs, leaning in to lower his voice. "I will tell her what happened, and that you need time before you are ready to discuss it."

"Will she be insulted if I don't tell her myself?"

As he rises, he squeezes my shoulder, a quick but meaningful touch of reassurance. "She will not. May I bring her to see you after we've spoken?"

"Please."

"Then that will be enough."

THIRTY-FOUR

Yep, I'm a big ol' coward. I throw Gray to the wolves and hide in the office until the low murmur of voices ends with Isla saying, "May I see her?"

"Of course. She wants to see you. I only ask that . . ." His voice lowers, and I don't hear the rest.

"I will."

They knock on the office door, and I call them in as I stand. Seeing me, Isla hesitates, her expression schooled to a pleasant but cautious smile, as if she's walking into the hospital room of a fragile patient. Which, let's be honest, I guess I am.

"Hey," I say. "I'm back."

She strides over and embraces me, whispering, "I am sorry for what you went through, but I am very glad to see you."

"I'm glad to see you, too." I hug her tight and then back up. "So . . ."

"Mallory would like to discuss the case," Gray says.

Isla turns a questioning look on me. "If that is what you want."

"It is. Please. The rest can wait. Apparently, I'm not going anywhere. We can figure all that out later. For now, we need to worry about Selim Awad."

Isla stiffens. "We will not let him get near you again."

"That's not it. He wasn't the one who attacked me," I say, and we catch her up on the story.

* * *

Halfway through my explanation, McCreadie shows up, which means starting over, both with the quick "how Mallory came back" story and then "how Mallory saw her attacker, who was not Selim Awad."

"I am relieved to hear it," he says. "Not as relieved as I am to have you back, of course. I was quite beside myself, worrying I had lost my detective-from-the-future advantage."

"That's what I was thinking too. The whole time I was gone. Oh my God, I need to get back so I can help Detective McCreadie or he'll never solve a case again."

We share a smile at that.

"It is good to have you back, Mallory," he says. "Also good to hear that it wasn't Selim Awad who attacked you. I rather liked Selim. Lord Muir, less so. It is always more satisfying that way."

"Well, we can't write off Selim just yet," I say. "Or pin Sir Alastair's murder on Lord Muir. My attempted murder, though? Definitely Muir. The problem is that if you arrest him, and it turns out he's holding Selim captive . . . ?"

"We might endanger one by arresting the other. However, if we wait before arresting Lord Muir, it weakens our case."

"Because my statement has more weight if I make it immediately upon waking. Can we get another detective in to witness my statement without moving against Muir?"

"I would rather not ask another officer to participate in any delay against Muir. However, you could give your statement to a solicitor, who can date and witness it."

"Perfect." I lift my hand to check my watch and curse. Yep, I'll be doing that for a while. "It's probably too late to get out and investigate tonight, isn't it?"

"Too late for you," Gray says. "There is nothing that cannot wait until morning, and it is already dinner hour. If you can stomach more food, you should do that, and then I'll have my solicitor come to take your statement before the delay seems suspicious."

When it's time to serve dinner, I decide I need to face the staff. It's too awkward to have Alice and Lorna serving the meal when I haven't even said hello yet.

I start easy, with Simon. He doesn't know my real story, so it's simply a matter of popping out to the stable and saying hello. He's glad to see me and doesn't seem disappointed that my latest injury didn't somehow return Catriona to him. Back in the house, I nearly crash into Lorna. That makes for an even simpler—if more awkward—reunion, as she feels obligated to express her delight at the return of someone she barely knows.

Now comes Mrs. Wallace. I'd rather speak to Alice first. Like Simon, she doesn't know my secret identity. Unlike Simon, though, she does have reason to fear the return of Catriona. Still, that will be easier than speaking to Mrs. Wallace. Yet I don't know where Alice is, and I do know where Mrs. Wallace is, so I can't postpone this conversation any longer.

I steel myself as I open the door to head into the basement. When I catch voices, I pause. Seems I've found Alice. She's talking to Mrs. Wallace, and she's upset about something.

About my return? Shit. I probably should have reassured Alice sooner.

"I want her gone," Alice says.

Something inside me tightens. I know Gray reassured them it was me. Maybe that doesn't matter—Alice has realized she doesn't want to take the chance of Catriona returning.

"And how do you think we'll manage that, lass?" Mrs. Wallace replies. "Mrs. Ballantyne would never let her go without good reason. Do you have a good reason?"

"I don't like her."

That knot tightens more. Alice and I have grown closer in the last few months, and I really thought she'd come to see me as a true "sister in service," part older friend and part big sister. Has she been tolerating me all these months, pretending to be friendly to keep a peaceful household?

"That's not a reason for letting her go, lass," Mrs. Wallace says gently. "I understand it feels as if it should be. You have been here longer, and if you do not like her, then you should not need to work with her. But it's not enough."

"She's nosy."

Nosy? Okay, yes, I am overly curious. Occupational hazard. Also, when I work with someone, I like to get to know them, and I'd struggled not to push that with Alice. Still, I did invade her privacy once. Kind of.

I followed her when I was concerned over a letter she received, and I ended up getting her backstory, which she may resent.

Is she nursing a grudge over that? I certainly didn't think so. Instead, it'd been the turning point for her to start trusting that I wasn't Catriona.

"Curiosity isn't a crime, Alice," Mrs. Wallace says.

"Dr. Gray and Mrs. Ballantyne are entitled to their privacy. They are . . ." Alice lowers her voice. "You know how they are, ma'am. They're not quite normal."

Mrs. Wallace lets out a sound suspiciously like a chuckle. "None of us are."

"I do not mean it as an insult. They are different, and being different makes people talk. You and me and Simon, we know not to gossip because people have gossiped about us. That's why she doesn't belong here. She *is* normal—too normal—and I fear she will not hold her tongue when she has interesting gossip to tell."

Normal? That doesn't describe me at all.

"I will speak to Lorna," Mrs. Wallace says.

I pause. Speak to Lorna about me?

No, wait. They are *talking* about Lorna. That makes more sense.

I exhale in relief.

Mrs. Wallace continues, "You are correct that she does not share our histories, and so she may not see the harm in a bit of tongue wagging."

"I do not see why I couldn't have been promoted. I would make a better housemaid than her *or* Mallory."

"You are too young to be a housemaid, and Mrs. Ballantyne has bigger plans for your future."

"Bigger plans for my *future*. That does not mean I cannot be a housemaid now."

I retreat and wait for them to finish the conversation. Now I understand Alice's animosity toward Lorna. She's upset that she wasn't promoted. Yes, she worries about gossip, too, which is a valid concern.

I recall Annis's objection to hiring someone who hasn't had trouble with the law. This is what she must have meant—that Isla's usual hires are less likely to look askance at their employers' eccentricities and gossip about them.

Once the conversation winds down, I open and then shut the door louder before clomping down the steps so I cannot be accused of sneaking up.

Alice glowers toward the stairs, until she sees who it is. Then she gives me a very gratifying smile—all the more welcome after my fear she was talking about me.

"You are back," she says.

"Yes, and I still remember that you owe me a thruppence from last week, when you needed extra money for that new hat at the market, so don't think you got away without paying me."

She rolls her eyes, but she relaxes into another smile, too. I don't give a damn about the thruppence. I'm just proving it's really me.

Mrs. Wallace hands Alice a plate of rolls for the table. "Off with you now. They are already dining late, and I do not want the roast growing any colder."

Once Alice is gone, Mrs. Wallace turns to the aforementioned roast, setting it onto the butcher's block and slicing a few pieces. I wait until she has the roast on the plate and turns to the potatoes.

"So you're just going to ignore me," I say.

"No, I am preparing dinner."

"That's fine. I can come back afterward, and we'll talk then."

"I have dishes to wash."

"I'll help. The perfect opportunity for a nice chat about what I said before being strangled."

"Are you taking back what you said?" She adds carrots to the platter, still not looking my way.

"Nope."

"Then I do not believe we have anything to discuss."

"So we *would* have something to discuss if I rescinded my statement?"

"Only if you are going to tell me the truth."

"Well, that's a Catch-22, isn't it? You'll only discuss it if I tell you the truth, but I already did tell you the truth, which you refuse to discuss."

She fishes out a carrot intent on escape.

I continue, "Catch-22. It means a paradox, a situation where you can't proceed without first having something that you can't get until you proceed. Taken from the novel of the same name, written by Joseph Heller in the middle of the twentieth century. The book is a satire about war. World War II, specifically, but the title refers to absurd bureaucracy. I can discuss the themes of the book if you like. That's the peril of having an English-lit prof for a dad. Would you like me to continue?"

She hands me the vegetable platter. "I would like you to take this upstairs."

"Alrighty then." I pause. "That's a phrase used to move past an awkward situation, popularized in the movie *Ace Ventura: Pet Detective*."

She pauses and then says, as if in spite of herself, "Pet detective?"

"It's a comedy. American. Most blockbuster movies—motion pictures—are."

"Take the vegetables upstairs."

"You *do* believe my story. I can tell. If you didn't, you'd challenge me on it and prove that I'm lying. But if Dr. Gray and Mrs. Ballantyne have accepted it, then you must, too, however difficult it is. Yet you can't bring yourself to admit you believe me, so you're going to ignore it and pretend you still think I'm lying. Got it. Taking the vegetables away now. But if you ever want to discuss mid-twentieth-century literature or late-twentieth-century pop culture, I'm your gal."

I walk out of the kitchen without another word. I won't say I've won this battle, but I have a feeling I don't need to worry about Mrs. Wallace holding me at gunpoint again. At least, not for a while.

We have another guest for dinner. Annis, who shows up, sees me up and moving about, and says, "You are alive then? Good. You are making a terrible habit of that."

"Being alive?" I say as we enter the dining room.

"Being strangled and left for dead. What is it about that pretty throat that makes people think they would like to throttle it?" She lowers into her seat. "Or perhaps it is not the throat but the owner of it."

"Annis . . ." Isla warns.

"That was no insult," Annis says. "I am certain many people have wished to do the same to me."

As we settle in, the door opens and Lorna enters.

"Ah," Annis says. "The new maid has not fled. Having second thoughts yet, child?"

Lorna freezes and looks about, as if Annis must be addressing someone else.

"Is there another maid here?" Annis says. "Of course I mean you."

"I . . . I am doing well, ma'am. Everyone is very kind to me."

Annis snorts. "Of course they are. They are all too kind by half." She lifts her wineglass. "Fill this and then be off with you. The adults have a murder to discuss."

After dinner, Annis leaves and the solicitor arrives to take my statement. Then it's a short evening before we're all off to bed. I don't have a restful night. Once dark comes, it drags all my fears and anxieties with it. Have I made the right choice? What if I really do never see my parents again? Was this worth giving up my former life for?

I think it was, and if I have doubts, then I need to make sure it's worth it. Immerse myself in this world and helping those around me.

First thing the next morning, Gray and I are off to the university. Mc-Creadie is busy with the search for Selim Awad. Isla has chemist orders to fill—she has arrangements with male chemists, where they pay her for medicine they pass off as their own. I'm sure Isla could spare the time to join us, but obviously "poking around a professor's office" doesn't strike her as exciting detective work. She's holding out for a real adventure.

Can't say I blame her. Universities aren't the most exciting place in the world. Now, I *do* have good memories of my years at one. I love learning, and university was far better at scratching that itch than high school had been. Yet for some people, just breathing the rarefied air of a university is exhilarating. For me, a university is like a law office. It's where one of my parents works, which takes all the mystique out of it. For Isla, university is also a place she was prevented from entering as a student.

Gray occupies a weird place within the academic structure. He's a graduate. A lauded one, too. Second in his class with dual degrees. He's also a published researcher in a new and exciting field. That should win him invitations to speak, even to join the faculty. But he's Duncan Gray, the doctor who was refused a license to practice his craft. I don't think the university knows what to make of him, so while he's permitted to attend lectures, no one's asking him to give them.

He is recognized on campus, though. Staff tip their hats to him. One professor smiles as we pass, another pauses for a quick exchange of pleasantries, while a third pretends not to see him and a fourth actively glares.

When we reach Sir Alastair's office, there's a constable standing guard. I've seen the man before, and like Iain, he doesn't have a problem with

Gray, which is probably why he's been assigned to this morning's shift. Gray greets him as I slip inside.

The room is dark and windowless. A small office, for a medical professor who is best known in a field other than medicine. The air is stale and chilly, the fire having been out for days. I flick on the gaslight, which doesn't do much to illuminate a room of dark wood. I can make out the desk—also dark wood—and it seems to have a lamp on it. I head that way, and I'm leaning over to light it when I catch sight of something on the desktop.

I light the desk lamp and then use a pencil to push the object toward it for closer examination.

"Found something already?" Gray says as he enters.

I point at the object. "It's the key from the King residence. Simon wouldn't have left it here. I'm guessing he returned it to one of the constables, who forgot to take it back to the police office."

"That key is still at our house. Hugh told us to keep it in case we had another idea where it might fit."

I tilt my head as I frown at the key. "Am I imagining that this looks like the same one?"

"No, it most certainly does."

So Florence King's key seems to be one for a university office. What was she doing with it, and whose office did it open?

Gray takes a handkerchief from his pocket, scoops it up, and leaves the room, locking the door behind him. A moment later, Gray opens the door, key still in hand.

The constable on duty calls over, "Oh, that's the key to this office. The secretary brought it around in case we needed it. Sir Alastair's went missing a while ago."

Gray looks at me.

"Seems we should speak to Sir Alastair's secretary," I say.

THIRTY-FIVE

Yes, the constable's story is correct. Sir Alastair's key disappeared a couple of weeks before his death. He'd been trying to remember where he put it, and in the meantime, he'd left the backup key with his secretary so he wouldn't misplace it, too.

After we finish speaking to the secretary, we tuck into a side hall.

"I thought the key we found might be for a different office," I say. "But it seems it was for Sir Alastair's. Florence nicked it and was hiding it under her mattress."

"To what purpose?" Gray muses.

"Well, we know Sir Alastair was leading the charge against the Edinburgh Seven. Maybe she was searching for his plan of action. Who he was trying to win to his cause. Who might have sent letters of support. Information Miss Jex-Blake could use to prepare for the fight ahead."

"Or information to *stop* the fight ahead."

"Ah. Digging for blackmail fodder to end Sir Alastair's campaign against the Seven. If that were the case, and Florence found something and confronted Sir Alastair with it . . . Looks like we might not be able to rule out Mrs. King that easily. Time to pay her a visit?"

"Indeed."

* * *

We'd had a hard time pinning down Florence after the murder, but she's home today, though she's preparing to leave for a study session.

We'd asked McCreadie to meet us at the apartment, to lend an official air to the interview. It's the right move, but I can see that it also sets Florence back, having the three of us descend on her tiny apartment.

"Is there something else you need?" she says. "I have told you all that I know. If you are having trouble verifying my whereabouts after Sir Alastair's death, I have thought of other people I encountered on my walks."

"No, we confirmed with the witnesses you provided," McCreadie says. "A well-dressed young woman out alone was memorable enough."

Her chin lifts. "It should not be, and the fact that it is demonstrates how far we need to go, when people look askance at respectable women without escorts."

"Agreed," I say. "However, that's not the problem we're currently trying to solve. Your whereabouts were verified, which is only marginally helpful."

She'll already know why. Confirming her alibi for the period *after* Sir Alastair died doesn't clear her in his death.

"I am sorry to interrupt," Mr. King says, hovering behind his wife. "Might I offer tea?"

"Thank you, but no," McCreadie says. "We hope this interview will be brief. You may be aware that your premises were briefly searched the other day, in accordance with proper procedure during a murder investigation."

"What?" Florence says. "When?"

McCreadie pushes past the part where I snuck into their bedroom while he was questioning her husband.

"We removed two items from your home," he says.

"Is that legal?" Florence says, and while it's a very inconvenient question, I give her credit for asking.

"It is a murder investigation," McCreadie says. "The items were located under your mattress."

She stops. While her attention fixes on McCreadie, mine can fix on her. When he says that, her expression is pure bafflement.

"The mattress? On our bed?"

"Yes, we found a key and note written in a cipher."

"A cipher? Is this some sort of joke?" She goes still again, her face now filling with dread. "Did someone place a coded message there? Trying to frame me for the murder of Sir Alastair?"

"No, the note was for studying."

Her face screws up. "Studying? Why would that be in a cipher?" A moment of thought and then her eyes flash. "If you are accusing me of cheating, let me assure you that we are not permitted to take anything into the examination room. A note—even in cipher—would be useless."

Across the room, Emmett King has stopped making tea. He's gone very still. Huh. I glance at Gray, who has noticed the same thing.

McCreadie continues, "We are not concerned about the study notes. It is the key that has become an object of interest, as it belongs to a specific door. That of Sir Alastair's office at the university."

"What? Why would I—?"

"He was leading the opposition against the admission of female students. We believe you were in his office for that. You may have been searching for details on his plan. Or information on his supporters. Perhaps even information that could discredit him."

"That . . . That is . . ." She shakes her head. "I should say it is preposterous, but I cannot help wishing I had thought of it myself, at least insofar as discovering his plans and allies. There are days when I am sorely tempted to explore more underhanded methods than Sophia espouses. However, I did not search Sir Alastair's office. Nor did I have that key."

"It was found—"

"I did it." Emmett practically throws himself in front of his wife. "I am sorry. I understand how this will look, but please know that my wife played no role in my scheme."

"Your scheme?" McCreadie says.

"I only wanted to help her cause. The cipher . . . Well, that is rather embarrassing. It was practice work." He turns to Florence. "Remember the time we discussed ciphers? We were playing with a simple one, and I said perhaps there was a use for such a thing. You said such a simple code would be too easily deciphered. I was learning a more difficult one. I thought perhaps you ladies could use it for communication." He hangs his head. "Yes, I was being foolish, and perhaps a little childish."

"And the key?" McCreadie asks.

Emmett straightens, still planted between his young wife and the detective. "Sir Alastair left it behind in the lecture hall, after I spoke to him. I took it to return it . . . and then I had another idea. I thought perhaps I could find something to help Florence and the others in their fight against

Sir Alastair." He glances at McCreadie, half sheepish and half cunning. "Is it still considered illegally entering his office if I had the key?"

McCreadie ignores the question. I highly doubt he's going to charge Emmett with anything, but it's in his best interests to give the impression that the outcome will depend on Emmett's cooperation.

"Did you find anything?" McCreadie asks. "Being a murder investigation, anything you might have uncovered could be useful."

"I fear I am a very poor detective," Emmett says. "That is why I had not mentioned it to Florence before Sir Alastair's death. And then after his death, well, I dared not mention it then and cause her to worry, particularly after she herself had been questioned in his death. It was a foolish thing for me to do, sir, and I deeply regret my recklessness."

Florence lays a hand on his arm. "I appreciate the thought, my dear, but you need to be more careful. Imagine if you'd been caught? You could have been expelled. As it seems unlikely that I will be able to practice medicine, one of us really needs that license."

"I know, and I had not even considered the consequences. I acted rashly, and for what? I found nothing helpful and have brought the police to our door."

"I believe I brought them first," his wife murmurs. "Behaving rashly myself outside Sir Alastair's party." She sighs and turns to us. "We have both acted like impulsive children, and I do apologize."

I speak up. "Was there anything that caught your eye in that office, Mr. King? Anything at all?"

"I cannot say there was." He pauses, as if he just thought of something. Then he says, "No, that was odd, but not useful."

"What is it?" I press.

"I found a letter in the trash, from a fellow who wanted to buy a mummy. I knew Sir Alastair was also an Egyptologist, and I am certain he hears from many wealthy people wishing mummies for their collections. Yet the letter did not look like it came from such a person. It was poorly written and ink-stained. So I continued reading, and it turned out the fellow didn't want that sort of mummy at all."

"That sort of mummy?" I repeat.

"He was asking Sir Alastair if he could buy any that were not found fully intact. I suppose he hoped to sell pieces to those who could never afford a full mummy, as a curiosity of sorts. The odd part was that he referenced Sir Alastair as a doctor and said he would understand."

"That, being a doctor, Sir Alastair would understand why the letter writer wished to purchase mummified body parts?"

"Yes. Is that not strange?"

Florence shakes her head. "He wanted them for mummia."

"For what?"

The young woman smiles. "Did you sleep through your course in medical history, Em? Mummies were once used in medicine."

"They were?"

She sighs. "The fellow wanted mummia for some medical purpose, and Sir Alastair wisely disposed of the letter rather than pursuing it. I cannot see that it bears any connection to his murder, though. I can hardly imagine anyone coming to Sir Alastair's house demanding bits of mummified bodies and killing him for refusing. The servants would never admit such a person."

Emmett turns to us. "That is all I have then, sirs and madam. I am sorry I made you chase down the clue of the cipher and the key for nothing. It was simply a young man behaving foolishly."

I wouldn't say it was for nothing. While Florence is right that stealing mummia hardly seems motive for murder, it might not be a coincidence that someone was pestering Sir Alastair for mummified remains shortly before those remains were stolen.

It reminds me of something else, too. I'd gone to the goblin market for a lead on mummia buyers. Time to talk to Gray and McCreadie about how vital that lead may be.

Gray and McCreadie are divided on this subject, in a split that I could have predicted. Gray sees no harm in asking Isla to help our black-market Miss Havisham. McCreadie is far less willing to let Isla commit herself to this "woman of criminal enterprise" for a lead that might prove pointless.

In the end, I realize that the choice really isn't theirs, and it was wrong of me to lay it there. Isla already suffers from an affliction too common in middle- and upper-class Victorian women. The affliction of having spent her life with men making decisions for her. First her father, then her husband, and now her brother. Her *younger* brother, no less. Legally, Scottish women have more rights than English ones, but in practice, even as a widow, Isla is under Gray's informal guardianship.

Isla may be less sheltered than most women of her class, but that only means she pursues her own interests, travels alone and such. Compared with me and most women of my time, she is still sheltered and sometimes naive. That makes it easy to take decisions away from her.

For her own good. Just looking after her interests.

That's infantilizing, and she'd be rightfully upset with Gray for doing it and even more upset with me, who should know better.

I tell Gray and McCreadie that we need to put the question to Isla, with the data she needs to make an informed decision. Back at the town house, we do exactly that. Not surprisingly, Isla would like to accept the deal. She does, however, want to be very clear on what services she will and will not provide and how they will be provided, with a layer of privacy for her. In other words, she makes the calculated choice.

Gray sends Simon to convey a letter to Queen Mab.

We are finishing lunch when a message arrives. My first thought is "that was fast." But it turns out to be Bob, Elspeth's errand boy, delivering a package from Jack.

"Oh, look," I say, waving the pamphlet. "It's the latest installment in *The Mysterious Adventures of the Gray Doctor.*" I lift it to show the cover, with a poorly done sketch of what I presume is me, frozen in terror at a mummy rising from an examination table. "Seems someone has a head start on the latest case. Think they can provide any clues?"

Isla takes the pamphlet from me. "Oh, this might actually prove useful. Listen. 'As Edinburgh's finest citizens crowded around the table, dear Miss Mitchell unspooled a strip of cloth to reveal the face of poor Sir Alastair, twisted in a horrifying grimace. She leaped back into the arms of our gallant Gray Doctor, who calmed her, while her alabaster chest heaved and she panted most prettily.'"

"'Panted most prettily'?" I imitate a dog's panting. "Like this?"

"You need to work on your panting," Isla says. "If you do not, Duncan will never wish to calm you. Remember that. A young woman must carefully craft her moments of hysteria, if she wishes to attract the right sort of attention from a man. Fainting is fine, as is pretty panting. But if you dissolve into panicked shrieks, you will never find a husband."

I roll my eyes. "At least we can rule out the writer as anyone who was actually at the party."

"Mmm. Do not be so quick with that assumption, Detective Mitchell," Isla says. "The writer describes your dress to a tee. Either they were at the party or they spoke to someone who was."

"How bad is the rest—?" I begin, only to be stopped by a knock at the door.

"I apologize for interrupting again," Lorna says when Gray calls her in. "But another message has arrived. This one is addressed to Dr. Gray."

She holds out an envelope. Gray takes it and excuses her. Once she's gone, he opens and reads it. Then he passes it to McCreadie, who scans it and curses.

"I surrender," McCreadie says, throwing the letter aside. "I am sorry, Isla, but it seems I have no choice but to move into your guest room, as people seem to be under the impression that this is my residence. Or, at least, I am going to tell myself that, as it is a far easier blow to my ego than admitting that people have declared Duncan to be the superior detective."

"Yet another reason to find whoever is writing those"—I point at the pamphlet—"and shut them down. I'm guessing that letter is another summons."

McCreadie is already getting to his feet, Gray doing the same.

"The writer claims to know where we might find Selim Awad," McCreadie says. "Which would be far more exciting if I didn't fear it was a false lead."

"Or a trap," Isla says.

"Yes," McCreadie says. "Considering who it was addressed to, someone might simply hope to lure Duncan and Mallory out to see them in action."

"May we accompany you?" Gray says. "In case whoever sent the note really does expect to see us?"

McCreadie's smile warms. "That makes a fine excuse for an adventure. Yes, come along. I will send word to the office for backup, but I should proceed there directly and could use the support."

According to the note, a young man matching the description of Selim Awad was seen outside a "land"—or apartment building—in the Leith

Wynd district of the Old Town. That area is known for prostitution, and from the careful language in the letter, we presume the building is a brothel. Or maybe "brothel" isn't the right word. That implies an organized business run by a madam. These buildings are mostly inhabited by sex workers, who seem to operate either independently or under the supervision of a "fancy man"—a lover who is usually also their pimp. According to McCreadie, there are three of these buildings triangulated in that area, locally known as the Happy Land, the Holy Land, and the Just Land. I really need the explanation for those names, but McCreadie is withholding it to tease me.

I find all this fascinating. I've been through this part of the Old Town, both in this time period and my own, but I wasn't aware of the stories behind the walls. I guess to know that, I'd need to be a prospective patron.

Even knowing what I do, I don't see anything out of the ordinary. Sure, it's only early afternoon, but McCreadie says that even at night, you wouldn't see scantily clad women lounging outside the buildings. There's no need for advertising. If you want to engage a sex worker, you know where to find them, or you'll be directed here by someone who does.

The women I do spot seem ordinary enough, though many are bleary eyed, as if they've just woken. Seeing McCreadie, a couple stiffen, seeming ready to slink back into the shadows, but he only tips his hat, as if they are ladies in the New Town. One perks up, hopeful, until she spots me, and then casts me an envious look before continuing on her errand. A few glance at Gray, but it's mostly with curiosity. McCreadie is the one catching their attention, which means they likely realize he's a cop.

We don't stop at any of the three buildings. The note said that Selim was spotted outside one "conversing with a young lady" but that he was "unsteady on his feet" and she helped him into a neighboring building.

Helping him? Or taking advantage of his drunkenness?

Of course, we don't know this is actually Selim Awad. There's a good chance they just saw a brown-skinned young man. We're also aware that this isn't a random tip. Whoever sent it knows the police are looking for Selim, and the fact that the letter came to Gray means they realize *why* the police are looking for him. That's not normally divulged, though in this era, we can't be sure one of the constables wasn't going around saying Selim is wanted in the murder of Sir Alastair.

The writer was very specific about the building Selim was "helped" into and also the apartment entered, which they'd noted because a light appeared after Selim and the woman went inside.

The building we need is actually the one beside the brothel lands, and we get inside easily enough. No controlled-access condos in this part of Edinburgh. The smell hits me first, and that's saying something, considering how the street had smelled. The stench of poverty is enough to have me wishing I carried a handkerchief. When something taps my hand, I jump, only to see Gray pushing a spare handkerchief into my pocket. I take it with thanks, although then I'm aware of the figure I must cut—the girl in a decent dress, daintily picking her way through the rubbish with a cloth over her nose.

This isn't the worst part of town, but this building must be the worst of it. The stink of unwashed bodies and unemptied chamber pots is so thick I understand the logic—however faulty—behind the miasma theory of disease.

When we reach a man half sprawled in an open doorway, I inhale sharply, which is a mistake. Gray and McCreadie calmly each take one of the man's shoulders and heave him into the room, which I presume means he's alive.

Gray flips a coin near the man's outstretched hand.

"You know he'll only use that for poteen," McCreadie says.

"Yes."

McCreadie sighs and drops his own coin beside the man before retreating and shutting the door. Yep, that money will probably go toward cheap alcohol, but that isn't something Gray and McCreadie can control, and probably not something the man can control either. At least waking to find the coins will be a bright moment in a dark day.

We take the stairs. The building must have been a private residence once, with its indoor staircase and makeshift rooms. We go up three levels and then McCreadie pauses, as if figuring out which apartment would be the one seen from the road. He starts forward, only to hesitate. There are three doors along this wall, and the middle one seems to be a closet, but the letter writer specified the second apartment from the left, which would seem to be that door.

McCreadie steps forward and raps on it. The door beside it opens, and an older woman scowls out.

"What's all that racket?" she says. "It's two o'clock."

"In the afternoon, ma'am," McCreadie says evenly.

"That's even worse." Her gaze travels across us and then narrows, her eyes glittering. "Are you from the society? I—" She hacks into her hand. "—have a terrible cough and cannot afford medicine."

"I am a doctor," Gray says. "If you can tell me your symptoms, I will make sure you get the proper medicine."

The glint leaves those narrowed eyes.

"Unless you would prefer to get it yourself," he says, holding out a coin.

She reaches for it, but he pulls it back.

"A few questions, first. This door here. Is it an apartment or a closet?"

Her look calls him daft. "An apartment, of course. No one's living there, though. Well, no one's paying rent. There's a fellow inside, drunk as can be. His friends dragged him in there last night. Haven't heard a peep from him since. Might be dead by now."

Gray hands her the coin as McCreadie grabs the knob on the narrow door. It's locked, and I hurry over to pick the lock.

Before the woman can retreat, Gray says, "May we knock if we have more questions?"

"That depends. Do you have more coins?"

"Naturally."

"Then knock. I'm awake now, thanks to you."

She retreats just as McCreadie decides to skip my lock picking and break the flimsy door down. He throws his shoulder into it, and the wood cracks.

"Good job," Gray says as he reaches through to unlock and open the door. "See? You are a valuable member of this team, Hugh. Never let anyone tell you otherwise."

As Gray starts pushing open the door, I grab his jacket. "Uh, trap?"

He frowns at me. I nudge him aside, hoist my skirts, and kick open the door while holding the others back. Inside, the window has been covered, and the room is pitch black. McCreadie lights a match, and we step in.

The woman might have claimed this was an apartment, but it's no bigger than a closet. In fact, I'm quite sure that's what it had been before the house was converted into apartments. At the very most, it was a small child's bedroom. It's a single room, no more than eight feet long and half that wide. There's room for a cot and nothing more. Except there is no cot. Just blankets piled on the floor . . . with a man lying atop them.

McCreadie lifts his lit match, and the face of the man comes clear.

It's Selim Awad.

THIRTY-SIX

We rush in then. With such a tiny space, there's no chance that someone is lying in wait to attack. Selim is on the blankets, with empty bottles beside him and something else. Something that I see Gray notice at the same moment.

I yank newspaper from the tiny window, and light floods in. When I glance over, I can see what that pale object is. A length of rope, lying right beside Selim.

Gray is already bent next to the young man.

"He's alive," Gray says as he checks for a pulse. He grips Selim's shoulder. "Mr. Awad? Selim?"

A low groan. Gray shakes him and says his name again. Selim falls over, head lolling. The stench of alcohol overwhelms the stink of Selim's unwashed body. There's another smell, too. Sickly sweet.

"Vomit," Gray says.

He shoves aside a filthy blanket covered in that vomit. Then he returns to trying to rouse Selim. When he slaps his face, I wince, but it does the trick. Selim jerks awake, blinking and looking around.

"Dr. Gray?" He blinks harder. "Miss Mitchell and Detective Mc-Creadie. Where—? Oh!"

He tries leaping to his feet, but staggers and needs to be held up by both men.

"Where am I?" Selim says, looking around. His gaze falls on the empty bottles. "What are—?" He looks about again. "How did I get here?"

"Well, according to a note I received," McCreadie says, "you were spotted entering here with a woman last night."

"What? No." Selim gazes about himself in horror. "That's not—I did not—" He points at the bottles. "Those are not mine." He sees the length of rope and goes still. "And that definitely is not mine."

"We have questions for you, obviously," McCreadie says. "But for now, we need to get you home to your sister, where Dr. Gray can take a better look at you."

While McCreadie goes outside to hail a hansom cab, I talk to the neighbor. Gray has given me coins to draw answers out of her. The saddest part is that they aren't even big coins. Pennies and ha'pennies are all it takes, and so I don't begrudge her demanding payment incentive. The real concern will be that she'll start making things up to earn more money. So I'm careful with my questions, and I pay her even when she can't answer.

Last night, two men brought Selim to the apartment. Definitely men, meaning whoever wrote the note was lying about seeing a woman take him in, which suggests the whole thing was a setup.

The neighbor can't describe the men beyond saying they were big and rough, like dockworkers. They didn't see her with her door cracked open, and she had the good sense not to throw it open and confront *them* with all the noise they were making. Also it was two in the morning instead of the afternoon.

Selim had been unconscious. Drunk, she said, the smell cutting through even the stink of the building. They put him inside the room, and then they left. Before they went, one said something very specific to the other.

"Did you leave the rope?"

I don't even need to question Selim Awad to know he was set up. We would have strongly suspected it from the note and from finding him unconscious and surrounded by empty liquor bottles. His boots are also missing, suggesting they were used to make the prints that seemed to tie him to the attack on me.

By the time I finish my questioning, the guys are helping Selim downstairs. I slip in after them to search the room. Gray has taken the rope. I scoop up the bottles in the least filthy blanket. I also realize Gray took the one with the vomit. Gross, but a good call.

The setup here was that Selim was dead drunk. That blanket may tell us what was actually in his system, be it alcohol or something else.

Once those items are removed, the room is empty save for two other blankets, which I shake out. Empty.

The men had dumped Selim in that room overnight. They'd staged it with booze bottles and rope, and then someone sent that note to Gray. McCreadie might grumble that everyone is passing the clues our way, but I suspect if there's any insult in there, it's not directed at McCreadie.

The serialized stories depict Gray as a brilliant detective, but also something of an adrenaline junkie, rushing headlong into danger. While the writer gets a lot of things wrong, they're dead-on with that part. Brilliant but also an adventure hound, much like his new assistant.

The clue might have been sent to the guy most likely to hare off after Selim without bothering to notify the police. Such a person would burst in, see the rope and the booze bottles, and go "Ah-ha! I deduce this is our killer and, in his guilt, he drank himself into a stupor." Because, obviously, if you've strangled someone, you're still carrying around the rope days later.

Whoever set this up fancies themselves a criminal mastermind when, like most self-declared criminal masterminds, they just make our job a whole lot easier with their clumsy attempts to stage a crime scene.

Selim is resting at his sister's and joking—sheepishly—about setting a record for number of times rendered unconscious in a week. Yep, there's a serious dose of déjà vu here. The guy was knocked out in the tunnels below and now, well, now it seems he was knocked out there twice.

Selim had been in the tunnel the night he disappeared. Speaking of amateur sleuths, he'd gone down hoping that being there might jog a memory. Had he seen or heard something the day before and then forgotten it after he lost consciousness? Could some clue to his brother-in-law's murder be locked deep in his brain?

Selim might not have set a record for number of times being knocked out, but he has probably set one for being in the wrong place at the wrong time. First, he'd encountered a fleeing killer while he was trying to sneak in to surprise the children. This time, while he poked around the tunnels for clues, someone was making off with the artifacts.

"I heard someone coming," he says. "I did not know what to make of that. Would the killer return? If so, for what reason? My indecision cost me precious moments, and when I did spot the thief, it was too late. I saw him with a bag and I grabbed it from him. It fell, and a roll of papyrus tumbled out. Then someone clubbed me from behind. The blow did not knock me unconscious, but it befuddled my mind, and the brute overpowered me."

"You saw the thief?" McCreadie asks. "Is it someone you know?"

Selim shakes his head. "I strongly suspect he is only working for whoever was stealing the artifacts, and I believe I know who that was."

He seems poised to tell us, because surely that will be our next question. Instead, I ask him to describe the man he saw. The guy was in his thirties, large and rough looking, and while I didn't get much from the neighbor, what little I did get matches this guy to one of the men who hauled Selim into that tiny apartment. It is not, however, the person who ambushed him in the tunnel after Sir Alastair's murder—Selim confirms that person was notably smaller.

"What happened next?" McCreadie asks.

Selim hesitates, probably confused that we're not asking him to name his suspect for the antiquities thief. But he answers, telling us how he was sedated, and briefly woke a few times in the darkness, bound hand and foot, before being sedated again.

Gray confirms that rope burns on Selim's wrists and ankles support this story.

After that, Selim remembers waking once, sick to his stomach, barely managing to vomit safely before falling back into a heavy sleep.

McCreadie grills Selim on everything he can remember about the person who grabbed him, the papyrus roll that fell from the bag, and the places he woke in. He has nothing on the last, and only what he's already provided on the first.

It seems the attack on Selim was, once again, just bad luck. But after he'd been knocked out, whoever was in charge of the theft decided he could be useful. Selim's attacker stashed the artifacts in the tunnel for safekeeping while he hauled Selim out. Then, the next night, Muir went back for the artifacts . . . and found that the so-called secret tunnel wasn't so secret, with people traveling to and fro like it's Toronto's underground PATH system after a Leafs game.

Me being down there with Mrs. Wallace had launched another scheme. Knock out Mrs. Wallace and strangle me the same way Sir Alastair had been strangled, so Selim could be blamed for both deaths, since they already had Selim in their keeping and could use his boots to make tracks. Hell, killing me might also affect the investigation, if the loss of his assistant—and his presumed lover—threw the illustrious Dr. Gray off his game.

Now comes the moment Selim has been very politely awaiting. He has told us that he knows who took him captive, and we haven't even asked for a name. That's because we have a feeling this will be the least surprising part of the story.

"Lord Muir," he says when McCreadie finally asks. "Now, before you say anything, I know it is a very serious charge to make. Worse, I have no solid evidence that he took me. I did not see him or hear him speak or even overhear my captors say his name. What I have instead are the results of my own detective work, which point to him as the person stealing Alastair's antiquities. It is entirely possible that this latest theft—and my capture—was undertaken by a different person. Yet even if it was, I must step forward with my suspicions regarding Lord Muir as I realize it might affect the investigation into Alastair's death."

Selim takes a deep breath. "Alastair believed Lord Muir was behind recent thefts of antiquities destined for museum collections and research. It put Alastair in a very difficult position, with Lord Muir being his patron. He had asked me to investigate, using my contacts in the antiquities community. I have been doing that, coming to visit the city whenever I can, under the guise of having a mistress here."

I think back to the letter Muir found. "Did Sir Alastair write to you about the artifacts?"

He frowns.

"We have heard something about a letter between you and Sir Alastair, urgently wishing to speak to you about the artifacts."

"Ah, yes. I was in London, and he had the note sent there. I returned here to discuss it. If that is important, I can likely produce the note."

"If you could, please."

"So you were in Edinburgh investigating," McCreadie says. "There is no mistress?"

"I will not pretend I am a monk." He notices me, and color rises in his cheeks. "Er, that is to say, well . . ." He clears his throat. "I have no mistress. I am too busy with my work for entanglements of that nature. When the time comes, I have aunts who will find me a wife, if I do not wish to find my own. The ruse of a mistress allowed me to slip about the city at night without my sister asking questions."

"You were helping your brother-in-law find the thief."

"Discreetly. *Very* discreetly. To even say they were stolen is . . . complicated, if the person taking them is the one funding the expeditions. I had the sense there were other points of contention between the two men, and it was all very . . ." He shrugs. "Complicated."

"So what did you discover?"

"Enough evidence that Alastair was mulling over the best way to handle it. I tracked down three of the missing antiquities. There were two dealers involved. One is well known for trading in high-value items, and I can provide his name. The other has proven more difficult to track. He operates deeply in the criminal world of antiquities trade. I had a lead on him, but it was something to do with an underground market, and I had not finished those inquiries. The dealer I did contact seemed to think the goods came from, well, from me. The man who delivered the antiquities was brown-skinned and claimed to be the Egyptian brother-in-law of an Egyptologist. I tracked down that person, and in a conversation with him, I became convinced his employer—and supplier—was Lord Muir, who also told him to pass along the story that suggested the young man was me. I told Alastair, and we planned to pay the fellow a visit once Alastair got past that blasted mummy unwrapping."

"So you would be able to tell me where to find this young Egyptian."

Selim rolls his eyes. "He is not Egyptian. He is not even African. His mother is from India."

He looks at Gray. "I am certain you know how that is, Doctor. One brown-skinned person can easily be substituted for another. But yes, I can tell you where to find him. I even have his real name." He nods our way with a slight smile. "I am no great detective, but an inquisitive turn of mind and a bit of charm go a long way in finding people and convincing them to talk. That is why Alastair set me to the task, in addition to my contacts in the community. Charm was not part of my brother-in-law's repertoire." He sobers. "He was a good man. A bit stolid and often frustratingly obstinate, but he cared for Egyptian history and for my sister, even if it was in that order. Work was everything to him, but he did not neglect his family. He cared about them more than he knew how to demonstrate."

An epitaph that could, I'm sure, be appended to the lives of many men in this world, and even in my own. Raised to embrace their careers, but not given the skills to do the same with their families, however deeply they might care.

Of course, McCreadie asks why Selim didn't come forward with this right away, as it gave Muir a motive for, if not plotting to kill Sir Alastair, at least getting into an argument that might have led to murder.

The question is not entirely fair, given the timeline. When Sir Alastair was found, Selim was unconscious in the tunnel. He spent a half day recovering . . . and then was kidnapped before the latest antiquities disappeared.

Still, McCreadie must ask, because if Muir is charged—even with just the thefts—his defense lawyer could use this delay as "proof" that Selim was the real thief and just needed time to formulate his defense, which resulted in sending Gray that letter to make it seem he'd been kidnapped.

The answer is simple. Selim didn't mention it because he saw no reason to suspect Muir of his brother-in-law's murder, which was the active investigation. We know Muir had an alibi for that. The theft was only discovered after Selim was gone.

Once Selim knew more artifacts had been stolen, he would have come forward. He just didn't get that chance.

"Oh, and there's one more thing," Selim says. "I had suspected Lord Muir might be using the tunnel to remove the artifacts. Of course, that seemed ridiculous—how would an earl know about an underground tunnel only used by children? I found the answer by talking to his daughter, on the pretense of ferrying messages between Alastair and Lord Muir. She's a lovely woman, if somewhat lonely in their country home, and she was happy to provide tea and conversation when I visited."

Yes, I'm sure she was. Selim isn't only charming; he's intelligent, educated, and attractive. His background adds the appeal of exoticism for a woman who may have never left the British Isles. And the fact that he is a baronet's brother-in-law makes him socially acceptable company, at least within the safety of Miss Muir's own home, surrounded by staff.

"I mentioned the tunnels once," he continues. "She particularly enjoyed little touches of adventure like that. When I spoke of them, she became very animated and wanted to share a bit of family gossip with me. Do you know how Alastair came to be sponsored by Lord Muir?"

"A family connection, wasn't it?" McCreadie says. "The families have known each other for generations?"

"Yes, dating back to the French revolutionary wars. Alastair's great-grandfather served under Lord Muir's grandfather, and saved his life. The family's fortunes became intertwined after that. Alastair's house was originally owned by Lord Muir's grandfather, who constructed the tunnel to sneak 'unsavory people' into his parties. While that does not prove Lord Muir knew of the tunnels, it is a fair bet, as he lived in that house when he was a child."

"And if there are tunnels," I say, "children will find them."

Selim smiles. "They will indeed."

THIRTY-SEVEN

I'm in the town house library with Isla, who is busy updating the household accounts while I . . . Well, I'm mostly just staring out the window, and she leaves me to it, after making sure I know that, should I wish to talk, she will happily take a break from her accounting.

After leaving the Christie house, McCreadie needed to go directly to the police office to speak to his superior officers about Muir. Deciding when and how to bring Muir in for questioning is tricky, given the earl's position. That might frustrate me, but it also frustrates McCreadie, so there's no point in grumbling.

Gray went with McCreadie, in case any parts of his story required backup. They invited me to join them, but I didn't see where I'd be any help, so I let them drop me off at the town house.

Now I am in the library and thinking. Doing lots of thinking. Putting together the pieces and fussing with them.

An hour later, Simon returns with a message from Gray.

> Have found one of Lord M's accomplices in the kidnapping. Bringing him to the station for questioning. Would you like to join us?

I consider the question for a few minutes. Then I return a simple message that does not even require writing down.

No, thank you.

I send Simon with the message and my thanks for delivering it. Once he's gone, Isla raises her brows. I tell her what Gray asked, which only makes those brows jump higher.

"You do not wish to question the man who kidnapped Mr. Awad? Who might provide a direct link to Lord Muir?"

"Hugh can handle it."

"I have no doubt he can, but Duncan asked you to come—not to help but to witness your would-be killer seeing justice."

I shrug and gaze out the window.

"You do not believe Lord Muir is the culprit?"

"I believe he kidnapped and framed Selim Awad. I also believe he is behind the theft of the artifacts. And I know, beyond any doubt, that he tried to kill me."

"What about Sir Alastair? Could Lord Muir have killed *him*?"

"He has an ironclad alibi."

"One of Lord Muir's accomplices then? The men who kidnapped Mr. Awad?"

"How likely is it that Muir would have sent one of them to murder Sir Alastair?"

"Also they are clearly not the person seen by Mr. Awad. Then who killed Sir Alastair?"

I stare out the window.

"You have ideas," she says.

"My mind keeps circling back to Selim Awad. We presume he was on good terms with his brother-in-law because Sir Alastair enlisted his help."

"Yet we only have Mr. Awad's word on that."

"Plus the letter, which he produced, but it's exactly what Muir said—an urgent summons to discuss the missing artifacts. It could be interpreted either way."

"Helping Sir Alastair investigate or confronting Selim with the theft."

"Yes. I don't doubt that Selim was kidnapped, by Muir, who also was responsible for the thefts, but the thief isn't necessarily the killer."

"The thief—Lord Muir—may have only taken advantage of Sir Alastair's death and a house in mourning to steal more artifacts. While Mr. Awad was found unconscious in the tunnel, that could have been faked. And he is a hale young man who could easily have overpowered Sir Alastair *and* could have easily gotten him into that storage room."

"His alibi also doesn't clear him."

She rises. "Let us analyze that blanket Duncan brought back. I might be able to confirm whether Mr. Awad was truly under sedation in—"

A rap at the door. Isla calls in Lorna, who has a letter in her hand.

"My, my," Isla says. "Endless messages today. Is that also for Miss Mallory?"

"No, ma'am. This one is for you."

Isla smiles and takes it with thanks. As she goes to open it, she pauses, frowning as she looks down at the envelope. Before I can ask what's wrong, she opens it and takes out a card.

"Ah," she says. "It is actually for the both of us, Mallory. It is from Queen Mab, who says your contact for the mummia will meet you in an hour at the Old Calton Burial Ground. My presence has also been requested, as I had questions before agreeing to her terms."

Isla looks over at the clock. "We have time then to change and be off. It is still daylight, so I presume this will be a safe location to meet?"

The cemetery is on Waterloo, an extension of Princes Street, near Calton Hill, perfectly fine for two women in the late afternoon. I say so and then we head off to change into walking dresses and clean up for the meeting.

I come downstairs just as Isla is telling Lorna and Alice that she wants them to dust the library thoroughly. While the room is dusted daily—a must in the era of coal and wood heating—what she means is the monthly task of a thorough dusting, and the library is the most time-consuming room to do it in, with all the books and knickknacks. I just dusted it two weeks ago, but I presume Mrs. Wallace has talked to Isla about finding tasks to put the two girls in forced proximity, in hopes they will become better acquainted.

Lorna, who hasn't questioned any chores so far, balks at this one. She has a bit of a headache and hoped for a lie-down. To my surprise, Isla doesn't grant it, instead only giving her headache powder.

Isla is not the sort of boss to give a bleeding employee a bandage and tell them to keep working. But is it my place to ask what's up? I might not be a housemaid anymore, but what exactly is my position in the house?

That brings thoughts of the future, which sends me into silence with its uncertainty. We leave the house and start to walk, and I'm so caught up in my thoughts that I don't even notice whether it's sunny or overcast, snowing or not. As we near Princes Street, I spot a mail carrier and give a start.

"Oh, I need to speak to you later," I say.

I explain the situation with my parents, with the plans of a letter under the floorboards and personal ads in the paper.

"Your parents are exceedingly clever," Isla says. "Yes, the newspaper notices should work, and it will allow them to know you are well."

She glances over as we step around a couple of tourists. "I am not going to bother you about what happened until you are ready to talk. May I say, though, that I am happy you returned to your time before your grandmother died? I am glad she lived so much longer than expected."

"Actually, she didn't. I woke up a couple of days after I left. Probably about the same time I woke up here the first time. Don't ask me to explain that. But, yes, I got to see Nan and tell her everything, including about here. She's the one who made me realize it wasn't a dream. And the one who pushed me to return."

"Did you . . . feel obligated then?"

"What?" I look over sharply. "Oh. Obligated to come back because she wanted that? No. It was . . ." I take a deep breath. "It feels weird to call it a choice when it happened so fast, but it *was* a choice, and I'm glad it did happen quickly. This wasn't the sort of decision you think through. My gut said I should take the chance if I got it again, and so I did."

Her voice drops. "Do you regret it? You may say if you do. It will help to have someone to discuss it with. I would never tell Duncan."

"I don't regret it." I cross the street with Isla. "In an ideal world, I'd have a door I could pass between. But at least I had the chance to say goodbye to Nan and to see my parents, and they know where I am. Also Catriona never showed up there, which is a huge relief. If she ever does, though, they're prepared."

"I do not think she will. I have no idea where Catriona has gone, and I feel some sadness for what I presume is her death, but I am not overcome by grief. I do not think anyone is, and that is what makes me the most sad. No one should die unmourned."

"Catriona made her choices, and I'm sure survival was at the top of her priority list but . . ." I shrug. "People survive in the harshest of circumstances without backstabbing everyone who shows them a bit of kindness. Catriona was wired differently."

"That she was."

When we pass a clock and notice we're running early, Isla slows to window-shop. Then she says, "I must speak to Duncan about your salary. I know he raised it when you began helping him, but it should be higher now that you are his assistant full time."

She waves at a drapers shop displaying fabric wares. "You are no longer expecting to leave at any moment, and so it is time to accept a higher salary and begin taking your proper place in this world." She looks at me. "If this world is to be your home, you must truly make it your home, Mallory."

"Yeah, about that . . ." I clear my throat. "This is the awkward part. I decided to live here without consulting the people who were hosting me. I've been thinking that I should find an apartment. Catriona had a bit of money saved, and I've barely spent any of my last two quarterly salaries. That should help me get settled."

Silence. Then, her voice careful, Isla says, "That is what you want? A place to call your own?"

"You didn't sign up for a permanent guest," I say. "If you want to negotiate room and board in my salary, I'm happy to stay, but I know it makes things more crowded, now that we have Lorna."

"I would understand if you need your own apartment, but we would very much like it if you stayed." She glances over. "I enjoy your company, if that is not perfectly clear, and the house is quite large enough for all of us. We should discuss moving you to one of the guest rooms, though."

"I'm fine where I am. And I'm happy to stay. I just don't want to inconvenience anyone. I wasn't inviting myself to be your permanent houseguest."

"You are not a houseguest. You may consider yourself a lodger, if you like, but we see you as a friend who has chosen to live with us, much to our delight."

"Uh, if you're including your brother in that 'we,' you'd better check with him first."

"No need. I am certain my brother feels the same. Now, after this is over, we will talk about your new salary and then we will make plans to visit a drapers shop for a new wardrobe, befitting your new and permanent position."

As with Greyfriars Kirkyard, I've been to both Calton Burial Grounds in the modern day. There's an "Old" Calton Burial Ground, and a "New" one that is, in this time, actually relatively new.

These are parish cemeteries from a time when that was the only way to be buried. Or the only way to be buried if you were a Christian hoping to pass through the pearly gates. Private cemeteries are relatively recent . . . and a source of newfound wealth for families like the Grays, who had invested heavily in this wave of the future.

For hundreds of years, every Christian in Edinburgh was buried in one of a handful of kirkyards. Yet there are only a few hundred gravestones in each. The answer to that mathematical impossibility is that the majority of the graves aren't marked. Such things are for the rich.

In this cemetery, the most obvious marker is the Martyrs' Monument—a ninety-foot obelisk to memorialize four parliamentary reformers who were transported to Australia. There's a rumor that it's so tall you can see Australia from the top, which would be quite a feat, with the thousands of miles between them and that whole "round earth" problem. At some point there will also be a statue of Abraham Lincoln, and if I ever heard why, I've long since forgotten. But while Lincoln was assassinated four years ago, there's no sign of that monument yet.

Queen Mab told us to meet our contact up on the hill. We head there, passing about a dozen people, a few paying respects but most just walking through. At the top, a woman in black kneels before a grave, her gloved fingertips pressed to the ground.

We're giving the widow a wide berth when she says, "Mrs. Ballantyne?"

The woman rises. She's dressed head to toe in mourning black, complete with a veil that hides her face. It's the veil that tells me this is our Miss Havisham. The White Lady, as Queen Mab called her.

As we walk over, I look down at the grave she'd been paying respects to.

"No one I know," she says. "It is a convenient way to have a private meeting here. No one wishes to intrude on my grief."

She motions to a bench nearby, and we take a seat. I stay quiet while she negotiates with Isla, answering her questions and then haggling over the amount of work she will receive in return. When they have finished, the White Lady turns to me.

"I presume you still seek someone who purchases mummy remains?" she says.

"I do."

"Then my answer is not going to please you, but be assured that I still have something of use."

"All right . . ."

"If there is a person trading in mummia within Edinburgh, I do not know them, and if I do not know them, I doubt they exist. So my answer is that no one purchases such things, as no one, to my knowledge, sells them."

My fingers clench the slab seat of the bench. "You said you had information. Our agreement—"

She lifts one black-gloved hand. "I said I had information. Someone came to me wishing to purchase mummia. I told them I do not sell it, and they wished to know who did. They were most insistent on an answer. They were in dire need of it and wished to make contact with a seller."

"I'm not looking for someone who wants to *buy* it."

She shakes her head, veil whispering against her dress. "They were not seeking to buy mummia. I realize that now. They wanted a seller because they had some to *sell*."

"When was this?"

"The day after Sir Alastair's death."

"So you've met the person who might have been trying to sell mummified remains?"

"I do not meet any customers outside of the market. This person contacted me by letter."

I lean forward. "Can you get in touch with him?"

"I have a method of communication. Also, it is not a he. The hand was feminine. However, I believe the sender is connected to a physician. Perhaps a doctor's wife or a hospital nurse."

"How so?"

"I often receive requests from physicians for ingredients that are rare or no longer in fashion. The letter was from someone who was obviously well educated and used medical terminology that suggested they were seeking it on behalf of a doctor. They even used the name of someone I previously employed to obtain . . . certain ingredients."

"Certain ingredients?"

Her sigh ripples the veil. "I had a contact at the medical college, who would provide me with ingredients from dissected cadavers. He is no longer there, but whoever wrote the letter used him as a reference."

"A doctor was selling cadaver parts?"

"A student, who has since graduated. Although I presume that makes him a doctor now. I will not give his name because he is overseas and therefore not connected with this, beyond being used to establish this letter writer's credentials. Put all that together, though, and you can see why I presumed the letter was a legitimate request."

"From a woman connected to a doctor looking for mummia."

"Yes."

"Do you have the letter?" I ask.

"No. I burned it, as I always do when someone writes anything that could land me in trouble. I can tell you how to make contact, though. You are to leave a letter here, in this cemetery, and she will collect it when she can. I will show you the spot."

THIRTY-EIGHT

Isla and I catch a hansom cab to McCreadie's police office. As tempting as it is to leave a letter while we're in the cemetery, we need to discuss it with McCreadie and also to have him assign someone to watch that spot.

We reach the police office just as Gray is coming out, preparing to return home. He ushers us back inside and updates us as we walk through the station.

"Lord Muir's man confessed," Gray says as he shows us into an empty room. "It was not an easy process, but once he heard that the earl had attempted to murder a young woman, he began to have second thoughts about protecting him. Hugh pretended we believe this fellow was an accomplice to the attempt on your life, which could put him on the gallows. A jury would take one look at such a rough fellow and decide that you were mistaken and clearly he was the one who strangled you."

"Good call."

"Hugh is now speaking to his superiors. But, of course, that does not solve the murder of Sir Alastair. I am hoping that whatever you have to tell us will help with that."

Isla and I tell Gray what we learned. As we explain, his brow furrows.

"And what does all that mean?" he says.

"I'm still working it out," I say. "We presume that whoever killed Sir Alastair took the remains and tried to sell them as mummia. But that's only a theory. Could someone else have found and taken the mummified remains, realizing their worth? Could it be sheer coincidence that someone reached out to the White Lady looking to buy mummia the day after Sir Alastair died? According to Emmett King, someone also reached out to Sir Alastair, but the penmanship and style were entirely different. For now, I can only suggest that we leave a letter at the cemetery along with police to apprehend anyone who comes for it."

"All right then," Gray says, his expression troubled. "I suppose that is indeed all we can do. Let me speak to Hugh. Do you wish to stay for that?"

I shake my head. "Isla and I should head back to the town house and think this through."

"I will join you shortly. Please tell Mrs. Wallace that I may not arrive in time for supper."

Gray doesn't make it back in time for dinner. He does make it for dessert, though, and I'll let him pretend that is accidental. It might even *be* accidental, given how distracted he is when he arrives. He settles in with Isla and me—McCreadie being busy at the police office—and proceeds to eat his lemon cake without a word to either of us.

"Hungry, I see," Isla says. "Would you like another piece?"

Gray blinks up at us. "Hmm?"

He's not hungry. He's just so wrapped up in his thoughts that he's eating on autopilot. Or maybe he's ingesting sugar to fortify himself for what is to come, because after a half-dozen bites, he says, "I fear I have a new suspect, and I do not like it. I do not like it at all."

"Florence King," I say softly.

His eyes meet mine. "Yes."

"Isla and I came to the same very uncomfortable conclusion. Florence knew what mummia was used for, and she is a woman with the medical knowledge to pen that letter."

"Mrs. King seems guilty of trying to sell the remains," Isla says. "And we hope that is all she's guilty of. We cannot find a strong motive for her to murder Sir Alastair. I know Lord Muir accused her of doing it to stop Sir Alastair's campaign against the female students, but as Mrs. King herself said, that is only stopping one person of many who oppose them. She would need a stronger motive."

Gray wipes his mouth with his napkin, the move slow and deliberate.

"And you have one," I say. "Damn, what did I miss?"

"A piece of evidence I had access to and you did not. One that has been troubling me since I first deciphered it."

"The study notes? The ones her husband . . . Wait, the penmanship suggested it was written by a woman. I completely forgot that."

"Because her husband took the blame for both the note and the key. Also, you did not see the deciphered notes, and even if you did, the significance might not be clear to someone who was not a medical student. As I said, it was a list of questions, the sort one might use for self-study."

"Right. I used to do that. I'd write questions on one side of index cards and answers on the other so I could test myself. If Mr. King wanted something to practice his cipher with, he might use whatever was at hand, and that could be a list of self-study questions. As for why he'd hide it under his mattress—" I stop. "Shit. Was it *only* questions? No answers?"

"Only questions."

"The sort one might expect on an exam?"

"Yes," Gray says.

"A list of medical-exam questions, written in a cipher, hidden under the mattress along with a key to Sir Alastair's office. Sir Alastair, who is a professor at the medical college. Wait. No. Mrs. King isn't taking medical classes yet. She only did the matriculation exams last month with the others."

I turn to Isla, who seems puzzled. "That list of questions could have been stolen from Sir Alastair's office. The last thing we'd want is to discover that one of the Seven was cheating."

"What about Mrs. King's husband? He's a year ahead of her, is he not?"

"He is," Gray says, "and he is an inferior student. My fear is not that Mrs. King stole the questions to cheat on her own exams."

"She stole them to help her husband."

"That would explain why she had them in a cipher."

"Using them to help him without him realizing it," I say. "Focusing his studying on the right questions."

"That would be a more laudable explanation than cheating for herself," Isla says.

"Unless it led to murder," I say. "Sir Alastair figures out that Florence stole exam questions for her husband. He threatens to kick Emmett out. As Florence has said, that's a problem—one of them needs to be a practicing doctor. She goes to Sir Alastair's house to speak to him. She slips in during the chaos of preparing for the party and finds him in the artifact storage room. She begs mercy for her husband. Sir Alastair refuses. In a panic—or fury—she kills him. Hides him in the mummy wrappings so the body won't be discovered until she's long gone. She already confirmed that she knows mummia is worth something. So she takes the remains—their apartment suggests they are typical starving students. Only she's worried about what will happen when Sir Alastair is unwrapped and finds an excuse for being nearby during the party."

Isla nods. "She then reaches out to the White Lady to sell the mummia, knowing of her association with a former medical student. And then, when the key and cipher are revealed to have been stolen, her husband leaps in to claim responsibility, with an awkward explanation for both."

Gray takes another slice of cake. "Yet that means that her husband either knew or suspected what she had done."

"Did he figure out that she'd stolen the exam questions?" I say. "Did he also know about the mummia? He claimed to have found that letter in the trash—the one from someone looking for mummia—which is awfully coincidental. Was that an awkward attempt to divert attention again—this time to some uneducated third party who might have the remains?" I shake my head. "Damn it. I'm stuffing square pegs in round holes. This felt like a solution, but Florence doesn't seem to fit much better than Selim Awad."

"Perhaps because we are looking at it wrong," Isla says. "At the wrong culprit, based solely on penmanship."

I stare at her. Then I let out a string of curses. "Of course. The cipher seemed to be in a feminine hand and so did the letter to the White Lady. For the one found at the King apartment, the obvious writer was Mrs. King. For the one sent to the White Lady, Mrs. King also fit. But we're basing all that on deciding that a woman wrote it because it *looked* like a woman's writing."

"When it could very well be a man with more typically feminine penmanship," Gray says. "One who fits the criteria otherwise and already took credit for the cipher."

"Emmett King."

As a suspect, Emmett King does indeed work better. I still don't like suspecting a pleasant young man who supported the pioneering efforts of his wife and other women. But otherwise, it works.

Emmett takes the key—which he already confessed to. He uses it to steal exam questions. He's caught, and he goes to speak to Sir Alastair, who winds up dead. This would be the same scenario we'd contemplated for his wife—he goes to beg for leniency, Sir Alastair refuses, and there is a fight, during which Emmett kills Sir Alastair.

Realizing what he has done, Emmett unwraps the mummy and wraps Sir Alastair so he won't be discovered until that evening. Then, seeing the unwrapped remains, he remembers that mummia was believed to have medical uses—he only pretended to have missed that part of medical history.

He also knows of an upperclassman who had a sweet deal selling body parts to a trader woman. That makes more sense than Florence knowing the White Lady's former contact. The majority of the male students won't exactly be tossing back a pint with their new female classmates, especially not while gossiping about selling human remains in a side gig.

Does Florence know what her husband did? Is that why she was outside the party? Possibly, but when I consider that more, I realize it's a dangerous ploy, one that initially brought her into our pool of suspects.

No, I think Florence had already been planning her protest, and her talk about the unwrapping party led her husband to realize Sir Alastair would be home that day and the house would be in chaos, giving him a chance to sneak in and speak to the man.

Emmett must either know about the tunnel or had discovered it. He enters that way and then exits that way, only to encounter Selim and knock him out. His stature fits the description Selim gave of the person he saw in that tunnel.

When we arrived at Emmett's door the next day, he must have had a heart attack. To his relief, we were there for Florence, whom he knew was innocent. Then we returned to ask about the key and cipher, and he made up a story.

Why claim to have found a letter about mummia in the trash? Diversion, if clumsily done. After all, he knows the mummified remains are missing, which hasn't been made public. Set us looking for some poorly educated scoundrel who might have killed Sir Alastair for that mummy. As for why the fellow wanted it?

Mummia? Never heard of it. You were right there when I said so.

I don't expect McCreadie will have any problem convincing the police to bring Emmett in. After all, he's not nobility. Or I certainly hope he's not.

I leave that to Gray. What I want now is to compare Emmett's handwriting with that cipher—and see whether it matches the White Lady's recollection—but all that will need to come after Emmett's arrest.

Once again, I'm trying to occupy my time, feeling as if I'm stalled. I'm satisfied with this solution, but I still feel sidelined . . . even though I put myself there.

I need to find my footing and solidify my position, personally and professionally. I can't step on McCreadie's toes, and I can't become a cop myself. I need to accept that I have chosen a life where being a woman will raise more barriers than it did in my old one.

Would I have felt better seeing Emmett arrested? No. In fact, I might have felt worse, watching a young man dragged away from his trailblazing wife.

I feel bad for Emmett and Florence, but this is justice, and maybe, in the end, I only wanted to be there because *not* watching his arrest feels like cowardice. But it isn't my place to witness arrests, and doing so would feel ghoulish. I'll be here if anyone needs me, but until then I'll change my mood by reading the latest installment of *The Mysterious Adventures of the Gray Doctor*. It might make me laugh, and it might make me want to spit nails, but a distraction is a distraction.

I settle in with the pamphlet Jack dropped off earlier. It's the first installment in our mummy mystery, beginning with the scene I already read, where I unwrap the face of the mummy and nearly faint into Gray's arms. That makes me smile again.

From there, the party scene devolves into pure fictional chaos, which is entertaining. Or it's entertaining up to the point where the chaos comes from McCreadie's inability to control the scene, when in reality, he handled it like a pro. For that, I'm outraged on his behalf, which is also usefully distracting.

On to the next scene, where Selim is discovered unconscious in the basement tunnel . . .

Wait, that never made it into any news reports.

Still, everyone at the Christie house knew. Someone must have talked.

I flip to the next scene and—

"What the hell?" I say, pushing to my feet.

I've been reading alone in the library, and when I hear someone outside the door, I freeze, hoping I didn't say anything too un-Victorian within Lorna's hearing. Instead, it's Isla who walks in.

"Ah," she says, seeing the pamphlet in my hand. "The cause of the outburst, I presume."

"Have you read this?" I say.

"I have," she says calmly. "And I am handling it."

"At first, I figured the Selim-tunnel bit came from a leak in the Christie house, but then I got to the scene where Lord Muir interrupted our breakfast the next morning. The details were spot-on. Same as the details on my dress the night of the party."

"I know, and I am handling it."

"Someone inside this house is supplying . . ." I trail off as the answer hits. The only possible answer. My gaze shoots to the door.

"We are safe to speak here," she says placidly as she takes a seat. "We no longer need to worry about Lorna listening at keyholes."

I curse as I remember how many times I'd found Lorna hovering outside a door, as if nervous about interrupting. How often she'd offered to help. How often she found an excuse to linger.

Alice had complained about Lorna being nosy, and like Mrs. Wallace, I brushed it off as Alice being protective of her employers' privacy.

"You've fired her," I say.

"Not yet. I want proof, and I am working on obtaining it. Until then, I have informed Mrs. Wallace, who agrees with my assessment. She is helping me keep Lorna busy at tasks that do not allow her to eavesdrop or follow us."

"Which is why you wouldn't let her go to bed when she had a headache. You figured she'd read the letter she brought and hoped to follow us."

"Yes, the letter was clearly unsealed, and if I had any further doubt, her sudden headache erased it."

I wave the pamphlet. "You think she wrote this?"

"Sadly, no. I say 'sadly' because, if she did, I would feel obligated to commend her resourcefulness and ingenuity. It would be hard to fire a young woman who took such efforts to fund an independent life. No, I am convinced she is only being paid to spy on us for the actual writer, who is likely Jack's rival, Joseph McBride, based on my analysis of the word choices and writing style. I have been working with Jack to confirm that."

"You've been busy."

"More like *you* were busy—you and Duncan—and I recognized these serialized adventures pose a threat to your investigations. I decided to delve deeper while you were otherwise occupied. It was only after reading this latest installment that I realized we had a spy under our own roof."

"Another housemaid gone, then."

"I am afraid so."

"Annis warned us. She said Lorna was too normal to work out . . . and the fact she *did* work out should have suggested something was up. Guess I'll be picking up my dustrag for a while longer."

Isla shakes her head. "I will speak to Annis and borrow one of her girls while I find another maid."

I don't argue, but I know that won't work. The Gray household—with its scientist siblings and former-criminal staff—can't have just anyone working here. That's why they kept Catriona for so long. As difficult as she was, she'd never been frightened off by the blood spatter or sold gossip about her employers.

"What we need—" I begin, when Gray comes tromping down the hall, the sound of his boots unmistakable.

I pop into the hall. "How did it go?"

"Hmm." He passes me and heads straight for the bottle of whisky on the desktop.

"That well, huh?" I say. "An ugly arrest?"

"No arrest at all. The Kings were not at home." He lifts a glass and waves it from me to Isla.

"Yes, please," we both say.

He pours three glasses and passes us ours. "The police are stationed at the apartment, as well as at the cemetery, in hopes Emmett King returns looking for a response from the White Lady. In the meantime . . ." He reaches into his pocket and withdraws a packet of tied papers. "You wished to see the cipher. I have brought that, along with the solution."

I take the pages. "Whoa. You traced out the cipher instead of bringing the original. I'm impressed."

"It was a bit of work, but it saved me from that noise of deep distress you make when we handle actual evidence."

"Thank you."

Seeing the cipher page again, it still looks like feminine handwriting, which only makes me kick myself for making such a gendered presumption. Yes, the penmanship is very small and pretty, with the sort of loops associated with women, but that would be like seeing a six-foot-tall figure and presuming it was male. I should be the one to question judgments like that, and I didn't.

I read over the list of deciphered medical-exam questions and then pass it to Isla. I don't blame Gray for mistaking them for study notes. That's the obvious answer . . . until you ponder why they were written in cipher. Emmett stole the questions for a medical exam, which he wanted to study without his wife knowing what they were, so he wrote them in a cipher, inspired by a conversation they'd had about ciphers.

"I'd like to get a copy of this to the White Lady," I say. "It'll need to go through Queen Mab, which could take a bit of time. I'd also like to compare it to a known sample of Emmett's handwriting. He confessed to writing this, but once it becomes evidence he may withdraw his statement."

"He might even blame his wife," Isla murmurs. "Claim he was covering for her."

"Let's hope not, but yes. I'd also love to help Hugh by proving this is Emmett's writing even before he's arrested. Where would be the best place to get a verified sample? The university?"

"It should be easier than that," Gray says. "The police are guarding the Kings' apartment, which means we will have access to it." He checks his watch. "It is getting late, but we could go now if you like."

"Please."

THIRTY-NINE

It is nearly ten when we arrive at the Kings' apartment. Two constables are watching it. They've staked out a spot where they'll see the Kings climbing the stairs to their home, and they can quietly swoop in before they reach it.

One of the officers is Iain, the young Highlander constable, and I suspect that's no accident. When an officer is friendly toward Gray, he's more likely to get picked for important tasks by McCreadie. It's a solid foot on the ladder to detectivehood, if this young man wants it. I hope he does.

McCreadie is accustomed to having a constable at his side, rather than the traditional detective partnership I'd had. He lost his protégé back in May, and he hasn't found a new one yet. If it turns out to be Iain, I'll be pleased for both of them.

We leave Iain and his partner outside, and we're in the apartment after a few moments of small talk. Well, I make the small talk, while practically holding Gray back from galloping up the stairs to the apartment. It'll be a long night for Iain and his partner, and they could use a bit of conversation, as well as a promise to find them something hot to eat after we're done here. I might even add a pint of ale to the inevitable hot meat pie. That'd be a huge no-no at home, but here "drinking on the job" means downing a bottle of whisky. A pint of ale—or even a hot toddy—doesn't count and will keep them warm and keep their spirits up.

It doesn't take long for us to find samples of both Emmett's and

Florence's writing. Florence keeps meticulous records, even in a time that predates the modern filing system. She has a small desk with pigeonholes for current papers and drawers filled with past papers. It's obvious that she handles the couple's finances and the correspondence, even to the point of dutifully writing to Emmett's parents. While those letters are signed by both, other letters signed by only Florence make it clear who the writer is. We do find samples of Emmett's writing, love letters to her, signed by him, which she had saved.

I try not to read those letters. Of course, I can't help but see a few lines, and it is enough to make me feel worse about what happened here. The tragedy of a young man pushed beyond his intellectual limits, resorting to cheating on exams and then killing his professor in what I can only presume was a blind panic. The tragedy, too, of a world where he was expected to be the doctor when his wife was obviously better suited to the occupation.

With those writing samples in hand, we can conclude, beyond doubt, that the ciphered notes were written by Emmett. Florence's handwriting is much different, measured and precise, much like the woman herself. Emmett's is more florid and flowing, and it is an exact match for the cipher. Now we need to confirm that this looks like the penmanship on the note sent to the White Lady. Either way, it wouldn't be Florence's, whose handwriting would never be categorically identified as a woman's hand.

I'm finishing my examination when Gray walks over and hands me a crumpled letter. "I found this hidden in Emmett's clothing."

I take it, scanning it. "Damn. Not unexpected, though."

"No, sadly, it is not."

The letter is from the medical school, warning Emmett that if his grades do not improve, he will be expelled. The only surprise there is the name at the bottom.

"It's from Sir Alastair," I say.

"Yes, it seems he was Emmett's advisor. That is why the tone is casual, encouraging even."

I would never have called the tone casual, but I'm coming to understand that is a very different thing in this world, where even letters between friends can sound far more formal than I'd jot off to my modern friends.

On second reading, I see Gray's point. A letter from the college itself would be cold and impersonal. This one is a warning from his advisor that he needs to improve his grades or risk expulsion. The "encouragement" is a stiff line that says Sir Alastair knows Emmett can do better and that he expects better of him. Not exactly warm and fuzzy, but in the Victorian world, I can see where it would be considered supportive. There's even a line at the bottom with Sir Alastair's office hours, which I presume is meant to suggest he's there to help Emmett.

That only makes the situation worse. Emmett was in danger of expulsion, and Sir Alastair had tried to help. This wasn't a cold professor cruelly refusing to hear Emmett's pleas after he was caught cheating. It was an ally, and yet one with a strong set of ethics that could not condone the cheating.

"There is more," Gray says.

He leads me to the far wall and then waits. Apparently *my* educational advisor is testing *me*. I can grumble, but I'd be grumbling more if he always pointed out what he sees without giving me a chance to develop my skills.

I touch marks in the plaster. Most are old, as if dented by previous tenants. Then I see a few recent dents, including one so new it still has plaster dust hanging from it.

I've seen walls like this before when I'm investigating a certain type of call. Dents in the drywall. Chips in the paint. All just above the height of my head. With these plaster walls, they're divots. Same pattern, though.

I'm backing up for a better look when something crunches under my boot.

"I should have picked that up," Gray says, "but I remembered you do not like me handling evidence."

I give him a hard look. "Then you can warn me before I step on it."

I lift my skirts and crouch. I find a sliver of rough china that I've crushed under my boot heel.

Gray sighs. "You do realize you are doing that entirely wrong."

I look up at him.

"You are supposed to bend over with your posterior in the air."

I snort. "You try doing that while wearing a corset. Now, would you hand me that lamp?"

He does, and I crouch lower to get a floor-level view. I can make out a few more slivers of china, along with drops of something.

"Can you help me up, please?" I say, lifting a hand.

"You really do need a lot of assistance today."

"It's the damn corset and skirts, okay?"

He sobers as he lowers his hand. "If you would prefer to dress like Jack, we could manage that. I know you were accustomed to trousers in your time."

I heave myself up. "Tempting, but it means I need to pretend to be a man, and I'm not sure I want to wear trousers badly enough for that. With this body, I'd need a serious binder to pass as male. It'd be nice to wear trousers now and then, though. Maybe at the town house, when no one else is there? If that would be acceptable."

"That would be absolutely acceptable. We will find you trousers and inform the others of your choice. They will not question it."

Which is, again, why we need a very particular sort of housemaid, one who won't be scandalized by a woman lounging in trousers . . . or won't run around telling others.

I remember that I'd noticed some spilled liquid, which is why I'd needed to get up in the first place. As tidy as this apartment is, I wasn't about to crawl over the floor.

I crouch again where I saw the spot. Then, when I'm pretty sure I know what it is, I reach down and touch it. My fingertip comes back red.

A drop of blood on the floor, still wet, along with several more that have already been absorbed by the wood.

From there, I find the trash and look inside. Right on top are the remains of a broken cup and a bloodied rag.

"Shit," I say. "I really did not want to see this."

"Hmm."

"Marks on the wall in the kitchen area. Right at what would be roughly head height. Someone routinely throwing things at another person, the latest being a cup, very recently. They cleaned up the big pieces but hadn't swept yet. Blood on the floor, and a bloody rag in the trash."

"I had not noticed the blood myself," Gray says. "Just the broken cup and the wall, the marks suggesting a pattern of behavior."

"A pattern of domestic violence by one partner against the other."

"Presumably Mr. King against his wife."

I nod. "Statistically, yes. She's just over my height, and the marks are consistent with that, but I need more. I want to speak to the neighbor on the other side of that wall."

When McCreadie and I first visited the Kings, Emmett had said their neighbors were the Ryans, the wife ill. Fortunately, that isn't the neighbor we need. The person living on the other side of the kitchen wall is an elderly widower. He's slow to open his door, but when I say that I'm concerned about Mrs. King, he readily invites us inside. It doesn't take much to get him talking. He's fond of Florence . . . and not nearly as fond of Emmett.

"He should be an actor, that one," the old man says. "Not a doctor. An actor. Has everyone in this building fooled except me. They all think he's such a nice young man, so charming and polite, while they think his wife a haughty little miss. She's a somber lass, serious and sometimes outspoken. But she is the one always running errands for me and bringing me a bowl of stew and letting me complain about my feet. *She* would make a good doctor. I wouldn't let him treat a stubbed toe. He'd likely want to take the toe clean off. He might seem friendly, but he has no time for anyone but himself and his lads."

"His lads?"

The old man waves a hand. "His friends from the college. If he's not out drinking with them, leaving her all alone, he's bringing them home to drink and driving the poor lass out."

I remember thinking Emmett's exhaustion meant he was up late studying. Guess not.

"He drives her out of the apartment with his behavior when he's drunk?" I ask.

"No, no. When the boy is in his cups, he's sweet as can be. But the girl has no peace with all that noise. She goes to study with her friends or slips out on one of her walks, and when she comes back, he's sober, and that's when he's a right tyrant."

"You hear them arguing?"

"Oh, he's careful. Never shouts. Barely raises his voice. He's too clever to let others hear him. Instead, he throws things about. Dishes and such, as if they can afford to buy more. Just tonight he smashed something against my wall. The poor lass left with blood under her nose. She tried to clean it, but I saw blood. I tell you, if I were twenty years younger, I'd thrash that boy. If I were thirty years younger, I'd whisk that girl out from under his nose. She deserves better."

"Could you tell what they were arguing about?"

He shakes his head. "My hearing isn't what it used to be, and the boy is careful. I only heard his voice, angry, and then something smashed. She came out not ten minutes after, and I asked if she was all right, and she said yes and that she was going for a walk. I stayed by the door to make sure he didn't follow. He never does, though. He lets her go off at all hours."

"So Mrs. King left, and her husband did not follow. He is gone, though. They both are."

"Oh, he left. He just did not follow her. He went out about twenty minutes later, wearing his good coat and hat. Heading out for a pint with his lads, as if nothing were wrong."

"His good coat?"

"Like yours there, sir." The man nods at Gray, who has been silent. "A long black coat and a black cap. He only ever wears it when he's going out on the town with his lads. He must think he looks dapper, but it does not suit him at all."

So the Kings had a fight. Emmett whipped a cup at Florence, and it hit the wall. He also struck her. She quickly cleans her bloody nose and leaves him to his foul mood. He lets her get a head start and then goes out himself, at night, dressed in a long black coat and black hat, invisible in the dark night.

I can hope Emmett really did go out for a pint, but I don't think he did. I really don't.

FORTY

We stop by the lodgings on Buccleuch Place, to make sure Florence didn't go there to study with the others. The young woman who answers the door says she hasn't seen Florence all day. We should look for her down along the Water of Leith. That's where she likes to walk . . . and that's also where we planned to go next.

From our earlier talks, when Florence had been establishing her post-murder timeline, I know the route she takes. She heads to Dean Bridge and then follows along the Water of Leith to Stockbridge, before she exits and heads home.

Just a few days ago, I'd walked along the Water of Leith with my mom, the Stockbridge entrance being near our rented flat on Royal Circus. It's a pleasant stroll down along the river, a place where, if there's no one else around, you can listen to the burbling water and enjoy the old architecture and imagine yourself living . . . well, around now.

However, that's during the day, and I'm not sure I'd walk along the river at this hour, and certainly not by myself. I definitely wouldn't in this time period. The Water of Leith may meander through the New Town, but that doesn't mean it's safe on a winter's eve as the clock nears midnight.

As we cross Dean Bridge, I spot a sex worker, keeping warm in a doorway. Yes, again, it's the New Town, but there are still parts like this, where you'll find the underground world thriving. You can put up pretty town houses and pretty private gardens across a mound dividing your world from the slums, but poverty isn't going to stay on the other side of that mound forever.

This sex worker wears a wool dress with extra petticoats for warmth. Her dress isn't scandalous by any stretch of the imagination, but her unbound hair and her makeup betray her occupation, as does the fact that she's tucked into that shadow, alone, at this hour.

"How much would it cost to buy her favors for an hour?" I ask under my breath as we pause at a street corner.

Gray looks startled. "How would I know?"

"I'm not asking for your personal experience, Gray. Just a rough figure."

He sputters and protests, and finally allows that he may have heard that for a woman on the street, it would be a few shillings for a well-dressed man.

I put out my hand. He sputters some more and then sets the coins in my palm. I walk toward her, letting my heels click to warn the woman we're coming. She looks over, her gaze traveling from me to Gray. When she realizes we're heading her way—and not scowling in righteous indignation—she steps out, smiling.

"Good evening," she says. "Looking for a little winter warmup party?"

"More like looking for a missing party." I hold up the coins. "A young woman likes to walk back here, and we have reason to be concerned for her well-being tonight. Any chance I could buy a few minutes of your time?"

"You're looking for Miss Flo?"

I slow. "Uh, yes."

The woman laughs, and as I draw closer, I realize she's older than I thought. Maybe midthirties, with a pleasant face and enviably sleek black hair.

"There's only one young woman who walks here at this hour, and you'd have every right to be concerned about her." She rolls her dark eyes. "That lass is living proof that intelligence and common sense do not go hand in hand. No matter what I say, I cannot keep her out of here. None of us can."

"Not exactly the safest place for a young woman on her own," I say.

"Please tell her that. Or perhaps if your gentleman friend here does, she might listen. Some women listen better to men. She is a sweet, sweet girl, and I envy her bravery but . . ." She sighs and shakes her head.

"Just because she ought to be *able* to walk around safely on her own does not mean she *can*."

The woman points a finger at me. "Exactly that, miss. Exactly that. Anyway, the answer to your question is yes. I saw her an hour or so ago. She tried to give me a few shillings, as she always does, in hopes I will take the night off. I won't take her money. She needs it more than I do."

"Did she say anything tonight?"

The woman shakes her head. "Hardly a word. She's never chatty, but she usually asks how I am doing, reminds me to take care against the pox, asks after my little ones. Tonight though, it was barely a few words. Her mind was elsewhere."

"And she headed down there, along the river?" I point.

"As always. If you're going after her—hopefully to talk her out of this madness—you can ask anyone you see. We all know her, and we take care of her." She sighs. "Which might be part of the problem. With us keeping watch, the lass never has any trouble down there. I don't suppose you would mind putting a wee bit of fear into her?"

"We're more concerned about her finding trouble on her own but, yes, it might help her to realize that she has only been safe because others have looked out for her. I suspect she would not want to be a bother."

"It is no bother. We only wish she would stop these mad jaunts. Or bring that husband of hers along. I cannot imagine how he allows it."

I really hope she *doesn't* have her husband along tonight. I don't say that. I just pay her the coins—despite a protest it isn't necessary—and then we head down the stairs to the path below.

This is a part of the city even Gray hasn't seen. He has taken these walks, of course, but only in daylight and only in areas where those of the New Town stroll along the river. It isn't only night today. It's winter, with newly fallen snow and a cold wind whipping along the open streets above. Down here, it's calmer and quieter. Too quiet for a young woman on her own, but I suspect Florence only sees the peace and the silence. It feels safe, especially with the pretty layer of white purifying even the dirtiest corners.

When we smell roasted chestnuts, we climb a set of stairs to find a bent and elderly woman closing up her little cart for the night. We're near a garden that's been decorated for the winter, and people would have been out enjoying the snowy walk earlier. We don't expect she'll have seen

Florence, but when we ask, she says yes, she knows the young woman, who bought chestnuts and paid double, as she always does. We take the last bag of her wares, already cooling off the coals, and thank her as we head back down.

We don't go much farther before Gray spots an old man, huddled in his blankets against the chill. He has also seen Florence, who gave him the chestnuts she bought. She didn't stop to talk, as she usually does, just said a few kind words and carried on. He points us in the right direction, and we give him our chestnuts before resuming our walk.

It doesn't take more than twenty steps before even the sounds of the city above disappear. I'm not sure where we are, but it's completely quiet now, even the river soundless as it runs along under a skin of ice.

When we reach a bridge, I look down. Earlier, I'd noted footprints in the new snow but there'd been too many to track. Now I see only one set, already filling in.

"We're not far behind," I say as we skip the bridge and continue on. "And there's no sign that anyone followed her."

"Good," Gray says. "Though even if her husband did not pursue her, we should strongly recommend that she doesn't go home."

"We'll take her into the police office for questioning," I say. "Hugh might not need to question her yet, but it's a good excuse."

"Agreed."

We follow the footprints until they stop, and another set approaches from the opposite direction. Then both sets head across a little bridge, toward the other side of the river.

"Those aren't Emmett King's footprints," I say.

"No, they are not."

When we realized we would be looking for Florence and Emmett, we'd found an extra pair of shoes for each of them. Florence's were smaller than mine, Emmett's longer than Gray's.

"I know people don't always wear the right size shoes here," I say. "They get what they can afford. Is it possible Emmett's feet are actually smaller than the shoes we found?"

Gray shakes his head. "I checked for unusual wear patterns on both and found none." Gray puts his own booted foot beside a print. This one is a size or two smaller.

"Unless *now* he's wearing boots too small for him," I say. "Damn it."

"Look at the print," he says. "These are new boots, but the wearer has a slight limp. I would expect to see . . ."

He takes a few steps and then points. "There."

He's indicating a divot in the snow. It's so small that, unlike the prints, it's almost filled in.

"A walking stick," I say. "A man with newish boots, a size or two smaller than yours, who used a cane." I follow the two sets of prints as they head, side by side, across the bridge. "Someone Florence would go with willingly."

"Or, at least, someone she would follow without fear of harm."

"Because even if she doesn't like him, he's an old man with a cane." I look over at Gray through the fog of our breath. "Lord Muir."

FORTY-ONE

Mere footprints can't prove this absolutely is Muir, but it sure as hell seems to be. Either he followed Florence or he knows she came down here. He approaches from the opposite direction. He "bumps" into her, which would be annoying, but she needs to be civil.

Wasn't that what she'd said in one of our first meetings? That she can't help thinking if those opposing the Seven got to know them, they would see that they were earnest and intelligent young women, no threat to them? It's a nice thought, and I can't count how many times I've had the same one. The hope that someone prejudiced against you would change their mind if they got to know you. I've won over older cops, either resistant to women on the force or resistant to working with "a millennial." That didn't mean they changed their minds about women or millennials. I was just different. An anomaly.

These women cops, expecting us to change things to suit them, can't even joke around on the job anymore. Oh, I don't mean you, Atkinson. You're different.

These millennials, don't know the meaning of hard work, blowing all their money on avocado toast. Oh, I don't mean you, Atkinson. You're different.

Lord Muir allegedly bumps into Florence. Maybe he says he's made a wrong turn. Maybe he's a bit anxious, being down here alone. He asks her to accompany him. Or she offers, because that's the young woman she is.

So what would be his plan? Why waylay Florence King? Does he still think she killed Sir Alastair? Is this more amateur sleuthing? Or something more sinister?

Once the footprints cross the bridge, they veer off the path onto a bare strip leading to . . .

"A tunnel?" I whisper to Gray.

He doesn't answer, which means he isn't sure either. All I can tell for sure is that the footprints lead to a gate under a building. A metal gate. And right at the edge of it, the footprints change, no longer two sets but a flurry of scuffs and drags that dig down into the dirt.

This is the spot where Florence realized something was wrong and tried to get the hell out of there. The arched metal entrance is shut but not locked, though a padlock hangs there.

I pocket the lock. Gray starts to lift his brows and then stops, remembering I've done the same thing before. Leaving an unclasped padlock behind is practically an invitation to trap me inside.

We slip through into darkness. Complete darkness, and I have to resist the urge to light a match. Wherever we are, it smells of damp earth, and when I scuff my boot, that's what I feel under it.

Gray eases the gate shut behind us. Once it's closed, I can make out the tiniest glow ahead. I get two steps before a voice sounds. Gray grabs my arm to hold me back, as if I might break into a run. I shake my head and focus on the voice, trying to make it out while an odd echo distorts it.

It's Muir. Undoubtedly Lord Muir. When another voice answers, I mentally curse.

Emmett King.

We ease forward, taking each step with care.

"I want you to fix this," Emmett is saying. "You promised you would fix any problems."

"Which is what I am doing, boy."

"You said you would talk to her. That if she figured out anything, I ought to tell you immediately, and you would speak to her."

Silence.

Emmett's voice rises. "You were supposed to take her back to your home for a conversation. This is not your home, and this is not a conversation."

"On the contrary. You and I seem to be having a conversation. Clearing up an obvious misunderstanding."

As they talk, we move forward. We finally reach what looks like a door, one that's strangely new for this old underground place. It's solid metal, and there's a hasp for a padlock, but no lock is there, and the door is slightly ajar, with a wavering light shining through.

"What misunderstanding?" Emmett is saying as I eye the opening, trying to determine whether I can peek through without being spotted.

"I said I would deal with it," Muir says. "Not that I would speak to her. That I would deal with her. That is what I am doing. She figured out what you have done—"

"She realized I cheated on the examination. That is all."

Despite the echo, I can tell the voices come from the far side of the room, and I decide a peek is safe. I crouch and put my eye near the opening. Inside is a storage room, solid construction, filled with crates and boxes.

This wasn't just a convenient spot to take Florence after Muir accosted her. Muir knew about this place, might even own it. He'd waited until she was close before he bumped into her on her walk.

When I shift, I can see Florence. She's bound and gagged and left sitting under a lantern, while the two men talk nearby, out of my sight. Her gaze is on them, her eyes wide.

"Well, that is a misunderstanding, indeed," Muir says in his smooth voice. "I thought you said she knew everything."

"No, I was very clear on that. I said she figured out that I had cheated on my exams, and that I wanted your help making sure she didn't learn anything more."

"That is what I am doing. Making sure she doesn't learn anything more."

"By taking her hostage?" Emmett says, voice rising. "She is my *wife*."

"Whom you married only for how she could help your studies. She is a dedicated scholar, from a group of dedicated scholars, all of whom would happily help you if you pretended to support their cause. Your wife would coach you and even write your papers, while you chased far more enjoyable pursuits, like ale and pretty girls. And then, when you finished your schooling, her father would take you on as an apprentice doctor. He can hardly refuse his son-in-law, can he? No matter how terrible a student the lad was."

Muir pauses. "Oh, I am sorry, Mrs. King. Is all that news to you? Did you think Emmett married you for love? No, you had begun to fear otherwise, which is why you stopped writing his papers and coaching him for exams. Your betrayal forced him to cheat. I hope you take responsibility for that. It is your job, as a wife, to assist your husband, and you did not. Look where it led him. He cheated on his exams and was caught, and then he—"

"No!" Emmett says.

"—murdered Sir Alastair. Oh, did you not know that either, Mrs. King? Dear me. That happens when you grow old, my dear. You just blather on."

"You *sent* me to murder him," Emmett grinds out. "You knew Sir Alastair had caught me cheating, and you offered me a way out, complete with a sizable payment. You told me where to find the tunnel and where to find him. You told me to pretend I came to plead my case, as if the servants had let me in, and then kill him and wrap him up like a mummy."

"I did not tell you to take the mummy bits, lad, and that is where it all went wrong. I promised you money, but you got greedy. You took the mummy, and the police are now at your apartment, waiting for you. There is only one way out of this. Flee the country. I will help, in acknowledgment of the service you've done me. Your wife, however? She cannot follow. She would not. She will be your undoing if we let her live."

I tug Gray's arm so I can whisper into his ear. "You are hearing all this?"

"Yes. Can you see them?"

"Just Mrs. King."

"That is enough," he says. "I propose we slip inside, and I will divert the men while you rescue her."

I nod. That was exactly what I was going to suggest. I have no doubt Gray can handle the elderly Lord Muir and young Emmett King. If he has trouble, I'll be there to help, but I'm fine with leaving the fight to him. Getting Florence out of there is the priority.

I move back to the door gap and analyze what I can see through it. The two men seem to be behind stacks of boxes. The light is inside the room. That means they shouldn't notice the door opening.

I test the hinges. If they squeak, I'll need to wait for Emmett's louder voice before I open the door. When he speaks again, arguing for his wife's life, I ease the door open another inch. It doesn't make any sound. Nor does either man notice. They're too wrapped up in their drama,

Emmett insisting that Florence will flee with him while Muir mocks his naiveté.

I pull the door another inch and then another, until it is open enough for me and Gray to creep through.

"Go on ahead," Gray says. "You get into position to protect her, and then I will storm—"

He turns, and only as he moves do I hear a noise behind him. Gray spins, fist flying out just as a huge shape lunges at him. Gray's fist makes contact, knocking the shape backward, but then another shadow grabs him. I fly at the second figure. I'm hitting blind, striking out in the near-darkness and praying I'm not hitting Gray.

Someone grabs me from behind. I kick and start to twist, but I'm already sailing through the air, thrown against the door, knocking it fully open and tumbling through.

I hit the ground, and my brain screams that this is the worst possible outcome. I've been practicing fighting in skirts and corset, and one thing I've learned—particularly if my opponent is male—is to stay on my damned feet. Once I'm flat on the ground, it takes work to get back up. I can't just vault to my feet, the way I would in my old body, my old clothing.

When I hit the floor, the first thing I do is yank up my skirts and flip over. That puts my bare knees on the ground, and from there, I can propel myself up. Or I would, if my attacker didn't use the opportunity to grab the back of my dress. There's a huge difference between fighting an actual opponent and sparring with Simon, who'll give me that second to get on my feet.

My attacker hauls me up, clearly ready to throw me again. I kick backward as hard as I can. My foot connects with his stomach, given his oomph of pain. I kick again, harder, and here's where Victorian clothing is better than modern-day, because a hard-soled boot in the gut is much more effective than a sneaker. One more kick, this one aimed lower, and with a yowl, the man releases me.

I start falling and somehow manage to land on my feet, if awkwardly. I spin to see a huge man, like the one McCreadie arrested. He's red-faced, doubled over, clutching the front of his trousers and spouting words I've never heard, all aimed at me.

I charge and punch him in the side of the head. That takes him down.

Behind him, Gray and his equally outsized opponent are inside the storage room and circling each other, both breathing hard, blood flowing from the other man's nose, Gray's lip split.

I'm charging in to help when there's a blur of motion beside me. A third man, smaller than the others. Shit! I forgot about Emmett.

I wheel, but it's not Emmett. It's Muir, and he's at the door. No, he's going *out* the door.

I leave Gray to his fight. His opponent might outweigh him, but Gray has it under control. I charge toward Muir and reach the door just as he slams it shut.

There's no handle on the inside. I push the door. Something clicks outside it. I shove hard, throwing myself against the door as my brain flashes an image of that empty padlock latch.

I'd grabbed the one on the exterior door, but the second one had been empty. Because Muir had it.

The door doesn't budge. Muir has snapped the padlock into place . . . leaving us locked in here with his two goons and Emmett King.

I spin toward Gray, who has his opponent in a headlock. Damn. I wish I'd seen how he managed that.

"Rope," Gray says, jerking his chin as he grits his teeth with the effort of holding the man.

I follow his gaze to see extra rope from when they bound Florence. I'm grabbing it when my former attacker stumbles toward me. Nice try, but he isn't walking too well, and a hard kick to his kneecap takes him down.

I bind the hands of Gray's opponent while Gray keeps an eye on mine, who has realized that damn door is shut and decided that's now his bigger concern. He's slamming meaty fists against the metal and shouting for Muir.

Once the other man's hands are bound, Gray says, "Emmett?"

"He must have run with Lord Muir."

Gray grunts and strides to the man still pounding on the door, so intent on his shouting that Gray has only to grab his hand. Well, grab his hand and throw him down, and then I help him wrestle the man onto his stomach and bind his hands.

When we have the man bound, I exhale. "Okay, so the next step is—"

"Getting me out of here," a voice says from across the room.

I look toward Florence, but she's gone and that wasn't her voice. I take a careful step around a pile of boxes to find Emmett with a rope around his wife's neck, his foot on her back.

"You are going to find a way out of here," he says, gaze fixed on Gray. "And you are going to let me leave first. Otherwise, I kill her."

Didn't he just argue with Muir to keep Florence alive? Surely he won't kill her.

But it's not that simple. He also led Muir to her, and he can claim he thought Muir was only going to talk to her, but how much of that speech was for her sake, so she wouldn't go to her grave cursing his name? Or for his own ego, telling himself he wasn't *that* evil, and if Muir killed her, at least he'd protested.

I don't think Emmett wants Florence dead. He might even care for her, in his way. You don't marry someone just to help you through medical school and get you a job. He doesn't want her dead, but if she has to die to protect him? Well, a man has priorities, right?

Emmett keeps talking to Gray. Variations on a theme. *I'll kill her if you don't let me leave. Really. I mean it.*

He's paying no attention to me. None at all.

I ease back. Emmett doesn't look over. Gray says something. I don't catch what it is, only trust that Gray realizes what I'm doing and continues holding Emmett's attention. I keep moving until I'm back around that pile of boxes.

As I creep across the room, I pass one of the bound henchmen. He's not gagged. He could warn Emmett. But he only glares at me and sets his jaw. He's not getting involved. There's nothing in it for him.

When Emmett's voice rises, I peer between two crates. Gray has advanced a step, and it's freaking Emmett out. I double-check my trajectory. I wish I could catch Gray's eye, but he's intent on his own part of the ruse—keeping Emmett's attention.

I reach up, count to two, and then shove the boxes.

The stack crashes over. Emmett yelps, and I catch sight of him staggering back, dropping the rope. Gray lunges and shoves him away from Florence. I push through the remaining boxes while Gray subdues Emmett. That happens quickly enough, and by the time I have the ropes off Florence's hands, I can pass them to Gray to bind Emmett.

"It's true then." Those are Florence's first words when I remove the gag. "He killed Sir Alastair."

That is what stands out for her, in all of this. Not that Muir wanted her dead or that Emmett threatened to strangle her. Maybe none of that came as a surprise. After all, there's still dried blood under her nose from where Emmett struck her earlier this evening.

What has tears in her eyes is knowing that Emmett killed a man, not in a fit of rage, but to save himself from expulsion and earn some money. I have a feeling that marriage to Emmett King had already been an erosion of hope for Florence. A dawning understanding of why he'd married her. Without divorce as an option, she had to deal with it and soldier on. Maybe he'd change. Maybe he'd get his degree and a job with her father and the stress would ease and he'd be a better man for it, the man she thought she'd married.

Now, with this revelation, her hope evaporates, and she drops her head in silent tears.

With the three men secured and Florence asking, softly, to be left alone, we have one more task. Getting out of this storage room. I don't think Florence has fully realized we're trapped in a windowless underground room, and I'm not telling her until I have to.

We circle the room, checking every bit of the walls, but it's as tightly constructed as it seems.

"The only way out is that door," I say. "With a padlock on the other side."

Gray squares his shoulders. "Then we need to open that padlock. I'll batter the door until it breaks."

"Or we could ask one of them to do it." I nod toward the two behemoths watching us.

"I volunteer," one rumbles.

"Yes," Gray says, "and once you have it open, you will run. No, I shall do this myself and—"

"And save the day?" a voice says as the door swings open and McCreadie walks through. "This time, Duncan, I have saved the day. And saved you, using fine detective work to track you down."

"Because we told Iain we were following Mrs. King," I say.

"Still required detective work to actually find you."

I smile. "It did. But you'll want to go after Lord Muir. He's the one who locked us in here and—"

"Iain has him right outside."

"Fine detective work," I say.

He doffs his hat in a bow. "Thank you. Now tell me what we have here."

FORTY-TWO

Emmett King will go on trial for the murder of Sir Alastair, and that's no longer the tragedy I thought it was going to be. Yes, it won't be an easy life for Florence, as the wife of a killer, but when the alternative seems to have been dying at his hands herself, well, that's not much of an alternative.

She's a sensible young woman with the willpower to get through this, and she has the support network to help. She plans to stay in school—even her husband's reputation isn't going to drive her out—and I overheard Gray quietly offering whatever aid he can provide. Earlier Jex-Blake had wanted to convince Gray to lend his support to their cause. I know why he can't—his own position is too precarious and he doesn't believe his notoriety would help them. Aiding Florence is something he can do. She's also considering moving to America afterward. That would let her practice medicine while escaping the shadow of her husband's crimes.

Lord Muir is in prison, on a charge of conspiring to kill Sir Alastair. I asked McCreadie to request that the procurator fiscal not press charges for Muir's attempted murder of me. McCreadie didn't like that, but he understood it would only drag Gray further into the limelight. Better to let Muir know that I identified him as my attacker, and I'll change my mind about those charges if he doesn't negotiate a satisfactory end to his business arrangement with Lady Christie.

She's decided to part ways with Muir and seek an Egyptian patron for their continued work. While the family wishes to continue living part-time in Scotland, they want the artifacts to stay in Egypt whenever possible.

The missing artifacts have been recovered, as well as most of the mummified body. Both will be repatriated. As for the remains, that's a bitter note. Sir Alastair had hoped to identify the person in those wrappings and send them home for a proper burial. Now the burial will come, but only part of the body remains, and any hope of identifying the person is lost.

As for why Muir set us on Florence's trail in the beginning, he isn't explaining that. McCreadie believes it's because Florence made such a poor suspect that we'd eliminate her quickly and, if clues later turned toward the Kings, the police would ignore them. Maybe McCreadie's right, but I also wonder whether he did that on purpose to spook Emmett. After all, having Emmett flee the country would have been to Muir's advantage, his only tie to Sir Alastair's murder gone.

That leaves us with one loose end, only tangentially tied to this whole affair.

"It's McBride," Jack says. "He's the one writing those adventures, and your housemaid has been spying for him."

We're sitting in the funerary parlor—Isla, Jack, and myself. Jack and Isla have been in charge of solving this particular mystery. I'm just here because I'm invested in the results, not only in stopping those serials but in learning Lorna's fate.

Gray isn't home. To him, this is a domestic concern, and so it is Isla's province. That might sound like a man washing his hands of "women's" work, but he's given his sister control of the household and the staff, and to take part in discussions like this would make it seem as if he's still in charge. If there's a man in the room, people will look to him for the final word.

"All right," Isla says. "Mallory, would you bring Lorna in, please? Jack, we appreciate all your help in this, and my brother will ensure you are adequately compensated."

"Oh, I know he will, but I am in no rush to leave." Jack stretches out, propping her feet on Gray's desk. "I'd like to see this play out. Also, feel free to blame me for uncovering the truth."

"Blame you? Or credit you?"

Jack smiles. "Either."

They're still talking as I head downstairs to where Mrs. Wallace has Lorna scouring pans.

"Lorna?" I say. "Mrs. Ballantyne and I could use your help in the funerary parlor."

She drops the pot in the water basin and fairly scampers after me. Before, I would have thought she was just tired of scrubbing pans. Now I know she's just leaping at the chance to hear something useful.

We walk into Gray's office. Jack is still seated behind the desk. Seeing her, Lorna tenses.

"What is *he* doing here?" A note creeps into her voice, and it isn't curiosity. It's the sound of hackles bristling. She might not realize Jack is a woman, but she seems to know Jack works for McBride's main rival.

"Jack is a friend," I say. "You have seen him before when he's dropped off notes."

"Notes which you read," Jack says.

Isla and I exchange a look. So much for the subtle approach.

Isla cuts in. "We know you are spying on us for Joseph McBride, who is writing the Dr. Gray serials."

"McBride even admitted it," Jack says. With a smug smile, she adds, "Or he did when I offered to give him better information, as I know Dr. Gray and have been involved in his investigations."

"So please let us skip any protests that you are not employed by Mr. McBride," Isla says to Lorna. "He hired you, knowing we were in desperate need of a housemaid, and he helped bring you to our attention. The question now is not whether it's true, but what we are going to do about it."

Lorna hasn't said a word. Nor is she cowering in fear of repercussions.

Few crime stories in Victorian Britain are as popular as those with domestic servants as the villains. These are the people allowed into a family's inner sanctum. One would sooner hire a lazy maid than an untrustworthy one. If Isla spreads the word of Lorna's betrayal, she'll never find another job. Yet she only stands there, stone-faced.

Isla clearly expects more, and her hand dips into her pocket for a mint, a sign of unease. She stops herself and straightens. "I believe we can come to an arrangement, Lorna, one that might not even see you losing your position. You have been a good maid, and we are willing to consider keeping you on—"

"One hundred pounds."

Isla stops and stares. "I beg your—"

"A hundred quid, *m'lady*." Lorna twists the last word. "That is the cost of my silence."

"Your silence in what?"

"Everything." The girl crosses her arms. "For one hundred pounds, I will keep all the secrets of this house."

Isla meets her gaze square on. "No."

Lorna blinks. Then she laughs. "If you are trying to negotiate, I would suggest you ask this one"—she waves at me—"to do it. You lack the backbone."

A muscle twitches in Isla's cheek. "Perhaps, but I am not negotiating. I am refusing to make any payment."

"So you want me to tell the world what happens inside this house?"

Now it's Isla's turn to laugh. "And what *does* happen here, child? We are odd, but all you can threaten us with is public embarrassment for our eccentricities. That only works on a family far more respectable than ours. Everyone knows we are eccentric. What else would you tell them? There is nothing truly scandalous happening here, and certainly nothing criminal."

Lorna's eyes glint. "What if I say different?"

"Who'd believe *you*?" Jack cuts in. "Whatever lies you tell about this household, there'll be a dozen people to say that you are lying. A dozen people far more respectable than a guttersnipe who . . ."

She stands and passes over a folded piece of paper. Lorna opens it and blinks.

"Where did you—?" Lorna begins.

"None of your bloody business," Jack says.

I sidestep to see the paper.

"Uh-uh, Miss Mallory," Jack says, taking it back. "None of your business either. Nor, with all respect, Mrs. Ballantyne's. This is between me and Miss Lorna." She turns to the girl. "You heard the lady. She is not accepting or negotiating your offer. She accepts your threat to spill secrets. I do not accept it, as that tidbit might imply. Tit for tat, girl. Tit for tat."

"Fine. I will stay on—"

"Yeah, not a chance." I stop and look at Isla. "Sorry."

Isla turns to Lorna. "Mallory is correct. Not a chance. You will pack and leave today. While you did not stay the full quarter, I will pay you the full quarter. That is not a bribe. I have done the same to the other maids who have not worked out. Now, go. Mrs. Wallace has your earnings."

Lorna doesn't leave quite so easily, but she's gone soon enough, and I'm sinking into the guest chair as Isla takes a whisky bottle from the shelf.

"Another maid lost," I say with a sigh. "I'm starting to think the others weren't so bad."

"I am sorry," Isla says. "We will borrow a maid from Annis until I find someone."

"So there's a job opening?" Jack says.

"Yes," Isla says. "If you know of any young women who might wish a fresh start in life, perhaps someone in trouble, I would love to meet them."

"Oh, the one I know isn't in trouble, but she will fit in much better than *that*." She waves toward the door where Lorna left. "I'm applying for the position myself."

Isla and I both stare at her.

"It's . . . a housemaid job," I say. "That means—"

"My parents were in service. I was even a parlormaid, once upon a time. I can do it, and I will, in return for special considerations."

"What . . . considerations?" I say carefully.

"I want something."

"Uh-huh."

Jack smiles, and I swear I see canary feathers sticking out of her teeth.

She picks up the pamphlet of our latest cases. "I want to be the official chronicler of your adventures."

"Oh, I'm sorry," I say. "But to do that, you'd need to be a writer."

She rolls her eyes at me. "Yes, fine, apparently I need to admit that you are correct."

"Correct in what?" I cup my hand behind my ear. "I can't hear you."

"I am Edinburgh's Foremost Reporter of Criminal Activities, as you guessed. Now I want to write . . ." She waves the pamphlet. "Something better than this trash. The official adventures of Dr. Gray and Miss Mallory."

"You'd work here to get the inside scoop?"

"The what? You mean the insider's viewpoint? Yes."

I glance at Isla.

"Hmm," Isla says, and Jack perks up before affecting an air of nonchalance, as if she isn't champing at the bit for this. "I presume you are open to negotiation?"

"Sure." Jack leans back, feet on the desk again. "Negotiate away, ma'am."

"You will fulfill the complete duties of a housemaid, leaving no extra burden on Alice or Mrs. Wallace. We do not generally require a full day's work, but it would range between four and ten hours a day."

"I was working ten by the time I was ten myself. I would only ask that if I finish in a half day, I will be permitted to leave early and not linger about, waiting for more work."

"Agreed. The pay is five pounds a quarter with board, double without."

"Let us split the difference, and I need only a place to lay my head now and then and the occasional meal. I'd like to keep my lodgings elsewhere."

"As for chronicling my brother's adventures, that will require his permission."

"Of course."

"And if he agrees to it, I will play the role of editor."

Jack stiffens. "I do not require—"

"Every writer does. As your editor, I will have the power to veto anything I deem unacceptable, either an intrusion upon our privacy or a misrepresentation or mockery of those involved."

"So I cannot have Miss Mallory raising her rump in the air?"

"If it sells papers, go for it," I say. "But you can't have me doing it to investigate nonexistent evidence."

She smiles at me. "That is fair."

"Speaking of selling papers," Isla says, "I will require a cut, as your editor. Ten percent to me and an additional ten to Mallory, who should gain something for the use of her adventures. Duncan will not care."

"Neither do I," I say. "Isla should take both cuts."

Isla looks at Jack. "Ten percent to me. Five to Mallory. Five to the running of the household."

Jack pretends to think it over, but I can tell she expected Isla to demand more.

"Sounds fair," Jack says. "You have yourself a new housemaid and a new chronicler."

"If Duncan agrees. Also, first we need to put the other chronicler out of business. At least in this endeavor."

Jack's smile is all teeth. "Leave that to me."

It's been a week since our adventure ended. A busy week for Gray, helping McCreadie and the procurator fiscal build their case. If one good thing came of those serialized adventures, it was that they brought more recognition to Gray's work within greater law enforcement. I'm not sure how he feels about it, and it's not something I can ask and expect an honest reply.

As for those serialized adventures, Gray has agreed to let Jack chronicle them. Someone will, and it seems better to have editorial control.

It's Gray's first full day off since everything ended, and he's taken me to lunch. Now we're walking home as I look toward the castle in the distance, glistening in the sun and snow.

"It's such a pretty city," I say.

Gray smiles. "With the snow to cover all the grime and soot."

Even without the snow, I see the beauty in everything from the city to the people. A world in flux, changes coming hot and fast, the world evolving within and beyond their borders. Some, like Gray, race forward to embrace this new world, and others, like Lord Muir, walk backward and try to pull the world with them. Not so different from my time. Maybe that's why I'm comfortable here. There's so much I want to see changed, but also so much that I already see changing. Just like my own world.

When we arrive home, Gray tugs off his gloves and says, with utter nonchalance, "Have you checked the floorboards today?"

I tense.

"I will stop asking," he says, "if you truly do not want the nudge."

I've written two letters for my parents and put them under that board. Both are still there.

"If they have not fetched them," Gray says, now studiously turning his attention to his boots, "that does not mean they cannot. They do not live in Edinburgh. They will only check periodically, perhaps no more than once a year."

"I know," I say, which I do know . . . except that time seems to work differently, and they'd have needed to stay awhile to deal with my coma, and renting the Robert Street town house would be wise.

"Even if they get them, the letters would likely still remain in this time," Gray says. "Perhaps they will pile up there until they read them in the future." He frowns. "I truly do not understand how this time traveling works."

I throw up my hands. "Who does? Whatever cosmic force threw me here forgot to drop off the instruction manual."

He chuckles.

"I will continue to write letters," I say as I put my winter boots away. "And continue to post personal ads."

"And trust they will receive them."

I nod. "But I'm also going to keep checking under that damned floorboard, even if it's futile."

"Then let us do that now."

I shake my head, but I do walk to the stairs and begin to climb. The house is quiet. Both Jack and Alice have a half day, and Isla had an appointment and couldn't join us for lunch. Our soft-soled boots seem to echo through the house.

"I heard Alice," I say as we climb. "When I was here in my time. I heard Alice's boots."

Gray sighs behind me. "She is so loud that the very walls still echo with her steps a hundred and fifty years from now."

I smile back at him. "That is exactly what I thought."

We reach my room. I've taken to locking the door again. Not that I don't trust Jack but . . . yeah, while I trust Jack not to steal my silver hairbrush, I do not trust her not to come poking about for secrets.

I head for the floorboard. I've moved the bed slightly, so one leg rests on that board. Yep, I'm being *super* careful. I'd joked to myself once that I didn't lock my door because I had nothing to hide—it wasn't as if I was chronicling my adventures as a time traveler. Yet that's exactly what I'm doing with those letters.

"I know it is difficult," Gray says as we shift the bed. "You made a very hard choice, and I would understand if there are times you regret it."

I shake my head. "I don't."

A soft exhale. "Good."

He moves to lift the floorboard but I wave him off, and he sits on the edge of the bed as I maneuver to the floor.

"I am glad to have you back, Mallory," he says. "I have said that, more than once, but I worry that my reaction upon your return was . . ."

I glance up to see him rubbing his mouth. Then I turn away and pull at the board.

"I feared it was not true," he says. "That I . . . wanted it too much and was imagining you waking. I dared not hope you had actually returned. I'd spent two days sitting there, hoping for some sign and telling myself that if you woke, I would tell you—" He stops short. "The letters are gone."

I look up at him. "You would tell me that the letters are gone?"

"No." He gets to his feet and points down. "Your letters are gone."

He crouches to check the space, as if the letters might have slipped into some unseen hole. Then he smiles at me.

"They are gone. Your parents have the letters."

I swallow. "But why would they be gone here? Shouldn't they just pile up—"

He lifts a hand toward my lips. "Your parents received your letters, Mallory. Do not question and second-guess and doubt. They know you are alive and well."

"And that we solved the case."

He smiles. "I think they will care more that you are alive and well, but yes, they will know you solved the case."

"*We* did. All of us."

As we rise, I look up at him, and my smile breaks into a grin. I want to throw my arms around his neck. I want to do a silly little dance of joy. I'm not sure why this is such a big deal, but it is. My parents know I am well. I can send them missives from the nineteenth century.

Gray takes my hand and squeezes it. "I am happy for you."

"Thank you." I look up at him. "Now, what were you saying before?"

"Hmm?"

"Before you saw that the letters were gone. You said that, if I woke, you would tell me something."

"Ah. Yes." He plucks at his collar. "I would tell you . . ." He rolls his shoulders. "I would tell you that if you could go home again, and you wished to do so, I would understand. I would understand that you might change your mind."

"I appreciate the sentiment. But I really have made a choice, and I don't regret it."

"Still, if you ever did—"

"No." I meet his eyes. "I need to make a life here, Duncan. Yes, I can't predict the future, but I need to commit to this *as* my future."

He meets my eyes, and something in his, some . . . I don't catch it before he glances away, busying himself with getting something out of his pocket.

"Speaking of the case," he says . . . which was not what we were speaking of at all. "I bought you a gift. You wanted this, and I agree that—after your attack in the tunnels—you need it."

He opens his hand to reveal a derringer pistol. I may let out the kind of noise others make on seeing a puppy. It's adorable, and unlike any derringer I've ever seen. It's silver—nickel-plated, I suspect—with scrolled engraving. The butt curves as if to fit around a finger.

I hug it to my chest. "I love it. Thank you."

"And you will learn to shoot it, as I presume it will be different than you are accustomed to."

"I will. Thank you. Really."

"You are very welcome. I thought to also buy you a pair of trousers, but they would not fit in my pocket."

I laugh. "True."

"Also, they would likely not fit *you*. You require a tailor's help. Jack has suggested one that might prove suitable. I suggest we head there to arrange a fitting. If that is acceptable to you."

I smile up at him. "It is all very acceptable to me."

He waves me toward the bedroom door. I tuck the derringer into my pocket and as I leave, I glance over my shoulder at that floorboard, those letters gone and with them a link to my life in the modern world. Then I turn my gaze ahead, and walk out the door, toward our next adventure.

ACKNOWLEDGMENTS

Thank you to my editor at Minotaur, Kelley Ragland, and my agent, Lucienne Diver, for all their help. You're both awesome, as usual.

Thanks to Elizabeth Williamson and Allison MacGregor for once again providing local reads and flagging things I got wrong about their city. And thanks to Elli F and Amanda KM for all their advice on Victorian fashion and moving-about-while-wearing-that-fashion. I sincerely appreciate the Edinburgh local and historical fashion advice. You guys have saved me many cringeworthy mistakes.

ΛBOUT THE ΛUTHOR

Kathryn Hollinrake

KELLEY ARMSTRONG graduated with a degree in psychology and then studied computer programming. Now she is a full-time writer and parent, and she lives with her husband and three children in rural Ontario, Canada.